Redemption

By the same author

Misfortune

Nancy Geary

Redemption

MACMILLAN

First published 2003 by Macmillan
an imprint of Pan Macmillan Ltd
Pan Macmillan, 20 New Wharf Road, London N1 9RR
Basingstoke and Oxford
Associated companies throughout the world
www.panmacmillan.com

ISBN 0 333 90469 9

A CIP catalogue record for this book is available from
the British Library.

Typeset by SetSystems Ltd, SaffronWalden, Essex
Printed and bound in Great Britain by
Mackays of Chatham plc, Chatham, Kent

For Nick

Acknowledgments

I could not have found the strength to write this book without the constant support and encouragement of Nick Ellison. I cannot imagine a better friend. His sage advice, constant empathy, and first-rate crisis management have guided me safely through various minefields. For his exceptional work as my literary agent, I am in his debt. For his attentive ear when I needed someone to listen, and his kindness and affection to my son, Harry, I am grateful beyond words. I thank everyone at Nicholas Ellison, Inc. for their kindness, professionalism, and hard work on my behalf.

I don't sit down at my computer without feeling thankful that my work has found a home at Warner Books. I thank Jamie Raab for her patience, her encouragement, and her constructive suggestions. She has made my words and story far better than they would otherwise be. I truly appreciate her brilliant editorial eye, her hard work, and her friendship. I thank Larry Kirshbaum and Maureen Egen for believing in my work. Thanks to Tina Andreadis for her tireless efforts and endless good cheer; Colin Fox and Sharon Krassney

ACKNOWLEDGMENTS

for their patience, kindness, and attention to every detail; Sona Vogel for her meticulous copy-editing; and Miriam Parker for her enthusiasm and dedication.

I also wish to thank Ulrich Genzler for his support of my work, his advice and encouragement, and for giving life to Frances Pratt in Germany. Many thanks also to Anya Serota for her very thoughtful editorial help on the manuscript for publication in the United Kingdom.

My two sisters help me in more ways than I can enumerate. I cherish their love and their loyalty, and hope they never doubt that they have mine. A day doesn't pass without Natalie Geary calling to bolster my spirits. Her insight and suggestions make seemingly insurmountable problems manageable. Her two daughters, Isabelle and Lily, are the most wonderful cousins Harry could have. Daphne Geary reminds me that chaos builds character, and that we are happier because our homes are filled with Labrador retrievers, dog hair and half-chewed pillows. I thank her, and her children, Christina, Natalie and William, for evenings filled with much-needed laughter and shared Matchbox cars.

I have relied a great deal on my friends and I hope they all realize the depth of my appreciation. Thanks to Missy Smith for her constant sense of celebration, her patience, and her trust; Amy Kellogg, Aliki Nichogiannopoulou, Christof Friedrich, Juliana Hallowell, and Mark Phillips for their long-distance encouragement, humor and love; Wing, Evan, Lucy, and Ella Pepper for opening their hearts and their home to me, and for their enthusiastic support of my work; and Claire and

ACKNOWLEDGMENTS

Bart Johnston for their loyality and warm welcome to Westchester County.

I thank the Reverend Lynn Harrington for helping me on my own spiritual journey. She infuses the entire parish community of St. John's Episcopal Church with a sense of compassion and awe. Her ministry, tolerance, guidance, and willingness to embark on discussions of even the most difficult questions have renewed my faith.

I am deeply indebted to Ruby Londono. Her excitement and energy fill our home with happiness. She has treated Harry as her own. Her loving care brings me tremendous security. Also many thanks to Ligia Betancourt for her hard work in keeping our house in order. Mucho Gracias!

During the writing of this book, I have reflected at length on what it means to be a parent. I thank Diana Michener, my mother, for the love she gives me regardless of where her travels take her.

Finally, I thank Harry, who brightens every minute of my day. His great spirit and laughter, his songs, dances, and his big hugs are the joys of my life. I feel blessed to be his mother.

JUNE

1

"You're a saint." Frances Pratt hung up the telephone still hearing Sam Guff's amused chuckle. She absent-mindedly twirled one of her brown curls around her index finger. Sun poured through her office windows onto the plush navy carpet and upholstered armchairs. She debated drawing the blinds but decided instead to enjoy the warmth. Summer was here. Finally.

Frances glanced at the cream invitation embossed with black script, the two envelopes, three pieces of tissue paper, and reply card that lay scattered in front of her on the large walnut desk.

> *Mr. and Mrs. William Waller Lawrence*
> *request the honor of your presence*
> *at the marriage of their daughter,*
> *Hope Alexandra,*
> *to Mr. John James Cabot III*
> *Saturday, the eighteenth of August*
> *Four o'clock*
> *The Church of the Holy Spirit,*
> *Manchester-by-the-Sea*

She turned over the larger of the two envelopes and examined the calligraphy: *Miss Frances Taylor Pratt and Guest, 1382 Plainview Road, Orient, New York.* Even her address seemed formal.

Leaning back in her leather chair, she ran her finger over the raised lettering. Manchester. She could envision her aunt and uncle's sprawling white clapboard house on Smith's Point, a small peninsula that jutted out into the harbor. The salty air peeled the paint from the dozens of black shutters and moss grew in the acidic soil between the flagstones of the patio. Although her brief visits to the New England seaside town had become less frequent in recent years, in an odd way it felt like home – a place infused with welcome. The mere sight of the oversize brass door knocker in the shape of a lion's head gave her a sense of belonging. It was a feeling she missed.

Aunt Adelaide, her father's only sister, had moved to Manchester with her infant daughter, Penelope, when she married for the second time. They'd moved into Bill Lawrence's family home and stayed there ever since. "I've set down my roots," she used to say with a polite smile whenever anyone asked how she could have left her birthplace. "And trees don't do well in Manhattan." Twenty-nine years later the rambling house, its rooms full of faded chintz mismatched furniture, was filled with her presence.

Summer "family reunions," announced as if the weekend promised hordes of distant relatives rather than the small brood of cousins that they were, had begun the year Frances turned nine. They'd offered the best of activities: camping on the private beach, eating Cheerios out of an aluminum foil-lined box in the early morning while still in her sleeping bag; scavenger hunts that sent her scrambling across the rocky shore in search of a piece of blue sea glass, a sea star, or a periwinkle shell; fishing expeditions in the canoe, dropping paper-clip lines baited with raw bacon overboard in hopes of snagging a flounder; late night games of charades in the paneled library of the Lawrence home with its sweet smell of bitter-orange potpourri. Frances could still recall the taste of her aunt's angel food cake, the sound of the porch door as it slammed shut, the creak of the floorboards in the upstairs hall that always seemed louder at night when she snuck in past her curfew. These were her happiest childhood memories.

Theodora Pratt, the family matriarch and Frances's sole living grandparent, had become a permanent fixture in Manchester, as well. After her husband died she'd moved from Ann Arbor, Michigan, to the guest cottage at the edge of the property. Frances remembered well the two frenzied days she'd spent listening to her grandmother bark directions as she'd helped to unpack her eclectic possessions. Teddy's collections of first editions and travel logs filled to overflowing the bookshelves in the sunken sitting room, and her Matelasse bedspreads brightened the two mildewed bedrooms. She remembered the sunny afternoon after they'd hung the last beveled mirror. They'd sat together in the screened-in porch, admiring the view of the harbor.

"I get my independence without any of the troubles

of home maintenance," Teddy had remarked. "And it works for them. They get rent. Not much, but it'll help with the taxes." She'd raised her eyebrows and said nothing further. As Frances now reflected, it was the only reference to money she'd ever heard made by any of her Manchester relatives.

It was hard to imagine that nearly five years had passed since that fall weekend. But hardly a Sunday came and went without Frances picking up the telephone to listen to her grandmother's stories, the words rattling in her two-pack-a-day throat. At eighty-two, Teddy drove to lunch at the Singing Beach Club, played mah-jongg Tuesday afternoons, volunteered at the checkout desk of the local library, and walked her three dogs every day. The sight of her with her silver-handled walking stick and her pack of canines – an Irish terrier, a dachshund, and a one-eyed pit bull she'd adopted from the North Shore Animal Rescue League after reading about its fighting injuries in a local paper – had to be a source of constant amusement to the residents on her route. And she still gossiped. It hadn't taken her long to know everything about everyone in Manchester-by-the-Sea.

She often spoke of raising her two children alone because their father had spent much of his career in the Far East and she had refused to go. "I know my conduct was viewed as scandalous. My loyalty was questioned because I wouldn't follow my husband to some tsetse fly-infested country with primitive sewers, but I wasn't about to have my children educated abroad. Generations before me worked bloody hard to get to this country and I intended to remain. Dick could do

what he liked. He always did anyway," she said, referring to her late husband. Frances remembered the note
of pride in Teddy's voice as she relayed her decision.
An independent woman was a relatively rare commodity "in my day and age," she liked to say.

Frances thought now of the last time she'd seen
anyone from the paternal side of her family. She'd been
sitting by her father's bed at New York University
Medical Center when Adelaide entered the room unexpectedly, her hazel eyes and high cheekbones partially
obscured by the oversize brim of a navy hat. Frances
had been startled by her frailty, her tiny waist cinched
by a leather belt and thin ankles covered by sheer black
stockings. They'd embraced quickly, Adelaide gracing
both cheeks with the faintest of kisses. Then she'd
removed her hat, approached her brother, and perched
gently on the edge of his bed. Under the fluorescent
hospital lights, the crow's feet surrounding her eyes and
the deep lines in her forehead betrayed her fifty-three
years.

Adelaide had taken Richard Pratt's limp hand in her
bony fingers. "My dearest, dearest Richard, I'm so sorry
this happened to you," she'd cooed with a particular
emphasis on "you." Frances thought she saw her father's
fingers move in response, a feeble gesture perhaps meant
to reflect the affection he felt for his younger sister, but
she hadn't been sure. "Tell me," Adelaide had continued
without looking at Frances, "tell me everything I need
to know about what happened."

Frances hadn't known how to respond. An intercere-
bral hemorrhagic stroke on the left side of his brain, a

ruptured blood vessel, extensive bleeding into the brain tissue . . . The doctor's words had echoed in her mind, but she'd had difficulty repeating them aloud. Instead, she'd stared blankly ahead, wishing her aunt would read her thoughts so that she could avoid articulating the diagnosis that condemned her father.

"Never mind. What happened isn't important. What will happen now is all that matters. Please forgive me. We must look to the future," Adelaide had reassured her as she'd moved toward her and gently wiped tears from Frances's face with a slightly perfumed linen handkerchief. Frances hadn't even realized she'd been crying, yet she could still remember the faint smell of tuberose, the feel of the cloth on her face. The gesture had seemed maternal, a tenderness that was foreign to Frances. She hadn't wanted it to end.

Now Hope Alexandra Lawrence, the only child of Bill and Adelaide's marriage, was getting married.

The telephone interrupted Frances's reverie, and she reached to pick it up.

"Fanny, it's me," Sam said. "Give me the date of that wedding again. I want to be sure we get a ferry reservation."

Typical Sam, Frances thought. Always efficient. The ferry from Orient Point to New London, Connecticut, the simplest way to get to New England from the easternmost tip of Long Island, was packed during the summer months, and a coveted spot on any weekend between Memorial and Labor Days had to be secured well in advance.

"I'll deal with it. It's enough that you've agreed to

come. Standing around in jacket and tie making small talk on a summer Saturday is not your idea of a great time."

"I'm honored that you want to take me," Sam said with his usual humility. "Really I am. I'm hardly the one you should have on your arm for such an occasion."

"What's that supposed to mean?"

"You should be escorted by some guy who wears Porter's lotion and suspenders, has two middle names, and is a fourth generation graduate of Groton. I'm just a potato farmer," Sam paused. "But I'll try to brush up on my stock-market lingo and pretend I have a portfolio." He lowered his voice and affected a lockjawed manner of speech. "Yukon Golds are my hot new commodity."

"Don't be absurd," Frances replied. "This is my cousin."

"That's what I'm afraid of. Your family."

Frances thought for a moment. She wished his words were true, that she had been part of the Lawrence household instead of just a visiting relative, so distant that she'd needed a guest pass at the Manchester Field and Hunt Club in order to use the swimming pool. As an adolescent, she'd spent many hours fantasizing that there had been a mistake, that she'd actually been Adelaide's daughter or that her aunt would adopt her into the intact family. But fate had dealt her a different hand.

"Actually, it'll just be us. Dad can't go," Frances remarked, thinking of her father's ever worsening condition. Missing his niece's wedding wouldn't help his already fragile emotional state. "And Blair's baby is due the twenty-fifth. I doubt she'll be able to travel," she said, referring to her younger sister.

"What about your mother?"

"No," Frances responded too quickly. Her parents had been divorced for more than thirty years, but that wasn't the real reason her mother would stay away. She appreciated that Sam didn't inquire further. He knew her well enough to know that if she wanted to explain, she would, without any prompting from him.

They were silent. Even so, Frances felt comfortable. They often spent time together without speaking. They could read, sit in front of the fire with their own thoughts, or work in her garden without a word passing between them, but she never felt isolated or alone. Sam managed to put her at ease with his ability to share in her privacy.

"How does vegetarian chili sound for dinner?"

"Is that my only choice?"

Sam laughed. "Aren't we getting picky? I'll see if I can come up with something else."

"Thanks. See you tonight."

"I love you," Sam added just before the line went dead.

Frances smiled to herself as she caught his words. Her romance with her neighbor had evolved after seven years of friendship, weekly Wednesday night bingo games, and many hours of gardening. Two misfits, perhaps, but they had a mutual adoration and a shared affection for her two dogs and a reclusive life. The small town quietness of Orient on the North Fork of Long Island suited them both.

In the grocery store parking lot the previous fall, Sam had first told her he loved her. Why here? Why now? "I figured if I could make a shopping plaza feel special, if you could feel swept away even amid bags of toilet paper and laundry detergent and dog biscuits, you'd trust me to fill the other parts of your life with romance." Since that first time, Frances craved hearing him say the phrase, and he didn't disappoint. He never ended a conversation or turned off the light at night without washing her with those words.

She had assumed that the magnetism of his smile, his voice, his touch would pass or that she'd discover a dark side, as she had with past relationships. But it hadn't happened. There were days when Sam seemed so kind that she asked herself whether he was a figment of her imagination, an idealized man whose sensitivity and insight she'd scripted in her mind. Wasn't romance a predatory dance, a mixture of hunting and mating, hurting and courting, until one creature emerged the stronger and the other was destroyed? It wasn't supposed to make you feel confident, was it? She wanted to relax, to feel safe in his embrace, to trust that nothing would change. But at moments her nerves flared. Was Sam really different?

Frances checked the "will attend" line on the reply card, sealed it in its prestamped envelope, and tucked the various components of the wedding invitation away in her desk drawer. Then she turned her attention to a legal pad covered in handwritten notes. The almost illegible scrawl formed the outline for her lecture to area law enforcement on how to respond to, and handle, domestic abuse cases. As president of the Long Island Coalition Against Domestic Violence, a job she had accepted shortly after leaving the Suffolk County District Attorney's Office, she regularly gave public awareness and educational seminars, and she could recite her key points by rote: how to take a thorough history from the victim, document physical injuries, obtain temporary restraining orders, and work through the morass of social services to determine what state-funded food, shelter, and other aid could be available. Occasionally, especially when the administrative responsibilities of her new job seemed overwhelming or she was forced to attend another fund-raising luncheon, she missed the adrenaline and excitement of constant court appearances, presentations before the grand jury, all the stages of investigations and prosecutions of criminal cases. But most of the time she was satisfied. Although her work consumed her week and a good portion of her weekends as well, the coalition and its mission were causes she believed in. That made the bureaucratic headaches and long hours worthwhile.

She made a note to herself in the margin: "Emphasize emotional abuse/psychological battery." Police officers, prosecutors, and even judges needed a black eye before they were willing to intervene in personal matters, to punish a husband or a boyfriend for losing his temper, but there was more to domestic violence than bruises or blood. It was her job to explain that. Insults, verbal abuse, and threats could be just as frightening as a broken bone.

The intercom buzzed and Frances heard her secretary's nasal voice announce, "Kelly Slater is here to see you. She doesn't have an appointment, but she says she'll only take a minute of your time."

"Send her in," Frances replied into the speaker box. She slipped her feet into the loafers under her desk, stood up, and tucked her gray blouse back into her pleated pants.

The door opened slowly and Kelly stepped inside. Wearing tight mauve leggings, thin-soled canvas sneakers, and a T-shirt emblazoned with the New York Giants logo, she stood in the threshold with her arms crossed over her chest. "I'm sorry to bother you," she said in a voice that was barely audible.

"It's good to see you." Frances extended a hand in greeting. Then she pushed a stack of coalition brochures onto the floor and indicated a chair. "Please have a seat."

"That's okay. I can't stay long." Kelly averted her gaze. Her stringy black hair, parted in the middle, looked wet, and her skin hung loose around her jaw.

"You've lost so much weight!" Frances said in surprise. Although she knew it was none of her business, the difference in Kelly's appearance was dramatic. "I hadn't realized it had been so long since we'd seen each other."

"Eight and a half months." At that time, Kelly had been so heavy that, after one meeting, the folding armchair had stuck to her hips when she stood up. Now her body had shrunk. "I've dropped over a hundred pounds. I didn't know there was a smaller me inside," Kelly added.

"Smaller maybe. But no less courageous."

Kelly forced a smile and then cleared her throat. "I thought I owed you an explanation," she almost whispered.

"For what?"

She hesitated before answering. "I've gone home. Matt and I are back together."

Frances barely contained her gasp. It wasn't possible.

Kelly had been a client of the coalition's for years before Frances ever met her. Her husband's violence went unpunished because she'd distrusted the young lawyer initially assigned to her case. Coalition lawyers fit a definite mold: fresh-faced women, mostly graduates of Fordham or Brooklyn Law School, who were willing to work for a meager salary because they felt they could make a difference but were naïve about the workings of the courthouse and unable to withstand the aggressive persistence of defense attorneys. Kelly's lawyer had been no different. Without the constant buttressing she needed, each time the date came for a hearing on her application for a restraining order Matt's intimidation prevailed, Kelly backed down, and the case had been dropped.

As the new president of the coalition, Frances had intervened when Kelly's husband broke her collarbone against a newel post and pushed her down the stairs. Perhaps Kelly had been impressed by her twelve years of experience as a prosecutor. Or perhaps it was the countless conversations over cups of coffee at a remote diner that finally won her confidence. But Frances had attributed her willingness to proceed to the evening Matt's temper turned on their daughter, Cordelia, a nine-year-old with a heart-shaped face, auburn pigtails, and a bucktoothed smile.

"That was no spanking." Kelly had whispered over the telephone. "I knew from the look in his eyes. He wanted to hurt her, hurt her bad. How could anyone do—" She'd broken off and started to cry. "Cordie's just a little girl. Worst thing she's ever done is spill cranberry juice on the carpet. If you'd seen her face, her tears." There was silence as she'd composed herself. "*She* doesn't deserve this."

You don't either, Frances had wanted to say, but she'd known the words were pointless. All the encouragement in the world couldn't give Kelly the self-esteem she lacked. Only when something finally mattered enough to compel her to leave, would she be safe. And that was the goal.

Several weeks and dozens of telephone calls later, she'd finally agreed to proceed. After obtaining the necessary restraining order, Frances, Kelly, and a police escort had hurried to Kelly's house in Riverhead. Frances remembered the apparent normalcy of the ranch-style home with its painted mailbox, automatic garage-door opener, satellite dish, and balloon valances in every window. As Cordelia waited in the back of the cruiser with a female officer who'd been dispatched to pick her up from school, Frances shoved toiletries, clothes, photograph albums, toys, and, at Kelly's insistence, her wedding dress into garbage bags while her husband stood in the corner next to a framed embroidery of the Twenty-third Psalm. As Matt ranted, Frances couldn't help but notice the blue scripted letters beside him: "The Lord is my Shepherd, I shall not want . . ."

"Who the fuck do you think you are?" he screamed. "You can't even see your feet over that fat. You'll never find anyone else. No one wants a moose." When he got no response, his tone softened momentarily, and he begged her to return.

"You're doing the right thing," Frances said under her breath to Kelly, who stood immobile beside her.

"Shut up, you bitch," he snapped. "Stay out of my life."

Looking at Kelly's tear-stained face and trembling body that day, Frances wanted to confront Matt, but she forced herself to stay quiet. There was no point in arguing the merits of a wife's departure with the husband who beat her.

The counselors and social workers got Kelly and her daughter settled in an apartment. Nothing fancy, but they were safe in a one-room studio. Cordelia enrolled in a new school district, and Kelly got a job, an assistant at a day care center. She had always loved children.

"I . . . I . . . We're in counseling . . ." Kelly stammered, now seemingly anxious to avoid her gaze.

Frances knew from experience that battered women often returned to the men who abused them. Despite the fear, the relationship was familiar, and the known held a powerful attraction. Once the particular cranial paths got imprinted, the recurring behavior was reassuring, even if frightening. Such relapses, the principal reason that many of the coalition lawyers and volunteers left in frustration for less emotional work, enraged Frances and fueled her determination to broaden the coalition's reach. But she had never expected Kelly to be one of the many who went back. Not after all her struggles.

"Well . . . let's just say there's a lot I'm coming to learn about myself. I didn't think I could make Matt happy, but I was wrong. I was just going about it the wrong way. Things are better. Really. He's changed."

"I hope so. For your sake." Her voice was flat. "And Cordelia's, too."

Kelly's gaze seemed to stare past Frances and out the window beyond. "She'd surprise you, how grown-up she's getting – almost an adolescent. But she needs a daddy. And Matt loves her. He says that to me over and over, you know, that the hardest part for him of my going away was not being able to be with her. He wants to take care of us both."

"You can take care of yourself. You've got options, other possib—"

"I don't want you to think it wasn't my choice," Kelly interrupted.

Frances rested a hand on her shoulder. She knew Kelly could sense her disapproval and wished she could be supportive, but it was impossible under these circumstances. Kelly had a master's in English literature, a family in Minnesota who would take care of her and her daughter if she returned home. But that wasn't enough to offset Matt's pleas, his promises. He had seduced her yet again, and Frances would have to steel herself for the call late some Sunday night, a call that could be days or even years away, but one that was inevitable: Kelly is hospitalized. Or dead.

"Our door is always open if you need anything," Frances said. "Just remember that. Anything at all."

"I won't need it. This time I'm sure." She paused for a moment, seemingly uncertain whether to continue. "But thanks. I appreciate all you've done." She nodded quickly before turning to leave.

Frances watched the door shut. Please let her survive, she thought. And spare Cordelia, too.

2

Hope Lawrence poked at the mound of tuna fish salad with one prong of her silver fork. The heavy sterling was Tiffany's Hamilton, the same pattern she had chosen for her bridal registry. "It's important to pick something classic," her mother, Adelaide, had advised as they'd stood in front of the velvet-lined glass tables studying place settings. Although she rarely followed maternal advice, Hamilton seemed a good choice.

She stared at the pinkish lump in the middle of the gold-rimmed plate. Rather than replace the more informal Spode china that had broken over the years, her mother now used her wedding service at every meal, and the gilt was already starting to wear off. Using luncheon china that had to be hand-washed seemed ridiculous, but it wasn't her problem. Kathleen, the plump, uniformed cook who had lived with the Lawrences for as long as Hope could remember, cleaned up.

"Please eat something."

Hope looked up and met her mother's worried gaze. "I'm not hungry." Why did her mother insist that so much mayonnaise be added? If she ate it, it would be more calories than she should consume in an entire day. No number of treadmill miles would make up for that amount of fat. She ran her fingers along her side, feeling the spandex of her black bodysuit, and counted her protruding ribs.

Hope's eyes wandered to stare at the portrait of Adelaide Lawrence that hung on the wall behind her. Painted years earlier, it depicted her mother on a damask settee, her fingers interlaced in her lap, her ankles crossed demurely, and her knees together pointing to one side. A large bouquet of peach roses in a cobalt vase was positioned on a table beside her. The setting seemed contrived, but the image served its purpose. No one would forget that her mother had been a beautiful woman.

"You're going to make yourself sick," Adelaide murmured. "Again."

"It's not like that," Hope lied, recalling the night before. She had locked the bathroom door, turned the hot water of the shower faucet on full blast, removed the filter on the drain, and, as the steam filled the room, repeatedly jammed her fingers down her throat. Chunks of partially digested pasta and tomatoes spilled out and disappeared down the pipe, pushed along by the scalding water. Her nails scraped the roof of her mouth as she persisted until all that came up was bloody bile. Her throat still burned from her purge.

Adelaide rested her silverware against the left side of her plate and reached for her daughter's hand. "Darling, I know you're nervous. Everyone is. But you'll be a beautiful bride. It will be a wonderful wedding. I promise." She opened her eyes expectantly. "This is what you want, isn't it?"

Hope didn't know how to answer. She had no doubt that Jack Cabot would make a good husband. He was that kind of person: reliable, kind, protective. She had known him since childhood. They'd attended sports group together at the Field and Hunt Club and won the twelve-and-under mixed doubles tennis tournament. Although she didn't sail, she'd often go down to the dock of the Yacht Club to watch him race in C class on Saturday afternoons. They'd dated since Jack's senior year at Groton, when she'd written copious letters in an effort to make the distance between Manchester and his boarding school disappear. She'd driven to watch his lacrosse games and felt filled with adoration when, after the clock had run, he'd scan the crowd, searching for her in the stands. She'd liked the way he looked with his sweaty jersey and black smudges of sun block under his eyes, and she'd sometimes hesitated before running down the bleachers into his arms so that she could just watch him, his tall frame and muscular thighs. After his games, she'd snuck into his dorm room and then lain perfectly still as they'd made love in his narrow twin bed.

She had gone to Pomona to be near him at college, had sat with his family at his graduation from the University of Southern California, and even then had been treated like the daughter-in-law she would soon be. Jack's mother, Fiona, invited her to go shopping in

Boston or to matinee performances at the Wang Center and had sponsored her for membership in the Daughters of the Mayflower Society.

Even during the two years in which they'd broken off their relationship, she knew this marriage was her fate. It was the virtuous course for her life to take. Jack was good and honest, and he made her feel that way, too. Their courtship had the support of both families. The Cabots and the Lawrences were social friends, members of the Field and Hunt Club, and parishioners at the Church of the Holy Spirit. Fiona Cabot and Adelaide Lawrence co-chaired the New England Horticultural Society's annual flower show. The Cabots invited them on vacations skiing in Waterville Valley, snorkeling at Leyford Cay, and, most recently, watching Jack play polo at Palermo in Buenos Aires. When Jack finally proposed, the families had toasted with a magnum of Taittinger and talk of two birds of a feather.

With her right hand she twirled the brilliant-cut diamond on her left finger. Her engagement ring had been exactly what she wanted: four carats, a platinum setting, all wrapped in a velvet box from Shreve, Crump and Low. A ring everybody noticed. But despite the seemingly perfect union, she felt hesitant. She needed to isolate certain feelings, relegate them to a place deep within her where they couldn't resurface, and all would be fine. She'd be the proper wife she wanted to be. She knew Jack was her way out of her past, and she wanted that salvation. But she couldn't deny that the thought of life as Mrs. John James Cabot III made her shudder.

Adelaide appeared to take her daughter's silence as

assent. Because her mother rarely pushed to find out what lay behind the failure to respond or what might be the import of an omission, Hope never had to disagree. Nor did she have to be totally honest. Silence was easier when the chasm between them was so enormous that it was impossible to bridge. Words were a waste of breath.

Adjusting her reading glasses on her thin nose, Adelaide reached for a typewritten sheet of paper next to her. "The band is confirmed. It'll be five-piece rather than seven-, but the woman I spoke to assured me we wouldn't hear the difference. Bess from Artistry in Flowers comes tomorrow at nine to finalize table arrangements and your bouquet. I've decided to go ahead with a sprinkling of baby's breath in the center-pieces to make them fuller, but don't worry – the overall effect is still roses." She furrowed her brow. "Do you want to ask Reverend Whitney to join in the discussion of the altar flowers?"

Hope glanced at the grandfather clock against the wall. The midday sun shone on its mahogany case. She liked the metronome regularity of its tick and the hourly chime, a surprisingly sweet, delicate sound. Twelve fifty-five. In five minutes its tone would fill the dining room.

"Well, I can call him if you don't want to."

Through the open window, Hope heard the sound of a motorboat in the distance, the steady purr of its engine as it made its way out of the harbor. Living by the water meant constant noise: foghorns, masts clang-ing as sailboats rocked on their moorings, bells on the buoys that marked the entrance to the harbor ringing with the ebb and flow of the tide, the caw of seagulls as they fought over mussels, bumpers squeaking as the Lawrences' dinghy grinded against the side of their pier. Although activity on the sea increased dramatically in the summer, fishermen and an occasional brave yachtsman kept the Manchester harbor alive year-round.

"Come to think of it," Adelaide continued, "I think we should get his opinion. It's his church after all."

Hope nodded. She needed to speak to Reverend Whitney, in fact had made plans to meet with him in his office later that afternoon, but it was not to discuss flowers. She needed advice. Desperately. More often than not, especially in recent months, she felt that only Reverend Whitney could provide answers to the myriad questions that spun in her mind. He was the one person with whom she felt safe to talk, the only person she could trust. He'd heard her confessions and tried to help her come to terms with her past. He'd promised that through faith she could be protected. With few options that could begin to offer as much, she was more than willing to make the church the center of her life. As long as she had that, she felt safe.

She rubbed her thumb in circles against her protruding hipbone and felt calmer.

"Teddy wants to give you a bridal lunch on the eighteenth. At the beach club, I'd assume. You should let her know if you want anyone in addition to bridesmaids and family."

"It's really—" Hope began.

"Teddy just wants to feel a part of the celebration. Let her do it. We have to have lunch somewhere."

Hope didn't reply. The last thing she wanted moments before her wedding was to sit under a faded umbrella at the Singing Beach Club, the bastion of octogenarians on the North Shore, eating petits fours with her grandmother. She loved Teddy and would forever be indebted to her. She'd kept secrets that no one else in her world would have, but now Hope couldn't take the risk that, given an audience, Teddy might be less than discreet. Not with the wedding so close.

"Oh, we have to get to Boston on Friday. Priscilla's called. Your dress is ready for a second fitting. What time is good?"

"You decide."

Adelaide leaned forward and removed her glasses. "Your effect has not gone unnoticed." Then her voice softened. "Please, Hope, tell me what's wrong. I'm your mother, after all."

A mother, she thought. What did that even mean to Adelaide? Hope didn't know how to respond and fought to avoid tears. She had wanted her wedding preparations, the plans, to bring them closer together, to give mother and daughter a chance to bond over the right registry selections, bridesmaids' dresses, and corsages. In fact, the promise of such an opportunity was the primary reason she had agreed to a large celebration at home. Instead, she couldn't generate interest in what was supposed to be the most important day of her life, and her mother's obsession with details that meant nothing to her only made her feel more estranged, isolated from the process. She envisioned herself as a plastic bride atop a seven-tiered white cake with ribbons of pink frosting and flowers: perfect to look at, but devoid of emotion.

She wished she could confront her mother, but each time she thought to start a conversation, the words disappeared. There was nothing to say after so many years and all that had happened. If her mother couldn't already understand, nothing she said would make a difference. She hated herself. "It's nothing. I just meant that whatever suits you is fine by me."

Adelaide made a note to herself. "Let's say ten o'clock." She rested a palm over her daughter's hand. "I've got bridge at Bonnie's house today, but if you need me, I'll cancel. I want you to know I'm here for you."

Right. Why would you want that now, when you've never been there before? she thought, but instead she said, "I'm fine. Really. You don't need to worry." Hope excused herself with the flash of a reassuring smile. She felt consumed by an overwhelming urge to vomit the two crackers and carrot stick she had eaten in a moment of weakness. Whether she could get them to come out after fifteen minutes in her system, or whether the crackers were already digested, she didn't know. But she would try.

3

Jim Cabot stepped back from the rope barrier as the eight horses thundered down the polo field, kicking up grass and mud in their wake. The sound of hooves was deafening. A chestnut collided with a dappled gray, and he watched its rider in a green-and-red jersey tilt precariously in his saddle in an effort to remain mounted. The horses foamed at their bits. Sweat glistened on their immaculate coats.

He scanned the crowd, recognizing the usual suspects: Robert Harrington Sr. wearing a Field and Hunt Club visor and a yellow cashmere V-neck sweater, stood beside his lovely blonde wife, number four she was, although, in Robert's defense, his third wife had left him for their landscape architect. That she had ended up with the house seemed a travesty, but the probate courts were tough on men. Next to the Harringtons stood Bunny and Cliff Taylor, she in oversize dark glasses. Their continued involvement with the polo circuit surprised him, given that their eldest son had been killed playing the sport less than three years earlier by a mallet to the head. An Argentine defenseman had been responsible. No surprise. The South Americans were known for their aggressive game. And there was Ray Burgess. He had to be ninety. Rain or shine, he showed up to watch the excitement with his frayed green-and-white-striped folding chair and his shaker of martinis.

Jim returned his gaze to the action in front of him. He heard the crack of a mallet against the wooden ball, followed almost instantly by a similar sound. The ball was intercepted, the direction abruptly reversed, and the players galloped toward the opposite goalposts nearly three hundred yards away. For a moment the noise subsided. But Jim had seen enough polo matches to know that any silence was fleeting. Within seconds, the enormous beasts and their athletic riders would reappear before him.

He wiped at the dirt that speckled his Nantucket red pants.

Jack, his only child, had been playing amateur polo since high school, then played competitively at USC. The University of Southern California had one of the best college teams in the country and plenty of practice time, given the near perfect weather. Jack thrived. He had a natural gift for the game, loved the animals, and lived for the excitement. By the time he graduated he'd earned a handicap of six, placing him in an elite group of top-ranked players in the United States and making his career preordained. Negotiations were under way with a reclusive Texan to make Jack field captain of his team. Jack was twenty-nine; it was time he made the transition from amateur to professional.

Although the cost of polo was enormous, Jim took no small pride in the fact that for his son it was not prohibitive. Jack had trained eight thoroughbreds into some of the best horses in the sport, and Jim paid upward of a hundred thousand a year to cover their feed, veterinary bills, and transportation, plus the salary of a full-time groomer and additional trainer. Winnings would start to defray some of the costs, but that didn't matter. There was enough money in various trusts to ensure that he could play polo until he was too old to mount. Unless, of course, Jack and Hope's marriage ended in divorce.

Jim reached into his pocket and removed his key ring, a silver horse hoof. He twirled the keys in his hand, thinking for a moment. He was proud of the money he'd earned for his family. In the last thirty years he'd converted a small inheritance into a net worth of more than $20 million by investing in alternative energy sources. Now he had several plants in Nevada and Colorado, as well as the largest fossil-fuel production center in the northeast.

His financial statement looked good, great by most standards. And it was no small accomplishment for a man who could have lived comfortably with no effort at all. His drive, ambition, and discipline, plus his desire to see future generations of his family secure, had been the reason he'd worked fifteen-hour days, often six days a week. Yet he'd achieved what he'd set out to do. He'd become a power. He'd made the cover of the *Boston Globe*'s business section several times, was continuously in *Boston* magazine's list of most-powerful people, and

served on the board of several prominent philanthro-
pies. His reward to himself was a 59-foot Hinckley, the
Lucky Day, big enough to be impressive in the harbor
but small enough for him to maneuver himself without
a crew.

He'd made only one mistake, but its ramifications
seemed increasingly severe as August 18 approached.
In providing for future generations of Cabots, he'd
established a series of irrevocable trusts. The income
went to Jack and the principal to "the issue of his body,"
his children. It was a complex legal framework, one
that had cost nearly $40,000 in legal fees to implement,
but it had seemed like a good idea at the time to
minimize future estate taxes. The problem that nobody
had anticipated when the documents had been created
more than a decade earlier was that if Jack's marriage
didn't survive, some bottom-feeding attorney could
extract half the income for Hope.

These legal creations couldn't be modified. Jim's rage
at Lloyd Barrett, his lawyer and adviser, who'd represented him in all his personal and corporate legal work
for his entire career, his demands for a solution, the
hours of angry telephone calls over the last few weeks,
reminding Lloyd that he was the firm's best client,
couldn't change the law. The whole point of an irrevocable trust was that it was irrevocable. The only possible protection was a prenuptial agreement, a contract
signed by Hope relinquishing any claims to those
assets. It seemed reasonable. Why was she entitled to
his hard-earned money if she wasn't a Cabot? But Jim

knew about greed. When money-lust was involved, anything could happen.

Jim saw the blue-and-gold number three jersey worn by his son heading back down the field. The sun shone off the black coat of Deliver Me, Jack's greenest horse, whose agility and strength gave every sign of her becoming a champion polo pony. Jack raised his mallet and whacked again at the ball, driving it in front of him. With his left hand he held the reins, managing to steer his horse by the pressure of his strong thighs. A defenseman charged, but failed to hook Jack's mallet because of Deliver Me's quick dart left. The crowd cheered as Jack and his mare flew past toward the goalposts. Jim thought he could see panic on the goal player's face, although from this distance, it had to be his imagination. A final hit, and the ball crossed the line.

The horn blew to announce the end of the chukkar. The game was over. Jack's team had another triumph, a boost to their confidence as they headed into the Hurling Ham season. Moments like this made Jim love even more the mountains of money he'd made.

Jack had dismounted and handed Deliver Me's reins to Ben, his trusty groomer and faithful employee. Ben would lead her back to the trailer, remove her tackle, wash her down, and get her settled for the short trip home. Jack took off his helmet, tossed his head back, stuck his crop in the side of his leather boots, and headed toward his father.

Jim smiled as he watched Jack's easy gait, arms

swinging from his broad shoulders and leg muscles showing through his tight jodhpurs. His son was a near perfect specimen.

So why had he picked so poorly? Hope wasn't the sort to marry. She couldn't be controlled. Jim was not about to risk losing his empire because of that girl.

"Great game," Jim remarked as his son approached. "Deliver Me looks awfully strong."

"She's responding well. Seems to have a sixth sense," Jack replied. His breathing was heavy, and he wiped a handkerchief across his brow. "Hotter than I thought it would be out there."

Jim rested his hand on his son's shoulder. "We've got to talk. And it's not a conversation I wanted to have at home." He paused. "Your mother is not part of this discussion."

"Shoot."

Jim started walking slowly away from the crowd, and Jack fell into stride. Whenever there was anything of import to discuss, father and son tended to walk and talk. They were both athletic, and words flowed easier when accompanied by physical movement.

"I'm happy for you that you've fallen in love," Jim began. "The Lawrences are an old North Shore family. Bill's a decent guy. But—"

"Dad, don't—"

"Let me finish," Jim interrupted. "You need to understand that a life with Hope won't be easy. She's not the simplest of women."

"I don't know what you mean."

"I think you do, son. Her troubles didn't start yesterday."

"Whatever problems Hope may have had, they're over. She's better."

"I'm not here to judge. My point is only that if you go through with this marriage, which I realize you are going to do, you need to open your eyes to potential pitfalls, or should I say land mines. You don't need me to tell you that marriage can be tough, even under the best of circumstances. Your mother and I have had our share of ups and downs, though she's one of the most pragmatic and organized women I know. Don't misunderstand me. I've never contemplated leaving her. She is a good wife and puts her family first. She keeps herself attractive and takes care of our home. Her values and mine are completely in line. I couldn't ask for anything more, yet we still go through bad patches from time to time."

"Hope and I are very close. I love her, Dad."

"I know you do. And I'm not trying to convince you not to." He was a father after all and not a stupid man. Guiding his son's emotional arrow was doomed to failure. But he could remind Jack of practicalities. "Lloyd says he hasn't heard from you about the prenuptial."

"That's right."

"I thought you'd agreed to speak to him."

"Well, I did, but I changed my mind."

"We had an agreement."

"You had something that you wanted me to agree with. But I don't. I'm not going to enter into my marriage anticipating problems in the event of divorce. I trust Hope. I want things to work, forever, and I'm not going to ask her to sign anything."

"Too much money's at stake." Jim felt sweat start to form at the back of his neck, his body's typical response to stress. He resisted the urge to wipe it away.

"But it's my money."

"It's yours only because I gave it to you."

"But it's irrevocable. You know the terms better than I do."

"Don't you dare throw that in my face, young man. Anything can be changed," he lied. "You'll end up with nothing, so I suggest you listen and listen well. You have to think about preserving Cabot assets for future generations. Your lineage."

Jack stopped abruptly and turned on his heels to face his father. Jim could see his face redden. When he spoke his words were flat, a tone he'd never before heard from his son. "Dad, nothing you can do or say is going to make me change my mind. Asking Hope to sign some stupid piece of paper is repulsive. I won't enter my marriage distrusting her so much. I won't hurt her by asking for a prenuptial. You may be pessimistic about our future, but I'm not."

"I'm trying to impart to you that you have an obligation to this family. She doesn't have the kind of money you do. The Lawrences put up a good front, but you know as well as I do that their situation isn't what it appears. Look at the condition of that house. They're thrilled their daughter's about to become a Cabot, as anyone in this whole town would be."

"They're thrilled because Hope's happy."

"Don't be naïve. That you're there to pay for a new shingled roof doesn't hurt."

"Adelaide and Bill are good people."

"Everyone has ulterior motives."

"Hope and I are going to be happy. Just stay out of it."

"How can I? Her conduct has . . . is . . ." he stammered. Even he couldn't find the right words to describe how loathsome he found her reputation, at least her sexual one. "And what about Carl?"

"That's over between them."

"So you think. But Hope threw that man in your face. You may be willing to forgive her, but it was reprehensible. And that relationship didn't end when you thought it had, so you can't know for certain it's over now."

"Hope wants to be my wife."

"As long as she stays that way, she'll be protected and included as one of our own. But if things change, you, son, have to remember that you're a Cabot first and foremost."

"I'm not having this conversation. I've made up my mind."

"Don't do this."

"No, Dad. Don't *you* do this!" With that, Jack pulled the riding crop from the side of his boot and whacked his heel.

Jim felt rage explode with the sudden snapping sound. Instinctively, he reached for his son's wrist and held it firm, feeling the pulse. He squeezed tighter, indifferent to the pain his grip caused. It was no small source of pride that even at the age of fifty-six he was stronger than his son. That's what fifty one-armed push-ups, a hundred sit-ups, and a three-mile jog every morning did for him. Discipline, that's what mattered.

"You've forced me to interfere. Hope is going to sign a prenuptial if it's the last thing she does. I won't have this wedding without it. If you can't learn to be a man, if you can't get your woman to do what you demand, you have no business being entrusted with Cabot wealth. She has to respect us. All of us."

Jack twisted his wrist, and Jim eased his hold. He looked at his son's face and thought he recognized the faintest sign of fear. There was something in his eyes, slightly wider than usual and possibly rimmed with tears. He hadn't wanted to threaten his son, that hadn't been his agenda when he'd set out this morning, but Jack's stubbornness left him no choice. Just like the friskiest foal, he needed to be broken. Jim had to establish that he was still head of the family. He was the dominant male. Jack could be the pride of his life, but that didn't mean he could be in control.

Jack dropped his head to divert his gaze. He had looked away first.

"Talk to Lloyd tomorrow. If you have any problems with Hope, you let me know. I'll take care of her."

As he walked away, Jim didn't have to look back to know that Jack remained standing where he'd left him.

4

Bill Lawrence slowed his navy blue Mercedes to nearly a stop in order to read the street numbers off the row of crooked mailboxes: 10, 10A, 10B, 12, 14A through 14F, the dented tin boxes snuggled as close together as the dilapidated houses to which they purported to correspond. He gazed across the street. On one porch an elderly woman wearing orange fuzzy slippers and a brass-buttoned housecoat shifted in her La-Z-Boy recliner to stare suspiciously at him. Then, apparently uninterested, she returned to her crocheting.

Frustrated, Bill pulled over to the side of the road, turned off his engine, and stepped out onto the hot pavement. He shielded his eyes from the sun with his right hand as he scanned the houses, three-family homes that differed little except for the amount of peel in the exterior paint and the degree of sag in the small balconies. Thank God Hope changed her mind, he thought. Or she could be living here. He tried not to imagine his youngest daughter as the wife of Carl LeFleur, a lobsterman with a future as bright as ebony. Although this working-class section of Gloucester at the tip of Cape Ann couldn't technically be called squalid, it was far from what a father would want for his little girl, and literally and figuratively miles away from the environment that Jack could provide.

Bill had visited Carl once before, but now in the bright daylight he didn't recognize the house. The previous time he'd had a police escort. Although Hope had been twenty-five and legally able to do as she pleased, the uniformed officers at the Gloucester station hadn't questioned his story that his daughter had run away. An infatuation with an older man, he'd explained. She'd lost her head and needed to be brought home before it was too late. He hadn't had to explain his fear that his daughter would disappear into a world of lobster traps and Budweiser beer with a forty-three-year-old ne'er-do-well who had nothing to show for his life but the contents of a second-floor walk-up, a rental at that. When they'd arrived at his apartment, Carl had opened the door without hesitation or resistance. Hope, fully dressed, had been sitting cross-legged in front of a Scrabble board. It was she who had become hysterical when her father had asked her to leave. He'd ended up carrying her out crying, her long, thin legs flailing about.

Had Hope heeded his instruction never to return? He would be the last to know.

"Bill Lawrence?" He heard a voice call from behind him and turned to see Carl on the second-story balcony of a red clapboard house. He was bare-chested and his prominent biceps and pectoral muscles flexed as he leaned against the railing. "You looking for me?"

Bill cleared his throat. Even though he had driven nearly thirty minutes in weekend traffic in order to talk to Carl, his sudden presence was unnerving. How had he known of his arrival?

As if reading his mind, Carl nodded toward the car. "Not many of those around here. Even if it is twenty years old."

If Bill could have afforded to trade in his 1982 Mercedes for a newer model he would have, but that was none of Carl's business. The diesel engine still hummed. Only the leather interior had needed repair after the first hundred thousand miles. "I tried to call first, but your line was disconnected."

Carl half smiled. "That's what happens."

"Could I come up for a moment?" When Carl didn't respond, Bill added, "Or could you come down? There's something we need to discuss, and I would rather not do it like this."

"If you can make it up the stairs, I'm all ears."

"Fine," Bill said, deciding to ignore the obvious insult. He opened his car door and reached in to remove the keys. As he did, he wondered for the hundredth time whether he should just walk away. But he didn't want anything to interfere with Hope's future.

The lock on the front door was missing, and the door swung open at the slightest push. The stairwell smelled of fish and onions, an oppressive odor in the heat. He held onto the handrail as he ascended, feeling the pain of the effort in his right hip. Thus far, he'd been able to live with the growing incapacitation of his arthritis, a slowly debilitating condition that all started from a hip fracture playing fives when he was in the tenth form at Groton. Adelaide had done her best to accommodate him. She'd moved their master bedroom and his study downstairs, compromising the water view considerably, bought him a golf cart with a beige canopy to get around their extensive property, and instructed Kathleen to make lime Jell-o with aspartame until he'd lost the twenty extra pounds he'd carried. But despite her best efforts, he wouldn't be able to postpone forever the total hip-replacement surgery he needed.

"I was expecting you to show up one of these days," Carl said from where he stood, leaning against the door frame. He had a slight lisp, and saliva shot through the gap in his front teeth when he spoke. With one hand he rubbed his head with a striped towel to dry his thick brown curls. His khakis hung low on his narrow hips, revealing the elastic of his underwear around his waist. Calvin Klein, Bill noticed. Designer briefs. He shuddered to think that they might be a present from his daughter.

Bill extended a hand. "Nice to see you," he said.

Carl laughed, then stepped away from the door to allow him to pass through. Inside, the room was exactly how he had remembered it from when he had come to retrieve Hope nearly eighteen months before. Two couches covered in batik fabric straddled a single window. In one corner was a square table holding stacks of well-worn books and a vase of daisies. Fishing paraphernalia – lures, a buoy, several oversize rusted hooks, a large whale's tooth, and several smaller shark's teeth – filled a corner hutch. An assortment of colorful porcelain pitchers lined the floor along one wall. The domesticity seemed odd, almost feminine.

Carl indicated for him to sit and offered him something to drink, which he declined. "Suit yourself."

"Let's cut to the chase," Bill began, crossing his arms in front of him. "I assume since Hope is about to be married, we can get this matter resolved quickly. She doesn't need you stirring up trouble."

Carl raised one eyebrow in seeming bemusement. His casual ease, his indifference, made Bill all the more uncomfortable.

"Is that what you consider me? A troublemaker? That's quite a statement coming from you, old man." Carl laughed again, but the sound was sinister, not humorous. He walked to the refrigerator, opened it, removed a bottle of orange juice, and unscrewed the cap. His tanned bicep flexed as he tilted the bottle and drank for what seemed like several seconds. Bill watched his Adam's apple move back and forth along his arched throat.

"Look, I'm not here to point fingers. All I'm asking is that you recognize that her life is taking a different turn. You mustn't contact her. No calls. No visits. It only complicates matters. Hope's vulnerable, susceptible to influence. *Your* influence," he said with particular emphasis, although he wondered whether, in an effort to make his point, he was actually empowering Carl in a manner he hadn't intended. "You both need to recognize that you've gone your separate ways."

"Thanks to you."

"What's that supposed to mean?"

Carl's gaze seemed to lock on Bill. "I should be waiting at the end of the aisle. That's what Hope wants. You know that, too, or you wouldn't be here."

"Don't be absurd. Hope is very happy with Jack, I assure you. You and she had . . . had . . ." He stumbled over his words – "very little in common."

"Because I'm older? Because I'm Portuguese? You're as big a prick as she said." Bill's surprise must have shown on his face, because Carl laughed. "Don't think I don't know how much your little girl despises you."

What had Hope told him? He shut his eyes for a moment, trying to remain calm. Even as the smallest child, she'd known exactly how to make him angry, but the difficulties between him and his daughter had been resolved. He'd taken his share of responsibility and extended his share of forgiveness. They had a good relationship now, as good as any father could have with a daughter. "Her marriage is a *fait accompli*."

"I'd be surprised."

Bill hadn't realized he was squinting from the sun filling the room until Carl moved to the window and drew the blind. As he did, Bill watched, recalling the first time he'd ever seen this mysterious, offputting man. It had been a lazy fall afternoon. He'd stayed at the club drinking Bloody Marys after his round of golf, then returned home looking forward to a night of outdoor grilling – a porterhouse steak and corn on the cob. He'd pulled in the driveway only to see Carl and Hope sharing a chaise longue on the flagstone patio. Hope was asleep, her head tucked into Carl's armpit, her thin leg draped over his, her bare arm wrapped around his neck. She'd looked blissful, her half-smile reflecting a peace she rarely displayed. As much as their public affection, her apparent contentment in the arms of an older man had enraged him.

Carl had been staring at the sky when Bill approached the two of them. He made no effort to get up and, when Bill began to speak, had warned him to lower his voice. "You'll wake her," he'd said softly, as if there were no worse fate. *Who are you to speak to me like that?* he'd wanted to say. Instead, dumbstruck by Carl's boldness, he'd turned and walked away.

Hope must have asked Adelaide if Carl could stay for cocktails, because he was still there that evening. He paraded across the Oriental rug in bare feet and sat on the damask couch, his legs spread, his right foot propped on his left knee. From where he sat in his armchair, Bill had to divert his gaze to avoid seeing up his shorts. He drank a beer from the bottle as Bill probed him on who he was, what he did, how long he had known Hope. Hope stood by silently, sipping orange soda through a thin straw, most probably dreading, if he had to project, the reprimand she knew would come upon discovery that this lobsterman was seventeen years her senior, one of six sons who left his family behind in Portugal, who had no 401(k) plan, no investment strategy, not a single indicium of success, and whose car insurance had been canceled for nonpayment of premiums. But Carl seemed unfazed as he made conversation, intermittently dropping literary references and reciting poetry.

Self-taught or not, he was, Bill thought at the time, an arrogant immigrant, a peasant who had no business touching his daughter.

Perhaps he'd been wrong. Perhaps Carl's confidence in the Lawrence family came from knowing their secrets. It was a thought he couldn't bear. Hope would have wanted to protect their privacy, wouldn't she? He cleared his throat. If not, what had all his efforts years before been about? His nerves were making his mind race, and he needed to refocus on the purpose of his journey.

"I know it's tough making ends meet in your . . . your . . . industry." He stammered slightly, not knowing exactly how to categorize a one-man lobster boat. "And I also know you're interested in starting an aquaculture business. Hope told me scallops."

"That was something Hope wanted, not me. Probably thought I'd do better in her crowd – better with you – if I was an entrepreneur."

"Look. I'm prepared to help you out," he said, realizing that his voice sounded more pleading than he intended. What was wrong with him? Getting some broken-down lobsterman to stay away from his daughter should have been nothing compared to what he'd had to deal with year after year during the forty-one he'd been a real-estate lawyer. All up and down the North Shore was evidence of the multimillion-dollar deals he had put together – the sprawling malls and condominium developments along Route 128, the expansion of the commuter rail, much of the early legal work to make way for the Central Artery, the biggest public-works project in history. That level of success hadn't been easy. Hardly a day passed in the legal profession without some degree of acrimony.

But looking at Carl, Bill had to admit to himself that he was intimidated. There was something about him, his bare torso and weather-worn face, his obvious strength, his easy carriage. Despite the conversation, he was comfortable, much more comfortable than Bill.

Carl walked to the corner cabinet and removed an oversize, rusty fishhook from the shelf. He laid it on his right palm and rubbed it slowly with his left. "Help me? How could you help me? I love Hope. I have since the day I saw her. And she'd be marrying me if it weren't for you."

"I don't know what you're talking about."

"I bet you do." Carl moved to where Bill sat and seemed to loom over him. "But that's the way you people operate. Wouldn't want to talk too directly about anything. Did she ever tell you about us? How great we are together? Not bad in bed, if you know what I mean." Carl stared at Bill for a moment before continuing. "No, I imagine she didn't. You wouldn't have wanted to hear it. Your worst nightmare: a guy with red instead of blue blood pulsing through his veins, exciting your daughter in ways she never thought possible. I may not be what you want, but if you were a half-decent father—"

"I won't hear this," Bill said, rising to his feet. He stood within inches of Carl, close enough to feel his breath and smell a trace of the anchovies he must have had for lunch. He struggled to balance. "I'm offering you ten thousand dollars. Start your business. Buy a new boat. Get the hell out of town. I don't care. I just want you to leave her alone."

"Where'd *you* get that kind of cash?" Carl had a smirk on his face.

"I don't know what you're insinuating." But even as he spoke, Bill wondered whether his words were emphatic enough to be convincing. Maybe his paranoia was getting the best of him. Hope wouldn't have relayed the sorry story of their finances to Carl, would she? But why else would he make such a reference? They still lived in a beautiful home. Even if his partners had forced him to leave his law firm, few people knew the catalyst for that decision. As long as no one discovered the pile of bills and late notices in the top drawer in his desk, or looked too closely at the peeling paint in the kitchen or the water spots that were now forming on the bedroom ceilings from the leaking roof, he'd appear to be the success he'd always been.

It was hard to believe that for nearly a decade he'd survived as a sole practitioner charging $175 an hour, half his former fee. He leased space from an office complex in Beverly Farms, shared a secretary and a conference room with a title examiner, and had enough work to keep him busy most days, especially since low interest rates generated plenty of refinancings. But Carl was right. The cash he was offering didn't come easily. Not anymore.

"You want to pay me – bribe me – to stay away from Hope. And you expect me to take it?"

"I expect you to do what makes sense under the circumstances. Hope will be very happy as Jack's wife.

He's a good man. And I know you could use the money. So we can consider it a win-win deal." He hoped his voice sounded firm. *If you love her, let her go,* he almost added, but he caught himself from acknowledging the intensity of Carl's feelings.

Before Bill realized what had happened, he felt the cool wetness of spit run down his cheek. He stood frozen, wanting to wipe his face but hesitant to make any dramatic gesture that might precipitate further reaction. Carl's black eyes were filled with rage.

"You wouldn't give your daughter a real choice because you and I both know she'd pick me. Then again, you've never acknowledged her will or her wishes. She does what you want or else."

Carl turned away, walked back over to the window, and parted the curtain slightly. Bill scanned the room, wanting to inventory the sharp objects he'd noticed earlier to make sure they were all in place. He couldn't read Carl's expression. Was he lost in thought looking toward the sea, or was he slowly boiling, getting ready to explode? Bill didn't want to wait to find out.

He reached into the pocket of his summer blazer and took out an envelope. Keeping his eyes on Carl, he leaned over and laid it on the table. "Think about it," he said, moving backward toward the door. He opened it and stepped into the hallway. A woman's voice shouting and a baby's high-pitched cry filled the narrow stairwell. He scrambled down the stairs, feeling tempted to skip steps but hesitant lest he fall. He wasn't afraid of the pain, only the embarrassment of seeming feeble. *Old man,* Carl had called him. Relief swept over him as he stepped outside and saw the sun shining on the hood of his Mercedes.

As he was fumbling for his keys, Bill heard Carl's voice call from above. "You don't know her as well as you think you do. She won't marry Jack Cabot. I can promise you that."

5

The Reverend Edgar Whitney unzipped the plastic bag and removed the pledge envelopes, loose cash, and checks, the mound of currency that constituted the yield from yesterday's collection plate. He organized the piles and began to count, feeling a rush of relief that the offerings remained consistently high. Judging by the numbers, the parish members were loyal. The Church of the Holy Spirit was one of the most fiscally healthy churches in the Massachusetts diocese.

Although Monday was officially his day off and the church office was closed, he came to work anyway. He did allow himself an additional half-hour to linger over his daily cup of coffee and rewarded himself with an extra slice of microwavable bacon, but otherwise his routine was sacred. He appreciated the quiet of the empty building, the privacy that gave him time to reflect. Silence bred the germ of his upcoming week's sermon.

What better pastime was there than to work on the words he would deliver, the message he would relate, to the congregation? His life was his work in service to

God. He'd made that pledge a long time ago, after he'd awoken night after night damp with sweat, panicked by the black abyss of his fate, and understood what it was to have his faith tested. From the dust and ashes of his destruction, he'd repented. Finally his prayers had been answered. After three years running a summer camp for violent boys in Barnstable, followed by a six-year struggle in an impoverished church in Lynn trying to lead a congregation plagued by drug addicts, alcohol abusers, teenage runaways, and single mothers, he'd earned his appointment as rector here, the pinnacle of his career. He'd arrived triumphant, a minister dedicated to improving the spiritual life of even the most desperate. No one in the parish would ever know all he had endured.

His quiet dreams over the years didn't begin to measure up to the joy and wonder of this place. This congregation had embraced him and made him their family. Even after the initial wave of social events upon his arrival, the various meet-the-rector cocktail parties, luncheons, and teas, parishioners had continued to call. For the first time in his life, he felt nurtured, appreciated. Certainly there was some status in including the Episcopal minister in one's social roster, but the members of the Church of the Holy Spirit had become his genuine friends. Mrs. Lundy, an elderly widow who had almost completely lost her eyesight, invited him for her lavish Easter supper. He said grace over the lamb and mint sauce before taking his coveted velvet-cushioned seat to the right of his hostess. He spent each Christmas Eve after the late church service at the home of Lars and Sandra Reardon, drinking champagne from Baccarat crystal and nibbling on triangle toasts with caviar in front of a roaring fire. He was the only non-family member invited. These were but a few of the precious privileges he now enjoyed. Hardly a week passed without several invitations.

The evenings he did spend alone were by choice. He welcomed his solitude, knowing he had a place where he belonged. He took comfort in the familiar surroundings of his office and his church and his concomitant duties and responsibilities. Seven more years until retirement, at which time he'd relax and supplement his pension with an occasional appearance as guest minister or retreat leader. Thank you, God, he prayed, for giving me a second chance.

He sat at his substantial desk and ran his hands across the leather top. Everything about the Church of the Holy Spirit seemed elegant. His office had plush carpeting, and a leather couch and two club chairs nestled into a bay window overlooking a carefully manicured garden. The ladies of the Flower Guild spent hours each week pruning and tending the plethora of plants so that their blooms and greens could adorn the altar each Sunday. As he looked out he noticed the delphinium, his favorite, beginning to bud. Good news. He was tired of pink: pink tulips, pink hyacinth, pink roses. The staple color seemed too feminine for the worship of the courageous, protective, and visionary man, Christ the Lord.

He stood, stretched his arms above his head, and sighed. He was stiff for reasons he couldn't quite locate, but he refused to scale back on his physical activities. Whether he carried boxes of canned goods that the congregation collected for distribution to the needy, rearranged the folding tables and chairs in the parish hall to prepare for a lecture on spirituality, or hauled stacks of hymnals upstairs for choir practice, labor in service to God was part of his calling. But he didn't want to throw out his back and be laid up in bed. He didn't want to become a burden to the people he was there to serve.

Besides, he was scheduled to lead his annual retreat in less than three months and needed to be in good health. Fasting, hours of silence, and long walks were all part of the week-long vigil that strengthened his faith and those of the people who joined him. During those seven days he often sat in darkness, imagining life as a troglodyte. He pictured himself buried deep inside a cavern, surrounded by blackness and damp, a deprivation that would heighten his piety and, should he ever venture forth, magnify the beauty of the Loire Valley. It was an image that he turned in his mind: solitude, scarcity, and extreme discomfort could only lead to a greater appreciation of the pleasure of God and His warm embrace. He couldn't bear to miss the annual experience.

Reverend Whitney walked over to the closet and opened the door. He ran his fingers down each of his official vestments: His two cassocks, starched albs, and elegant chasubles in the various liturgical colors of red, green, white, and purple. His cinctures hung on two pegs just inside the door, and he gripped the rope for a moment. It felt soft and smooth against his coarse hands. Everything was in place, just as he'd left it when he'd departed after midnight the previous evening. Then he moved to the small storage closet and turned the knob. Much to his surprise, it opened. He glanced inside and felt relief as he realized nothing had been disturbed. He thought he'd been careful to lock it, but this brief experience reminded him that he always needed to double-check.

He returned to his chair, opened the top drawer of his desk, and removed a package of trail mix, dried apricots, cranberries, and cashews, the weekly stash that he bought by the pound at the health-food store in Beverly Farms. Even though she had never been to his services, the clerk with the brown pigtail who rang up his purchases addressed him as "Father," spoke in a soft tone of deference, and threw him a gum-filled smile as he departed with his brown bag. He liked the sound. He felt blessed to have a paternal role in young lives.

He split a cashew between his teeth and chewed slowly. His secretary had left him a pile of messages – a parishioner wanting to add a family member to the prayer list, a request that funds be allocated for the youth group's trip into Boston, a postponement of the Buildings and Grounds Committee's annual inspection of the facilities, minutes from the last vestry meeting that required his review and signature. Nobody expected responses from him today, but he liked to look at the blue slips with his secretary's perfect scroll. The last thing he wanted was to disappoint a parishioner by a tardy reply or an oversight.

His planner was open to the upcoming week, and he glanced at the checkerboard page. Hope Lawrence and Jack Cabot were coming in for their third and final premarital preparation session on Thursday. He leaned back, exhaled, and cupped his hands behind his head. It would be a difficult meeting. Sadly, Jack had no real interest in life as an Episcopalian. Hope was the opposite: pious, devout, precisely the kind of meek person God rewarded with an abundant inheritance. Her life had been a series of sufferings, poor girl, and she'd had more than her fair share of torment, but she'd managed to make a meaningful life within the church. "My faith has saved me from myself," she'd said. "It is the only component of my life I truly trust." How well Reverend Whitney understood her words. If anything, he worried that she was too puritanical. It was painful to hear how she chastised herself for her perceived shortcomings. He'd tried to explain that the Lord forgives, but he knew she hadn't really heeded his words or his explanation.

His task as marital adviser presented a difficult challenge. It was his duty to highlight the spiritual differences between Hope and Jack and the hurdles she would inevitably face in a relationship of one-sided faith. Although an unbelieving husband could be sanctified through the believing wife and produce clean children, he feared that Jack would prevent her involvement with just those factors that drove her life of faith. The noise of his agnosticism would drown out the whispers of belief.

Although he wanted her to understand, he had to be

careful. In this community, all couples married in a church regardless of their feelings toward organized religion. The father of the bride paid the fee, filled the pews, and got the pleasure of walking his daughter down the aisle, her last saunter of innocence. A secular alternative for those without faith would be the subject of scorn. Weddings were a huge source of revenue to the Church of the Holy Spirit, and if Reverend Whitney were seen as an obstacle, people would simply go elsewhere. He didn't want to jeopardize in any way the fiscal health of his church.

This week's session was supposed to address issues of sexuality and procreation, difficult subjects with any audience. He opened his copy of the New International Version of the Holy Bible, the translation he preferred. "It is better to marry than to burn with passion," Paul wrote in his letters in 1 Corinthians. Perhaps Father Whitney could use these words as a starting point.

A knock ended his musing. He recognized Hope's voice through the door and called out for her to enter.

"What brings you here today?" he asked, rising from his chair. Although she was a frequent volunteer at the church, he never expected to see a soul on Mondays.

"I was hoping to find you."

"Please, have a seat," he said, steering her into a chair and resting his hand gently on her shoulder. He hated that in the politically correct world he had to be concerned about inappropriate physical contact. She looked miserable, and he wanted to hug her, to comfort her, but such touching was out of the question. He had to maintain boundaries. "Tell me what's wrong."

Hope dropped her head and put her face in her hands.

"What is it?"

She shook her head. "I can't tell you."

He'd seen her upset before, many times, but she'd always been eager, almost frantic, to confide in him. Her reluctance today was different.

He remembered a conversation they'd had more than a month before. Through tears and garbled prayers, she'd asked him, "Will brimstone and fire be sent from heaven to destroy me?" The question had been offputting, and he'd tried to find out what lay behind her fears, but she'd offered nothing more. He'd failed for not being able to reach her. Now, as he watched her shoulders shake and listened to her sobs, he wondered whether something new had upset her or whether the same sadness had been resurrected. "You can tell me anything," he urged. "Whatever it is."

"No. No."

"Your secrets are safe. You can trust me. You know that."

She raised her eyes to stare at him, and he could see the puffiness in her face and the dryness of her lips. "It's . . . It's . . . I don't want to believe it." She hugged her knees to her chest. Looking at her bony arms and rail-thin legs, Father Whitney could see what a wisp of a woman she'd become. "Tell me it's not possible."

He took a step back and crossed his arms in front of his chest. "I wish I could read your mind right now, but I can't. Only God knows your pain. To me you have to explain."

"You do know. I know you do. I found . . . I saw . . ."
Her tears prevented further words.

Father Whitney took a deep breath and felt the air
pass through his lips as he exhaled. "Found what? Saw
what?"

"The box," she whispered. "All the documents. How
could you let it happen?"

He felt a sudden shortness of breath as he understood
her reference. He didn't know why she would have
gone in the storage closet or what would have prompted
her to open the sealed box, but the reasons hardly
mattered. She'd misunderstood. He'd done nothing
wrong. What had happened wasn't his fault. He just
needed to explain, to put the information in context so
that she wouldn't be afraid.

"The church is supposed to help people."

"It does. Hope, listen to me. You mustn't lose faith.
We all make mistakes. We're all mortal." His mind
searched for words to begin but found none. Please,
God, he prayed. Help me once again.

6

"Dr. Frank will see you now."

Fiona Cabot replaced the well-thumbed copy of *People* that she'd found in a pile of otherwise strictly medical journals, issues of *New England Journal of Medicine* and *Psychiatric Annals*. As she stood up, she glanced around the sunny office. An elderly man wearing a checked shirt picked at the cuticles on his left hand. Beside him, a young woman with lips carefully outlined in red pencil and dark circles under her eyes clutched her coffee cup. Two potted palms were the only decoration in the room.

Fiona nodded to the man and woman. They'd been there when she arrived. If they were also scheduled to see Dr. Frank, should she be seen first? Perhaps their problems were more pressing, emergencies even. Then again, hers was, too.

Fiona followed the blonde receptionist in her flowered sundress through a set of double doors into a wide corridor. The hall was impressive, with high ceilings and chair-rail molding. A faded Oriental runner somewhat muffled the sounds of their shoes on the wooden floor. Fiona glanced at the rows of doors, each marked with a different name followed by its series of credentials, MD, or RN, or MSN, or CS, or IAAP, or some combination thereof. To the right of the name, a small rack held a card indicating whether the therapist was in or out. One door was partially open, and despite the placement of the "out" card, Fiona could see a red-haired woman in a white medical coat slouched over with her elbows on her desk and her cheeks in her palms.

The receptionist must have caught her glancing inside. "It's been a particularly difficult day."

"Why is that?" Fiona asked.

"We lost a patient last night. A young girl."

"How?" The question came out automatically.

"She hung herself. That's how they usually do it. Oh, my God—" The woman covered her mouth with her hand. "I can't believe I said that. I just wasn't thinking, you know. I've only been here six months. Oh no, and Dr. Frank's talked to me repeatedly about patient privacy and all." She forced a smile and quickened her gait. "This is truly a wonderful place. Most patients are able to get real help here. The kind they need to change their lives."

Fiona nodded, wanting to seem reassuring.

"Dr. Frank's a remarkable man."

"He and my husband went to college together. Harvard," Fiona added, eager to be able to contribute something to the conversation.

"Is he a psychiatrist, too?"

"My husband? Oh . . . no. Not at all."

"Too bad." The girl smiled. "I hear they make great spouses. Then again, mine's a math teacher, so I really couldn't say." Her melodic voice reminded Fiona of a lullaby. She paused in front of a door marked "Peter Frank, MD." "Here we are."

Just as Fiona was about to turn the brass knob the door opened. "Peter," Fiona said, startled. He looked different from the way she remembered, taller, gaunter. He had loosened his tie and rolled his shirtsleeves to the elbows.

"Come in."

Fiona stepped into the cramped office. Stacks of papers, journals, and files buried a large rolltop desk. Books stuffed vertically and horizontally into shelves covered two walls. Light from the single window splashed onto an armless couch with a piece of paper towel covering the headrest. Dr. Frank indicated a chair, one of two plaid wingbacks, and settled himself opposite with his feet on a small stool.

She smoothed her pink skirt under her and sat with her cream handbag on her lap. She was nervous and wanted something to hold to stop her hands from fidgeting.

"How long has it been?" Dr. Frank mused, running his fingers through his thinning hair. "I don't think I've seen you since Jim and I had our thirtieth reunion. Hard to imagine so much time has passed."

"It is," Fiona agreed. Her eyes drifted above his head to where his medical diplomas and various certificates hung, each slightly askew. The clutter made her claustrophobic, and she questioned how anyone could find emotional stability in this disorganization. Then again, she knew almost nothing about psychiatric medicine or how it worked, if it even did. Hope was hardly a model of its success.

But she could certainly understand why the Lawrences had selected Dr. Frank to help with their daughter. He had both impressive credentials and an excellent reputation in the Greater Boston area. He'd gone to Harvard as an undergraduate, then to the medical school, after which he'd been awarded a fellowship at Yale–New Haven Hospital, was appointed to the staff there, and returned to Boston only when he was asked to become chief of the psychiatric unit at Massachusetts General Hospital. For the past two decades, he'd run the Avery Bowes Institute of Mental Health, one of the largest private psychiatric hospitals in the country. He was also a tenured professor at Harvard Medical School, had published dozens of papers, and had received several awards from the American Psychiatric Association. Fiona knew she had a tendency to be overly impressed with Ivy League degrees – she hated to admit that she'd barely survived junior college – but by any standards his resumé was overwhelming.

"And how's Jim?"

"Busy. He's always busy. Healthy. Still works out every day."

"I won't quickly forget his one-armed push-ups."

Fiona tried to laugh. Her husband's daunting exercise regimen seemed compulsive, although she wasn't about to admit that in the company of a psychiatrist. "Our son's getting married."

"Yes, you mentioned that. I understand you wish to discuss something about his fiancée." Dr. Frank leaned back, removed his glasses, and briefly massaged the bridge of his nose.

"That's right. Yes. And I know you've treated her, so now I'm hoping you can help me. To understand, that is."

Dr. Frank reached into his pocket and removed a folded piece of taupe stationery, which Fiona instantly recognized. Having struggled over what to say, she recalled precisely the note she had sent the previous week:

> I'm sorry to impose upon what I'm sure is an overly demanding schedule, but I truly need advice. Your patient Hope Lawrence is our future daughter-in-law. Given her emotional difficulties, Jim and I are concerned for our son. We're also extremely concerned about our future grandchildren. I don't have personal experience with psychiatry, but your friendship with Jim makes me trust you. Any time you could give me would be greatly appreciated. Of course, I expect to provide more than appropriate compensation for your services. I suspect we can both benefit by the discussions.

The part about a friendship with Jim was a bit of an exaggeration. Although they'd been college roommates and both members of the Porcellian Club, they hadn't kept in touch other than the briefest exchange of pleasantries at reunions. But she wouldn't be the first person to exploit a distant connection.

REDEMPTION

She would never forget the look in her husband's eyes, his rage that Saturday night almost a month ago. Their son wasn't even supposed to be home for dinner. He was taking Hope into Boston for a birthday dinner at the trendy restaurant Biba; they were to spend the night at the Four Seasons Hotel, but for reasons Jack never offered, they'd canceled that same day. So he'd stayed home for a family dinner, the first in a long time.

Perhaps alcohol consumption at the Caswells' cocktail party had fueled Jim's rage. He rarely ate hors d'oeuvres, couldn't stand canapés, miniature quiche or bacon-wrapped scallops, and had consumed gin and tonics on an empty stomach. Plus, he and Elliot Caswell had gotten into a lengthy discussion of whether the old Mercy House on Main Street had historical significance. If so, was it proper for the new owners to tear it down or should the town intervene? As a lifelong Manchester resident who'd watched the town grow and change, Jim considered himself an architectural historian and was vociferous in his defense of preservation. Elliot opposed government interference of any kind, especially interference by a local historic commission peopled by self-important retirees. "Private property means he can damn well do what he pleases," she remembered him saying. "He bought the place, for God's sake."

Fiona had listened intently, trying to follow the conversation but distracted by the seven-thirty supper she'd planned at home, a special occasion given the rarity of Jack's presence.

The Cabots finally settled down to overcooked

63

salmon and limp asparagus, a result of their tardiness. Fortunately, Jim didn't appear to notice the culinary imperfections, and Fiona was able to relax, pleased to have a moment alone with her family, her handsome son to her right, her husband at the opposite end of the long cherrywood table. Jim recapped his discussion with Elliot with renewed vigor.

"Typical Elliot. I'd like a buck for every hedge-fund manager who's moving up here," Jim said, pouring himself another glass of merlot. "And you know why they're coming? Because people like me keep this town desirable. We're the ones who have preserved its integrity, its beauty. Christ, if it weren't for us, we'd have a bunch of condos at the entrance to the harbor."

She was surprised Jim noticed when Jack mentioned Hope's therapist in a brief remark, a passing reference, the context of which Fiona couldn't even remember. How many nights had Jim sat at the dinner table studying the label on the wine bottle, swirling sour cream into his broccoli soup, or appearing to count the prongs on his sterling fork? Most dinners he was lost in thoughts of business, or his sailboat, or, as he was that evening, engaged in a monologue to explain and re-explain his views on any given subject. But that Saturday he seemed to have an extra degree of attention, an uncanny hearing. As soon as Molly had passed the pound cake with raspberry sauce and returned to the kitchen, his eyes turned hard.

"She's seeing a what?"

"Dad, it's not a big deal. Just some doctor she talks to when she's upset or anxious."

"Who talks to a stranger about their problems?"

"A lot of people do," Fiona volunteered.

"Stay out of this," he snapped. Although Fiona had endured more than her fair share of his temper, his tone that night was particularly menacing.

"Do you know anything about him?" he asked Jack.

"No. I don't even know his name. And I'm not about to ask."

"Well, you should. You'll be footing the bill soon enough."

"Forget I said anything."

"Forget!" Jim bellowed. "It seems like I'm supposed to forget everything about the woman you're planning to marry. You may have your head up your ass, but I don't."

Jack got up from the table, balled his napkin, threw it on his plate, and walked out. Fiona remembered her own feeling of panic, the knot in her stomach and sudden dryness at the back of her throat, as she watched her son stride away, defiant. She desperately wanted to remedy the situation but feared her husband's further wrath if she tried to placate their son. As she sat alone with Jim in the dining room, she could think of no words to soothe his temper.

"I can't believe of all the girls in this area, Jack picked her. There've got to be women who would kill to marry into this family. Instead, she shuns our boy for that Portuguese lowlife."

"She didn't choose Carl—" Fiona began.

"Don't even try to justify her conduct. Jack should never have taken her back, never proposed. Where was his pride?" Jim said, rising from the table. "And now that this event is actually transpiring, we learn she's a Looney Tune. She'll ruin us, mark my words."

He went to bed without even saying good night.

Fiona sat in silence for what must have been an hour after he left the room. She stared at the cake in front of her, now soggy with sauce. Several times Molly came into the dining room with a tray to clear the table, but with a brush of her hand Fiona indicated for her to leave. She needed to think.

Born and raised in Springfield, Massachusetts, a working-class city in the westernmost part of the state, she'd been nineteen when she met Jim Cabot. Her father had been a dentist until his retirement last year at the age of seventy-four, and she was the youngest and prettiest of his five daughters, with strawberry blonde hair and a figure that fluctuated between sizes zero and two. The family was comfortable in a center-entrance Colonial on a quarter-acre lot, and a two-week rental every August in Yarmouth on Cape Cod, but she'd resented its decidedly middle-class nature: her overweight mother, who got an up-do once a week at the local barber shop, gave herself pedicures, and thought dinner out was a meal at Howard Johnson's; and her good-natured father, who delighted in talking with whatever boys came around the house, played poker once a month with his hygienist's husband, his receptionist's uncle, and the guard at the parking lot, and insisted his girls spend at least part of every Sunday on a brisk, lengthy walk with him. "A constitutional's good for circulation," he always said.

REDEMPTION

Fiona's aspirations far exceeded those of her siblings, for whom she felt almost nothing but disdain. Eloise, the eldest, joined a convent at the age of seventeen. She'd moved to Rome several years ago to work in the Vatican. Two of her sisters had worked as au pairs for years until they eventually married – one to a contractor and the other to a state representative. They were still in Springfield in modest homes with above-ground pools, Corian countertops, and bedroom sets from Ethan Allen. The fourth sister, just ten months older than Fiona, had actually died in childbirth from an unforeseen complication. She'd insisted on giving birth at the local community hospital and ended up the tragic heroine of a Victorian melodrama. Only Fiona had soared beyond her roots, and it was all because of Jim.

Her life had been transformed the night she'd gone into Cambridge with her cousin. A party sponsored by the exclusive Porcellian Club, an invitation extended through a friend of a friend. Standing against the bar with a paper cup of beer in his hand, John James Cabot II had regaled the crowd with stories. His humor and cleverness were second to none. She'd had no idea at the time that he was third-generation Harvard, with all it implied. Although they'd eloped to avoid the shame of the middle-class wedding that her family would throw and the awkwardness of inviting members of North Shore society to a function at the VFW, her marriage meant a listing in the *Social Register*, an invitation to join the Daughters of the Mayflower, and a position on the board of the New England Horticultural Society. The Cabot lineage had been her escape. In

67

exchange, she did everything in her power to keep Jim happy.

And so her mission to preserve the Cabots began. Her work was crucial to prevent Jim's further rage, to preserve their assets, and, most important, their blood-line. She hadn't come this far to be ruined by her son's choice of mate.

Information was power and she needed more of it, so she'd scheduled a visit with Adelaide, nothing unusual given the impending nuptials. They'd been friends for many years and were about to be in-laws. "Hope's such a wonderful girl, but she seems sad at times, withdrawn a bit. Is there anything I can do to help? She feels like family already. I'd do anything for her, you know." Fiona had probed Adelaide on the nature of Hope's problems. Despite her slight pang of guilt at her duplicity, she'd coaxed normally reticent Adelaide until she'd opened up.

Sitting on a love seat together with a pot of Earl Grey tea and a plate of shortbread carefully arranged on a decoupage tray, Fiona had shared what had to be some of Adelaide's most closely guarded secrets: the details of her younger daughter's mental health, her lengthy hos-pitalization for an eating disorder, its recent resurgence, a diagnosis in something called the *DSM-IV*, with which Fiona pretended to be familiar. As Adelaide spoke, she'd taken Fiona's hands in hers and thanked her friend for listening, for caring. "I'm so relieved to have someone to talk to. This has been terribly hard for Bill and me. But knowing how much you and Jim love Hope makes things easier," Adelaide had said as she'd wiped a tear from the corner of her eye with an embroidered handkerchief.

Patting her palm, Fiona had tried to sound comforting. "It's not your fault. You're a wonderful mother, and Hope is a beautiful girl. There's nothing to be ashamed of. Besides, it's nobody else's business." Even as she'd said the words, Fiona knew she was lying.

Fiona had imagined herself in Adelaide's shoes, facing the table of ladies who made up their weekly bridge group, sixteen women who prided themselves on having raised accomplished, uncomplicated children. Anyone could manage a household staff or volunteer for a charity, but these women all had perfect families, sons who went to Groton and daughters who went to Miss Porter's. The North Shore children weren't supposed to have issues. Look at Jack. Life had been easy, the way it was supposed to be. He'd never had a problem in his life. Weren't Hope's efforts to starve herself evidence of Adelaide's bad parenting?

Dr. Frank seemed to be waving the letter at her. "I'm not quite sure how you found out that I am Hope's therapist," he said.

She wanted to respond but needed to choose her words carefully. She didn't need to be a medical ethicist to know there were issues of patient confidentiality, but she was prepared. Although she'd never be thankful for a friend's divorce, Betsy Witherspoon's unfortunate circumstances put her in a position to recommend a very good private investigator. The plump Irishman who worked out of his home in Revere had been as successful in probing Dr. Frank's background as he had been in uncovering Doug Witherspoon's Swiss assets, his rented apartment in the North End, and his twenty-three-year-old girlfriend, a ten-dollar-a-cut hairdresser at that. Fiona had paid handsomely to learn that Dr. Frank had almost lost his medical license. Although most of the details of the hearing before the Massachusetts Board of Registration in Medicine couldn't be disclosed – the records were under seal except as to the parties involved – she had learned that his defense had cost him financially and professionally. But more than the external damage it had done, she hoped it had bred in him an urge for revenge, a need to extract blood. If he was like most people, he'd stop at nothing to make sure that Bill Lawrence was adequately punished for his stream of baseless accusations.

"Adelaide Lawrence is a dear friend," she said, hoping he wouldn't notice the deliberate vagueness of her response.

"Any opinions I may have formed about Hope are confidential. She's my patient. I have duties to her."

She'd anticipated resistance. "I just want to be able to advise my son about his future, his family. He has a right to know."

"That's a conversation you should have with Hope."

"Peter, I don't know quite how to say this." She clasped her hands, wishing Jim were having the conversation instead of her. He'd know how to handle this situation gracefully. "I can help you, too. Jim and I are prepared to pay handsomely for your consulting services."

She liked the sound of that sentence, liked the idea

that she had something to offer this pedigreed doctor. For all his WASP heritage and credentials, she had more money than he'd ever see. Her husband's reputation wasn't marred. It gave her a feeling of power.

She'd never forget the conversation she'd overheard, so many years before, between him and Jim, when she'd arrived at their dormitory a half-hour earlier than expected. "I own her," Jim had said, laughing. "She's lucky to have me, and she knows it. You'd get a woody just listening to what she does for me. I'll take a Springfield girl any day." Peter had laughed, although she hadn't cared. She'd gotten what she wanted. But it did feel good that now, sitting across from him, he treated her with respect.

Dr. Frank stood and walked to the window. She couldn't see his face, but she wondered whether he was thinking about the numerous late payments he'd made on his mortgage or whether he was adding up the tuition bills for his two youngest children, who had yet to enter college. The investigator's report had been comprehensive.

"The information is only for us. For our family," she coaxed.

"This conversation is inappropriate," he remarked, although the tone of his voice made clear he was trying to convince himself more than her.

Silence fell between them as Fiona tried to think of a different approach. "It's actually in Hope's best interest, too. Having Jack know and understand the extent of her problems will certainly help her. He loves her and wants her to be happy. He's a very compassionate boy.

And Jim's a kind man, much more so than Bill Lawrence, as I'm sure you're aware."

He rubbed his eyes. "Even if I agreed with you, what you're suggesting violates every canon of ethics. It's also against the law."

"Isn't the Hippocratic oath first and foremost about helping patients?"

"And you think Hope would benefit by my disclosure?" Was his tone sarcastic or suspicious? She couldn't tell.

"I do. As I said, I think she needs people to understand her. With your help, we will." She stared at him. His resistance seemed to be crumbling, but she couldn't be certain.

"I'm sorry, I can't be of more assistance. I could lose my job."

"As you almost did?" She knew she was out on a limb, but it didn't stop her. He had information to disclose, information that might finally make her son realize he was marrying into a disaster, and her radar had locked. She would get what she'd come for, as always.

He looked around, as if nervous the conversation penetrated the walls. The color had drained from his face. "Who's to know?" she said, leaning toward him. "It could be our little secret. Don't duties ever get excused, even for psychiatrists?" She reached into her handbag, removed a calling card nestled between the pages of her alligator-skin Filofax, and rested it on the edge of his desk. "Why don't you think it over? Here's my number."

Standing up, she straightened her skirt. "I look forward to hearing from you," she said, knowing she would. The only question was whether his information would come in time to convince Jack to stop the wedding.

7

Her father had demanded she be home at two o'clock so they could "have a chat." It was just the sort of paternal mandate that she hated, one issued as if she actually had a choice. Even though they hadn't had a confrontation in years, she tended to avoid being alone with him, and she felt increasingly apprehensive as the hour approached.

She'd changed her clothes three times, standing in front of her full-length mirror trying to imagine how he perceived her. The first blouse was too babyish, the second too seductive. She settled on a pale yellow golf shirt, a blue sweater, and khakis, her hair pulled back in a ponytail. Anonymously preppy, perfectly aloof. She would certainly need to change before her bridal shower that afternoon.

As the grandfather clock in the dining room chimed, she made her way into the library. Bill was already seated comfortably on the sofa, the business section of the *Boston Globe* spread in front of his face.

"I'm here," she said softly. "As you requested."

He folded the newspaper and placed it on the cushion beside him. She sat in the chair opposite and crossed her legs to try to keep her left foot from jiggling. "There's no reason to be nervous," he said. "I'm your father after all."

Hope forced a smile. He liked to remind her, as if reaffirming his paternity could keep her in her place. "What did you want to talk about?"

Bill laughed. "I've certainly raised you to be direct." He crossed his arms in front of his chest. "Are you pleased with the plans?"

"Yes." She knew this small talk was a warm-up. He hadn't paid the slightest bit of attention to the wedding preparations that had consumed hours of her mother's time. After setting a strict budget for the party, he'd stayed away.

"Good. Your mother's been working very hard."

"I know."

He reached across for her hand, but she kept it in her lap. "My baby's getting married. I knew one day this moment would come, but I still feel unprepared. It seems like yesterday that you walked around in diapers and red slippers and I could bounce you on my knee."

His words made her cringe. He could hold on to that image of her childhood, but she had other memories.

He sat back. "You deserve everything to be beautiful. This is going to be your special day."

Special day. The words haunted her. She knew why she was allowing this to happen – it was her way out of a life of hell – but she didn't want the celebration, couldn't bear her future. All she could envision was the finality.

Bill pulled a small pouch out of his pocket and filled his pipe with tobacco. He lit it, puffed several times on the end, and then watched the thin curl of smoke waft upward. He'd smoked the same tobacco since before she could remember, infusing the house with its sweet scent, indicating to her that he was relaxed and otherwise occupied. Its familiarity comforted her. Once when she mentioned to Jack how she actually liked the odor, he'd laughed. "Now I know why I love you. You're the only woman I know who likes pipes."

"I wanted to speak with you before you and your mother left," Bill said. His tone had changed, and he spoke with a deliberate cadence. "Much as I still think of you as my little girl, you're not. You're about to be married and living on your own. I'm proud of you and I want you to be happy."

What do you really want to say? she wanted to scream, but she kept her mouth shut. She'd seen this ritualistic dance before – once when he'd disapproved of her continuing to see Dr. Frank and again when he'd wanted her to end her relationship with Carl. He had a predictable way of approaching what he considered hard topics, father–daughter differences, and she could always tell when the explosion was about to occur. Then his tone would change to an artificial sweetness, a transparent friendliness, as he forced himself to remain in control.

"I think you're aware that the Cabots want you to sign a prenuptial agreement. Jim called me a second time last night. I want to make sure you understand what the document is and why it's important to them."

76

"Jack and I have discussed it. He doesn't want it and neither do I." She felt relieved. If this was the issue, this conversation could end quickly. She glanced at her watch. In forty minutes they'd be leaving for Boston for her bridal shower, another unwelcome ritual, this one hosted by her half-sister. But anything was better than prolonging this discussion. Or almost anything.

"That's not the point." He puffed again on his pipe and then removed his tortoise-shell glasses. "I want you to sign it," he said with a particular emphasis on "I."

"Why?" She stared at him. According to Jack, the Cabots had imposed the prenuptial as a way to control them both, and to keep her in line, as if she cared about his money. If she'd learned anything in the last year, it was that the things that mattered had no price, high or low.

"Because the Cabots don't want you two to marry without one. I think under the circumstances we should abide by their wishes. And quite frankly, I don't blame them. You're lucky to still have Jack after your stint with that fisherman."

"Carl is a lobsterman," she said, knowing it hardly made a difference. To her family, Carl was a blight, regardless of his occupation.

"That's not my point. What I am trying to explain to you is that given your foolishness, your recklessness, whatever it is you want to call that . . . that . . ." he stammered.

She wanted to defend her relationship with Carl but knew she couldn't. That he brought her pleasure in a way she'd never imagined possible, that she could

escape reality by losing herself in rapture, were qualities she couldn't admit even to herself. And she also
knew that despite the joy of an hour here or there, a
moment stolen with him where she could feel trans-
ported, the relationship filled her with nightmares.
Feeling his arms around her could just as easily evoke
the darkest, most hateful moments of her life. Continuing involvement with him meant eternal damnation.
The circumstances of her life had to change, but it
didn't mean the end didn't hurt.

Bill stood up abruptly. He walked to the fireplace and
stood with his back to her. "Your mother and I have
tried to impart our sense of values to you. We've had
high aspirations for you. We've wanted you to belong to
this community, this society, to continue our heritage.
Our friends have worked hard to accomplish a great
deal. While they and we have succeeded, we haven't
become gaudy. Our community isn't ostentatious,
and that's important. Modesty, a commitment to phil-
anthropy, an understanding of history, we've wanted
you to appreciate these qualities." He turned and stared
at her. "The Cabots are part of this society. Jack is
precisely the type of man you should marry."

"Jack thinks the prenuptial is unnecessary," she
repeated.

"His parents just want the certainty that you're not
going to run off, abandoning their son and taking his
money, too."

Where would I go? she wanted to ask. Certainly not
home. "I would never do that."

"You and I know that, but they don't know you like I

do." He walked over and touched the top of her head, running his fingers along her scalp. It sent a ripple of repulsion through her. "Just make them happy. This marriage is in your best interest. You don't want him to change his mind. So I think you should accommodate whatever conditions are placed upon it. You've been raised in privilege. You don't know what it's like to worry about money. As Jack's wife, you won't have to. Don't jeopardize that." She thought she heard him sigh as he walked to the bookcase, unstopped a crystal decanter, and poured himself an ounce of Scotch. "If you'd stayed with Carl, it would have killed your mother. Me, too. We couldn't bear to see you with someone so unworthy, someone beneath you."

Kill him? If only it had.

"You may put blinders on to the way the world works, but your life would've been ruined. You would be ostracized from the community you know and relegated to a life of hardship. You may think you could have survived on love alone, but you can't. That's unrealistic. Romance ends quickly, I can assure you, and if you don't have shared values, a shared social life, and a mutual interest in establishing a household, it's over. You and Carl had none of that, but you and Jack have it all. You'll be friends long after the honeymoon's over."

What did her father know about marriage? She'd rather be alone than in a relationship like that of her parents.

"Hope, you're a dreamer. But it's time I gave you a lesson in practicality. Jack is the best thing that's ever happened to you. You'll be very lucky to be his wife and you can't forget that. Not for a moment. He'll take care of you."

She heard the subtext of his comment: *You're damaged. You're complicated. You have secrets nobody knows or should know. Take what you can, because you may end up with nothing.* He wanted to pass her off safely and quietly to Jack to live happily ever after as pillars of society. She could think of all she wanted to say but couldn't force the words from her mouth. Once again she'd failed to defend herself. She was weak, emotionally paralyzed, and she deserved to be the sacrificial lamb. "You care more about Jack than you do about me," she said quietly, wondering if she would faint.

"Don't be absurd."

She stood and walked over to him. His face was flushed, and the lines around his eyes had deepened. He suddenly looked older. You have to accept who I am. It's not who you want me to be, she thought. "If Jack had asked me to sign it, I'd feel differently. But he didn't."

"Jim and Fiona are going to call off the wedding."

"Then we'll just live together."

"Over my dead body!" he shouted, raising his hand. She closed her eyes, flinching in anticipation. They were silent. She stood frozen, waiting for the sound of a slap, the burning sensation on her cheek, but they didn't come. He had moved away from her, lived up to the deal he'd struck to remain in control. When he spoke again, his voice was low and firm. "You're going to do what is required of you to see that this marriage happens. Do I make myself clear?"

She stared at him, realizing that she wanted never to be fearful again. Despite his words and his temper, she couldn't let herself be terrorized. That period in her life was over. She didn't have to obey.

Penelope Lawrence's hands trembled as she placed the last platter on the table. The pile of thinly sliced, lightly toasted, crustless sandwiches, each with a minuscule slice of salmon, a dollop of cream cheese, and a piece of watercress, was one of more than a dozen delicate snack foods arranged on sterling trays around a centerpiece of white lilies. Several bottles of champagne chilling in silver coolers, a glass pitcher of orange juice, and a three-tiered white cake with buttercream trellis and roses adorned the sideboard. In the bay window gifts wrapped in white, pink, and gold paper with oversize bows were stacked three boxes deep. *The perfect bridal shower; how lovely of you to do this for your half-sister*, she could hear the guests say. As if she'd had a choice. Her mother had made it clear in no uncertain terms that she was to give the party. "That you're making this effort means the world to Hope," she'd added disingenuously.

The whole idea of a bridal shower seemed absurd. Hope and Jack had invited more than three hundred people to their wedding. They had received dozens of gifts already, more sterling, crystal, porcelain, toasters, carving sets, guest towels, and 310-count linens than any couple could ever use, plus so many duplicates that anything they might need could be gotten with the exchange. Yet Penelope had spent her entire week getting ready for this gathering of women to bring more presents. They would pass the day cooing over one another's selections, laughing at Hope's staged reactions, drinking too much, and lavishing the bride-to-be with praise and attention she didn't deserve. Penelope wanted to scream.

Her eyes wandered around the room, the high ceilings and detailed molding of the single space that served as living and dining rooms in her Marlborough Street apartment. She'd bought the two-bedroom floor-through on the sunny side of the street in Boston's Back Bay two years before, when her bonus for billing nearly three thousand hours covered her down payment. It was a good investment, a prime location between Arlington and Berkeley Streets just steps from the Boston Public Garden. She liked urban living but occasionally wondered whether her money would have been better spent on new construction, something with an office, a separate guest bedroom, and a backyard for her two cats to explore, a home in an affluent western suburb along the Massachusetts Turnpike with an easy commute. She wouldn't consider the towns along Cape Ann. Too many bad memories. There were times when she felt as if she'd barely made it off the North Shore with her sanity and judgment intact. Visits home were more than enough to remind her of why she'd left.

But the houses she'd looked at in Wellesley and

Weston reinforced that she was alone. Only married people moved to the suburbs. They wanted good school systems, safe neighborhoods. They wanted a house with a family room. Even the realtor seemed apologetic when she showed her house after house with kitchens that opened into a casual living area. She didn't need her old maid status thrown in her face more than it already was.

The doorbell rang.

She glanced at herself in the mirror. She'd been told she'd inherited the Pratt family's handsome features – chestnut hair, dark eyes, and full eyebrows. "You're exotic," Adelaide had said, trying to be comforting, but the comment had hardly diminished her feelings as an adolescent that she didn't fit the norm. Manchester was filled with blonde girls with button noses and complexions that looked radiant in pale pink. Even though she'd grown accustomed to her reflection over the years, she'd never adjusted to the real import of Adelaide's comment, her implicit suggestion that she was the lesser daughter. While she could tell her that she loved both girls equally, in the words of George Orwell's pigs, Hope was more equal. Whatever she'd accomplished – her *magna cum laude* law school degree, her appointment to head the corporate law section of the Women's Bar Association – seemed inadequate to elevate her status. She wasn't born with Bill Lawrence's genes, and nothing could change that simple fact.

She forced a smile of welcome and opened the door.

Her living room was filled with just the sorts of women she'd imagined when she'd sent out the invitations to a guest list supplied by Adelaide: There was the older generation, friends of Adelaide and Bill's, who'd known Hope her whole life, women with bleached, immobile hair that seemed to stand up off their foreheads, wide gold necklaces and wrists engulfed in bangles, legs encased in flesh-toned stockings despite the summer weather. These women wore bright pink lipstick and cardigan sweaters. Then there was the flock of Hope's friends, preppy, thin girls in capri pants or Lilly Pulitzer wrap skirts with a single strand of pearls around their necks, girls who wanted to know every detail of Hope's big day. She was one of the first among her peers to marry and so was showered with all the pent-up attention of twenty-somethings each anxious for her own walk down the aisle.

Four bottles of champagne had been drained and most of the food consumed, but not a single compliment had been thrown Penelope's way. They seemed to take for granted the preparation, flowers, monogrammed paper napkins, all the trappings on which she'd spent time and money. In fact, she'd been made to feel as if her presence were irrelevant. She hadn't been asked a single question about her legal work, her recent election to the firm's associates' committee. Nobody seemed to care that she was scheduled to close on a $200 million deal to develop a mixed-use parcel on the South Boston waterfront, a deal that had been more than three years in the making and had required so many late nights that she'd used her own money to buy a couch to sleep on in her already cramped office. All the news she would have been so proud to share went unspoken.

Matters worsened when she overheard Fiona remark with some degree of disdain in her voice that the decor was "clearly contemporary. Not what we're used to on the North Shore," she said, her laughter causing a slight snort to escape through her nose. The other woman, whom Penelope didn't recognize, glanced around the room at its neutral tones, sisal rug and embroidered throw pillows and nodded in agreement. She'd wanted to defend herself and her choice of understated furniture. It was meant to highlight the eclectic art and sculpture that she'd gathered on her travels – treks in Nepal, Patagonia, wherever she could go with an organized tour that had space for a single woman. *Interior design isn't only about chintz and English antiques*, she'd wanted to shout, but such an outburst seemed futile. Instead she sank farther into her chair.

"Penelope . . ." Her mother's stage whisper broke into her musings. "I think you should know that your behavior isn't going unnoticed. At least not by me."

"I'm not sure what you mean. If consumption is a benchmark, everyone seems to be having a wonderful time."

"You know exactly what I mean. You may have picked the finest strawberries DeLuca's had to offer, which I appreciate, but you've exuded hostility from the moment we walked in the door. This is supposed to be a joyous time, and you are not being joyful."

Penelope glared at Adelaide. How dare she? The

efforts and generosity of the shower were the limit of her pretending. Her emotions couldn't be scripted, too. As she looked at her mother's pinched lips and stern expression, she felt a surge of rage, an anger born of living under such controlled pretense for years.

"Now pull yourself together and join in the celebration," Adelaide said, moving away from Penelope through the crowd.

The bride-to-be looked serene in a loose linen blouse, cropped pants, and needlepoint loafers as she perched on an ottoman surrounded by wrapping paper. She opened a box from Victoria's Secrets and held the white lace negligee against her chest.

"Oh," Adelaide exclaimed loudly, covering her mouth with her hand in feigned embarrassment. Several women giggled.

Hope blushed and put the lingerie back in its pink tissue.

"Jack will love that," Penelope said, knowing her words were true.

It had been nearly two years since she'd slept with Jack, but she cherished memories of that summer. He and Hope had broken up when he'd discovered her infidelity. If she'd been honest with herself, she should have recognized that she could never take Hope's place, but she'd welcomed the attention nonetheless. He'd bought her the only fancy lingerie she owned – a pair of silk French knickers with white lace in just the right places. For months after their breakup she'd written to him, asking – no, begging – him to take her back. She'd highlighted the deficiencies of her younger sister, her vulnerabilities and neuroses, and outlined her own strengths. Even after he'd proposed, she'd sent several letters pleading with him to reconsider: she would make the better wife; she would never cheat on him. But he'd neither responded nor even acknowledged that he'd received them.

Penelope excused herself to no one in particular and then stood for a moment, wondering if someone might offer to help with the cleanup, the coffee preparation. Nobody appeared to notice her exit. She slipped into the kitchen and began to clear plates, wrap the few leftovers, and load the dishwasher. As she turned on the cycle, the sound of the water filling her Bosch reminded her of that day.

She'd been ten the summer of Hope's seventh birthday. The day before, Adelaide had errands to run, and they'd been left with some two-dollar-an-hour baby sitter. Why hadn't the sisters gone to the Field and Hunt Club to play by the swimming pool, order grilled cheese and boxes of spearmint leaves, and pass the morning? Penelope couldn't remember what had kept them from their likely destination. Instead, they'd gone to Singing Beach. They'd dragged their feet in the soft sand to hear the chanting sound for which the place was named. Penelope had helped Hope splash in the salty waves as their baby sitter flirted at the lifeguard station.

Waiting on line at the Good Humor truck, Hope looked up and stared directly into her eyes. Penelope could still remember her slightly sunburned cheeks, the smattering of summertime freckles. "Mummy and Daddy love me more than you," she'd said matter-of-factly.

"How do you know?"

"I can't tell you, but I just do."

Penelope hadn't protested or been able to challenge her sister. Whether Hope had overheard her parents talking or whether she'd learned from some other source, Penelope knew the comment was true. She'd felt a sinking feeling, a weight so heavy that she couldn't even nibble her toasted almond stick, then a wave of nausea and pressure behind her skull as her sadness had turned to anger.

After lunch they'd climbed the enormous rocks at the far end of the crescent-shaped beach. Penelope had watched the waves break against the jagged stones and the thick patches of seaweed flow with the tide. Hope had scampered over the surfaces, looking for flat rocks to sit on or gulls' nests to stare at, oblivious to the hurtful impact she'd had. As Penelope had struggled to keep up with her, her thoughts turned. A delicate seven-year-old could slip and easily fall, disappear below the ocean's surface in a fleeting moment, the sounds of the waves obscuring any cry for help. A horrible accident, but one for which Penelope couldn't really be blamed. If anything, the distracted baby sitter would suffer the consequences. She'd imagined the fall, limbs flailing, perhaps a finger struggling to grasp hold of a crag on the way down. It took every ounce of her rational side not to set such a course in motion with a push.

REDEMPTION

Several summers later, she'd been out in the Day Sailer with Hope and her cousin Frances, who'd come for her annual visit. The wind had taken them far from shore, and they'd had difficulty tacking their way back. When the sky grew overcast and the rain started, Hope had begun to cry, her teeth chattering between her blue lips. The strong tide and offshore breeze slowed their progress even more. The swells grew. Coming about, the boat had capsized. Hope had fallen into the sail and become entangled in the various ropes.

She remembered the bleeding cut on Frances's forehead from an oar strike as the boat capsized. "Swim to the beach. Get help. We need a motorboat. I'll find Hope," Frances had directed. Although Penelope had wanted the words to be muffled by the wind and the waves, she'd heard the instruction. A strong swimmer, she'd gotten to shore, but hadn't run to the house, hadn't called for anyone. Instead she'd stood gazing out to sea, watching the struggle. Despite the cold wetness that had saturated her shorts, T-shirt, and sneakers, she'd felt a sense of relief. Again the fate of her little sister was within her control. With no assistance, the ocean would let the first child triumph by swallowing the second, smaller body forever.

But Frances had saved her. She'd seen Hope's bright orange life preserver through the dense rain and loosened her from the morass of canvas and rope. With her elbow looped under Hope's chin, she'd towed her to safety. Penelope would never forget the glaring look in Frances's eyes as she'd turned to face her cousin. Holding Hope bundled in her arms, she'd asked only one

question: "Why didn't you go for help?" Penelope had
no response, and Frances knew it. Perhaps she'd even
surmised Penelope's intent. But despite the significant
punishment doled out to Frances, who as the eldest was
considered the most irresponsible in putting the other
girls in harm's way, she'd never said another word
about the incident.

Penelope now stared through the doorway and listened as the women's laughter and chatter grew louder,
more boisterous. The rage she'd experienced a decade
ago, the nausea in her stomach and pressure in her
skull, returned. Nothing had changed. She'd achieved
success, while her half-sister was useless. But Hope
would always be the favorite. She'd won the heart of
Jack and everyone else, no matter what Penelope did
or how perfectly she managed her life. It wasn't fair.

She let her weight fall into the doorway and sighed.
Sometimes she felt she'd suffered long enough.

8

"Why? That's all I want to know." Sitting beside Hope on the sagging couch, Carl had his hand on her thigh. He squeezed a little harder. "Give me an answer."

"You don't understand." Barely able to see through the puffiness of her eyes, she stared at her reflection in the black glass of the window.

He stood and walked to the closet, removed a clean undershirt from the stack on the shelf, and pulled it on over his head. "I'm sick of your lies, your bullshit."

"I'm not lying."

"Then why? Why not me?"

"Because . . . well . . ." She didn't know what to say. The conversation had been going around in circles for the last hour or more, with her rising desperation only fueling his anger. She thought he knew her so well that she'd be able to make him understand why she had to marry Jack, even acquiesce in the decision, but she'd been wrong. He didn't believe in sin. He didn't understand guilt. He took what he wanted and consumed her with a voracious appetite, never realizing how their pleasure tormented her. Coming to his apartment had been a mistake.

It had been weeks since they'd been together, since they'd made love, and she'd tried to convince herself their separation was for the best. She was about to be married. Her ongoing affair with another man violated the Ten Commandments; it was a betrayal of Jack's trust. Her involvement with Carl, the hedonism of their relationship, made it all the worse, but she couldn't help herself. She'd tried in an indirect way to turn to Father Whitney for guidance, and she prayed to God every day to give her strength. Both had failed. She couldn't contain her thoughts of Carl; they'd spilled out of the urn into which she'd entombed them.

"Please believe me. I'd be with you if I could."

Carl banged his fist against the door, and she heard the wood splinter. "Don't pull your victim act on me. You're a coward. Your parents sold your pussy to the highest bidder and you never objected."

"Don't," she said, her voice shaking uncontrollably.

"You make me sick."

"I love you." With all her self-doubts, she knew these words were true. She often felt Carl was the air she breathed, so consumed was she by his scent, his touch, his voice. But she couldn't break her engagement. Not now.

"Then tell me what you're doing marrying that fuck!" he yelled.

The blackness in his eyes as he stared at her made her cringe. She couldn't contain her sobs, and she felt her body nearly convulse. *Hold me! Help me!* she wanted to say, but she knew her pleas would only anger him more. She wished Hope Lawrence could disappear and she could lose herself and the torment of her past. She needed a new identity. She needed to feel worthy. She wanted to belong to someone she could trust. And she prayed that becoming Mrs. John James Cabot could give her what she craved. But as her wedding day approached, she realized she couldn't live without Carl, too.

"The truth is so repulsive, even you can't utter the words." He opened the freezer, removed a fifth of vodka, and took a swig from the bottle, then another. "Get out."

"No . . . no, please. I've told you everything," she lied, but her lies came from desperation, not an intent to deceive. "Please don't send me away." Hope slid off the couch, moved over to where he stood by the refrigerator, and knelt at his feet. "I love you," she said again. "You're everything to me. I'll make it worth it to you." She reached for the zipper of his pants.

The force of his hand slapping her cheek toppled her backward, and she felt something sharp pierce her side. Her face stung, and for a moment she saw spinning stars. She lay still, feeling her heart pound in her chest. "It's okay," she said, although her voice sounded foreign. Then she got up on all fours and crawled back to him. "Please," she begged. "Let me."

Her slender fingers moved slowly back up his leg, rubbing his calf, then his thigh, then his groin in slow circles. "Let me show you." She hesitated, waiting to gauge his reaction, but he didn't move. Slowly she undid his fly and reached inside.

He put his hands on her shoulders, and she felt his grip tighten. Was he pushing her away or holding her still? She couldn't tell. She buried her face against him. His hair and skin were soft and slightly moist. His smell filled her nostrils. She glanced up at his face and saw that his eyes were closed. Perhaps she could make him peaceful again. Perhaps everything could be all right.

She ran her tongue up and down him, feeling the texture of his skin. She made small circles with her fingertip and felt him grow even harder beneath her touch. She knew this was wrong, but for the moment she didn't care. All she wanted was for him to let her stay in his life.

His fingers dug into her back. The pain sent a twinge down her spine, making her neck muscles contract. Did he want more? He had one hand on her head and looped her hair around his finger. Suddenly he pulled, and she struggled to keep from uttering a sound. She didn't want to interrupt his pleasure.

He seemed swollen, larger than she ever remembered. He moaned, and for a moment she felt joy wash through her at his obvious excitement. Then she felt pressure on her neck and realized his hands were around her throat.

"Be gentle with me," she whispered. "Please."

*

REDEMPTION

Jack ejected the Robert Palmer CD from the disc player. Through the partially opened window of his black Porsche, he could hear the sound of crickets breaking the silence. Their persistence seemed to mock him, and he wondered again why he'd spent the last two hours staring at Hope's Volvo parked on the street just below the lighted window of Carl's apartment. Because of the distance, and the fabric covering the glass, he couldn't see inside, but he didn't need to. He could imagine everything.

His father was right. She had lied when she'd said her relationship with Carl was over. He just hadn't wanted to believe it. When he'd asked her directly the night before, she'd kissed his cheek, gently run her fingers across the front of his pants, and smiled. Her loving gestures had reassured him. So why had he followed her here? Why had his instinct been to distrust her?

A part of him knew even when they got engaged that her feelings for Carl would never disappear. She'd told him so. They'd gone skiing for the weekend, but the mountain had been covered in sheets of ice, so they'd never made it onto the slopes. Lying on the shag rug in the rented condominium, she'd tried to explain that loving someone else didn't make her love him less. As he stared at the gas fireplace, watching the symmetrical flames leap from the artificial log, he'd listened intently, desperate to be convinced. But it didn't make sense. Didn't loving someone mean wanting to be monogamous? How could he share his lover's heart and body and not harbor some resentment? How could anyone?

The light in the window went out. He continued to stare up at the dark apartment, as he felt himself perspire. Each moment he expected her to appear, get in her car, and drive home. But the minutes passed and Hope remained inside.

"What's wrong with you? Aren't you a man? What's happened to your pride?" He could hear his father's words. "Everyone knows what's going on. You may say she has emotional problems, but the girl's a slut, pure and simple. You're better than this."

But loving an unfaithful woman wasn't about being less of a man. It was accepting that he was less, so much less that she'd turned to someone else for her pleasure. He couldn't tell his father, but he knew Carl had opened Hope's body, elevated her sense of the possible. He'd freed her from the constraints she'd felt her whole life and allowed her to explore. Jack only reined her in by who he was and what he wanted.

"No son of mine is going to be cuckolded!"

Why couldn't his father understand? Of course he was angry. He wouldn't be human if he didn't admit that there were moments when he harbored violence toward Carl for making him feel inferior or toward Hope for her betrayal or toward them both for simply being in love; but aside from the one time that he'd thrown his favorite photograph of her across the room, shattering the glass, his rage dissipated as soon as he saw her.

"What more do you need to know before you realize she isn't worthy of you, Jack?" his mother had asked that afternoon. "Doesn't it matter to you that she's ill?"

He hadn't known what she'd meant by that comment, but he hadn't wanted to hear another word. "Why are you saddling yourself with this burden? You are our lineage, our future," he'd heard her call out after him as he left the house. He had to lose himself and knew of only one adequate distraction. He craved the familiar smell of oats, hay, and manure that filled the stable. He needed to sit in his well-oiled saddle, feel the smooth leather reins between his fingers, and run his hand through Deliver Me's silky mane. His champion pony wouldn't disappoint him. Or desert him.

But instead of seeking that solace, he'd felt compelled to drive to Gloucester, to torture himself by confirming Hope's presence at the lobsterman's apartment.

"You'll find someone else." That's what everyone had said that one summer he'd had the courage, or perhaps the stupidity, to end their relationship. He'd tried to forget her, but even her sister wasn't a distraction. She was sexy – he gave her that – and she'd thrown herself at him, been willing to do anything and everything to please and pleasure him; but she had an ambition, an efficient competence to her, that eventually repelled him. He didn't want a successful professional. He didn't want to hear about her climb toward the partnership. He wanted a wife.

Hope had a fierce spirit but a gentle nature, a sweetness born of the pain he knew she'd suffered, although she'd never been totally open about her experiences. Even if he couldn't appreciate her poetry or understand her intense depressions, there was nobody like her. She needed him. Her vulnerability, her fragility, were intoxicating. The bottom line was that he loved her so much, he would take whatever part of her she was willing to give.

He closed his eyes, exhausted, but rather than drifting off to sleep, he found himself picturing them together. He could see her slender body, feel her soft skin and silky hair. She'd unbutton her blue jeans slowly, pretending to be tentative, shy, even as she undulated her hips in rhythm to the tune she'd hum quietly. She'd pull her T-shirt over her head, revealing her thin torso and small breasts. Then she'd turn away from him and bend over ever so slightly. That was his invitation.

Carl would hold on to her protruding hipbones and press himself against her. She might lean against the wall for support when his weight and thrust threatened to topple her. Carl would listen, as Jack had so many times before, to her irregular moans, perhaps low and erotic, perhaps high-pitched, revealing a hint of the pain she experienced before she relaxed and was lost in pleasure.

As Jack sat staring into the black night, he felt lonely in a way he'd never before experienced. Nobody understood; he wasn't sure he could explain his relationship even to himself, but he was incapable of diminishing the intensity of his feelings. By loving her, he'd be forever isolated. And that scared him.

He turned the ignition and shifted the car into first gear. As he pulled into the road, he glanced once more at the window. He thought he saw shadows moving, the figures of Hope and Carl intertwined, but he knew it was only his imagination. As he pulled out into the street, he felt a flash of rage, an overpowering wish that she could experience the same torture that she inflicted on him with such seeming indifference. Only if she understood his pain, only if her heart could be twisted, too, would her involvement with Carl ever end.

AUGUST

9

Frances adjusted the drawstring on her sage silk pants and turned to check her backside in the full-length mirror. She frowned, wishing her sweater were a few inches longer.

"You look beautiful from any angle," Sam said.

She turned and smiled. Sam was perched on the edge of the sagging mattress. He adjusted his position and pulled at the collar of his dress shirt. At his insistence, Frances had selected his unoriginal but appropriate outfit: pressed khaki trousers, a navy blue blazer, and a polka-dot tie. Despite his discomfort, he did look handsome.

"We better get going."

They had arrived at the King's Arms Motor Lodge on Route 128 that afternoon and checked into a room with two double beds, wall-to-wall plush carpeting with a stain just inside the door, and a television set in a wood veneer cabinet. The balcony overlooked the parking lot. Although the room was reasonably priced given its location thirty minutes north of Boston, the motel otherwise had little to recommend it. This weekend, however, it was full, packed with guests of the Cabot–Lawrence wedding party; like Frances and Sam, most had checked in that day.

"I guess I'm as ready as I'll ever be," Frances said, glancing again in the mirror. Fortunately, her slight weight loss did show in her face. With a suntan and Sam's reassurance, she didn't feel half-bad. She grabbed her clutch, the cardkey, and the neatly printed directions to the rehearsal dinner, a buffet at the Field and Hunt Club hosted by Jim and Fiona Cabot. The scrolled paper tied with a white satin ribbon was one of several items in the welcome basket that had been left in their room.

"Better than Christmas!" Sam exclaimed as he gazed at the contents: a seaweed face mask, zinc oxide, a road map and guide to antiquing in the area, a lobster-shaped refrigerator magnet, two T-shirts and matching baseball caps with *Jack and Hope. August 18. Manchester-by-the-Sea* emblazoned across the chest in navy script. Typical of Adelaide's attention to detail, Frances thought. That she would select each wedding souvenir, pack each basket, and even leave extra baskets for them to take home to Blair and her father were just more examples of her generosity. It reminded her of how Adelaide ran her household: there were always homemade chocolate-chip cookies in green tins by the toaster, fresh flowers on the table in the entrance hall, and Floris soaps wrapped in tissue in the guest bathroom. Such details made life at the Lawrences' seem perfect.

"What are the Cabots like, anyway? You've barely said a word about them."

"I don't know them well. You have to remember that most of my visits here were brief. Dad brought us up for a couple of days to see Adelaide and our cousins. It was family time," she said, and smiled, thinking how odd the word sounded in the context of her upbringing. A sense of family was something that seemed to belong to everyone else. "Jack was always around. I think he fell in love with Hope when they were still in diapers. But other than a cocktail party now and then, the Cabots weren't much of a fixture. They're very rich. She talks a lot and he's aloof."

"Doesn't that describe virtually every couple you grew up with?"

"You are dreading this event." Frances laughed. "Don't worry. It'll be over soon."

"That's what you always say, Miss Fanny. And it's rarely true. But that's why I love you."

"Why? Because I'm always wrong?" she teased.

"No. Because nothing's simple, but you never stop hoping it will be." He opened the door for her to leave and gently patted her backside as she passed into the hallway.

"You're not welcome here," Bill Lawrence warned, keeping his voice deliberately low. He didn't want Adelaide, whom he'd left in the library when he responded to the knock, to hear any commotion. Nor would he tolerate any disturbance to the evening. Carl's unexpected arrival just moments before they were to leave for the rehearsal dinner threatened to be just that.

"I want to see Hope."

"We're late for a party. I've told you once, get out of my house." He tried to shut the door, but Carl blocked it with one hand. Bill stepped back, releasing the pressure. The last thing in the world he needed was a physical confrontation on his doorstep that evening. He momentarily debated some greater exertion, an effort to grab Carl's lapel or make some bolder gesture, but realized its futility. "Please leave," he repeated.

Carl reached toward him and, before Bill could assess what was happening, grabbed his throat. He felt a squeeze on his trachea and pressure on his Adam's apple. For a moment he was still, trying to relax, to breathe some oxygen despite Carl's powerful grip; but his head pounded, his vision blurred, and he started to feel dizzy. Was he going to faint? God forbid Adelaide should appear now. Time seemed to have slowed, and Bill tried to remember what the martial arts experts said about using the energy of the enemy, or something like that. He had no other choice. He managed to wedge his palms against Carl's chest and, with all his forearm and elbow strength, pushed against his torso with a single heave. Carl released his grip and stepped back.

Bill rubbed his throat. He couldn't think of anything to say and was reluctant to speak for fear his voice would betray him. What a night! They were late for the Cabots' dinner, and he'd almost had a fight with a fisherman twenty years his junior, a man who could probably break his jaw or neck or spine without too much effort. Even as a teenager he'd avoided fights.

The world of physical intimidation between men was foreign. Calm down, he told himself.

"Take your money."

Bill instantly recognized the crumpled envelope in Carl's hand. "We had a deal." It had been nearly two months since he'd been to see Carl and left the cash behind. Not a day had passed that he didn't wonder if his plan had actually worked, if ten thousand was enough to keep Carl at bay. If so, it was less than the cost of the lighted tent that now filled his backyard.

"You can't buy me."

Everyone has a price, Bill thought, but he caught himself from speaking aloud.

"Our deal should be that I now break your fucking neck," Carl said, his voice flat. "I've held on to your putrid money because I wanted to show Hope, to show her what her father was really made of. Now I have a chance."

"I forbid it. You can't—"

"I'm not leaving until I see her," he interrupted.

Bill shook his head. "That's out of the question." He straightened his tie knot. "Don't force me to call the police."

"You can't stop me. Your daughter loves me, and I have a right to that love. If you make her go through with this wedding, if you force her to betray me for a better balance sheet, she'll be in trouble. Trouble that won't go away, because I won't go away. I can promise you that. I know what you are and you can't control me."

"Don't threaten me."

"Take your fucking money!" He thrust the envelope at him.

Startled, Bill took a step back. The crumpled envelope dropped at his feet just inside the threshold.

Bill stared at this man whose black eyes were difficult to read. He seemed so exotic in the Caucasian enclave of Smith's Point. He hated that he'd been intimate with Hope, hated that they'd been so involved that she'd obviously confided things to him that he should never have been told. Carl was a scourge from whom Hope needed protection. She couldn't become Jack Cabot's wife soon enough.

He heard the click of Adelaide's heels behind him. At that moment, Carl stepped back just enough for Bill to shut the door in his face. With his velvet loafer, he pushed the envelope under a skirted table to the right of the door. He turned to face his wife.

"Who was that?"

"Nobody . . . nobody at all," he said again, as if to reassure himself.

"Please, Jack, just talk to me for a minute." Penelope grabbed his arm.

"Don't do this." Jack glanced quickly around the porch, wondering if anyone noticed the wild look in her eyes or the tight grip she had on his wrist. Fortunately, the evening air was unseasonably cool, so none of the guests loitered outside the clubhouse. They'd forgone a view of the ninth hole and hurried inside to enjoy the music, the lavish hors d'oeuvres, and, most important, the well-stocked open bar.

"You can't just walk away from me. I've been trying to contact you for days and you don't even return my calls."

"Penny, stop! I'm about to get married." He lowered his voice. Her harassment felt like some bad rewrite of *Fatal Attraction*, and he wanted her to go away. But he also didn't want to cause a scene. Few people knew of his brief involvement with her, if it could even be called that, and he wanted to keep it that way.

"What we had was a long time ago, and it's over. I care about you. I truly do. And I'm sorry that you're hurt. But I'm in love with your sister. Don't make this any more awkward."

"How can you love her? Don't you see what she's doing to you? You've been used."

With his free hand, he took hold of her shoulder. Her eyes had filled with tears and her lips looked swollen. He needed her to calm down.

"Don't you see how much I love you? I'd be everything you want. I'd be faithful to the day I died. I'd take care of you. I'd do everything in my power to make you happy. That's what you deserve."

"I'm flattered. I truly am," Jack said, struggling to find the proper words. He hadn't anticipated this outburst. He'd thought that if he ignored her endless correspondence, the whole problem would simply disappear. But he'd been naïve, stupid, or a combination of both. He should have addressed her lingering attachment a long time ago.

"Don't turn me away. I promise you won't regret being with me. Didn't I make you feel good? Didn't I bring you pleasure? Tell me what you want and I'll do it."

What could he say now? His mind floundered, unable to come up with polite words to tell her he didn't want to have anything further to do with her and that if she weren't Hope's sister, he'd be perfectly happy never to see her again. "It's too late," he said at last. "Hope and I are going to be married in less than twenty-four hours. Our opportunity's gone." He hoped his slight change in tactic would soothe her, that it would make her feel better if he appeared disappointed, too.

"Is that it? Is that the only reason?"

"Penny . . ." He tried not to show the exasperation he felt. "We can't do this. Please. You'll meet someone else. You'll find someone good enough for you. I know you will. You're a wonderful woman, and you deserve a man to treat you well."

"She's always won out over me!" she cried. "I won't let her do it again. If you love me and I love you, we should be together. Tell her, Jack. You tell her or I will."

He felt himself giving up. There was no way to get rid of Penelope without hurting her, but he couldn't listen anymore. He twisted his arm loose. "I'm going inside now to celebrate with my bride-to-be. I'm sorry you're upset. But I love Hope and I want to make my life with her."

"That's not what you said. You said if it weren't for her you'd be with me."

"That's not the case," he said, being deliberately vague. He leaned forward and kissed her cheek, feeling the clamminess of her tear-soaked skin. "And she is here, so all of this is moot. Goodbye," he said, turning to go inside.

Frances and Sam navigated the thick crowd to make their way to the bar.

"This is quite a spread," Sam remarked as he gazed about the ballroom. Surrounding the parquet dance floor were more than thirty tables, each with a vase of cream and peach-colored French tulips in the center surrounded by flickering votive candles. At every place was a hand-painted plate that read "In celebration of Jack and Hope," plus four forks and three different knives in shining sterling. Ten men in tuxedos played big band music. The Cabots hadn't skimped on a single detail.

Frances glanced down at the calligraphy on the white card she had picked up by the door. They were seated at table six, wherever that was. "Who are all these people?" she wondered aloud.

"Don't ask me," Sam said, "but I think when we get to the end of this line, we better order two drinks each. Judging from the expressions on Fiona's and Jim's faces, we'll need one for each hand."

Frances smiled. It had been odd. The Cabots had been waiting at the entrance to the ballroom to receive their guests, but neither Jack nor Hope had been with them. And it had hardly been a greeting, more like a brief handshake and minimal pleasantries. Even after she'd reintroduced herself, there wasn't a trace of the socially effusive welcome she would have expected from the parents of the groom.

"Do you mind if I look for Hope?" Frances asked. She wanted a chance to see her cousin before they were seated and the evening slipped away.

"Go ahead. I'll wait on line for the bar."

"If dinner gets announced, I'll meet you at the table."

"Assuming I can find it." Sam winked.

Frances circled the ballroom. It was hard to move, and her progress was slowed by familiar faces: Adelaide's and Bill's friends asking about her father, a few of Teddy's well-preserved peers reminding her that they knew her when she was only "yea high." Eventually she spotted Hope, who stood alone, staring out a bay window at the golf course beyond. She was almost hidden by thick folds of the floor-length drapes, and Frances wondered whether that was her intent. In the dusk light she looked pale, her cheeks drawn.

"I wanted to offer my congratulations before you were swallowed up by the evening," she exclaimed, approaching her cousin.

Hope seemed startled, as if she didn't recognize her relative. Then, without any words of transition or pleasantries, she declared, "Mum tells me you work with abused women now."

"Yes."

"How did that happen?"

It seemed neither the time nor the place to discuss domestic violence, but Frances felt obliged to respond.

Hope was the bride, after all. This was her evening. "Sort of by happenstance, if the truth be told. When I left the Suffolk DA's office last summer, I had a brief period of doing nothing before I realized that gardening and my dogs weren't enough to fill the day. The Coalition Against Domestic Violence was looking for a new president, and the search committee asked a cop friend of mine for any recommendations. I didn't have much experience with battered women because I didn't do violent crime at the DA's office, but I went and interviewed. And here I am." She smiled. "I think they liked that I'd been a prosecutor for so long and had a lot of contact with law enforcement."

"You tell me, then, why women stay." Hope stared at her with an intensity that almost made her uncomfortable.

Frances had heard the question a hundred times before, but never had it seemed so difficult to articulate a response. "Well . . . uh . . . it's hard for someone who's in a loving relationship like yours to imagine how scary, how painful, and how difficult it can be to be abused by your partner." She paused, trying to gauge Hope's reaction. Shouldn't they be discussing the honeymoon or the trousseau instead of the plight of battered women?

"Go on," Hope said. Her directness was unnerving.

"I think there's a disconnect that happens in the mind of a victim, an inability to process that her husband has beaten her, or tormented her, or yelled at her, or isolated her in order to control her. The horrible acts – the crimes – get split off from the person the woman has fallen in love with. Somehow the batterer isn't responsible for the consequences of his actions. Instead the woman takes responsibility. She's not good enough. She shouldn't have been flirting. Her dinner should be more elegant or her dress prettier. Some of the stories are really shocking."

"Tell me the worst."

Frances forced a laugh, nervous at Hope's insistence. "Do you really want to know?" Hope nodded. "Well, there was an awful case just outside Riverhead. He was an engineer and she owned a clothing store. They'd been married four or five years and had a two-year-old son. One Sunday afternoon the guy cut his wife's head off and put it on a stake in the backyard. Neighbors having a picnic next door had heard her crying, apologizing over and over for burning the macaroni and cheese, but by the time anyone realized what was happening, it was too late. When the police began interviewing, they discovered the abuse had been going on for years. She had a hospital record three inches thick from various lacerations, burns, a broken arm, but nobody had put two and two together." Frances paused. "Why am I telling you these horror stories? We should be talking about the joy of your wedding."

Hope leaned toward her. "No, we shouldn't," she whispered. "This is much more important."

At that moment some young woman in a pink sundress rushed at Hope. "This party is so awesome!" she shrieked. "You look totally beautiful and totally happy!"

Frances reached out, meaning to touch Hope, but her hand only brushed the fabric of her dress. "I'll catch up with you later," she said.

Hope said nothing as Frances set off into the crowd in search of Sam.

"I told you I wanted that prenuptial signed or this wedding wasn't going to happen." Jim pulled up his zipper and moved to one of the several marble sinks to wash his hands. He'd surprised Jack by appearing in the men's room.

"I did everything I could," he lied. He'd had a difficult evening already, and he wasn't sure how much strength he had to take on another battle.

"I don't think so."

His father's tone was hostile and Jack looked around, hoping someone would interrupt them. Unfortunately they were alone. "What's that supposed to mean?"

"That paperwork is going to get delivered to me before anyone walks down the aisle."

"Can't you let it go? There's nothing you can do to come between us. Nothing you say is going to make me change my mind about the woman I love."

"Did you hear one thing your mother said to you this afternoon?"

Jack didn't have to be reminded. Just hours before the rehearsal dinner was scheduled to begin his mother had been on a crusade, a mission clearly designed to have him call off the wedding at the last possible moment. She'd relayed all kinds of personal details about Hope's life, details that baffled him. How did she know such things? Why had she gathered this extensive information? The final blow had been her claim that

Hope couldn't have children. With that, he'd left. He wouldn't listen.

"Yeah, I did. Every word. And you know what? All I could think about was how manipulative she'd become. My own mother! But you know what? I shouldn't be surprised. She's been married to you a long time."

"Hope can't get pregnant and hasn't had the decency to tell you. Why can't you process that she's lied to you again and again?"

His mother had to be wrong. He and Hope had discussed a family on several occasions. He found it impossible to think she would have omitted such a crucial detail as together they'd imagined a little boy riding a pony on a lead line or a little girl sitting at a piano, banging out "Heart and Soul" on the keys. Once Hope had even told him how she'd wanted to decorate a baby's room with stars and moons painted on the ceiling. "So that she can dream of flying far away," she had said. Had it all been an act?

"Why can't you two stay out of my life?"

"Your mother and I have never interfered in your life. We've supported choices that you've made, even ones that have cost us a considerable amount financially. But let me make one thing perfectly clear. My future is not going to be tied up with her," he hissed in a stage whisper. "And I suggest, son, that you accept that."

10

"Penny! Penny!"

Penelope stopped at the top of the stairs and turned around at the sound of the loud whisper. Hope stood at the threshold of her bedroom, the silhouette of her lithe body prominent through the lace slip. Her white knuckles gripped the door frame as if they were barely able to hold her upright.

Penelope glanced at her wristwatch. The day of Hope's wedding, with a luncheon scheduled in less than thirty minutes, and she wasn't nearly ready. Typical Hope. So self-absorbed, the time never occurred to her. The day before, she'd been late for the rehearsal. The wedding party – the bridesmaids, ushers and flower girls – had stood idly among the pews, reluctant to express irritation at the bride. Even Adelaide, the queen of social grace, had run out of small talk with Reverend Whitney. Then, more than an hour after the scheduled run-through of the service and without a word of apology or explanation, Hope had appeared from a door near the sacristy, accepted a kiss on the forehead from Jack, and turned her attention to the minister's instructions as if nothing unusual had transpired.

"Why aren't you dressed?"

"I need to talk to you."

Penelope sighed. Her half-sister had never chosen to confide in her before. Why today? "I'm not sure this is the best time."

"Please." Her eyes were swollen and her upper lip quivered.

"All right. But you'd better make it quick. Teddy's disagreeable enough without you keeping her waiting."

"Aren't you coming, too?"

"No. There's too much left to do," Penelope lied. This day – Jack's wedding – was the hardest of her life, and lunch with her grandmother at a stodgy old club wouldn't help. She didn't need to be subjected to a minute more of cooing about the bride-to-be; she'd heard quite enough the night before. "I already called to cancel." She entered Hope's room and heard the lock on the door turn behind her.

The normally immaculate bedroom was in disarray, with clothes piled on the canopy bed, shoes strewn across the floor, and pillows from the love seat pushed aside. The floral area rug was askew on its pad. Makeup and powder covered the skirted dressing table. "What's going on?"

"I don't know what to do," Hope said, her voice trembling.

"Everybody gets nervous," Penelope replied, realizing how dismissive she sounded.

"It's not about the wedding. I don't even care about that anymore."

Penelope was silent. How was she supposed to be empathetic when she'd trade places in a minute? All her life she'd dreamed of a big, dramatic wedding with large bouquets of roses, a fabric-lined tent with white lights and decorated poles, a crowd in black tie, everything Hope was now getting. She had no father to walk her down the aisle and knew that if ever the day came, Bill wouldn't go to this expense, this effort, for his stepdaughter. Hope was spoiled and selfish. *Try being thirty and single before you complain*, she wanted to say. "You're being irrational."

"You don't understand. My heart's racing. I keep changing because I can't stop sweating." Hope walked over to her bed and flopped down on the pile of clothes. "I should have said something before now. I don't know why I didn't."

"What are you talking about?"

"Have you ever thought you knew someone, really knew them, but then realized you'd been deceived? It's as if the world has been split down the middle and your legs are spread straddling some abyss. I can't manage." She put her head in her pillow and Penelope could hear the muffled sobs.

"Maybe you should talk to Mom. Or Bill." Your parents, Penelope thought. They're the ones who are supposed to know and understand you. But she knew Hope's prewedding jitters wouldn't be well received. After a ten-month engagement consumed by planning and preparation, their mother wouldn't hear of a cancellation, and Bill would tolerate Hope's anxiety and intense emotional state for all of a half-second. Make a decision and don't second-guess it. If you can't trust yourself, your own judgment, you can't trust anybody else. That was his advice in just about any situation.

"I can't. They're liars. They've lied to me for years. Everyone has. I want this to end. You've got to help me."

Penelope glanced out the window at the dogwood below. Its branches seemed to reach up, covering a portion of the glass. It had always been her favorite tree on the expansive property, an ironic selection given that it grew just outside Hope's bedroom. As a child, she'd climbed it and spent afternoons nestled in its boughs, enveloped by its pungent flowers.

Her ranting made no sense. Penelope would have thought she'd thrive on all the attention. She usually did. Instead she was having yet another fit, another one of the emotional tirades that the entire family had dismissed over the years as simply Hope being Hope. Why didn't Jack give up on her? Why was he willing to tolerate the hysteria? It wasn't fair. "What do you want?" she said with a sigh.

Hope sat up on the edge of the bed. When she spoke, her voice was so low that Penelope could barely hear. "Mum has some Equanil in her medicine cabinet. I need it. Please get it for me."

"Equanil?"

"It's antianxiety medication. Like a tranquilizer."

Penelope was surprised that their mother, the personification of social grace and composure, needed a sedative. And how come she hadn't known? "I can't go snooping in her bathroom." She walked over to Hope and took her arm, which felt tiny in her grip. "Let's get you dressed. You can go have a glass of wine. That'll calm you down."

"Please."

"Why don't you get it yourself?"

"I can't. I can't run into anyone like this."

"If I could get away with it, why couldn't you?" She realized she was using logic on someone whose distress made her irrational. It was a pointless conversation.

"Please!" Hope nearly shrieked. Her body shook and she hugged herself, rubbing her upper arms with her hands as if she were freezing. "It's all I ask."

Although Penelope felt sorry for Hope, her sister's weakness and fragility empowered her. While recognizing how tragic she appeared, that the Lawrence princess was begging to be anesthetized at the precise moment when everyone was watching, gave Penelope a thought. Maybe this time Hope could be a disappointment. She'd cause some scene no one could ignore. Maybe then their mother would be forced to acknowledge how irresponsible and unstable she really was. Maybe Jack would realize the true extent of her pathology. Maybe her opportunity wasn't gone. Maybe, finally, Penelope would be the winner by comparison.

"Have you taken it before?"

Hope shook her head. Then she started to cry. Her lips quivered and tears ran down both cheeks. "I need your help," she blubbered.

She forced a reassuring smile. Just when she'd least expected it, her time had come.

"I don't know what I'd do without you," she heard Hope say, as she headed down the hall toward the master bathroom.

Frances scanned the round tables sprinkling the lawn at the Singing Beach Club, but between the plaid umbrellas and the myriad straw hats it was difficult to discern the faces underneath. She debated checking the dining room adjacent to the buffet but remembered her grandmother's words: "If it's nice, we'll be outside. Inside gets claustrophobic. Plus everyone else can hear your conversation, but you can't. The acoustics are terrible." Given the cloudless sky, they had to be here somewhere.

Finally she spotted Teddy and Hope seated on aluminum chairs. Teddy wore a frayed straw hat, a pink-and-yellow long-sleeved dress belted oddly under her large bosom, and a pair of flesh-toned orthopedic shoes. Her cane rested against the back of her chair. Frances glanced at her watch. Lunch was scheduled for noon and it was just now ten past, but they'd obviously already gone through the buffet line. Teddy's plate was piled with cucumber sandwiches, deviled eggs, and tomato aspic.

"You're late," Teddy admonished as Frances approached. "We couldn't wait, but get yourself some lunch and join us. Penny canceled at the last minute,

Adelaide's apparently running even later than you, and the bride-to-be here has said nothing since she sat down, so I could use an addition to the conversation. I'm hoping you'll have something of interest to tell us."

Frances laughed to herself. Old people seemed to get away with comments and criticisms that no one else would dream of uttering aloud. She went inside, lifted a warmed, slightly damp plate from the pile at the left end of a long table, and proceeded through the buffet. The menu hadn't changed since Frances had come to the club as a child, and she could almost close her eyes and remember the sequence: hot and cold soup, carrots, celery sticks, canned olives on a clear plastic tray, deviled eggs that looked as if they'd been set out an hour too soon, chicken salad, sweaty cold cuts, aspic, and Jell-o. Nouvelle cuisine hadn't made an appearance. Although well situated on a bluff overlooking Singing Beach, the clubhouse was equally outdated. The white-painted walls had yellowed and the furniture in the main sitting room had faded. There was mildew in the changing rooms, and a constant smell of stale cigarettes permeated the air. Why anyone wanted to belong, or would remain on a more than five-year wait list, baffled Frances. She helped herself to a cup of vichyssoise.

"You see, I got known as a pearl wearer," Teddy was saying. "My mother said it was the oil in my skin. I never knew if she was right or whether it was all hogwash. But everyone admired the pinkish color of my pearls. Acquaintances began to ask me to wear their pearls for them, hoping the color would turn, too. So I did. And before long, wouldn't you know, I was walking around with seven or eight strands at any time."

"Are you ready?" Frances said to Hope, settling herself in one of the vacant seats.

"As I said, Hope's not talking. I've tried," Teddy replied. "She wouldn't let me give a proper bridal lunch, so here it is, just the three of us. She's not eating anyway."

"I'd be nervous, too." Frances tried to sound reassuring. She looked at Hope, who stared down at her plate. "Is there anything I can do this afternoon?" She took a sip of her soup. It was overly lumpy and tasted like flour.

"Adelaide's got everything in order. The house is like a military base," Teddy replied. "You should've eloped. It's not as though Father Whitney's blessing would help a marriage anyway."

Hope looked up at the mention of the reverend's name.

"Aren't we a little cynical?" Frances asked. Her cousin looked so pale and forlorn that her natural instinct was to defend her. As much as she adored her grandmother, Teddy could be harsh.

"Oh, please. Don't tell me the religious bug has bitten you, too. One fanatic in the family is enough."

"Teddy doesn't like that I volunteer at the church. But I guess you could figure that out," Hope said.

"When I was bedridden with my broken leg last summer, I didn't get a single call from that man. What kind of minister is that?"

Frances remembered hearing of her grandmother's accident. The terrier had tripped her on a walk. She'd fallen on the path and lain there for hours before being discovered by the neighbor's gardener. When she finally got to the hospital, X-rays confirmed multiple fractures and she'd had a cast for nearly eight weeks.

"I had a terrible time. Even missed Clio's funeral, although I can't say I was heartbroken. I never understood what your father saw in that woman." Frances contained a smile at Teddy's bluntness about her stepmother. Her candor seemed to increase with age. "They never did figure out what happened, did they?"

"It's a closed case. The lead investigator determined it was a suicide."

Her grandmother snorted in disgust.

"Father Whitney probably didn't come to visit because he knew what kind of a reception he'd get from you. Why go where you're not welcome?" Hope said quietly.

"You're entitled to your view." Teddy lifted a bite of aspic to her lips, but it jiggled and rolled off the spoon. She didn't seem to notice and inserted the empty flatware into her mouth. Frances could hear her dentures hitting the stainless steel. "Why, speak of the devil."

Frances turned to see a minister standing at an adjacent table. Despite the heat, he wore his black cassock. He excused himself from his conversation and approached the table. Resting a hand on Hope's shoulder, he asked, "How are you holding up?"

She said nothing.

Father Whitney introduced himself to Frances. "I'm

sorry to break up your lunch, but I do need a moment of Hope's time and her mother said I'd find her here."

"I've got a lot to do," Hope said. "I can't now." Her voice was soft, and Frances noticed a slight slur to her words. Had she been drinking? Her glass seemed to hold iced tea.

"I only need a minute. There's a part of the service we need to discuss. Jack has asked that we delete that portion of the service that allows a member of the congregation to object to the marriage. It's rather last minute, I'd say, but I think we three should discuss it. I told Jack I'd come find you."

Hope kept her face down as she stood and pushed her chair back from the table. Frances reached for her wrist. Her skin was cold and clammy despite the warm day. "Are you all right?" she asked.

Hope's eyes met hers but revealed nothing. Father Whitney nodded, then turned to escort her out.

"What's that all about?"

"I'm not the least bit surprised. I know several people who might cause a stink if given a chance. And I'm probably unaware of others, knowing how this family keeps secrets." Teddy reached for a deviled egg. "Jack's not as dumb as he looks."

I am Resurrection and I am Life, says the Lord. If we have life, we are alive in the Lord, and if we die we die in the Lord. Hope straightened her back and realized what pain she was in. She'd been crouched over her vanity using the mirrored top as a desk for the last hour, and her muscles were sore. Adjusting her position on the stool, she heard the sound of a tear as the hand-sewn folds of her silk Shantung train snagged. Look what you've done, she thought.

Why had she bothered to dress so early? She was Miss Havisham, perpetually waiting for a wedding. Although unlike Dickens's heroine, she wanted it never to transpire.

She put down her pen and gently rubbed the cover of her diary, a well-worn red leather book with lined pages. Flipping back through the last fifteen, she saw that she'd scribbled the same sentences over and over. She'd been unable to stop. The forced repetition seemed the only way to block out the voices that screamed in her head. How could she not have seen, have known, that she could trust no one? Why did she find it so difficult to accept further deceit? More to the point, why did the people in her life continue to betray her?

She'd sought answers in the Episcopal Church. Even though the church had always been a part of her upbringing, it had only been in the last several years that she'd truly immersed herself in its teachings. She'd studied the Book of Common Prayer. She'd read John Booty and other theologians. She'd felt as if she'd absorbed their words and adhered to their instructions. But it hadn't worked. No matter how much she prayed, no matter how she tried to be pious, she'd failed in her quest for redemption. The betrayals she'd discovered were her fault. She'd obviously gotten what she deserved. She was bad, evil, and would be forever damned to hell, the place for sinners and infidels. She shut her eyes and imagined her body burning, her skin peeling from her skeleton as she writhed in pain, acid destroying her sight.

She stared at the pen in her hand, the fragmented letters it created. She'd started keeping a diary years earlier and wrote every day, often more than once. She'd hoped it would help her to purge her fears, that the process of reducing her emotions to writing would clarify her feelings, but she'd found just the opposite resulted. Now the pages were filled with the thoughts that tormented her, evidence of the world's wickedness and her weaknesses. The past volumes were safe, protected from discovery, but this current one remained. Now it was too late to stash it away.

If she was honest with herself, she knew that part of her wanted her secrets to be discovered. She wanted her mother to find the book and to read of her agony. Maybe then she'd understand the full consequences of her years of silent tolerance. She wanted her father to know the pain she'd endured.

She reread the last complete entry and then reached for the medicine bottle, her mother's Equanil. Shaking it slightly, she listened to the pills rattling inside. She'd taken two earlier to calm her nerves, but the dosage hadn't been enough. She'd felt nothing. Now she poured the remaining contents into the palm of her left hand, leaned toward the mirror, and opened her mouth. One at a time, she began placing pills on her tongue, making an arrangement in the shape of a heart. *Go on Hope, do it. Don't be weak about this too*, the voices screamed. *A sip of Pellegrino and they can all disappear. You can, too.*

REDEMPTION

She closed her eyes and felt momentarily calm, the first peace she had experienced in days. She tried to remember the sensation of overwhelming excitement she'd had when Jack had invited her on their first official date. Dinner at 7 Central. In the smoky, informal pub filled with underage drinkers – girls in flower-print summer dresses and Jack Rogers woven sandals, boys in black T-shirts with pictures of the Grateful Dead and Aerosmith on them – they'd talked until closing time, drunk Sam Adams straight from the bottle, and shared their visions of a future, Jack's dream of an Olympic polo team. There had been an ease born of years of friendship, a safety in their intimacy. That had been the best summer. Walks along Singing Beach hand in hand, rainy days in Rockport exploring the twists and turns of little shops along the waterfront, the blistering hot afternoons spent in Jack's air-conditioned library drinking vanilla frappes and watching *Family Feud*.

She felt a tear roll down her cheek and realized she simply couldn't muster the vision or energy to imagine such pleasure now. Her future promised no such delights. She'd tried as hard as she could. It felt as if she'd been trying to claw and scrape her way out of an abyss of anger and distrust, and then, just as the edge seemed within reach, she'd slipped and fallen back. She knew she would never get as close again.

She shut her diary and hugged it close to her chest. She felt the pills on her tongue pressing against the roof of her mouth. Just then the doorknob turned. The noise startled her. "Hope," a familiar voice called. "Hope, open the door. It's me."

Wait, she wanted to say, but she couldn't speak. She spat the pills into the palm of her hand and then transferred them to a tissue, which she tucked into a corner of the vanity. Saved for later. There was still time.

Although she knew she shouldn't, she found herself unlocking the latch.

11

Organ music filled the Church of the Holy Spirit, a celebratory prelude before the "Wedding March" began. The late afternoon sun lit the stained-glass windows, sending an array of color onto the white walls. Bouquets of pink roses and clusters of blue hydrangea tied with oversize tulle bows decorated each pew. On either end of the altar, white candles burned next to floral arrangements that exploded from silver urns.

Frances sat in the third row next to Sam. An usher in a morning suit with gray satin lapels had escorted her to their place on the bride's side of the aisle. Although Frances was surprised to be seated so close to the front, she realized that the Lawrence–Pratt family was small, and its present contingent was even smaller. Teddy sat in the front row, wearing a bowl-shaped pale blue hat and matching knit suit with four separate strands of pink-hued pearls dangling around her neck. Aside from her, Adelaide's only other relative was Frances. Bill Lawrence had had two siblings, but his sister had died several years earlier of lung cancer. The remaining brother, Stephen, with his wife, Maggie, occupied the second row. At the Cabots' party the night before, they'd boasted in hyperbolic prose to whoever would listen about how their sons' accomplishments kept them from the wedding. One was a decorated pilot in the navy and couldn't obtain leave because his reconnaissance missions were crucial to United States security; the other, a graduate of Columbia Business School, worked for an investment bank in Hong Kong. Pressing financial decisions with tremendous impact on world currency markets kept him away. "Hope and Jack surely must understand that," Maggie had said without a hint of apology. The small contingent of relatives didn't translate into an intimate gathering, however. Several hundred friends, out-of-town guests, and business colleagues filled the pews to witness the celebration.

Despite the overhead fans, the church was warm, and Frances could see several women fanning themselves with the printed programs. She glanced at Sam, who appeared to be in a meditative trance as he sat stiff-backed and perfectly still. She touched his forearm lightly. "Are you okay?"

He nodded. "Just thinking."

The space was quiet except for the strains of music, the click of heels, and the crinkling of taffeta as well-dressed ladies settled into their seats. She opened the program and skimmed the order of service, pausing at the reading from the Song of Solomon: "My beloved spake, and said unto me, Rise up, my love, my fair one, and come away." She'd never thought of marriage as a departure, but rather more of a journey. What was it that Hope was about to leave? Childhood, parental control, Frances considered the possibilities. Or, she thought as she reread the verse, did the passage mean movement toward another, come away *to me*?

Frances stopped herself. She didn't care to indulge whatever kind of holy spell was causing her to contemplate doctrinal interpretation. Religion had never been important to her. In fact, just the opposite was true. She couldn't understand blind adherence to beliefs and had never been willing to embrace as true the resurrection of Christ when her rational mind told her that it couldn't have transpired. Maybe she was missing something, but she didn't think so.

Her eyes drifted back to the program, the excerpts from the Book of Common Prayer: "Let their love for each other be a seal upon their hearts, a mantle upon their shoulders, and a crown upon their foreheads." She couldn't ask for a better companion than Sam, but Frances still had no particular interest in giving up her single status. Would she ever be ready? She harbored the notion that the cloak of love was supposed to make two people together – the couple – greater than the sum of the individuals. But maybe her expectations were too high, and marriage wasn't about magic anyway.

She sighed. The heat must be getting to her. Her watch read 4:31 and still the wedding hadn't begun. Even the organist, who'd presumably allowed for only thirty minutes of introductory music, began to repeat her repertoire.

Penelope appeared at the end of the pew, looking elegant in a bright green suit with a full skirt. She

smiled awkwardly as Frances and Sam shuffled sideways to make room for her. Leaning toward Frances,
she whispered, "I gave up waiting with the wedding
party. Everyone's getting restless. Adelaide's nerves are
shot."

Frances wanted to probe, but she refrained. Although
this wasn't a formal Eucharistic service, church protocol
probably precluded chatter.

She looked over at Sam again, who stared straight
ahead as if he didn't want to miss the possibility that
the bride might spring from the ornate cross that hung
above the altar. How much longer would he have to
wait? Frances thought.

Jack Cabot adjusted his waistcoat, then wiped aimlessly
at nonexistent dust on the front of his trousers. Brad
Farley, his college roommate, the number two player
on his polo team, and now his best man, paced back
and forth along the length of the sacristy. His baggy
morning suit hung off his wiry frame. He ran his fingers
through his sandy hair and stared at the floor.

"You still have the ring?"

Brad stopped, opened his eyes wide, and feigned
panic. "Uh . . . uh . . . I left it at the barn." Then he
smiled. "You've asked me that at least a dozen times
since you gave it to me, and I've still got it," he said
with a smile, as he produced the single gold band from
his right pants pocket.

"I don't understand what's holding us up."

"Come on, when have you ever known Hope to be

on time?" Brad laughed. "Don't get me wrong. I love your bride. We all do. But prompt she is not."

"Even for her wedding? I just kind of assumed Adelaide and Bill would make sure things ran smoothly."

"Maybe they had pictures to take beforehand. Relax. She'll show up any minute."

"Speak for yourself. You're the one who's pacing like a caged animal. Don't tell me you don't think this is a little strange."

Brad stopped, went over to his friend, and rested both hands on his square shoulders. "Jack, everything's going to be fine. For all you know, she's doing last-minute packing or she got a run in her stocking or her mascara smeared. Think of all the crap that women go through getting dressed. And believe me when I tell you they won't be rushed. I don't know what Amy does in the bathroom for hours," he said, referring to his own wife. "All I can do is appreciate the result. And you will, too."

"Just go see if the limo's outside."

"A limo? They practically live across the street."

Jack shrugged. "She and her dad are taking a car because Adelaide didn't want any dirt getting on her veil." Brad looked skeptical. "Hey, it's a long driveway." Jack smiled. "Please go look. Make yourself useful for once."

"Anything to make you happy, big guy."

"Thanks."

Jack leaned against the wall. He wanted to calm down, but he was much more anxious than he'd realized. She'd been late for dinner last night, too, although when she did arrive, she looked more beautiful than ever. Her red dress with buttons down the back hugged her thin frame. The high-heeled black pumps accentuated her slender calves. With her hair pulled back in a ponytail and virtually no makeup, she'd had an innocent, fresh look that he found irresistible.

But something had been wrong. She'd hardly been able to speak, and she diverted her gaze whenever he tried to catch her eye. She'd resisted holding his hand, squirmed away from him when he put his arm around her, barely kissed him after he gave his toast, and rode home with her parents, refusing his offer to drive her. She'd been so aloof that he decided to postpone telling her about his wedding present to her: a secluded, three-bedroom carriage house set back from Masconomo Street with a beautiful lawn, mature trees, and plenty of privacy. Although it needed a fresh coat of paint, masonry repairs to the front steps, and furniture to fill the nicely proportioned rooms, they could move in when they returned from their honeymoon. Their first home together. Because he wanted her to be excited, appreciative, happy, he would wait until tonight, when the wedding was over and they were alone, when he could hold her in his arms, whisper her new address in her ear, and hand her the key.

He looked at his gold pocket watch: 4:37. Where was she? He felt his heartbeat accelerate. Had something happened? No, it wasn't possible, he reassured himself. More likely, nerves had overcome her, and she was lying down until she could muster the courage to get through the service. Her life was changing irrevocably. That had to be scary. He was apprehensive, too, if he allowed himself to admit it.

Or, most likely, she was praying. He hadn't paid attention to, or perhaps hadn't wanted to recognize, how important religion had become to her, because the abstract notions of virtue and sin, the incredible stories of seas parting, water turning into wine, and octogenarians giving birth, and the impossibility of adhering to at least several of the Ten Commandments made Christianity too esoteric for him to take seriously. He knew his eyes glazed over as she talked about the Bible or focused on something from a sermon, and their marital preparations with Father Whitney had only highlighted their differing views. Nonetheless, he was willing to accept its importance to her and had even agreed that he would accompany her to church each Sunday. Neither she nor the minister had seemed as pleased as he'd expected when he'd made that concession.

Once again he checked his watch: 4:49. He dreaded seeing the faces of his family and friends sitting in the rows of pews on the left-hand side of the church, the groom's section. Despite his repeated efforts to forget the conversation he'd had with his father back in June, the words reverberated in his ears. *A life with Hope won't be easy. She's not the simplest of women.* His father had had no business making that remark.

That insult was nothing compared to the drama that had unfolded earlier that day. Jack had come into the kitchen after his morning ride to find his mother in tears. She wouldn't explain, just held a handkerchief to

137

her bowed face and muttered something between her sniffles about how she would never be able to explain. He'd walked through the swinging doors into the pantry and on into the dining room, where his father sat alone at the table, a day-old *Wall Street Journal* in front of his face.

"Why's Mom upset?"

"Because I'm not coming to your wedding."

"What?"

"You heard me. Don't make me repeat myself."

"Why?"

"A signed prenuptial was a mandatory condition of this union. Not an option," he'd said coldly without looking up from an article on the advantages of syndicate financing.

Jack had stared at the sheets of the fine black newsprint stretching in front of his father's face and watched him reach around them for his coffee cup without even acknowledging his son's presence. The sight had filled Jack with a rush of anger he'd never before experienced. His parents should be supportive of his decision, regardless of any misgivings. This was his choice, his life, the woman he loved. He'd stepped over to his father's chair and, in a sweeping motion, grabbed the paper and torn it from his hands. He remembered now the tearing sound it made. Then he'd bent over and, leaning toward him, studied the startled expression on his face. He knew Jim Cabot was used to being in control. His outburst was unprecedented, but he felt a rush from even this small rebellion. "Goddamn you," he'd said softly. Then he'd dropped the paper on the floor, turned, and walked out. They hadn't spoken since.

As he counted down the hours to his wedding, Jack had tried to block out his father's disapproval. This was his celebration after all. He didn't need his father there, he told himself. He loved Hope, and at least her parents embraced the marriage. Once they returned from their honeymoon, he felt certain the sea of charged emotions would have calmed. But although he was determined to put up a good front, standing in the alcove waiting for his bride, he felt empty inside. He'd made them proud over the years, and both of his parents should share his joy on this special day. Instead, his mother was there to keep up appearances by explaining to anyone who inquired that Jim was suddenly ill. "Food poisoning, can you believe it?" she said over and over. Her shock actually seemed genuine. His father could sit in his paneled library in a rage and abandon his only son, but nobody in Manchester would know the truth.

His pocket watch showed 4:53. Could the Roman numerals be wrong? There was still no sign of Hope, and Brad had yet to return. Hope was emotional, erratic at times, but she wouldn't have stood him up at the altar, would she? *Cuckolded*, his father's antiquated word resonated. *Cuckolded. Cuckolded.* Had she decided to be with Carl after all? Was it possible, after all they'd been through? As the minutes ticked away, he couldn't bear to acknowledge that maybe his parents were right.

*

"Frances." She turned in response to the whisper of her name. Bill Lawrence stood at the end of her pew, indicating for her to come with him.

"I'll be right back," she said to Sam. As she followed Bill toward the front of the church, she knew all eyes were upon them. People had to be wondering, as she was, what accounted for the inordinate delay.

Once they stepped outside, Bill's face dropped. "I need you to go get Hope." Frances must have looked puzzled, because Bill explained, "I was waiting, but every time I went up and knocked on her door she told me she needed more time. I asked her if she was all right and she said she was, that she wanted some privacy. The last time I checked on her, she'd locked the door and refused to answer me. This is absurd now. Adelaide is very upset. Our guests are beginning to think something's wrong, and we just can't tolerate further delay."

"Has Adelaide talked to her?"

"No. She doesn't want to leave the church because she doesn't want the bridal party to get alarmed."

"Why would she respond to me?"

"She told us last night on the way home how pleased she was to see you. How much she missed you."

"That may be—"

"I'm not the right person to get through to her," Bill interrupted. "I don't know how to say it more clearly than that. If your father were here, I'd make him talk to her. He had a way of getting things done."

Had. Frances noticed the past tense. Although said without a hint of malevolence, the implicit reference was to her father's stroke, to the difference between the man he was before and what he had become. His stroke and the tragedy of his wife's death had stripped him of the robust, assertive qualities for which he'd been universally admired. Now she was supposed to fill his shoes.

She looked into her uncle's walnut eyes. He'd been a background character in the drama of family visits. The focus had been her aunt and cousins. Bill left in the morning to take the commuter rail to work in Boston, and he often returned after dark. But his first act upon walking through the door was to kiss his wife on the forehead, a tender ritual that hadn't been lost on Frances. She recalled other mannerisms that made him seem kind, affectionate, more interested in his family than her own parents had been: He smoked sweet-smelling tobacco out of a pipe while he bounced Hope as a toddler on his knee; he seemed genuinely interested in hearing all the details of their day, asked questions to prove he'd been listening, and laughed at the adventures they relayed; he pitched and covered the outfield for the team of girls when they arranged softball games on the wide lawn.

"I'll see what I can do."

12

Frances opened the front door of the Lawrence home and stepped into the marble-floored entrance. The scent of lilies from several large bouquets and a garland woven around the banister of the elegant staircase filled the room. Although she could see no one, she heard voices, the clatter of china, and the sounds of footsteps as the caterers and bartenders hurried to complete their setup.

She climbed the stairs and knocked on Hope's door. As expected, there was no reply. She turned the knob, only to confirm that it was locked. "Hope," she called. "It's me, Fanny. Are you okay?" Silence. "Do you want to talk?" Still nothing. Frances leaned against the wall and thought for a moment. What help could she possibly be? She hadn't spent much time with Hope in the last several years and knew nothing about the intricacies of her relationship with Jack. If she was having second thoughts, if she wanted to cancel the wedding, it seemed unlikely that she'd open up to Frances.

If your father were here. Bill's words filled her head, making her feel overwhelmed by the task assigned. She put her face close to the door. "I'll tell you something that very few people know about me," she began, hoping to get an immediate response so that she wouldn't need to delve into personal experiences she was reluctant to share. You can't hold back, Frances told herself. She would certainly fail if she exercised her usual closemouthed self-protection. "I was engaged once, many years ago. I thought the guy hung the moon. I didn't think twice when I accepted his proposal." She paused, listening for any sounds from behind the door. Nothing.

"In the months after our engagement, though, things changed. Maybe it was my own insecurity at the idea of being someone's wife. I didn't understand what that meant. Could I still be me? How would I have to change? I became very sensitive to references he made, comments that I would perceive as criticisms. I got the feeling he wanted a wife with a Rolodex like the *Social Register*, with loafers that matched her purse and perfect skin. I got increasingly paranoid. He'd tell me he liked some woman's outfit, and I viewed it that he thought I was drab, unattractive. He'd change the subject while I was talking, and I thought I bored him. It finally came to a head because he asked me to convert to Catholicism. He came from a very religious family, and instead of embracing the fact that he wanted me to share in what mattered to him, I took it that he wanted me to be different. That he didn't like who I was. I wasn't good enough. I broke our engagement."

Frances stopped, momentarily overcome by the power of her own memories. She'd never spoken such thoughts aloud, not even to Sam, and for a moment she regretted sharing them now. But each minute that passed without a response from Hope increased her agitation. "I'm not saying that's what's happening with you. Maybe you've got your dress caught in the bathroom door and can't get out, and here I am rambling away." She forced a laugh. "But I'm telling you about my experience in case you're scared. In case you don't see a way out. You don't have to do this. Your parents may be upset for a few days, but they'll get over it. And Jack will, too. Ultimately everyone just wants you to be happy."

Frances sighed. Hope wasn't going to open the door. She tried the knob again. Should she? She thought for a moment. Over her years of work with the police at the district attorney's office in Manhattan and in Suffolk County, she'd learned a few investigative tricks. Perhaps it was time to use one. She opened her purse and shuffled the contents in search of a hairpin or needle, but without luck. Fortunately, a mint-scented plastic toothpick from the Field and Hunt Club remained at the bottom of her clutch from the night before. She removed its plastic wrapper and stuck it in the lock. Gently, so as not to snap the less than perfect tool in two, she fiddled until she felt the fastener give. The knob turned.

Frances stepped inside and scanned the disarray. There was no sign of Hope. She moved to the dressing table, its surface covered with makeup, hairstyling gels and creams, a brush, and several pairs of earrings. Instinctively, she reached down to right the overturned stool. As she did, she caught sight of a white plastic bottle cap with a safety guard rim and several small pills lying on the floor. Her heartbeat quickened. "Hope!" she called, even though she knew there would be no reply. "Hope!"

She opened a door and looked into the adjacent bathroom. Aside from a pile of towels on the floor, it appeared clean and orderly. A narrow closet held rows of perfectly folded sweaters and racks of shoes arranged in matching pairs. Glancing once more around the bedroom, she noticed another door and pulled it open.

She gasped as she nearly walked into the shantung-wrapped torso. Frances felt her knees collapse, and she grabbed the door frame. Dressed in her white gown, Hope hung from a noose secured to the light fixture, an electric candle encased in a pewter ring. Her hair partially covered her face, her head was tilted to one side, and her tongue hung out of her mouth. Satin-slippered feet turned pigeon-toed and rolled at the ankles moved slightly as her body swayed.

A surge of adrenaline spurred Frances to movement. She grabbed a side chair and climbed up to try to dislodge the rope, but it was surprisingly smooth and slipped from her grasp several times. Frustrated, she wrapped one arm around Hope's slender body and elevated the weight to allow some slack. With her free hand, she struggled to release the noose. She pulled the rope over the back of Hope's head, desperately wishing her cousin would cry out in pain or respond; but Hope remained limp, silent. "Oh God!" she heard herself exclaim, but her voice seemed disconnected, an echo from someplace far away. Again she tried to pry the knot loose.

Frances heard a crash. Hope's body crumpled in a heap, followed by a smattering of plaster as the light fixture came out of the ceiling. She jumped off her chair and reached for Hope's wrist, knowing that it would be exactly as she feared: cold. The pulse was gone.

She looked up at the gaping hole, then at the exposed wire, the still body, the folds of white fabric, tulle petticoat, thin, silk-stockinged legs, curled hair, and delicate face, unrecognizably mangled by the destruction of her death. Frances felt tears burn in her eyes and covered her face in her hands.

The crowd had grown restless, obviously confused by the delay which exceeded ninety minutes. After Adelaide had left the church, several guests had risen from their pews and mingled in the entrance or just outside, reluctant to wander too far, but impatient all the same. However, whatever irritation had been brewing at the wedding's tardiness quickly dissolved when a uniformed policeman appeared. Removing his cap, he made his way down the aisle with a brisk pace and long strides, identified himself to Fiona Cabot, and invited her to follow him. Watching the young officer as he waited for her to rise, Sam could see his hands shaking. Whatever duty he'd been given was not one he relished.

Once they were out of sight, the buzz of whispers quickly filled the hallowed space. What was wrong?

What had happened that required law enforcement? Moments later, Father Whitney appeared and stood in front of the altar facing the congregation. He rocked slightly from side to side. His eyes were bloodshot, his face puffy, and he clasped his hands together so tightly that his knuckles turned white. As startled by the priest's demeanor as he was by the policeman's appearance, Sam looked over his shoulder, searching the church for any sight of Frances, but she was nowhere in sight.

"Ladies and gentlemen," Father Whitney began. His voice trembled. He cleared his throat and repeated, slightly louder, "Ladies and gentlemen." Silence fell over the audience. "In my seventeen years in ministry, this is the saddest day of my life. I must inform you that Hope Lawrence is no longer with us. We pray for her soul."

Somebody screamed. Gasps, sobs, and other sounds of astonishment instantly filled the church. Sam could hear a buzz of voices, a mixture of alarm and tears. Several people got up from their seats and went running down the aisle. He stood, too, an almost spontaneous movement, and swiveled on the spot, not knowing where to go or what to do. Where was Frances? He scanned the crowd for someone he knew, but the faces were a blur of unfamiliar features.

Next to him, Penelope flopped forward and covered her face with her hands. Instinctively, he reached over and rubbed her back, but when he tried to say something, no words came out. What was going on? How could this be happening?

He turned back toward the reverend, hoping for some direction.

"Adelaide and Bill Lawrence have asked me to refrain from discussing further details at this time and, instead, to lead us in a moment of prayer for Hope. We pray too for her family, as well as what should have been her future, the Cabot family. The Lawrences invite you back to the house. They feel that at this time of terrible tragedy, you may want to stay together for comfort." Father Whitney looked away and rubbed his eyes. "Let us pray."

Much to Sam's surprise, the audience actually appeared to follow directions, positioning themselves on the needlepoint cushions that were available under the pews. Robotically, he too slid out a black rectangular cushion embroidered with a red cross and knelt awkwardly. He steepled his fingers and rested his forehead on his thumbs.

"O God, whose mercies cannot be numbered: Accept our prayers on behalf of your servant Hope Alexandra Lawrence, and grant her an entrance into the land of light and joy, in the fellowship of your saints; through Jesus Christ our Lord . . ."

Sam couldn't listen to the words. The entire scene felt surreal. That a young bride was dead on her wedding day as hundreds waited to witness her special event seemed incredulous. Equally bizarre was that her parents actually expected people to return to the house for a reception. What did they plan to do? Precut the wedding cake and serve it with coffee?

Frances had told him several times about the emphasis her family placed on maintaining composure. She'd relayed stories about being injured as a child and having her father tell her that her skinned knee or bruised elbow didn't really hurt, that she shouldn't cry. She'd been in a swimming race at the age of seven and swallowed so much water that she'd thrown up while her father cheered in delight at her efforts; she'd fallen off a horse and broken her arm, but her father had insisted she jump the fence successfully before going to the hospital. She'd seemed amused as she recounted moments in her life in which anyone else would have collapsed, or at least stayed in bed for the day, while she carried on, trying to pretend nothing had happened. Her stoicism was a quality he admired, but he also knew that certain tragedies warranted a display of emotion. That there would be a reception under these circumstances was a morbid elevation of appearance to a loathsome pinnacle. He had to find Frances and take her home.

Tiny white lights hung from each edge and pole of the enormous tent. Underneath, the crowd hovered on the parquet dance floor, sipping drinks and staring vacantly at the round tables set for ten that formed a barrier to the outside. Although the band had set up, there was no music, just a lone guitar on a stand, several microphones, and a drum set. The only activity seemed to be surrounding the long bars, where guests stood quietly on line and the bow-tied bartenders worked at a feverish pace to keep glasses filled.

Sam led Frances to the far corner and pulled a white bamboo chair away from an empty table so she could sit. She perched, feeling awkward and unwilling to disturb the elaborate place settings, specially folded napkins, and white boxes monogrammed in gold that each held a champagne truffle. Sam sat beside her, holding his Corona with both hands and sipping occasionally from the long-necked bottle. She knew if this had been the real reception, he would have ordered his beer in a glass, but there were enough pretenses in operation at the moment. She found his ordinary habit comforting.

Young servers in black pants and starched white shirts passed trays of hors d'oeuvres. At first people seemed unwilling to admit they wanted food and politely refrained, but as the minutes passed, more and more guests reached for the various canapés, the water chestnuts wrapped in bacon, cherry tomatoes stuffed with crabmeat, and spinach in filo pastry. Several times Sam offered to get her food, to refill her glass, but she wanted nothing. She had no interest in mingling and needed silence to remind her that Hope's death was real.

"I don't understand this charade," she said finally, no longer able to contain the confusion she felt. Through the clear plastic sides of the tent, she could see that the driveway was still lined with police cars. Although she'd spoken to the officer in charge when he'd first arrived, the police had little to do once Hope's body had been removed. She wondered whether they were loitering for a free drink or a handful of bite-size quiche Lorraine.

"People mourn in different ways. Maybe making small talk about Hope's wonderful qualities are just ways to deal with the sadness, to process the loss."

Frances looked at Sam and raised her eyebrows. Moments earlier, a heavyset woman in an orange suit had remarked within earshot as she twirled the link strap of her Chanel bag, "I can't bear this for Adelaide. How is she ever going to find the courage to leave her house after *this*?" She'd also overheard a thin man with white hair and a pen in his blazer pocket remark as he stood in line at the bar, "What a dreadful waste of money. Can you imagine?" If these snippets were manifestations of grief, she didn't want to know.

"At some level even the strangers here feel so familiar," she remarked. "I guess because I've been around them in some capacity for so long. I remember once during college I went to an opening-night benefit for the New England Horticultural Society at the Expo Center in Boston. It's one of these deals where various garden clubs, landscape architects, and nurseries put together elaborate displays so that hordes of people get to see beautiful flowers in bloom in the middle of winter. It can be magical. I used to go every year for the smell, the sense of impending spring, and the visual spectacle. Adelaide was on the board for years, and for the kickoff dinner Bill had bought a table. We'd all settled down and wine had been poured and this platinum blonde a few seats from me raises her glass. 'To the North Shore,' was her toast. That was it. As if that said it all."

"Hmm," Sam responded. It was his way of showing

her he was paying attention, empathizing, when he had nothing verbal to add.

"I get the same impression now. What are we doing here?" She sipped her drink. "Once when I was at the DA's office, this cop's wife died. He showed up the day after and testified at a trial. A cocaine case, I think it was. Everyone was talking about how great he was, how strong he was because he didn't take off any time to grieve. Why is that a virtue?" She knew her mind was racing, her thoughts a jumble, but she needed to talk.

Sam finally spoke. "Think of the time we saw that woman outside of Our Lady of Poland crying and screaming. Remember last winter? Who knew what was wrong? She might have lost a family member or she might have just lost a blackout game. But you were shocked at how hysterical she was. It's not just others who try to cover up, Fanny. It's us, too."

Frances leaned over and rested her head on his shoulder. She knew he was right. She'd spent most of her life trying to keep her feelings in check. She was no different from the hundreds of guests now trying their best to contain their sorrow. "Why can't we change, then? What are we all so desperate to hide?" she asked.

Sam ran his hand along her cheek but said nothing. Out of the corner of her eye, she saw her uncle slip through a slit in the plastic siding and head toward the house. "I better go check on everyone," she said, although the prospect of talking with any members of the Lawrence family at that moment seemed a monumental challenge.

"I'll be right here," Sam said. "Not changing."

She smiled. "In your case, that's good."

"It's out of the question!" She heard Bill's voice as she ascended the staircase.

He stood on the landing, leaning against the newel post. Next to him was a broad-shouldered man in a trench coat with his arms crossed over his chest. The tonic he used to hold his black hair slicked in place had a pungent odor that wafted toward her. As Frances approached, both men turned to stare at her.

"Maybe you can help clear this up," Bill said without offering an introduction. "I'm being told there has to be an autopsy. But Hope is our daughter, and it should be our decision. Adelaide and I strongly object."

"Detective Mickey Fleming. Manchester PD." The stranger extended his hand. He had an almost non-existent chin and day-old beard growth. "It's standard procedure under the circumstances."

"What circumstances? Can't you see what's happened? There's nothing to be gained, and I don't want her disturbed. We've been through enough."

Frances turned to the detective, anxious to hear a full explanation.

"I don't mean to be morbid, and I certainly understand the family's concern over the sanctity of . . . of . . ." He struggled for an appropriate euphemism but evidently found none. Frances nodded to indicate she understood. "Where there are suspicious circumstances, the medical examiner needs to be involved."

"Suspicious? Is that all suicides?"

"No, ma'am, but we've made a determination in this case. The deceased was young, healthy, and about to get married. Not a typical suicidal scenario. I'm sorry to say that it's not a private decision at this point. It's protocol."

"This is outrageous! Leave us alone. There's nothing suspicious here, and I won't have you investigating this family." Bill's face had turned red. "I won't allow it. I'm calling a lawyer."

"I'm sorry you feel that way, sir. You're certainly entitled to do what you need to do, but as I say, this is standard procedure. Again, you have my condolences, Mr. Lawrence." He headed down the stairs.

Frances and Bill watched him descend. "Where's Adelaide?" Frances asked when the detective was gone.

"In her room. She's been sedated. There's a nurse with her." He rubbed his eyes. "Tell me something," he said quietly. "What can an autopsy tell them that we don't already know?"

"It'll clarify the cause of death."

"There's nothing to clarify. Hope took her own life. We have to accept that. She should be allowed to rest in peace. I don't understand how they can proceed without our consent. That detective barges in here and tells us what's going to happen as if she isn't our daughter."

"Is it possible it wasn't a suicide?" The question sprang from her prosecutorial mouth before she could contain it. She had no reason to insinuate anything and immediately regretted her inquiry as the color drained from Bill's face. Why would she ever have had such a thought?

"What are you suggesting?"

"Nothing. I don't know why I said that. I was thinking about autopsies in general, how much information you can learn about someone. But it's not relevant here, so I don't know what I was thinking," Frances said, recognizing that her comment had made him visibly agitated. "I'm sorry."

"What do you mean?"

"That my question was inappropriate. The last thing I want to do is make this more difficult. So I'm sorry."

"No, I mean about learning information."

"Oh . . . nothing. As I said, it's not important here."

"But what? Tell me."

"Really, it has nothing to do with Hope."

"Please," he insisted.

Frances sighed. "Part of establishing the cause of death is history of the body: its condition, prior injuries, everything from a pierced ear to surgical scars, all the marks that reveal what's happened to a person over a lifetime."

At that moment, Bill lurched forward as if he were about to collapse, and Frances grabbed his arm to support him, realizing immediately that she'd been too graphic. Too many years as a prosecutor had made her immune to the impact of gruesome explanations. "I'm so sorry. Let's get you to a chair."

13

Frances was alert by the second knock on the door of her hotel room. She pushed back the floral bedspread and reached for the Pashmina she had left in a heap on the floor when she'd hastily undressed the night before. She could see the first light of morning through the partially drawn blinds but knew it couldn't be later than five.

"What's going on?" Sam asked, propping himself up in bed.

"Someone's here. I'll get it."

Frances wrapped the shawl around her shoulders, moved to the door and, without removing the latch, opened it partially. In the hallway stood Jack. He still wore his morning suit, but the tail of his shirt hung out of his pants and he'd removed his jacket and tie. His eyes were black as he stared intently at Frances. "I need to talk to you."

She hadn't seen Jack the previous night and assumed he'd gone home. He'd been wise to avoid the morbid reception. After the police left, she'd sat with her uncle in his library as he'd poured vodka and tonics in quick succession. Perched on an ottoman next to his chair, she'd looked with him at a leather-bound photograph album with gold trim, a snapshot album of a family trip to Bermuda. Hope had been twelve, and there was page after page of carefully arranged images of a tanned girl with a huge smile and brightly colored sundresses standing on a beach with the turquoise water behind her. "Wasn't she beautiful?" he kept repeating.

She'd stayed with him until nearly midnight, listening to him recount stories from Hope's childhood: her first steps across the magnificent lawn at Smith's Point, the father–daughter procession at her debutante cotillion, the first time they'd waltzed together at a benefit for the Brigham and Women's Hospital held in the grand ballroom of the Ritz-Carlton Hotel, a bicycle trip into town on her eighth birthday for a double scoop of rocky road ice cream, the hours spent at the Field and Hunt Club, where he threw tennis balls over the net while she attempted to swing a racket nearly as big as she was. The memories weren't chronological, but they painted a vivid picture of an adoring parent and a beloved daughter. With each detail, Bill looked around the room as if she might suddenly appear. Then, disappointed, he'd slump a little farther in his chair and start on the next tale. She'd finally convinced him to try to sleep and left him slowly making his way up the curved staircase.

"Come in," she said as she shut the door, undid the safety chain, and reopened it. Jack walked past her into the room, seeming not to notice her, Sam, or anything else about his surroundings, and with his hands in his pockets he began pacing back and forth in front of the television cabinet. She didn't move. From the corner of her eye, she saw Sam slip out of bed and disappear into the bathroom. Then she heard a toilet flush and the sound of running water. When he emerged, he was dressed in a pair of wrinkled khakis and a T-shirt, his travel clothes, although they hadn't planned to leave until seven that morning. He gave her a perplexed look, and she shrugged. They both waited for Jack to speak.

"Hope didn't kill herself," Jack announced after several moments. His voice was flat.

"I think—"

"Please," he interrupted. "Hope wasn't suicidal. She had problems – ones perhaps I wasn't even fully aware of – but she wanted to live. She loved me. She wanted to get married. We had a lot of plans for the future."

Frances stared at Jack, not knowing what to say. How was it possible to explain to this man she hardly knew that whatever dreams he had, his wife-to-be apparently didn't share them? Despite his efforts and desires, his love for Hope hadn't been enough to sustain her, to save her. Then she felt a tingle in the back of her throat, a physical reaction seeming to prompt her to ask questions. No, she told herself. You gave up being a prosecutor a year ago. Those days are over.

"You're the lawyer, look at the evidence," Jack continued, seeming to know exactly what to say to engage her. "The police say she might have taken some sort of pills because there were some loose ones lying on the floor, but no one knows for certain. Then she rigged up a noose to the light fixture and hung herself. That's absurd. First off, Hope's tolerance is zero. One glass of wine and she's gone. If she'd taken anything, she wouldn't have been able to function, let alone do something mechanical. She wasn't about to set up that apparatus you found. And she couldn't have done it in advance. Tons of people were in and out of that room, helping her get dressed and who knows what else. She always complained she had no privacy. 'A huge house and not a single, solitary spot,' she used to say."

Suicidal people can be very resourceful, Frances thought. "Jack, this is probably not the time or the place to discuss the details, but it's not at all clear what happened."

"The other thing that you couldn't know is that she was afraid of the dark. She wouldn't have hung herself in a closet."

"That doesn't mean . . ." She let her sentence drift off.

"And there was no note. People usually write suicide notes. Don't they?"

She didn't respond.

"Hope was a compulsive writer. She wrote poetry. She kept journals. She would have wanted to tell us something about her decision. I know it." His voice cracked.

Frances moved toward him and reached to touch his arm, but he stepped away to avoid contact. "If you still don't believe me, take a look at the knot."

"The knot?"

"Of the noose!" he yelled. "Didn't you see it? You found her. I'll never forget the sight of that knot, not as long as I live. It was a bowline. It's a common nautical knot used because it tightens with pressure or weight. But Hope didn't know anything about sailing."

His powers of observation startled her. The discovery of Hope's body had been so traumatic that she now struggled to recall even the most obvious details – the sight of Hope's open mouth, the sense of white fabric enveloping the small space, and the sound of the light fixture as it crashed to the floor. Her inattention to the scene now angered her. "Are you sure?"

"Yes. Practically everybody around here has boats. But she refused to go out on the water. She'd had some bad experience when she was little. She wouldn't even ride in our Boston Whaler, and those things never flip." Jack ran his hand through his hair. "I'd bet my life on the fact that Hope couldn't have tied that rope, not like that."

Frances squinted slightly and studied his face. He'd set his jaw and appeared to be grating his teeth, because she could see his cheeks undulate slightly. She knew what he was suggesting.

"There's one more thing. Hope wasn't wearing her engagement ring when you found her."

"Are you sure?"

"Absolutely. It was a huge diamond. You couldn't miss it. That's what she wanted."

"Is it possible she took it off for the ceremony?"

"Maybe. But I looked in her room and couldn't find it anywhere. Besides, I can't imagine she wouldn't have wanted to wear it to the wedding because I think it made her feel special. Somehow the bigger the stone, the more I loved her. Too bad her finger couldn't hold a boulder or that's what she would have gotten." He looked away, and she thought she saw tears fill his eyes.

"Why would anyone want to hurt her?" Frances asked softly.

Jack said nothing. He walked over to the window and parted the drapes with one hand. Outside the light was gray. The black top of the parking lot was dappled with drops from the slight drizzle. "I need your help. You've got to find her murderer."

"Why me?" she said, even though she could guess the answer.

"Because she's your family and I think you care, and because you don't owe my family anything."

Frances paused for a moment, trying to digest the import of his words. "I'm really not sure—" she began, but cut herself off. She looked at him, wishing for once in her life she could mind-read. How could he be so certain about Hope's death when the obvious signs pointed to suicide? Were the odd details that he'd recited the only bases for his conjecture, or did he know something else that he wasn't sharing? If so, shouldn't he be talking to the police? What did he mean by her not having an allegiance to the Cabots? She remembered her own question to Bill the previous evening and wondered for a moment whether some part of her subconscious had known this was coming. "I don't know quite how to say this, in part because you and I don't know each other well, but you need to realize you're asking a lot."

"I don't care what I'm asking. I'll get to the bottom of

Hope's death, her murder, with or without you. I just thought you could help. I thought you'd want to know who killed her, too."

"Can you think of anyone who would want to?"

"Yes." He stepped in to face her. They were only several inches apart, but Frances didn't step back. "The question in my mind is who got to her first." He turned and walked out, closing the door behind him.

"Fanny," Sam said as soon as Jack had left. "I'm not trying to be unfeeling. Your aunt and uncle are going through hell. But you can't do this to yourself. You agreed to leave this morning, and I'm taking you home."

"What choice do I have?"

"You have to make the choice to protect yourself. You can't make everyone else's agony your responsibility."

Frances had nothing to say. She knew he was right. When Clio, her stepmother, had been murdered, she'd felt compelled to seek out the killer even though it had cost her a job and at least one relationship. She'd done it for her father, thinking it would help him and their relationship, but it hadn't. In fact, what she'd discovered during that investigation only made it worse for both of them. She feared a repetition of her errors. The Pratt–Lawrence clan had suffered enough, and she couldn't bear to contribute to or magnify the pain.

"I'm fully aware that there's a lot about Clio's death that you've chosen not to tell me, and I respect that. You're entitled to your secrets. But I also saw what happened to you. You lost confidence in yourself. You thought you'd failed. And you've just begun to get your life back together, back to a place where you experience joy and excitement and the things that make life worth living."

"Shall I get the violins?" she mumbled half-heartedly, knowing Sam was right. She still remembered the day she learned who had murdered her stepmother. She'd felt physically unable to function, as if her limbs weren't attached to her body. If Sam hadn't driven to Southampton to pick her up and take her home, she might still be sitting at the corner of Job's Lane and South Main Street. The last twelve months she'd struggled with anxiety over how to honor her father's wishes and keep information she knew to herself, with anger at the primitiveness of her family, and with confusion over her own values. Over the last twelve months, she'd relied on Sam and her position at the Coalition Against Domestic Violence to give her a new sense of stability and direction. Now just the thought of an investigation was enough to rekindle emotions she'd fought to suppress. "You heard what Jack said. I can't just ignore that."

"He should tell everything to the police, then. You know that, and he does, too, Frances," Sam reprimanded her. His tone, as well as his use of her formal name, reflected his seriousness. She knew he could tell her mind had already begun to race with possibilities.

"But why hasn't he?" She walked over to Sam, tucked her arms around his narrow waist, and rested her head against his chest. She could feel his heartbeat. "Just one more day," she whispered. "Give me one more day here, and then we'll leave. I promise."

Sam softly rubbed her hair with his hand. "You and I both know you can't make that promise."

She smiled, a mixture of exhaustion and contentment. At last someone else knew her better than she knew herself.

"They're expecting you," said Kathleen as she answered the door. The Lawrences' cook and de facto family member, given her decades of devoted service, wore a black uniform with a white collar and apron and balanced the dirty dishes of a tea service on a decoupage tray. Her eyes were swollen in her round face, and she swallowed repeatedly, struggling to keep her voice steady. "They're in the library." She indicated the direction with a tilt of her head.

"Thank you."

The door was open and Frances could see a roaring fire, presumably lit to drive away the dampness. Although the heavy striped drapes were held back with velvet ties, the dense fog that had drifted in from the water obscured any view out the window. Adelaide sat in a winged chair, a partially completed needlepoint canvas on her lap. Bill stood by the fire, staring at a silver-framed portrait of Hope on the mantel. In his hand was a pipe, but he didn't appear to be smoking.

As Frances quietly shut the door behind her, Adelaide looked up and extended a hand. The loose sleeve of her silk blouse slid up her arm, revealing her delicate wrist, bony elbow, and liver-spotted skin. Frances leaned over and embraced her.

"Can we offer you anything?"

"No, thanks."

"I hate to see you go. It's been so long since we were all together. Now it's hard to imagine . . ." Adelaide's lips quivered. She stopped speaking and covered her mouth with her hand.

"I'm so sorry."

"Hope always looked up to you. She said she was so proud to have a cousin doing such interesting work, helping so many people. You made quite an impression on her."

"I wish she and I had spent more time together recently," Frances said. Her family was small enough. It would have been wonderful to know her cousin better as adults.

"So do I," Adelaide replied.

The room was quiet except for the crackle of the fire. Adelaide picked up her needlepoint but set it down without adding a stitch. Frances moved toward the mantel and settled herself in a chair opposite her aunt. She glanced at the coffee table piled high with an assortment of catalogs from the Museum of Fine Arts, several books on container gardens, and a pile of Patrick O'Brian novels. Her uncle was apparently a fan of Captain Jack Aubrey.

"I just want you both to know that I think this autopsy is important," Frances began. There was no easy way to broach the subject. The mere word caused pain.

"Oh," Adelaide exclaimed. "Oh," she repeated, looking around and appearing to search for something.

"There's nothing unclear about what transpired," Bill remarked. His voice was flat.

Frances thought for a moment. She wanted to be delicate, but at the same time she needed to explain to them that the results could be important. "So much was happening yesterday, the sorrow and sadness is so overwhelming, I think we're all in shock. I'm not sure we focused on what actually happened."

"I can't bear—" Adelaide began.

"That's absurd," Bill interrupted. "What we need is to hold onto Hope's sanctity, her integrity."

Adelaide gasped again.

"I don't know how to say this, and the last thing I want to do is upset either of you more, but Jack came to visit me this morning at the King's Arms. And he pointed to very specific details from Hope's bedroom, from her . . . condition." Frances paused, hoping they wouldn't ask for particulars. She couldn't bear to repeat what Jack had relayed about Hope's body.

"Look, I care about him. For God's sake, he was about to marry my daughter. And I can understand why he wants a different explanation of her death. We all do. But –" Bill paused – "I think it's intrusive and unnecessary. I've already contacted a litigator, someone I've used before who's good. He'll intervene."

"Don't. Let the police do what they need to do. Don't try to stop them. The procedure can be done quickly. It won't interfere with any funeral or memorial arrangements you want to make."

"But if she didn't kill herself, what happened?" Adelaide's question hung in the air, because at that moment the door opened and in walked Fiona Cabot. She wore gray linen pants and a black hat with netting that partially covered her face. Ignoring Frances and Bill, she swept through the room to Adelaide's chair and knelt beside it with her Nantucket basket purse in her lap.

"My dearest, I've been up all night thinking of you and Bill and this horrible tragedy. At this morning's service Father Whitney led us again in prayer. Everyone was there for you. People are anxious to help if there's anything they can do. Bunny Taylor offered to send over her cook. The Reardons said they have a friend with a lovely funeral parlor in Beverly who can help with quick arrangements."

"That's . . . very . . . kind. I think I can . . . manage," Adelaide stammered.

"And we want to start a trust in Hope's memory. We want you to pick the charity, whatever you and Bill think would have made Hope happiest."

No one responded. Frances wondered whether her aunt and uncle were remembering Jim's failure to appear the previous evening. Food poisoning or not, few parents would miss their child's wedding. His absence was apparently being overlooked in light of all that had transpired.

"It's the least we can do. Jack's polo team plans to raise a million dollars for it. So between Jim and Jack, it will be generously funded," she continued. She twirled her double strand of pearls around one finger.

"Has Jack told you he doesn't think Hope took her own life?" Adelaide said.

Fiona leaned over and rested her hands on Adelaide's knees. "Yes. But my dear, you mustn't listen to Jack's rantings. He's distraught, as I'm sure you realize, and angry. He doesn't know what he's saying. I begged him to keep quiet, not to bother you. It's the last thing you need."

"He spoke to Fanny, not us."

"Really." Fiona looked up at Frances, acknowledging her presence for the first time. "You're not going to allow an autopsy to take place, are you?" Even as she directed her question to the Lawrences, she glared at Frances in a manner she couldn't read.

"I think they should," Frances said.

"You know you're making a mistake." She stood up and pulled at her trousers to adjust the pleats. "You don't know what box you're opening. All the details of her personal life will be exposed. The sooner you lay her to rest, the more your privacy will be respected."

"I'm not sure, frankly, that privacy has much to do with what we're talking about," Frances said, wondering why she suddenly felt so tense.

"We can't permit it."

"The procedure has nothing to do with you."

Fiona turned back to Adelaide. "You're wrong. It is my business because my son was involved with Hope. What she's done, the damage, reflects on him. He doesn't need to be embarrassed or humiliated any more than he has been. And we all have to keep on living here."

"Bill shares your view," Adelaide said softly.

"I'd imagine so."

Frances was puzzled. An autopsy was a strictly medical procedure designed to determine the precise cause of death. What was there to hide? She looked at Fiona's pursed lips, the lines of agitation showing in her forehead. What secrets lay within Hope's body that nobody wanted revealed? The subtext of this conversation was clearly something she knew nothing about. She thought again of the issues Jack had raised – Hope's fears, her lack of whatever technical skills were involved in constructing a noose, the missing ring. Was he right in his assessment, or did he just want to close his eyes to the truth of Hope's pain? And why did his mother think that pain was a better alternative to knowing something else? None of it made sense.

"We were fond of Hope, too." She pushed her purse up on her forearm. "We'll schedule a meeting with our attorney about the memorial trust as soon as possible. Please don't hesitate to call if there's anything we can do. Anything at all."

"Tell Jack to come over any time. He's always welcome here. I want him to know that. We consider him family," Bill said.

"He's home now. His father is with him. But I'll let him know," she said as she turned to go.

The father who couldn't be with him at the wedding, Frances thought. He'd apparently had a miraculous recovery.

After the door closed behind Fiona, Frances saw Bill's and Adelaide's eyes meet. They seemed to communicate silently for several moments in a language undecipherable to those outside their orbit, one developed over decades of marriage. Then Bill spoke softly. "Tell the police we won't interfere. We'll authorize this procedure."

14

The Church of the Holy Spirit was empty. Frances waited in the back as her aunt walked up the aisle, dipped one knee briefly, then slipped into a pew. As Adelaide bent her head in prayer, the thin fabric of her scarf slipped off her head and dropped to the floor, but she made no effort to replace it.

She'd asked Frances to take her to church after lunch; Frances was only too happy to oblige, to have a concrete task to perform, as well as a chance to get out of the house. Since the Lawrences had decided not to try to prevent the autopsy, the air in the Smith's Point home felt even heavier, the atmosphere gloomier, than it had before. Frances had often wondered why uncertainties surrounding a death made the grieving harder. That questions could increase the pain in many ways made no sense, since answers never brought the deceased back, but Hope's death seemed just one more example of this phenomenon.

As they'd walked down the drive, around the bend, and across the street, Adelaide had slipped her arm through Frances's. "Your father and I used to laugh at our girls. You, Blair, and Penelope were much more grown-up. Hope was the pipsqueak running behind the three of you in those red bedroom slippers she always wore. I remember her little voice, that squeal of delight she used to utter when she called, 'Fanny.' It amused her so, your nickname. Your father and I spent many hours watching the four of you. You were such a good little mother to her, always checking to see if she was all right, making sure she could keep up. You had remarkable instincts for parenting. I miss those summers."

"I think we all do."

Once inside the church, Adelaide made no effort to draw Frances up to the pew. "I'll just be a few moments."

"Take your time."

She glanced at her watch. It was nearly noon. She needed to call Sam and tell him what was happening. She didn't want him to worry, or at least not more than usual. Although in their daily life together she welcomed his concern and caring attention, she didn't want her prolonged absence from the motel to be a source of anxiety. She was all right, wasn't she?

Waiting for her aunt in the entrance alcove, she thought of the handful of times she'd been in a church of any denomination, other than her weekly bingo games at Our Lady of Poland. The first time Kathleen had taken her to Catholic Mass. She recalled descending the staircase and seeing the family's cook waiting by the door in a short jacket with pearl buttons and pink cording along the sleeves. She had curled her hair so that the soft rolls framed her face. Perched gracefully on top was a round white hat that resembled an upside-down dog dish. Her thick ankles were encased in opaque stockings despite the ninety-degree heat. "Where is your hat?" Kathleen had asked.

"I don't have one," Frances had replied, feeling instantly self-conscious.

Kathleen had eyed her bare legs, knobby knees, and dirty sandals. "Never mind," she'd muttered, steering Frances out the door.

Kenny, the Lawrences' elderly, rail-thin gardener at the time, was sitting behind the wheel of his mauve sedan with the engine idling. He got out when they approached and opened the back door. "What's she doing here?" he'd asked in reference to Frances.

"No one else around here seems concerned with this girl's religious training, so I'll just make her a Catholic. She'll be better for it. The religion of our great president, may he rest in peace, is plenty good enough, even for the Pratts."

Frances remembered sitting in an enormous church with mural ceilings and bright stained-glass images of the Virgin Mary, the Last Supper, and the Crucifixion. Kathleen had crossed herself before kneeling in prayer. "Do you pray for yourself?" she'd whispered.

"For the forgiveness of my sins. And yours," Kathleen had retorted.

Her reverie was broken by the sound of her name, and she turned in the direction of the voice. Father Whitney emerged from a small doorway to the left of where she was waiting. Without the religious vestments he'd worn for Hope's wedding, he looked younger, handsomer, and his appearance startled her. Were it not for his collar, he could have been mistaken for a golfer at the Field and Hunt Club.

"I'm Father Whitney. We met briefly at the Singing Beach Club."

"I remember."

He glanced down the aisle. His gaze rested on Adelaide as she knelt quietly in the pew. "I'm glad she came. She wasn't here this morning at service, and I was worried. I don't want her to be ashamed."

"Ashamed?"

"Adelaide is a deeply spiritual person. Her daughter was, too. And I'm concerned about how she will handle this."

"She's strong."

"Yes. Yes, I know." He furrowed his brow. "Our Lord forgives us all."

"What do you mean by that?" Frances asked, regretting the snap in her voice, but she didn't like the implication of blame.

"The Sixth Commandment tells us, 'Thou shalt not kill.' Suicide is a sin. Human life is sacred, precious. But Hope is forgiven. God has forgiven her. She's walked through the valley of death and into eternal life. Adelaide, as the survivor, must feel guilt about what happened. I just want her to know she mustn't feel that way."

But what parent wouldn't?

"I want to come by the house, if I'm not imposing. Adelaide and Bill must understand that this congregation supports them completely, and that I am here for them if there is anything at all I can do to help, to console. My prayer is that they don't lose faith because of this tragedy," he continued.

"That's very kind," Frances said, wanting the conversation to end.

"Don't misunderstand me. Please. Even among the most ardent believers, it's hard to hold onto our faith in a time like this. We're like Job. He questioned the tests that God put him through. 'Even today is my complaint bitter,' he exclaims as he calls out in search of God." He paused for a moment. "I don't suppose you've read *When Bad Things Happen to Good People*."

"I haven't."

"It's an examination of how we maintain our faith in God when circumstances are more horrendous than we could possibly imagine. I find the book extremely helpful in times like this. I was wondering if you could give it to Adelaide from me, from all of us here at Holy Spirit." Frances hadn't noticed anything in his hand, but he extended his arm and gave her Rabbi Kushner's thin book. The cover was torn slightly at the edges.

"I'm sure she'll appreciate it." Frances tried to smile. She flipped the pages of the book. "For everyone who has been hurt by life, here's a book that heals," the jacket cover read. That applied to just about everyone she'd ever met.

"Hope's faith was extremely important to her. In exploring and building that, she grew to trust me. We were friends. If there were things she wanted to say, she could tell me in confidence. If in any way I can help her parents assimilate her experience, her suffering, I want to do so." He glanced up the aisle at Adelaide. "I'm sorry I can't stay until she's finished, but I must deliver Eucharist to our shut-ins, the members of our parish who can't make it to church," he explained. "I'll call to check on her this afternoon. May God bless you and keep you safe."

"Thank you." Frances watched him leave. She fingered the small book, his offer of comfort, as she thought of what he'd relayed. If he knew Hope so well, why hadn't he seen her death coming? Or, as she mulled over his words, was he really echoing Jack's view that Hope hadn't killed herself? Was his implicit message that since she was such a pious church member, she wouldn't have taken her own life – so someone else must have done it? If that was the case, it appeared that he, like Jack, was drawing a different conclusion about Hope's death.

"Meaty. Meaty, it's Fanny. Fanny Pratt." The crackle and static in the telephone line made Frances feel as if she were calling Tibet rather than a cellular telephone in Riverhead, New York.

"And how many Fannys do you think I know?" She heard the familiar sound of Meaty's deep laughter. "Where the hell are you?" he asked.

"In Manchester, Massachusetts. It's about thirty miles north of Boston. On Cape Ann."

"So where have you been? I haven't heard from you in ages."

Frances realized he was right. Although they had worked together for seven years at the Suffolk County District Attorney's Office, Frances hadn't been able to bring herself to attend his retirement party at the end of April. She'd meant to call when she'd received the computer-generated invitation, an oversize announcement promising a pot-luck supper at the veterans hall and plenty of roasts to say goodbye to a career law-enforcement officer. But she wasn't good at parties and hadn't known quite what to say, so she'd stayed away.

But she missed him. Meaty Burke was one of the few friends she counted. He'd run every major investigation that Frances had prosecuted during her term as chief of financial crimes in the district attorney's office. She knew that he'd recommended her to the board of the Coalition Against Domestic Violence. No one had been more supportive of her career or had more faith in her professional judgment.

She assumed that now, with both a federal and a state retirement pension, he was doing what he loved to do: going to New York Yankees' games with his twelve-year-old granddaughter, buying refrigerator magnets, snow globes, and Christmas tree ornaments from Long Island tourist traps for his wife of forty-two years, and sitting out on his all-weather deck, eating plenty of floating island meringue desserts. She'd heard he and three other cops had bought an impressive twenty-seven-foot cigarette boat at a United States Customs Department auction of drug-related seizures, a boat they wanted to use for deep-sea fishing, complete with all the navigational equipment, sensors, and radios money could buy. She imagined Meaty behind the wheel, weaving in and out of another boat's wake, laughing with his buddies that they had a bargain because some low-level cartel member hadn't been able to avoid the Coast Guard. She hoped he was happy.

"I guess I owe you an apology," Frances began, remembering his dozens of unreturned telephone calls in the months following her stepmother's death and her departure from the district attorney's office.

"Forget it."

"I just—"

"Look. I'm always gonna love you, kiddo, so don't bother explaining. Now, since you're not in the neighborhood and I haven't heard from you in almost a year, I expect you haven't called to tell me you're missing the waters of Long Island Sound. What's on your mind?"

"You always know." Frances paused. There were few people like Meaty. "I need some help."

"What's up?"

She explained as best she could what had happened in the last twenty-four hours. "Who'd you say was the one that raised questions about her death?"

"Her husband, or rather the man she was supposed to marry. Jack Cabot."

"Hmm."

"Why?"

"What do you know about him?"

"I've known him a long time, but not well. He's from

a wealthy Manchester family. He's a polo player. He and Hope grew up together."

"How does he seem?"

"Upset. Angry. What I'd expect." Although as she spoke, she realized she'd never known anyone to commit suicide and didn't know what to expect.

There was a brief pause. "Well, the statistical likelihood – if the death turns out to be murder – is that the killer is Jack. I don't need to tell you that. You're the domestic violence expert these days."

"But . . . but . . ." Frances stammered. She hadn't called Meaty to raise suspicions of Jack or anyone else. All she wanted was some help, someone in Massachusetts with connections to the office of the medical examiner and, perhaps, the Essex County District Attorney's Office. She felt out of her league and needed a contact.

"Do you know anyone in this area whom I could call for information? Someone who might treat me as law enforcement?"

"Yeah. A guy named Elvis. Elvis Mallory. He's actually a relative, married Carol's cousin a few years back, although you won't believe it when you meet him."

"Is that how you know him?"

"No. He and I go way back, maybe fifteen years. We worked together on a mob case, a chop shop in Lynn. There'd been a hit on the owner and his head was actually sent to Manhattan by mail. Anyway, Elvis was part of the organized crime division for the US Attorney's Office in Boston, and he contacted our office for help. He's a character, a little quirky, but a very good guy, with a heart of gold."

"And he married Carol's cousin?"

"Yeah. I ended up introducing them. Margaret – Maggie – now she's a pistol, but that's another story. Anyway, they've been together for years but only recently married."

"Can you get me his number?"

"I'll call for you. But remember, Fanny, it's Sunday. That's the day of rest for most of us. I may not have an answer until tomorrow." He paused a moment. "Aren't the local police already involved?"

"Yeah. They say an autopsy is standard procedure under the circumstances, whatever that means, but her parents aren't seriously considering alternatives to suicide. None of us had much reason to doubt the obvious."

"And you're playing private eye again?" Meaty laughed.

"Hardly. I just seem to have found myself in the middle. The bologna in the sandwich," she added, trying to sound lighthearted. "If you could help me out, I'd be eternally grateful." She gave him her cellular telephone number as well as her aunt's home number. "You can reach me either place."

"Hey, kiddo, before you go . . . are you all right?"

"What do you mean?"

"I mean—" He interrupted himself. "I just want to know how you're holding up."

Frances smiled into the telephone, grateful for his

concern. "I'm hanging in there, but I sure could use the sight of your pretty face."

"Flattery will get you everywhere."

Frances watched Sam place his suitcase into the back of his Jeep and slam the hatchback closed. There was a grace to his movement as he bent over, lifted his suitcase, and placed it inside.

He turned to face her and squinted slightly. The fog had finally burned off and the late afternoon sun glared against the blacktop parking lot of the King's Arms Motor Lodge. "I won't say it again," he said, although Frances knew he would. "I think you should come home."

She closed her eyes, envisioning what he meant: the farmhouse with its creaky porch, her scattered flowerbeds, her two dogs, Felonious and Miss Demeanor, by her feet, a fire, a single-malt Scotch. Home . . . She hummed the word for a second before forcing her mind to focus. She'd planned to take a few days off after her cousin's wedding. Now her vacation would serve a purpose beyond much-needed rest. She put her arms gently around his neck and leaned against his chest. "I can't."

"You may have your reasons, but I still think you should."

"I'll call when I know what's going on. Give the dogs a hug for me."

Sam walked to the driver's side, opened the door,

rolled down the front window, and settled himself behind the wheel. "You sure you don't want me to take the rental car?"

"Yes. I'll return it in New London and take the ferry across."

"I'll be there to meet you." He started the engine but let it idle. "Look, Fanny. I don't know what I'm supposed to do – stay or go. I want to do what's best for you, but for once you're going to have to tell me because I can't read your mind."

She rested her hands on the car door and leaned toward him. "Go."

"Just say the word and I'm back in a flash." He covered her fingertips with his large palm. "I love you."

Frances smiled but didn't reply. He shifted his car into gear, and she watched as the shiny blue Jeep drove out of the parking lot and turned onto Route 128. For a moment, she had the urge to run after him, to forget Hope's death, Jack's concerns, and the autopsy, and to return to the familiarity of life on Orient Point. But she knew she couldn't block out the information she'd learned.

She wrapped her arms around her waist to try to thwart a chill despite the warming temperature. Sam was right: even if the autopsy demonstrated that Hope's death was not a suicide, there was little she could do. She was no longer a prosecutor. Even if she were, she was out of her jurisdiction, with no Massachusetts contacts except some aging cop Meaty knew. So why did she feel compelled to immerse herself in the tragic situation?

REDEMPTION

Frances thought of a late July weekend in Manchester when Hope was a toddler. It had been a Thursday night near the end of the Pratts' visit that summer. Her father had been forced by pressing business to return to New York City for twenty-four hours, so Adelaide had decided to take the girls for a treat. They'd all piled into the Volvo station wagon, and driven to the Sundae Shoppe in Beverly Farms. For ninety-nine cents a dish, the renovated railroad car with blue Naugahyde banquettes, Formica tables, and slowly turning overhead brass fans offered all the necessary ingredients to build an ice-cream sundae. Adelaide had helped the girls pile hot fudge, butterscotch, whipped cream, and candy so high that the vanilla ice cream underneath was barely visible. Then they'd crowded into a single booth. Frances remembered the feeling of her bare legs pressed against Blair's, the look of delight in Hope's eyes as she ate with her hands and smeared her pudgy cheeks with chocolate, and the laughter that appeared to fill the restaurant. An unsuspecting stranger walking by the table would have thought it was one family. And for that evening, Frances had allowed herself to believe the same.

Back at the house on Smith's Point, her aunt had perched on the edge of Frances's bed and rubbed her slightly distended belly. The gentle touch had soothed her stomachache.

"Can I always come back here?" she'd asked.

"What a question! Of course, you may," Adelaide had said, laying a hand across her forehead as if to check for a fever.

"Always?" she'd insisted.

"Absolutely. We'll be here forever, and we'll always want you with us. Whenever you want to come."

Frances remembered pulling the blanket-cover up under her chin and smelling the sweet fragrance of Adelaide's laundry detergent. Although technically a guest bedroom, it felt more comfortable than her room at her father's house. The twin beds, oval braided rug, wooden bureau with Lucite knobs, and lace curtains stayed the same year to year, always seeming to welcome her back. She'd closed her eyes, wanting to savor the night.

"Will you stay with me until I fall asleep?"

"Yes." And true to her word, Adelaide had remained rubbing her stomach as she'd drifted off.

Over the years, as her own fragmented family caused her more and more pain, she'd harbored nostalgic memories of her aunt's home, her maternal warmth and embrace, and her uncle's good-natured participation in the family activities. She'd needed such an ideal. Now that the seemingly magical family was beset by a nightmare, she realized how fundamentally disrupted she felt, too. It wasn't just the pain of Hope's death; it was the loss of her family myth.

But there was something else, too, something that drew her to stay. If Hope's death was a murder, Frances realized with anguish that she had possibly destroyed the crime scene. So frantic to find her cousin, and then so distraught when she had, she'd opened and closed doors, touched items in the room, and, worst of all, removed Hope's body from the noose. The details that

Jack remembered only highlighted how little she could recall of what she'd seen. She doubted now whether any crime scene analysis could be done, and she couldn't bear the thought that Hope's killer might go free because of her recklessness.

15

The front door was ajar, but the house was dark by the time Frances returned. In the evening light she made her way into the library. Embers still glowed, but the flames from earlier in the day had subsided. The drapes were drawn. The television, which Frances hadn't noticed before because of its concealed spot behind an elegant paneled cabinet, showed the evening news. The screen cast an eerie blue light.

She scanned the contents of the built-in bookshelves. The library was impressive: leather-bound copies of Walter Scott, Washington Irving, Thomas Carlyle, James Fenimore Cooper, and Charles Dickens, plus atlases, dictionaries, encyclopedias, and a slew of reference books, a section devoted to nautical history and picture books of the sea, and several shelves of contemporary fiction. Interspersed among the volumes were family photographs: Bill and Adelaide on a golf course in Scotland; Adelaide standing beside Hope in a graduation gown; Jack in his polo uniform mounted on a beautiful bay pony with Hope standing next to the horse and holding onto the reins; several slightly soft-focused black-and-white portraits of Hope as a child in a white lace dress playing in the sand. Frances paused at a picture of a group of young teenagers standing in front of a tennis net, a motley crew of freckle-faced boys and girls of varying heights and builds. They all wore white polo shirts with "F&HC" on the left pocket. She picked up the frame and searched the faces, recognizing Blair, then herself, a sullen-faced Penelope, and Hope, the tiniest child of all, in the front row of Field and Hunt Club tennis students. Why that summer had the Pratt girls been in Manchester long enough to enroll?

She remembered her father telling her of a business trip, an important one to Saudi Arabia, Kuwait, and then the Far East. He had to go during July, his month with her and Blair. That had precipitated a series of calls from her mother to her father. Why should his daughters come to visit him when he wasn't there? Why should they stay with their stepmother? The resolution had been to spend the two weeks with Adelaide, the constant, and the Lawrence family, which didn't have to fight over schedules.

She heard footsteps and turned to see Penelope holding a glass of red wine.

"Mom and Bill took dinner upstairs. They want to be alone."

"Of course. I hope I'm not bothering you."

"I should head back to Boston," Penelope said, seeming to ignore Frances's remark. She settled on the love seat and took a sip. "But I don't feel like driving. Not tonight. Can I offer you a drink?"

"No. Thanks." She glanced at the television as the weather forecaster began predicting warm-air fronts for the next several days. "Was there anything about Hope's death on the news?"

"No. But Bill asked me to look. He and Mom are concerned about media attention. You'd think that would be the least of their problems." Penelope slipped her feet out of her chartreuse mules and tucked them under her, but not without flashing her pedicure, the toenails painted fire-engine red.

Frances walked back over to the array of photographs. The last twenty-four hours were a blur. Part of her had failed to even process that her cousin was gone. Seeing images of Hope smiling, it was easy to forget; her absence was due to her honeymoon, the two-week trip to Europe that Jack had planned. "The three of us got the Pratt genes, and then there was this fair-haired, delicate girl. I always wanted to dress her and brush her hair. She seemed like a Madame Alexander doll come to life." She remembered the elegant brides and ballerinas in the glass cases of FAO Schwarz that she and her sister had collected.

"Madame Adelaide's doll. That she was."

The log cracked, and Frances turned to see the popping orange embers.

Penelope wiped her eyes with her hand. "Hope should've gotten help. That's what she needed more than a wedding."

"What kind of help?"

"A better psychiatrist than that shrink she'd been

seeing. Bulimia was the disease du jour, but her emotional problems were never under control."

"Bulimia?"

"Yeah. Everyone thought she was anorexic because she was so thin, but I heard her gagging herself in the powder room during her bridal shower. The party was at my apartment, and the half-bath is right off the kitchen. She turned on the water, tried to hide it. Probably assumed nobody would hear because everyone was talking in the living room. She didn't realize how close I was."

"Did Adelaide know?"

"We're WASPs remember? We don't talk about problems. But I don't see how she couldn't have known. I thought of telling her point-blank, but I figured it would only unleash hostility. Mom needed Hope to be perfect – they both did – and she wouldn't hear anything to indicate otherwise. Perfection is the torment of the upper class." She closed her eyes. "There used to be a comedian on *Saturday Night Live*. I can't remember his name. But his line of banter was about all these problems that privileged people have because they can't worry about the kinds of things everyone else worries about, like where the next meal is coming from. I remember him saying, 'Ever heard of lactose intolerance in Ethiopia?' It was a funny line, but it's true. Mom focused on whether the cocktail napkins matched the floral arrangement at the Garden Club's opening reception because there wasn't anything better to fixate on. She needs to feel like the worthless stuff that consumes her day is actually important. Either that or she's hoping a pristine exterior provides good cover."

"For what?"

Penelope laughed. "All of our neuroses."

Listening, Frances felt protective of her aunt. Penelope may have taken Adelaide's hospitality and graciousness for granted, but at one time or another they'd all been beneficiaries of it. To make people feel welcome and loved, was that superficial? She often wondered as she spent hours in her garden what constituted a wasted life versus one that had some sort of intrinsic meaning, but no matter how many weeds she pulled, she had yet to find an answer.

"Was Hope like that?"

Penelope stretched out farther along the couch. "Hope had a flightiness to her, too. That's why she liked the church. She could volunteer and feel as if she were contributing to something worthwhile, even though it was only a few hours a week at her own choosing. But I think she saw life with Jack as a responsibility she couldn't handle. Sort of like full-time employment. She was marrying into the same rigid social structure she'd been struggling with all her life, a world where she couldn't let down, but she was too emotional to keep up appearances."

"I had no idea she was so unhappy."

"You don't know the half of it. I'm not sure anyone does. But earlier this summer – must have been July, I can't remember exactly, but I was out here for the weekend – I'd gone into town to get tons of bug spray, and when I got back she was screaming bloody murder at Mom. Calling her all sorts of names. Telling her she was the worst mother in the world because she hadn't even bothered to protect her own daughter."

"From what?"

"Who knows? Some perceived horror or another. Life . . ." Penelope paused. "Kathleen ended up consoling her. Hardly in the job description, but we must be ever thankful for the hired help," she said sarcastically. "Mom didn't know what to do. That night Bill came into the library where I was reading. I'll never forget it because it was the only time either of them acknowledged that I've been the better daughter. 'She thinks it's my fault, our fault, but it's her. You were never like this.' That's what he said. He said he and Mom were at the end of their rope." Penelope's words hung in the air, and Frances closed her eyes, trying to drive away the image of Hope hanging in the closet.

"Did Hope ever talk to you about why she was upset with Adelaide?"

"No. Who around here shares anything? Everyone's always cheerful and gracious and reserved. But I think that pressure was what got to Hope."

"I can't imagine that Adelaide wouldn't have tried to talk to her," Frances mused aloud. Adelaide's affection and warmth made her seem infinitely approachable. Listening to Penelope, she thought it was almost as if they were talking about two different people.

Penelope paused and seemed momentarily distracted. When she spoke again, she turned her gaze to the fireplace. "Adelaide did better than talk to her. She finally shared her own helpful hint on how to survive Manchester life."

"What was that?"

"Prescription drugs. Plenty of them. It's how she gets through all these social events. You can't drink too much in this crowd or people talk. But a good tranquilizer lets you relax. Even get to sleep."

What was Penelope talking about? Was she drunk? Frances was shocked. Her aunt struck her as the bastion of health – high-strung, perhaps, but she'd always seen that as energetic. Then she remembered the bottlecap and pills she'd seen on the floor in Hope's bedroom. Could they have been from Adelaide? "I find it hard to imagine." She hadn't meant to utter her thoughts aloud.

"That's the point. You need solutions no one can see."

"Where does Jack fit into all of this?"

Penelope took a long sip and swirled the remainder around in her glass. "Jack's Jack. Mom and Bill wanted nothing more than to see them together. They spent more money than they had to make that statement. He was supposed to tame her spirit, keep her calm. What's that horrible expression? 'Make an honest woman of her' – something like that. Plus he's worth a fortune, and they needed that. They certainly can't provide for either of us."

Frances suddenly remembered her grandmother's comment about paying rent for the cottage. She'd had no idea money was an issue. "Were they wanting Jack to support them?"

Penelope snorted. "Don't sound so shocked. It could have been done without anyone really noticing. Hope and Jack move into the big house. Mom and Bill move into the cottage."

"And what about Teddy?"

"She won't be around forever."

Frances was quiet. She wondered again if Penelope's candor was fueled by alcohol. "What do you think of Jack?" she asked.

She looked up. "You don't know, do you?"

Frances shook her head.

"I went out with him. A couple of years ago he broke up with Hope because she wouldn't stop seeing this other guy, an older man who lived in Gloucester. In retrospect, I should have known it wouldn't work. Jack doesn't want a successful woman. He liked Hope's neediness, but I fell for him. Big time. I'd marry him tomorrow if he asked me. Who wouldn't?"

Penelope's insensitivity under the circumstances was especially painful. "What happened?" Frances asked.

"As soon as she decided to grace him with her presence again, he dropped me like a hot potato. I shouldn't have been surprised. Hope was selfish. She took him back so I couldn't have him. She had to make sure I knew I was less good, less desirable. I had to be reminded constantly that she was the focus of everyone's adoration."

"You don't think she loved him?"

"What difference does it make now?"

They were both silent. Penelope refilled her glass. "I guess we always go for the one who's not available. Jack did. That Hope was never really going to be his, that she would always be elusive, was part of her appeal. Isn't that a lot sexier than being with the person who cares? Loyalty and constancy are qualities one wants in a pet, not a lover."

Frances thought of Sam. That wasn't what character- ized her relationship, but she decided to keep her disagreement to herself.

"I think I've always known that as long as Hope was around, I had no chance with him. I was only the runner-up, the second-best contestant, who got to jump in if the winner failed to carry out her duties and responsibilities being Miss Perfect. 'Close, but no cigar,' as Bill says. That's me. That's what I've lived with since the day I entered this elegant abode," Penelope said sarcastically. "As long as I was Hope's sister, I fell short by comparison. You and I are Pratts, but *she* was a Lawrence." She swung her legs to the floor and stood up. "I'm heading to bed before I talk too much and get myself into trouble." She tipped her head back and exhaled audibly. "I'm only a corporate lawyer. No con- test for a prosecutor."

After Penelope left, Frances remained immobile, replaying the conversation in her mind. The depth of Penelope's jealousy and resentment seemed greater than just everyday sibling rivalry. It was difficult for Frances to listen to the anger that Penelope evidently still harbored toward her now dead sister, and she wondered again about Sam's comment on different reactions to grief. Could it help Penelope grieve to remember her rage? Frances had a hard time ignoring her instincts, but something didn't feel right.

Before turning out the light to go upstairs, Frances removed the Field and Hunt Club tennis photograph from the bookshelf and scanned it a final time. What was it about the faces of Blair, Penelope, Hope, and herself that left her feeling unsettled? What was she looking for the picture to reveal? The answer eluded her. But she already recoiled from the ugliness and animosity she was discovering.

16

Frances stretched her fingers to touch the awning of 7 Central. It was a childhood habit: She'd run down the street, jump off the pavement, and try to reach signs, overhangs, anything dangling overhead. Now that she was grown, it was easy. She raised her hand to block the sun and looked up and down Central Street. She didn't know exactly what to expect, but she had the feeling that Elvis Mallory's arrival would be dramatic.

He had called her on her cell phone after speaking with Meaty. In a gentle, high-pitched voice, he'd spoken so fast that she'd missed several words, but she'd understood the gist: he had canceled his fishing trip to help her out. "I actually don't like to catch anything, so this is a good excuse. I just can't bear to see those majestic creatures flailing on the deck as they die. Blues aren't so bad, but the occasional swordfish or marlin breaks my heart. My buddies give me plenty of guff 'cause I'm a cop working organized crime and I don't like death, but I know I'm tough as the grease under their nails when I have to be."

Frances didn't bother to respond as he paused for a

moment to catch a breath. "Here's the deal," he continued. "I talked to the first assistant in Essex. He's a good guy, knows your old boss by reputation. I explained the situation, your connection to the victim, and your connection to Meaty. He's willing to have you come along, but remember we're not learning anything that the DA's office isn't going to get, too. I guess I'm here to insure that, kinda like a liaison." He made a clicking sound with his teeth.

Frances wondered exactly what Meaty had said about her. Apparently more than she'd expected. But she'd hardly intended to conduct an independent investigation. Elvis was only establishing the obvious – that his first loyalty was to his job.

"I've known Meaty a long time," he continued. "Actually, my wife and Carol are related, but he probably told you that. My wife's a physician. She left private practice for the medical examiner's office about ten years ago. She got tired of patients, plus she loves administrative work. Says typing is therapeutic. Whatever. The career change has helped our relationship, so I'm not complaining. She's less critical of me now that she's surrounded by stiffs. Anyway, long story short, she'll get you in if I get you to Albany Street."

Frances didn't need or want to witness Hope's autopsy, but at Adelaide's urging, she had agreed to wait at the medical examiner's office while the procedure was being conducted. Apparently her presence provided some comfort to her aunt, some sense that the integrity of the corpse would be preserved, and Frances didn't want to disabuse her of that notion. She was surprised, though, that it was getting under way so soon. The crime laboratory for the state police in Boston was famous; it was apparently living up to its reputation.

A lilac Cadillac convertible came to a stop at the light on Pine Street, then turned left onto Central. From oversize speakers propped in the backseat blared Hootie and the Blowfish. Before the car even pulled to the curb, she knew it was Elvis.

Without turning off the engine, he jumped out and extended a hand. "Elvis. Elvis Mallory. My pleasure." He was small and wiry, with a buzz cut of gray hair and ears that stuck out from his narrow face. His baggy shorts and navy polo shirt with the emblem of the police department seemed too big for his slight frame. Frances couldn't help but notice his enormous feet. In proportion to his body, his Tevas looked like rubber fins.

She introduced herself. "Thanks for coming."

"I'm real sorry about your cousin. 'Sorry' doesn't mean much under the circumstances, but the death of a young girl is about the sorriest thing I can imagine. I guess that's my way of saying I'm happy to help. Besides, Meaty's a good friend. My kind of guy. And he thinks the world of you, that's for sure. Now get in. We're running about eight and a half minutes behind schedule because there was some construction just off exit 16 that I hadn't anticipated. We'll make it up, I've no doubt about that, but it's going to require some precision driving."

Frances walked around to the passenger door, wondering what that meant. The white vinyl interior had warmed in the sun, and Elvis quickly laid out a striped beach towel for her to sit on. "I like a little heat on my ass, but a lot of people don't," he said, flipping the car into gear.

She fastened her seat belt as the car lurched forward.

The humid wind blew in her face and rock music filled the air as the two sped along. She glanced over at Elvis occasionally, but his gaze remained fixed on the road, and he seemed lost in the sound of his voice as he sang along. Then, as they approached the toll on the Tobin Bridge and sped through with a flash of his E-Z Pass, he abruptly turned off the stereo. "We should talk. Tell me what you know."

Frances quickly summarized the events of the last several days.

"But you found your cousin. What do you remember?"

"Not much, unfortunately." She didn't want to admit to her trauma-induced amnesia. She'd already chastised herself repeatedly.

"Well, you know the drill. Treat yourself like a witness and walk yourself through the details. See what comes back. You say the body was hanging from a light fixture."

"Yes."

"Can you tell me anything about the color of her skin, angle of her head, position of her neck?"

Frances closed her eyes, but her vision seemed a blur of silk shantung and dangling limbs. She couldn't even picture Hope's face.

"Do you remember where the knot was located?"

"What do you mean?"

"Left, right, or facial centerline."

She tried to remember pulling off the noose from around Hope's neck. Had she pulled the rope from its knot? She couldn't have untied it completely, or Jack, arriving later, wouldn't have observed that it was a bowline.

Responding to her silence, Elvis said, "Okay. What about the body? How high was it off the ground?"

Frances thought for a moment. In the recesses of her mind, she recalled Hope's feet, crooked and sideways on the floor. "Her feet were touching the ground."

Elvis seemed momentarily lost in thought, and Frances had the sinking feeling that she'd given the wrong answer. "Is that significant?" she finally asked.

"I suppose it does us both a disservice if I'm anything less than candid. If a body's not suspended, the over-whelming statistics indicate a suicide. A person who wants to kill himself just bends his knees and lets the pressure of the noose asphyxiate him. People have been known to hang themselves simply by sitting in a chair and reclining slightly away from the rope. That's why I asked you if you remembered where the knot was. On the right side, it would cut off the blood supply to the brain through the carotid artery. A person can lose consciousness in only a couple of seconds. A left-side knot is also pretty efficient because it blocks the jugular vein. But a centerline knot is slow and painful because it blocks the trachea. I'd be surprised if that were the case here, given what you tell me about the timing."

Frances wanted to ask him how he knew so much about hangings but decided not to interrupt. The wealth of information that many of the best investigators stashed in their minds never ceased to amaze her.

"A murderer, on the other hand," Elvis continued, "now he'd want his victim completely suspended. Possibly even a drop hanging, because then the neck breaks and you're talking maximum chance of lethal result." He honked his horn and swerved into the right lane to exit onto Storrow Drive. "Granted we're talking probabilities here, and there's always the case that beats the odds. A couple of years back, I remember a mob hit that was a nonsuspended. Turned out they'd hung a noose around the guy's neck but held a gun to his head, forcing him to asphyxiate himself. That had to be a grueling death. Think I would have let them shoot me."

"How'd you find out it wasn't a suicide?"

"An informant. Described every gory detail from his tears and pleas to the shit in his pants. Poor son of a bitch."

"But there was no way to tell by the autopsy?"

"No. When we found the guy in his body shop, we thought it was a suicide. Didn't mean we weren't going to try to put together a case because we thought he'd been threatened or intimidated. Something drove him to do it, but the autopsy gave us nothing."

"I see." Frances turned away from him and looked out at the array of sailboats on the Charles River. Six or seven seemed to form a white line, as if they were sailing in formation. The esplanade was filled with joggers and people on Rollerblades modeling an impressive collection of spandex and sports bras. A blond dogwalker kept up a brisk pace with a motley pack of leashed canines. If she didn't know better, life seemed peaceful.

"We're almost there," Elvis said as he put on his blinker.

Elvis pulled to the curb in front of 720 Albany Street, a drab modern building that was part of the Boston Medical Center complex. Parked directly in front were several state trooper cruisers and a white van with the Medical Examiner's logo stenciled on the side. Elvis rang the bell, waited for the buzzer, and pushed the heavy door open. Frances stepped inside.

"Elllvisss," said a bald cop with rosy cheeks, stretching out the word. From behind the reception desk he grinned. "What brings you to these parts? Looking for your sweetie?"

"For once your sleuthing skills are accurate. Where is she?"

"In the back. Her usual room."

Elvis started in that direction, but the cop stopped him. "You may be the big girl's husband, but you've still gotta sign in your guest. Police procedure."

He bent over and entered Frances's name in a large ledger. "Frances Pratt, meet Officer John Johnson. And yes, it's his real name. His parents lacked imagination."

Elvis headed down a long corridor and she followed a few paces behind, listening to the sound of his Tevas squeak on the linoleum floor. He stopped at a door marked "22," knocked, and opened it without waiting for a response from within. "Mags, we're here."

Maggie Mallory stood up from behind a steel desk and removed her metallic half-glasses. She had an imposing presence: tall, with broad shoulders and large breasts and a mane of blonde hair that cascaded half-way down her back. She walked around to where they stood, leaned over, kissed her husband, and then extended a hand in greeting. "I'm sorry about your cousin," she said.

"Thank you," Frances said. She thought she detected a family resemblance to Carol Burke, Meaty's wife. Perhaps it was the wide forehead, but something about Maggie Mallory's manner struck Frances as familiar.

She indicated a chair, which Frances took. She could see Elvis standing behind her, swaying slightly from side to side.

"I took a preliminary look at Hope Lawrence," Maggie began, obviously happy to skip the pleasantries. "She was twenty-six, is that right?"

"Twenty-seven. Her birthday was in May."

Maggie jotted a note in a three-ring binder. She flipped to the next page, replaced her glasses on her nose and scanned the sheet in front of her. "Five feet six inches and a hundred and two pounds," she mumbled, before shutting her notebook. "Look, I'm talking to you candidly because of Meaty," she said, directing her comments to Frances. "He's family, and he tells me you're family to him. So I guess that makes us related in some metaphorical sense. It's odd working with someone you sort of know. It's happened to me a couple of times, but never like this, I mean, where the victim's your relative on top of our connection through Meaty. I want to help, but be forewarned that this isn't pretty."

"I appreciate that," Frances replied, feeling suddenly as if the oxygen had been pumped out of the room. There was an odd smell – a mixture of ammonia, grilled cheese and air freshener – that nauseated her, but she tried to concentrate.

"Okay, then. Remember I've done nothing formal, so this is preliminary. But one thing struck me right off the bat. Blood's pooled above and below the ligature. You can see it in the skin coloration of the neck. That shouldn't happen if hanging is the cause of death. The bruising on her neck – the pattern of grooves on her throat – appears more consistent with strangulation than hanging."

"What . . . are . . . you . . . saying?" Frances found herself stammering.

"My off-the-record suggestion to you both is that you don't waste your time with me. You're not likely to find the murderer here."

17

As Frances approached the Lawrences' house, she heard her grandmother's voice beckoning from the patio. Teddy sat in a wicker chair clutching the bent wood handle of her cane. Her large straw hat partially covered her face.

"Have you been swimming?" Frances asked.

"Yes."

"With or without a suit?"

Teddy was a notorious skinny-dipper. The local paper had done a feature story on her several years before with the prominent headline "Michigan Grandma Brings Nude Bathing to Manchester" and a picture of her floating in the harbor in her straw hat as the Coast Guard's boat passed in the background. Perhaps it was her age or the bluish black color of the water, but the town seemed unusually tolerant of her favorite pastime. Even the local fishermen were discreet enough to divert their gaze if their boats passed Smith's Point as she happened to be getting in or out of the sea.

"Can you sit for a moment?" Teddy asked, ignoring her question.

Frances could tell from the rattle in her throat that she'd been crying. "Of course." From where it was positioned facing the ocean, she pulled a chair slightly closer to her grandmother. The breeze chilled her. Assuming Teddy had something to say, she sat patiently, not wanting to rush the conversation. She gazed at her grandmother's arm, the pronounced age spots giving the otherwise porcelain skin a mottled look. After several moments of silence, she heard Teddy clear her throat.

"So what happened to Hope?"

The directness startled her, and she paused to collect her thoughts before responding. "It's still preliminary."

"Lawyer gibberish. I've been around enough of them to tell. You're a bad liar, Frances Pratt. Just like your father."

She should have known Teddy couldn't be assuaged with a noncommittal line. She'd always been blunt to the point of insulting and expected the same in others. "If you want the truth, I just met with the medical examiner in Boston. Hope was strangled."

Teddy inhaled quickly, turned her head away, and covered her mouth with her hand. Frances reached over, but Teddy shook her head before she ever touched her. With crooked fingers she pulled at her hat to lower it on her face. "That poor girl. That poor dear girl."

"I have to tell Adelaide and Bill today, but I don't know how. Or rather I can't face it. I can't bear to add to their pain."

Teddy said nothing in response for several minutes.

When she did speak, her voice was labored, her words slow. "At least they can't blame themselves. Adelaide's been catatonic struggling over what she did wrong, or should I say everything she did wrong." She coughed, then reached into a canvas bag for her cigarettes. She fumbled a moment with the package but removed one, lit it, drew a long inhale, and exhaled smoke out her nose. "I've buried a husband, but I haven't yet had to bury a child, and I never expected to bury a grandchild."

"I know how close you were."

"She was my granddaughter, just as you are, but since I moved here I've seen her almost every day," Teddy replied. "She had a passion for life, an energy and excitement – let's call it a spirit, for lack of a better word, although I'd prefer a secular one." She drew on her cigarette and sputtered slightly as she exhaled. "There was a period when she came over nearly every afternoon. She had some sort of diet soda and I had an excuse for an early cocktail. Occasionally she'd read her poetry. Between you and me, her skills in that area were lacking, but she read with a sense of high drama, lots of vocal intonations. I often had to suppress laughter. She could be quite melodramatic."

Frances was silent, imagining the scenes Teddy described.

"She reminded me of myself. I nearly forgot she wasn't our blood."

"What's that supposed to mean?"

Teddy cocked her head. "Don't tell me you didn't know Hope was adopted?"

"No." She'd never thought one way or the other about

it; Hope was Adelaide and Bill's baby. It was true that she had no memory of her aunt pregnant, but that didn't seem odd given the amount of time that passed between visits.

She remembered her father telling her that she had a new baby cousin and that they were all going to travel to Manchester to see her. But a few days before their departure, he'd been on the telephone with Bill, and when he hung up his eyes were red. He'd seen that Frances was listening and hugged her tight while he explained that the baby was in a hospital in Boston, seeing a specialist. She needed surgery for a congenital heart defect. He was going to be with his sister, but she and Blair wouldn't be coming. Not right away. No one mentioned that the new baby with heart trouble had been adopted.

"No surprise, I guess. Practically nobody knows. Adelaide and Bill were so secretive."

"Why?"

"Shame, perhaps. It was a trauma for both of them that Adelaide couldn't get pregnant."

"Is Penelope adopted, too?"

"No. But that made it worse. Don't quote me on any of this, for God's sake. Remember, I was in Michigan, and your aunt has never been much for confiding, even in her own mother, but the bits and pieces she let drop made it clear that Bill's ego was threatened. Some notion that Morgan was more virile, or something absurd," she said, referring to Adelaide's first husband.

"Did Hope know?"

"I'm not sure. Several times over the years, I tried to

convince Adelaide that Hope was entitled to know, but she and Bill were adamant. They thought she'd be obsessed with finding her biological parents and didn't want her to have that torment, not on top of the other struggles she had. But I think they also were afraid that she'd reject them."

"So she never knew?"

"If she did, she never said a word to me."

Frances was quiet, trying to digest the information her grandmother had just disclosed. She didn't like that this revelation made her disoriented. Whether or not Hope was a blood relative should make no difference, but she wondered nonetheless how she would have reacted if she'd been told as a child.

"Did she ever confide in you?"

Teddy paused, as if debating whether to answer. "She did when she was seeing that fisherman."

Frances leaned forward. "Who was that?"

"A Portuguese fellow named Carl something-or-other. But she fell for him like a brick off a building."

"What happened?"

"Well, as you might expect, she got quite a reaction from her parents. He wasn't at all what they had in mind – at least a decade her senior and probably without two coins to rub together – but he was charismatic."

"You met him?"

She waved her hand as if wanting to stop the conversation. "She brought him by on occasion."

"When?"

Teddy's glance seemed to ask whether Frances

wanted the official or the real answer, but she said nothing.

"Were they seeing each other recently?"

"How many times have you been in love?" Teddy asked, ignoring her question. "I'm not talking about a great friendship with a man or a compatibility. I'm not even talking about the kind of ease, the familiarity that comes with years of marriage or raising a family. I mean the kind of mesmerizing chemistry that can leave a girl breathless. Where even the thought of the man makes your heart race. Most of us never have that. I certainly didn't have it with Dick," she added almost as an afterthought. "Although I've often wondered whether marriage sounds the death knell for love. John Stuart Mill, the English philosopher . . . do you know him?"

Frances nodded.

"He once said something along the lines of, freedom is the ability to choose whom to love. With absolute freedom comes true love. I think the idea is that if every day you wake up and choose to be with someone, to share your life not because of a legal or financial obligation but because of real choice, that's love. Hope and that fellow had something like that. I saw it the few times I was with them. He was a physical man. Even in front of me, he couldn't keep his hands to himself."

"You invited them over?"

She frowned. "Of course not. But every so often, Hope would call and ask if she and her friend could come for tea. That was her code. Anyway, I'd say yes, and they'd show up a minute later, as if they'd phoned from the end of the footpath. We'd sit and make pleas-antries for several moments, and then she'd remind me that I was late for mah jongg. I'd excuse myself and they would stay behind, offering to clean up."

"And?"

"Must I explain everything? My word, Fanny. You should get off that peninsula of yours every once in a while."

Frances smiled. She never would have imagined her grandmother as a willing participant in a clandestine tryst. "Why'd you do it? Play along, I mean."

Teddy took another drag of her cigarette, and Frances watched the ash, which seemed to dangle pre-cariously over her lap. "In my day, marriages were arranged, or at least practically speaking. You were bloody lucky if you could tolerate the man you were with, never mind love him. I saw how Hope was with Carl, and frankly, I didn't see anything wrong. Passion is a precious commodity. She was lucky to find it, and I wasn't about to stand in the way."

"But she was seeing Jack."

"That was her business, not mine."

Teddy sounded so pragmatic that Frances almost didn't recognize her. Perhaps age had brought with it a certain freedom, a liberation of thought, but she hadn't expected to hear evidence of it under these circum-stances. "Why didn't Bill and Adelaide approve?" she asked, although she was quite certain she knew the answer.

"He was from a different class, had a different back-ground, little education, and no money. We'd like to think those factors make no difference. We pretend to look at the person, the qualities of the individual, not the framework surrounding them, but it doesn't happen that way. The world hasn't changed as much as we'd like to think it has. Besides, Jack Cabot always had a sneaker for her. They were the perfect match. Everyone thought so."

"Did she ever ask you for advice? You know, Jack versus Carl."

"No. But Hope was not a dumb woman. She had to know that a life with Jack would be easier. She felt tremendous pressure to leave Carl. And some of it was for good reason."

What reason could there be if, as Teddy described, their relationship was so perfect, so filled with passion? Wasn't that every woman's dream? But even as she ruminated, Frances knew she was being naïve. She could hear the conversation, the gossip, at the Field and Hunt Club, the criticism circulating through the Manchester cocktail party circuit, the glares thrown at the Lawrences by fellow sailors at the Yacht Club. *Did you hear? Hope Lawrence is marrying a fisherman, a poor one, and Portuguese at that.* It would have been painful for Bill and Adelaide, an elegant couple who kept a tidy life. Marriage into the Cabot clan would perpetuate the fairy tale.

"When was the last time she saw him?"

"I can't recall, although I've been trying to reconstruct events over the past two days."

"They stopped coming here?"

"Yes. But that happened for different reasons. Or at

least I think it did. We had a rather sad disagreement about six months ago, and Hope stopped visiting me almost completely. She certainly didn't bring him."

"What was the disagreement?"

"My dear, there's an old adage that says never discuss religion, politics, or in-laws with anyone you care about. Believe me, it's accurate. I just couldn't help myself."

"Did you fight about the Cabots?"

"Don't be absurd. Those people aren't worth fighting over. Ordinary, that's what they are. No, our disagreement involved that church. Hope spent more and more time there, and one afternoon I questioned her involvement."

"Why did you think it was wrong?"

"'Wrong' is not the word I used. You of all people should pay better attention."

Frances felt the sting of her grandmother's words. Part of Teddy's mystique was to keep people ever so slightly on edge, but she had a way of humbling her audience. Frances recalled a trip to Ann Arbor when she was ten. Teddy had seemed genuinely thrilled to see her, but after a few minutes she'd asked her whether she'd brought her flute. No, she'd replied. "It would have been an improvement," was the retort. Frances could barely get out of her grandmother's living room before she'd burst into tears.

"Hope was looking for an answer," she continued, indifferent to the impact of her admonishment. "She wanted to be told that if she did A, B, and C, she would be rewarded with happiness. She was looking for the church to provide her with those steps. To tell her how to be a good person. I got worried about her. I don't have anything against the Episcopalians. They're generally honest, tend to remain employed, and throw excellent cocktail parties. But I didn't think puttering around that old building inhaling mildew and mold on vestments that haven't been washed since Kennedy was president was going to convince Hope of anything. She had to do it herself." Teddy took another drag and seemed, this time, to hold the smoke in her lungs. As she spoke, it spilled from her mouth. "What she needed was structure, a focus to her energy. We all do."

Frances looked at her elderly grandmother and realized that for all her biting comments, she had a sensible nature. She could see to the core of a problem and find its solution. "Is that what you told her?"

"Hope and I never discussed the matter. I tried. But she didn't want to hear it from me. After that, she didn't want to hear much of anything."

"What did you think of her engagement to Jack?"

Teddy made a face that Frances couldn't interpret. "Jack's a good-hearted boy. I think he was genuinely fond of her, probably would have made a decent enough husband. Though his family leaves something to be desired."

"What's wrong with them?" she asked. There seemed no shortage to the amount of information Teddy could offer.

"They're obsessed with their money, their lineage, their blue blood. Reptiles have blue blood, I've been tempted to remind them. Fiona puts on so many airs – airs under the guise of hospitality and good manners, which is even worse – you'd think she was royalty." She leaned toward Frances and continued in a loud stage whisper, as though someone from the house might hear. "I'm suspicious of people who try so hard to set themselves apart with distinctions, classes. We're no better than the caste system in India. Hope's fisherman was an untouchable, and Jack is the landed gentry."

"You're a member of the Daughters of the May-flower."

"Was," Teddy scoffed. "All that connection means is that your ancestors were crooks or religious zealots. England wanted to get rid of them, so they came here. Not something to be particularly proud of, in my view."

Frances had to laugh. She remembered hearing a story once of Teddy opening a restaurant to raise money for the troops in World War II. She had tried to solicit the help of her society friends, who scoffed at the thought of waiting tables, but when she announced that she was doing the dishes, they were shamed into agreement. She even received some sort of medal for her assistance, although every time she was asked about it, she laughed and waved her hand dismissively.

"Then there was that stupid issue of the prenuptial agreement."

"What was that?"

"Something the Cabots wanted. They convinced Bill and Adelaide, too, although Hope and Jack refused to sign it. As I understand it, there was quite a scene here one night. I – thank God – was peacefully unaware at the time, but I had to hear about it ad nauseam for the next month."

"What happened?"

Teddy shrugged. "It was absurd. Jim had given Bill an outline of the proposed agreement. The four of them – Jim, Fiona, Bill, and Adelaide – met to discuss it. They're such idiots; they never bothered to consult the children. Greedy and foolish, they are, the lot of them. Hope came home and discovered the four of them in the library, marking documents with red pen, and she went crazy. She said her own parents were plotting against her. Nobody had faith that she would make a decent wife, so they were dealing with her demise in advance. She refused to talk to her parents for days afterward."

"What about Jack?"

"I don't know what he knew or didn't know at the time. I'm quite sure the thing never got signed, though."

"Did she ever tell you what happened with Carl?"

"No. And I wasn't interested in bringing up the subject. I wasn't going to be accused of meddling."

"But they were seeing each other six months ago?"

Teddy said nothing. She set her jaw, making it clear that Frances would not get a response.

"Can you think of how I could find him?"

"No. Perhaps Adelaide knows, or knew. But he was the sort of transient type that may not have stayed very long in any one place. Or at least he struck me that way."

In the distance, Frances heard the blast of a foghorn. Given the clarity of the sky, it must have been the starting signal for a sailing race. Looking across the harbor, she could see someone standing at the base of the Yacht Club's flagpole. She and Teddy fell into silence as they watched him lower the Stars and Stripes to half-mast.

"If Dick were here, he'd tell them to keep the flag flying. 'Never mourn the dead. Celebrate the living,' he always said. Then again, that's coming from the man who wanted 'Roll Out the Barrel' played at his funeral." She dropped her cigarette onto the terrace and stomped out the butt with the end of her cane.

"I never knew that."

"My dear, apparently that's not all you don't know."

Father Whitney appeared in the doorway just as Frances was about to go inside. She stepped back, startled. When she extended a hand, he clasped hers in both of his. His palms were warm. "I was just visiting with your aunt. She told me how much it means to her that you've stayed." His smile was soothing. "We were discussing the memorial service."

"When is it going to be?"

"Friday evening. She and Bill want some time to make sure all the police involvement is over." He paused and leaned in toward her. "Is it really necessary?"

Maggie Mallory's words echoed. It seemed as though fate once again had made her the messenger of terrible news. She looked at the minister, his large face and kind eyes, and fought to hold back her tears. "Yes. And it might not be over for quite a while."

"What do you mean?"

217

"I . . . I . . ." she stammered, wondering whether she should confide in him. He had enough work simply ministering to this grief-stricken family; he didn't need the worries of an investigation, too.

"Tell me," he urged, reading her mind. "Please. It's all right."

She knew how much Hope had relied on him. Maybe he could help her to break the news to Adelaide. "She was murdered. It wasn't suicide."

His mouth opened, and she watched his eyes get bigger in apparent disbelief. His grip on her hand tightened, and he wobbled for a moment, unsteady on his feet. "Are you sure?" She nodded. "How do you know?"

Frances relayed the little bit of information she'd learned from the medical examiner. "Who? Why?" He seemed about to cry.

She said nothing. She had no answers.

"Dear God," he whispered.

"Can you help me? Adelaide and Bill don't know. I need to explain to them what's going on."

"Nothing can explain this horror, this violence. But together we will pray for strength."

Frances needed that more than ever.

18

Frances had barely slept. In her dream, she'd been walking down a long center aisle of a dimly lit church. The interior was unfamiliar, but white lilies adorned the edge of every pew. The overpowering scent burned her eyes and the back of her throat. Above the altar, light shone on the gilded wood of an oversize cross. Each end was wrapped in white rope, tied and knotted. She walked slowly, carefully placing one foot in front of the other. As she approached the end of the aisle, she knelt in front of the altar. Staring up at the cross, she could see the knots beginning to bleed. The liquid oozed between the turns in the rope and dripped to the floor, leaving a pool of red. Frances reached out to touch the blood but awoke before her fingers made contact.

After propping herself against the pillows, she fingered the eyelet bedspread as she watched the light brighten through the lace curtain. Scattered bird chirps were the only sounds in the still of the early morning. Glancing at the alarm clock by her bed, she resisted the urge to call Sam. No doubt he was awake, but his morning routine made him unreceptive to interruptions, even from her.

She pushed back the covers, swung her feet to the floor, and sat up. She reached for a T-shirt and shorts from the bureau drawer. Then she grabbed a towel from the adjacent bathroom and tiptoed down the stairs.

Outside, the air seemed thick with the smell of salt, and she could see the gentle waves rolling onto the narrow strip of beach. She climbed over the low stone wall that separated the Lawrences' expansive lawn from the ocean and set out for a walk, relishing the feel of sand underneath her feet and the slight breeze on her face. The sun sparkled on the water, and she watched the changing coloration of the beach as the waves washed to shore, then retreated back to sea, leaving it momentarily darkened. Every few yards, she stopped to pick up yellow periwinkles, pieces of green or blue glass softened by the waves, or pink and gray moon shells scattering the beach. Expectantly she turned them upside down to look for any trace of the creature within, the mucous textured animal that she admired and envied for its ability to carry its whole world on its back. How many times in her life had she wished for just the sort of freedom that came with limited possessions and total mobility?

Frances rolled the moon shell in her palm. The animal was lucky indeed. If it had a bad experience in one tidal pool, it could pack up its spiral shell and move on with no trace of the past.

She sat down and wiggled her toes to bury them. Her

feet looked odd – two ankles disappearing into the sand – and she remembered the joyful hours spent covering her legs, her chest, sometimes even her whole body. When the weight or her own restlessness became overpowering she would extricate herself, a Houdini moment of reclaiming her limbs. These games seemed so compelling that she'd never tired of them.

As she settled herself on the beach, she thought about her conversation with Elvis the night before. He'd called shortly after she and Father Whitney had told Adelaide and Bill about the medical examiner's preliminary conclusions. When her cell phone rang, she'd moved out of the library into the hallway, not wanting them to hear her responses for fear it would aggravate their shock, disbelief, and pain, but as it turned out, she had little to say. Elvis had issued instructions. He would contact the caterer and the wedding planner and get the names of all employees with access to the house in the hours preceding Hope's death. The Essex County crime scene team – a group of forensic specialists, photographers, and detectives – would be dispatched to the house the next morning. Frances should begin to probe the family members, to learn what she could about Hope's relationships with her future in-laws, her fiancé, even her own family. Elvis had spoken slowly, carefully, as if he were dealing with someone suffering from a terminal illness.

She didn't know where to begin. For the hundredth time in the last twenty-four hours, she wondered who would have wanted to kill Hope. Manchester seemed so serene, a peaceful New England town with a penny candy store that still sold one-cent gumballs, a matronly policewoman who held an orange sign on Elm Street to assist with school crossings, a Ferris wheel on the Fourth of July, a place where violence wouldn't enter. Like Southampton, New York, where Richard Pratt had spent the majority of his vacation time with his daughters, Manchester felt completely safe: Frances had ridden her bicycle without ever worrying about traffic; later she and her cousins drank beers on Singing Beach and strolled home after dark without ever looking behind them. That danger lurked was unthinkable. This vision of the world, of the safe haven of the Lawrence home, had been shattered in an instant.

She stood, momentarily dizzy as the blood rushed from her head. After brushing the sand off her bottom and the backs of her legs, she continued to walk. The warmth of the sun began to spill through the cirrus clouds that striped the sky, and Frances felt herself start to perspire. She needed a swim. She glanced both ways down the beach and, seeing no one, pulled off her clothes, inhaled twice quickly, than ran into the ocean, stumbling slightly as the sea level rose to her thighs. She fell forward and felt the shock of cold spill over her. Immediately she began to churn the ocean with her arms, pulling her hands through the water and propelling herself out to sea. The temperature and her own exertion allowed her momentarily to forget the tragedy she wanted so much to leave behind. Only when she stopped and, treading water, turned back to look at the shore and the majestic Lawrence house rising from behind the stone wall was she reminded that she needed to get back. She wanted to be at the house when the police arrived.

As she walked back along the beach, her cell phone rang. The noise surprised her. She hadn't realized she'd brought it with her in the pocket of her shorts.

It was Elvis. "I'd say good morning and how are you and all that, except it's not a good morning and I doubt you're doing that well," he said. "The crime scene guys are on their way. I suspect they'll be at the house in the next twenty minutes or so."

"Frankly, I'm nervous they won't find anything. People have been in and out of here constantly."

"Nothing we can do about that now. They'll do the best they can. See what they come up with. But I've got something that might interest you. We've run CORI information on the caterers' employees."

"Criminal Offender Record Information?" Frances asked, wanting to make sure she understood the acronym.

"Yeah. That's right. We had a couple of hits, but only one that's worth checking out. Guy by the name of Michael Davis. He's got a criminal record a mile long, juvenile and adult, and goes by various aliases. He's currently on probation."

"For what?"

"Robbery and assault and battery."

Frances thought of the missing engagement ring. "Did he do time?"

"Yeah. Eighteen months. But he was supposed to be a witness in some federal drug case, so he got paroled early. The Assistant US Attorney in Boston tells me the case fell through because there was a problem with the chain of custody on the drugs, but they'd already struck a deal with this fellow, so they followed through."

"Government has to live up to its word," Frances said. She hoped her sarcasm was obvious despite the poor connection.

Elvis emitted the briefest of chuckles before continuing. "Far as I can tell, he's been in and out of prison since the age of fifteen. His juvenile record's got a number of minor offenses, but also two A and Bs and a larceny. Held up a 7-Eleven. His compatriots were over eighteen, so they took most of the heat. Anyway, I spoke to the owner of the catering company, an operation called Best Laid Plans." He paused, and she could hear pages turning in the background. "Christine Bridges," Elvis went on. "She employed this guy part-time. This was his third job with her. She's had no problems with him, says he's hardworking and strong enough to carry racks of dishes, which is what she needs. He gets twelve dollars an hour."

Not bad money, Frances thought. Then again, the people who used caterers to feed their guests probably didn't need to resort to minimum wage. "Didn't she know about his record?"

"In this state, even if you've got a pedophile applying for a job at a day care center, it's tough to find out a criminal history. She had no way to know."

"Have you spoken to him yet?"

"No. I thought you might want to come along for that."

"Where is he?"

"Lives in Lynn."

Lynn, Lynn, city of sin . . . The childhood rhyme popped into Frances's head. She remembered driving north along Route 1 from Logan Airport and seeing the gaudy restaurants offering tiki bowls and live entertainment. If memory served her, it was also the site of the track for greyhound racing, a sport that made her stomach turn.

"I'll meet you there. Just tell me where and when."

"Four o'clock. I'll meet you just off the Route 1 exit. You can follow me to his house."

"Fanny, I've been looking for you." Bill stood on the front step, dressed in pressed khaki slacks and an Oxford shirt. "I need a moment of your time," he added.

The chill of the Atlantic water had settled in her bones, and Frances wanted to excuse herself to shower, but the immediacy in Bill's tone trumped any thoughts of comfort that might add delay. She followed him inside to the breakfast room, an alcove where blue-and-yellow valances ballooning over the tops of the mullioned windows partially obscured the view of the garden. An array of newspapers covered one end of the cherrywood table.

"Coffee?" Bill asked, reaching for a white carafe.

"Please. Black's fine."

The smell of java filled the air, and Frances watched the steam rise from a porcelain mug. Bill settled himself in the chair opposite Frances.

"The police will be here shortly, but I hoped we could speak for a few minutes alone because I believe I know who might have killed Hope. His name is Carl LeFleur."

Frances could tell by the look on his face that he referred to Hope's lover, the one Teddy had described.

"At one time he was someone Hope saw socially. It never amounted to much in her mind, but I think he became rather obsessed with her. And she was impressionable, and . . . well . . . we all make mistakes."

"Why would he have killed her?"

"I'm quite certain Carl was looking for Hope to be his meal ticket. He had considerable difficulty accepting the reality of her marriage. He's a rough man . . . coarse . . . an immigrant after all. Violence would not be out of the question."

"Was he at the wedding?"

"Hope wanted to invite him, but her mother and I wouldn't hear of it. We didn't need to consult Jack. I know he would have agreed with us."

"Do you have any reason to think he came anyway?"

Bill paused for a moment, fidgeting his clasped fingers and appearing to squeeze his palms. "Carl tried to see Hope the night before the wedding. Came to the house just moments before we were to leave for the rehearsal dinner. But I refused to let him in."

"Did he say why he'd come?"

"I think that's obvious. When I told him to leave, he attacked me. Actually tried to strangle me. Nearly did, if the truth be told."

"Really?" Why hadn't anyone said anything earlier? "Did you tell anyone?"

"No. At that point, I thought I was preparing for a celebration. If I only . . ." His voice cracked, and he covered his mouth with his hands.

Frances didn't know whether to get up to comfort her uncle or to give him his privacy during his momentary wave of emotion. She never seemed to know which was best and often withdrew herself; the simple reason was, she felt helpless when faced with immense grief. He didn't need to speak for her to know his agony. She was sure that a day wouldn't pass without him wondering why he hadn't had Carl arrested that evening.

He reached into his breast pocket, removed a monogrammed handkerchief, and blew his nose. "Besides, Hope's ring was stolen, and Carl needed money. And he didn't have a prayer of accessing legitimate funds. But a four-carat diamond might have given him a jump start. The police should talk to him. Maybe you could give them this." He handed her a piece of paper with a Gloucester address scrawled in black marker.

Traffic was bumper to bumper along Route 1, and Frances looked again at the dashboard clock. She was already more than twenty minutes late to meet Elvis, but she had wanted to stay for as much of the initial crime scene investigation as possible. The team dispatched by the Essex County District Attorney's Office – four men and two women in navy blue windbreakers and latex gloves – had gone to work on the Lawrence house as if it were an archaeological dig. They'd begun in Hope's bedroom, carefully bagging and labeling dozens of items from the dressing table, including the pills Frances had seen, a compact, a lipstick, two hairbrushes, several bobby pins, and a piece of torn fabric. They'd dusted the top and mirror for fingerprints, plucked fiber samples from the carpet with a pair of oversize tweezers, searched drawers, and taken some of what they'd found within. Then they'd moved to the windows, looking for fingerprints or evidence of forced entry or hasty departure. By the time Frances realized she needed to leave, they'd worked their way to the closet where Hope's body had been found. Detective Fleming, whom Frances recognized from the day of Hope's wedding, offered his business card and promised her a copy of the completed inventory. "Give a call if you've got any questions," he'd said as she departed.

The green exit sign for Lynn loomed over the eight-wheeler in front of her, and she quickly changed into the right lane. She instantly recognized Elvis's convertible parked on the shoulder at the bottom of the exit ramp. She pulled onto the grass behind him and rolled down her window as she saw him approach.

"I was here early, so I took the liberty of heading over there myself. There's not much to do to kill time in Lynn," he said, leaning against the side of her car and peering in the open window. "Our man's gone. So is virtually everything but his white catering jacket. According to his landlady, he bolted first thing Sunday morning. Packed up and hauled out in a black pickup, but she can't give us the make. He's been renting this

REDEMPTION

place since mid-May, but he's paid up through September, so she's thrilled."

"Does she have any idea where he went?" Frances asked, immediately realizing the stupidity of her question. A criminal wasn't likely to leave a forwarding address. "Did he pay cash for the apartment?" she added quickly.

"Yeah. Up front. Six hundred a month. I also asked whether he had any friends or people he hung out with, but she doesn't know. Our only hope is that he reports into his probation officer, but I have a feeling that isn't going to happen. I've put out an APB. See if any of my esteemed colleagues can track him down." Elvis chuckled, seemingly amused by the prospect. "In any event, you can turn around. There's nothing for us here. Sorry you wasted the drive."

"Any news from Maggie?"

"Not yet. And she's been avoiding my page."

"Is it worth going by? Maybe by the time I forge through this traffic, the autopsy will be complete."

"Any other woman, I'd say sure. But not Maggie. She doesn't like to be rushed, and I don't feel like being ripped a new asshole."

Frances couldn't help but laugh at his burst of crudeness. It was always hard to tell about other people's marriages, and the dynamic between Maggie and Elvis Mallory had her completely baffled. "Can I ask you a favor? It's a little out of the way."

"Anything."

She reached into her pocket and removed the piece

229

of paper her uncle had given her: "From the desk of Adelaide Lawrence." "There's someone I need to talk to, and I don't think I should go alone."

As Frances got out of her car she stretched, arching her back to rid it of its stiffness. A pain shot down her leg and she silently cursed sciatica, her affliction since she'd taken up jogging the past spring. She knew there was a reason she hated exercise. She scanned the row of houses and found the appropriate number. "This is it," she said to Elvis.

The series of buzzers were unmarked, so, guessing, she rang the first one. In response to the sound, a dog barked, and she heard a harassed voice call out in a language she didn't recognize. After a few minutes a woman opened the door. She wore a flowered smock, red socks, and blue plastic jellies. A bandanna covered her hair.

"We're looking for Carl LeFleur," Frances said in a voice that was surprisingly timid.

The woman ran her tongue over her lips in a gesture Frances couldn't interpret, but she said nothing.

"*Habla español?*" Although she assumed the woman spoke Portuguese, her high-school Spanish was the best she could do under the circumstances.

She shook her head.

"Does he live here?"

This time she nodded.

"But he's not here? Do you know where we could find him?"

Frustrated, Frances was about to return to her car when she noticed a small child appear behind the woman, leaning into her leg. No more than six or seven she was, with flowing black hair that seemed longer than she was tall. The calves of her skinny legs and her bare feet were covered in dirt. Her enormous walnut eyes stared up at Frances.

"Can you help us?" Elvis asked, squatting.

The girl nodded, an exaggerated gesture where her chin almost touched her chest.

"Do you know Carl?"

"Yeah."

"Do you know where he might be?"

"The dock. He's always there," she said in a melodic voice. "His boat's broken."

"Thank you very much," he said, and she smiled an array of white teeth.

Dusk had started to settle over the fishing pier. In the distance, Frances could see cawing seagulls circling overhead in anticipation of bait morsels as a group of bare-chested men hauled netting off a rusty-hulled trawler. Two others sat on the edge of the dock, their legs dangling idly as they sipped from long-necked beer bottles. A gray-haired man with the stump of a cigar in his mouth hosed empty lobster crates with fresh water. Latin music poured forth from one of the boats anchored at a slip and seemed to float with the tide out to sea.

Across the parking lot, a refrigerated truck waited with its engine idling while several sweatshirted men loaded ice into the back. Even with the distance, the odor of the day's catch filled Frances's nostrils.

"I'll check in with the harbor master," Elvis said.

"Meet me down by the boats."

Approaching the dock, she felt the sets of eyes on her. Whether it was her slightly sunburned skin, her outfit – a loose gray sundress and black sandals – or her gender that set her apart hardly mattered; she suddenly felt as if she'd sprouted a second head. She glanced back at the shingled building into which Elvis had disappeared. Scanning her options once more, she selected the seated men as the likeliest candidates to talk. They seemed the most peaceful and, she hoped, the most cooperative, but their noncommittal reply came as no real surprise.

"Excuse me, sir," she said, moving on to the man with the hose.

He turned in response to her voice and sprayed her slightly with water. Even as she instinctively leapt back, she smiled, a gesture meant to convey that his mistake was excused.

"Do you know where I could find Carl LeFleur?"

He tilted his head to the right. Removing his cigar, he muttered, "His boat's the *Lady Hope*. She's got a green hull and black bumpers."

She turned in the direction he indicated. From a distance, it was hard to tell which one he meant. "Thank you," she said. Hearing a whistle as she passed, she descended the planked walkway with her sandals smacking loudly against the wood. Out on the floating dock, she shaded her eyes with her hand to block the reflection of the last rays of sun on the water and surveyed the fleet. The *Lady Hope* had barnacles along her water line, and a davit protruded from the cabin roof. Her deck was covered with a pile of painted buoys, each tied by a warp to an empty lobster trap.

She wondered for a minute whether she should wait for Elvis to catch up with her, then decided against it. He was minutes behind her. What could happen? Besides, she wanted a moment to talk to Carl alone.

"Mr. LeFleur?" she called out as she drew near. She could hear the bang of a sledgehammer on metal, the clanking and sputtering of an engine trying to turn over, followed by more banging. A vise grip, pliers, and several other tools lay in a heap by the opening to the cabin below. She called again.

A man emerged, wiped his brow with a dirty rag, and hoisted himself onto the deck. "Who's asking?" Even with grease smeared across his forehead, he was hand-some, with a prominent jaw, black eyes, and carved musculature on his bare chest.

Frances introduced herself and extended a hand. He didn't return the gesture. "I wanted to talk to you about Hope Lawrence."

"Hope Cabot, now," he muttered. She thought she detected a quiver in his voice. Did he not know? Hope's death had been in all the papers. It would have been nearly impossible to miss, especially for someone who might have had reason to look for a wedding announce-ment on Sunday morning.

"No. Actually. Hope . . . she, uh . . ." Frances stammered.

"What happened?"

She willed herself to utter the words she wished weren't true. "She's dead. I thought you knew. She died shortly before her wedding," she added, as if that might make it easier for him.

For a moment he seemed frozen, unmoving, but then he covered his face with his palms and said nothing. His breathing was labored. She could see his fingers tense, pushing into his hairline and the perimeter of his face, his giant hands seeming to strain to bear the weight of his head. When moments later a drop of blood appeared on his cheek, she realized he had dug his nail into his own flesh. She took a step back and stumbled slightly on a pile of rope that she hadn't noticed before.

Carl looked up at the sound of her movement. His face was twisted and he clenched his teeth. He stared at her. His eyes were cold and hard.

"I'm sorry. I truly am. I understand you and Hope were once quite close and I'm sure this is difficult." Frances struggled with her words. How many times had she had to console a victim's family, comfort a witness decimated on cross-examination, but such nurturing had never been her strong suit. She believed that it did no good. Language couldn't placate or ameliorate emotions in any real way. Pain healed, or rather dulled, but ultimately it was a lonely process. She knew that all too well.

"Why are you here?" he asked.

She hadn't expected such a question to be his response, and his directness startled her. She took a deep breath. "I need to talk to you about the last time you saw Hope."

"And what if I don't want to talk to you?"

"Well, that's your prerogative. Um . . . you don't have to."

"I know what prerogative means."

There was no reason to talk to this man as if he had an elementary vocabulary, she chastised herself. It was an instinctive reaction based on what she'd heard of him, what she'd assumed. She'd thought she was better than that, but apparently not. "Did you see Hope on Saturday?"

Carl didn't reply. He crossed his arms in front of his chest and appeared to look past Frances to the sea beyond. "Who sent you? Bill?"

Frances didn't respond.

"You didn't come to tell me Hope's dead. Nobody in the Lawrence family would do me that favor." He lowered his voice. "So Bill must think I killed her."

She felt a shiver down her spine as his words echoed in her ears. How did he know? Only a handful of people were aware that Hope's death would be considered a murder; the papers had universally labeled it "self-inflicted," the polite phrase for suicide.

"Well, damn him. Damn them all." He stepped past her, walked to the stern of his boat, and leaned over the side. He reached into the water and pulled out a bunch of seaweed floating on the surface, pressing the pillowed pieces between his large fingers. Frances could hear the popping sound as air escaped, releasing a tiny burst of salty water. She stared at his hands. They were calloused and dark like the rest of his body, except for a lighter band – skin apparently unexposed to the sun – around the left pointer finger. She wondered for a moment what ring he'd removed.

"When was the last time you saw her?" she asked, trying to refocus the conversation.

"I see her every day. I close my eyes and see her face, smell her scent, feel her skin. She was everything good." Then he paused, dropped the seaweed back over the side of the boat, and turned toward her. "The corpses of drowned men float facing up, but women face down. Someone once said it was to respect female modesty, but I disagree. A woman expects the worst. When she dies, she faces the direction she knows she'll go, the blackness of her destiny. A man assumes he's going to heaven, so he looks up. Arrogant pricks, aren't we?"

Frances wanted to understand his point but felt that there was a philosophical subtext she was missing.

His tone changed dramatically as Elvis's arrival interrupted them. "I don't know who you are or where you've come from, but I don't want you here. Get off my boat." He picked up a wrench from near his feet and slapped it against the side of his leg.

"I . . . I think you've misunderstood," she said, slowly moving backward. She could feel her pulse rise and mentally prepared to dive into the cold water. "I loved Hope, too. I want to find out what happened, and I thought I might start with you."

"Don't feed me crap. Why me, unless I'm a suspect?

And why'd you bring a cop? I've got nothing to say."
With the word "nothing," spittle shot between his teeth
and landed on Frances's chin. She reached up and
wiped it with her finger. "Go ahead. Arrest me. But
you're wasting your time. None of you ever wanted to
understand what was really going on with Hope."

"Hope is my cousin. I do want to understand. Tell
me." Then a thought came to her, and she added,
"Teddy told me you could help." It wasn't exactly a lie,
given her conversation with her grandmother earlier in
the day. Teddy had understood something about the
relationship between Hope and Carl, enough that she
had sheltered their romance beneath her own roof even
while Hope was engaged to the apparent pick of North
Shore princes. Perhaps Carl would have sensed her
compassion, her empathy.

Instead he snorted a burst of laughter, dropping the
wrench down into the cabin. It clanged as it hit the
floor. "And what if I could?"

She didn't know how to answer and looked to Elvis
to respond.

"Think of Hope. Don't let her killer get away," he
said.

Carl didn't acknowledge the comment and began to
stack the empty traps in an ordered fashion at one end
of the boat. Frances stepped out of his way repeatedly
to avoid being hit by a swinging lobster buoy. He had
nearly completed his job before he stopped and said, "I
know you don't have the goods on me or we'd be talking
at the precinct house instead of here. I've never known
a cop who settled for a house call if he didn't have to.

But I don't trust you and I don't trust your friend here. So, I'll tell you what: You offer me something and I'll tell you stuff I couldn't possibly make up. That's my deal." With that, he swung himself back down into the cabin.

Frances pondered what she could say to change his mind, but nothing came to her. He'd obviously had enough experience and perhaps run-ins with the law to know what it could and couldn't compel him to do. Whether Elvis's presence had reinforced that experience, she couldn't say, but she realized that they needed information that either could exert pressure on him or would be of interest to offer. She clearly couldn't win him over otherwise.

They left him with their telephone numbers, knowing full well he wouldn't call. With Elvis a few steps behind her, she walked slowly back up the planked walkway, conscious of the squeaking of the wood as the tide flowed underneath. The light had started to fade, and the fog danced on the water as it rolled into shore. The temperature had dropped considerably, and Frances hugged herself as she scanned the pier once again. Seagulls, most with shells held tight in their beaks, paraded around the end of the dock. To an outsider, the scene should have seemed serene, but she felt an ache of unease.

"Now what?" she said to Elvis once they were back in the parking lot.

"I'll find out what I can about our fisherman friend. In the meantime, see if your uncle is willing to press an assault charge. That way we can pick him up. He clearly knows more than he's saying."

"You think he'd talk in custody?"

Elvis smiled. "Sometimes our timing's bad and we can't find a magistrate to set bail. We end up having to keep a suspect overnight. Then things happen." He winked. "You know how it is."

Despite the hour, police cars still lined the driveway at Smith's Point. Frances pulled onto the lawn to keep her car out of the way and idled the engine, hesitating before entering the house. She looked at the array of official law enforcement vehicles. Some were marked. Others – mostly Crown Victorias – were not, but it hardly mattered. Who else drove them?

She hadn't expected the team of crime scene personnel to work so late and wondered what they might have found. There had been so many guests, plus all the people hard at work to make a reception; it seemed impossible that anything worthwhile could be salvaged. But that was the magic of police work. A fingerprint, a hair sample, a fabric fiber – the tiniest particle left behind could hold the key to unlocking the mystery. She hoped for her aunt's sake that it could happen quickly.

She closed her eyes and leaned her forehead against the steering wheel.

Girls, come back! She remembered her father's voice calling from the beach. She and her sister had been diving off the dock, swimming out into the harbor, and returning to repeat the exercise again. Hope had stayed behind, smiling and laughing as her cousins floundered in the black water, jumping up and down each time they returned. She'd been four, five at the most, and by the end of the summer her blonde hair had a greenish tint from hours spent in the heavily chlorinated swimming pool at the Field and Hunt Club. Seeing her father's waving arms, Frances and Blair had turned around. As Frances had pulled herself up onto the float and wrapped herself in a towel, Hope had extended her arms. "A piggy, pleeeease," she'd said in her little voice. Frances had knelt down to let her cousin climb on her back. She could still feel Hope's pudgy hands around her neck, the warmth of her skin as she held her thighs, and she could hear the giggles as they'd trotted back along the dock to the beach. "Go, Fanny! Go!" Hope had exclaimed. Twenty years later, her death seemed impossible. Frances almost expected to see her scampering up the steps from the beach. More than anything, she wanted to hear the soft pad of little feet on the wood floors of the expansive house.

Tears welled. How could this have happened? The fleeting moment between great joy about the wedding and sorrow at Hope's shocking death emphasized the fragility of life. Frances knew all too well that nothing could be taken for granted, because it could disappear in an instant, that just when the world seemed ordered and peaceful, chaos returned. She rubbed her eyes. She couldn't let herself mourn, or at least not yet.

*

"I've told you twice now, we don't know anything about that," Bill said. He and Adelaide stood in the entrance foyer with Detective Fleming, who held a thick envelope in his latex-covered hand.

"Fanny!" her aunt exclaimed. "Thank God you're here."

Frances nodded in recognition to the detective as she approached her aunt and uncle.

"There was ten thousand dollars in an envelope underneath this table," Adelaide said, indicating a round skirted one close to the door. "I can't imagine where it came from, or when."

"We're going to take it to the lab," Detective Fleming said. As if its existence needed to be confirmed, he extended the envelope toward her. "Maybe a print will tell us who it came from."

"I was the one who picked it up. Ask Officer What's-his-name. I turned it over. So what's that going to tell you?" Bill's raised voice was just shy of a yell, and several officers finishing up in the adjoining room moved quickly into the foyer. "My daughter's dead, and I'm sick and tired of the police turning our lives inside out. We're private people. Leave us alone!" He turned and headed up the stairs.

Adelaide's lip quivered, and her voice cracked as she spoke softly. "I apologize for my husband."

"No need, ma'am," Detective Fleming said as he put the envelope into a clear plastic bag. "We'll be in touch."

Frances wanted an opportunity to talk with him alone, to find out what, if anything, they'd found, but she didn't want to abandon her aunt. They stood together, watching the police carry the last of their boxes and equipment out to the waiting van. It seemed an endless procession.

Where had that money come from? What was it for? Frances wondered. Had Bill inadvertently destroyed whatever clues the police might have found? Removing anything once the crime scene unit had begun its search was reckless. Even in his distraught state, he should have recognized that. Unless . . . could he have meant to alter the condition of the envelope? She pushed the thought from her mind.

19

Frances sat in the breakfast room drinking her second cup of coffee. Sun poured through the windows, and she repositioned herself so that her body cast a shadow and she could read the papers in front of her, pink sheets from a triplicate pad. They were the crime scene's lengthy inventory list, the list of items removed from Hope's bedroom. Her eyes scanned the scrawl. At the bottom of the second page, she paused at item number 47: "key attached to wine cork by wire." Was that a homemade key chain? What did it open? She wondered what forensic significance it held.

There had been no trace of Bill or Adelaide when Frances had awoken that morning, and the house seemed eerily quiet. Although it had only been six days since she'd left Orient Point, Sam and home felt miles and years away. She leaned against the down cushion and rubbed her temples.

Hearing a nearby knock, she looked up. Father Whitney stood in the doorway.

"Morning," he said.

"Good morning," she mumbled, getting up.

"Please . . ." He gestured for her to stay. "I'm sorry to bother you. I was looking for Adelaide."

"I'm not sure where she is. I haven't seen her or Bill this morning. Can I offer you anything?"

"No. Thank you," he said, coming into the room. He perched on the edge of the chair next to her and placed a small leather book on the table. "There's something I need to tell you, to give you. This is very awkward."

"What is it?"

He pushed the book at her but didn't remove his palm from its cover. "I never intended to show this to Hope's family because it had been her wish that it remain confidential. But now that you tell me about her . . . death, it didn't seem right. There may be something of importance to the police."

"I don't understand," Frances said, staring at the book.

"It's Hope's diary."

Why did he have it? The expression on her face must have been revealing, because he immediately offered, "I found it on my desk after her . . . after her body was discovered. There was a note attached that just said, 'Please keep this safe.' I don't know when it got there. I assume she left it when she and I met earlier in the afternoon, and that in my haste I hadn't noticed it before."

"Have you read it?"

"No. It was given to me in confidence, and I would do anything to preserve that. It's part of my role. So it never occurred to me to disclose it when I thought she'd committed suicide. I'm sure its contents will be extremely painful for her family, and it didn't make sense in my view to add to how much they already suffer. But now that the circumstances are different, well, I think I'd be remiss to withhold it."

What did it contain? Would it reveal Hope's fears? Did she disclose who had a motive to kill her? Frances couldn't bear the thought.

"It was Hope's possession, and her family should decide what to do with it." He got up to leave. "I should have given it to you earlier, but you have to know the torment I've been in over how to handle this. I've prayed to God for strength to do the right thing. I hope it's not too late."

Frances tried to smile. He looked exhausted. This trauma had wreaked havoc on an entire community and, as its minister, he was supposed to pick up the pieces. But who tended to him? Who cared for the caregiver? She didn't envy his role. "Thank you. You've done the right thing."

After he'd left, she fingered the cover of the book and then hesitantly opened it. Perhaps she should wait for Adelaide and Bill to return, but she couldn't. It seemed too important.

The pages had buckled with the pressure of a ball-point pen on the thin leaves. Some entries were in black, some blue, and as Frances flipped the pages, she noticed that even the handwriting varied. Certain paragraphs slanted heavily to the right, others were more vertical. She glanced at several sentences on the last day and could make out no more than a word, a name, and references to Jack amid illegible scribbles. She turned to the first page, dated August 2.

> I can't be who he wants me to be. And when I tell him so, he threatens me. His whole life, he's gotten what he wants, what he demands. I hate myself for my inability to satisfy him, but I hate him, too.

She turned the page.

> Jack wants a prenuptial agreement. As if I would take his money. Doesn't he realize that's the last thing that matters to me? That what I want and need have nothing to do with the materialism he worships. But I also wonder why relinquishing my marital rights is important to him.

She reread the entry and dog-eared the page, remembering her discussion with Teddy.

> August 14: I must tell Jack I can't go through with it. I know he will be upset, but I can't imagine life as his wife. He makes me feel inadequate. I am the constant disappointment. And even though I've tried to protect his feelings, he will be hurt. But it must be either him or me. Am I being too selfish? Should I be sacrificed?

Frances paused. Her own words, the ones she had shouted through the door of Hope's room just moments before she'd discovered her body, resonated in her mind. Were their feelings that similar? It seemed a strange coincidence. The entry continued:

I will tell him. If he's angry, there's nothing I can do. Perhaps if he hits me or lashes out, it will be easier. Maybe I'll be raped. His violence is easier, easier than his sorrow.

Frances thought she'd misread and pored over the words several times. That Hope would consider the possibility of rape, that she would even use such language was shocking. But then she remembered the conversation she'd had with her cousin less than a day before her murder. At the rehearsal dinner Hope had seemed eager, almost frantic, to hear stories of domestic abuse. *Tell me the worst.* Her words echoed in Frances's mind. At the time the conversation had seemed odd, inappropriate, but now the memory of it was haunting. *You tell me, then, why women stay.* Had Hope been seeking an answer for herself?

She couldn't imagine Jack as violent, but her brief time at the Coalition Against Domestic Violence had taught her that looks could be deceiving. She remembered Meaty's words: *The statistical likelihood . . . is that the killer is Jack.* Had Hope spoken to Jack? And if so, what had transpired? Had he been hurt enough by Hope's rejection that he'd lost control? Did he have a history of escalating violence? She hated that phrase – the escalation of violence – as if a fist or knife or gun were riding a moving staircase to some inevitable end. But she also knew that what could seem relatively minor, a shove or a swipe across the arm, could become more serious. Even deadly.

She had to stop her mind from racing. She pictured

Jack pacing in her motel room, the apparent earnestness of his despair. Had that been an act? If so, she was a poor judge of character. None of it made sense. She tucked the diary in her knapsack. She needed to show it to Adelaide as soon as possible, but in the meantime perhaps Jack himself could provide some answers to the morass of questions that jumbled in her mind.

"Oak Tree Farms" was inlaid in the left stone pillar of the entrance to the Cabot estate, and a small sign with black lettering staked into the ground read "Private." As Frances turned her rental car into the drive, she realized that the property bore little resemblance to any kind of a farm with which she was familiar. A white split-rail fence outlined the perimeter of what had to be more than a dozen acres. Carefully pruned oaks with massive trunks dotted the well-manicured lawn. Bright orange carp were visible in the clear water of what appeared to be a man-made pond with an elaborate bluestone surround. Wearing green monogrammed blankets, two horses, a chestnut and a bay, grazed. Even the long gravel drive had been recently raked.

The stone house with enormous columns on either side of the front door loomed as she rounded the bend. The structure seemed to stretch forever, and Frances quickly inventoried the thirty windows on the front side alone. Some were partially shrouded in double-sided drapes, the triangles of colored fabric brightening the otherwise ominous façade. She parked in front, approached the house, and rang the bell. Its timbre echoed.

Moments later a thin woman in a black uniform and white apron opened the door. Wrinkle lines made rivulets in her face, and her thin lips appeared almost blue. "May I help you?" she asked.

"Yes. My name is Frances Pratt. I was hoping to find Jack at home."

"He's not," she replied, offering nothing more.

"When do you expect him?"

"I can't say."

Whether the comment meant "couldn't" or "wouldn't" was unclear from her tone. "Are Jim or Fiona in?"

"Mrs. Cabot is here."

"Could I see her?"

"I will have to ask whether she's receiving guests, as I'm quite sure none were expected," she said, gesturing for Frances to enter. "You can wait in the drawing room. Follow me."

Frances walked slightly behind as she was led through the marble-floored foyer to a large set of double doors off to the left, which the housekeeper opened using two hands. "I'll return momentarily," she said, and headed up the wide staircase.

The drawing room resembled a decorator's showcase, so coordinated and filled that it made Frances claustrophobic. A thick wool rug with a trellis pattern covered most of the dark-stained wood floor. Three different seating areas of overstuffed chintz furniture and tufted ottomans made it difficult to navigate. Several oil paintings in gilded frames, including a life-size portrait of Fiona in a chiffon ball gown, hung on the dark green walls. A ginger-jar lamp rested on each end table, and stacks of magazines, Limoges pillboxes, and photographs in tortoiseshell frames covered the three coffee tables. Porcelain topiaries stood in a row along the carved marble mantel.

As she waited for Fiona, Frances worked her way around the perimeter of the room. Predictable bestsellers filled the bookshelves, and she scanned the titles, realizing how little popular fiction she'd read since leaving the Suffolk County District Attorney's Office. Moving along, she glanced at the day's brightness through a set of French doors that opened onto a brick patio. To the left of the doors was an English writing desk, its green leather top covered with a blotter, a sterling letter opener, and a pile of mail, including several small envelopes, the sender's return address embossed on the back flap. Frances ran her finger along the pile, some of which had already been opened. "Barcley and I cannot tell you how sorry we are about Hope's passing." "George and I write to send you our deepest sympathy during this difficult time." "Hank and I are keeping Jack in our thoughts and prayers." The ladies of the North Shore were prompt in sending condolence letters.

Frances stopped herself. It wouldn't look right if she was seen prying into the Cabots' mail. She was about to step away when one envelope caught her eye. Addressed to Fiona, it was business size, and the return address printed in the upper left-hand corner read "Avery Bowes

Institute." Even without living in Massachusetts, she was familiar with that facility's reputation, but a psychiatric hospital seemed an odd correspondent. Should she? She glanced toward the door, which remained shut. Was this just curiosity? No, she rationalized. She needed to know everything possible about the people surrounding Hope during her last days, and Fiona fell into that category. Keeping her body positioned toward the entrance to the drawing room, she unfolded the 8½-by-11-inch sheet with one hand. The letterhead read "Peter Frank, MD, Medical Director."

It was an invoice. "Dates of service: June 26, 27, 29, 30. Consultation. $5,000."

Frances had never seen a psychiatrist, but even to her untrained eye the bill seemed unreasonably high for four visits. Maybe consulting fees were higher. If that was the reason, she couldn't help but wonder what Fiona had consulted him about.

She jumped when she heard the lock click and, without thinking, stuffed the invoice in her pocket. In the process of distancing herself from the desk, she tripped over a leather bull footstool. She caught herself before falling, but the stern expression on Fiona's face as she walked through the door gave every indication that the mistress of the house didn't appreciate her clumsiness. Or perhaps her snooping.

Fiona extended both arms, and when Frances did the same, she leaned forward and kissed her cheek. But despite the gesture of welcome, when she spoke her tone was flat. "How nice of you to drop by. Could I offer you anything?" she asked, settling into an armchair.

She reached to ring a crystal bell on the table beside her.

"No, thank you," Frances replied as she sat on the adjacent couch. She felt her thighs and back sink seemingly forever into the cushions, and she held onto the arm to keep upright. "I wanted to speak with Jack."

"He's out riding, which means it's impossible to know when he'll return," Fiona said, striking a match from an embroidered box and turning to light a Rigaud candle. The wick lit, and Frances instantly smelled the distinctive perfume. "His horse seems to be his only solace right now. He barely eats, so I can't even promise he'll return for lunch, but you're welcome to join me. Vichyssoise and crab cakes, if that appeals."

"I can only stay a moment," Frances lied, although the air was so sweet in the room that she did intend to minimize any delay in her departure.

The housekeeper entered and set a tray with tea service on the table between Fiona and Frances. Fiona poured herself a cup and added a single slice of lemon. "I don't suppose there's any news from the police."

"Not yet."

She leaned against a down pillow and closed her eyes. "It's almost inconceivable that this should happen here in Manchester."

"Or anywhere."

"But Manchester especially."

Frances watched her raise her porcelain cup to her lips and take a sip without even the tiniest of slurps, an amazing display of manners. Emily Post would be proud.

"Cabots have lived in this area practically since its founding. If not the oldest family, we're certainly one of. Before Jim and I had Jack, we lived on Beacon Hill, Louisburg Square. Are you familiar with it?"

Frances nodded. Even the hick from the north fork of Long Island that Fiona presumed her to be could recognize the toniest address in Boston.

"We moved here when I became pregnant. We always intended to live here, but the prospect of a child hastened our exit from the city. We wanted this community, these values. It's a wonderful place. Everyone knows everybody. Jim and I could be confident that Jack's peers were . . . like us. Maybe that sounds insensitive, but doesn't every mother want to protect her child? All the school shootings and drugs you hear about nowadays. I can hardly bear to read the paper." She sipped again. "But I suppose we've taken the blessings of our life for granted."

"Mmm."

"I'm very concerned for Adelaide. She's a lovely woman. But I think she and Bill made a huge mistake letting the police proceed with that autopsy. Something like this is best laid to rest quickly. Otherwise people jump to horrible conclusions. Between you and me, there's already talk. Wondering why. When I ran into Lily Bowler yesterday at the club, she asked me if there had been abuse. Sexual abuse," she added, whispering the words.

"Why would someone have thought such a thing?"

"People speculate, and it can be quite unkind. Of course I told Lily there wasn't, or at least none of which

I was aware." She looked at Frances, seemingly to invite concurrence. "But something odd happened to that girl. And my guess is it happened a long time ago."

Hope had been murdered. What was she talking about? "What do you mean?"

Fiona leaned forward. "Can I be blunt?"

"Please," Frances nodded.

"Hope had a very serious eating disorder. You must have known that. Anyone could tell by looking at her. And she had other problems, depression and the like. Sadly, she was seriously unbalanced. She wouldn't have made anyone a good wife, Jack especially."

"But he loved her."

"Love is blind. And make no mistake that Hope kept her secrets well hidden. But I can assure you that Jack would never have gotten involved with her if he'd known the truth."

"Secrets?"

"Hope couldn't have children. But she never told Jack that. She misled him, I assume because he wants children and should have them."

"How do you know?"

Fiona's face went blank. She paused for a moment and swirled her tea with a small spoon. It appeared that she planned to ignore the question. When she finally spoke, her words came slowly, carefully chosen. "Our family has a history of accomplishment and respect. Our Jack is part of that success. And he needs a wife who won't be a drain, a woman who is capable of supporting him and their home so that he can excel. He deserves no less."

Her matter-of-fact delivery sent a chill down Frances's spine. She'd never known someone to be so cold. She had assumed that both families had blessed this union, but for the second time in as many days, she chastised herself for making assumptions that colored her evaluation of the people with whom she was dealing and their possible motivations.

"Jack will be a wonderful father someday, just like his father. And Jim wants grandchildren. This family's lineage should be continued. But he wasn't about to listen to reason." She picked up the bell again and rang it. Apparently Frances was being dismissed. Within moments, the door opened and the housekeeper reappeared. "You'd best be going now."

Frances stood up, wondering why the conversation had halted so abruptly. "Please ask Jack to give me a call when he has a chance," she said.

"And why is that?"

Frances needed to talk to him about the prenuptial, his parents, and his relationship with Hope, but she didn't want to spell out any of that to Fiona now. "Just a couple of questions, no big deal," she said dismissively. "Thank you for your time."

Outside, her breathing came fast and she held onto the door of her car for support. Although she felt somewhat soothed by the sound of water percolating from a marble fountain in the middle of the circular drive and the vibrant colors of the hibiscus, lavender, lilies, and assorted dahlias that filled the well-established perennial bed, her conversation with Fiona had been disturbing. She reached in her pocket for her car

keys and, instead, felt the letter she had hastily stuffed
inside. She removed it and stared again at the letterhead, the dates of consultation, and the exorbitant fee.
Who was Dr. Frank? What had he done to earn $1,250 a
session? And was there any reason to think this psychiatrist was connected to Hope's death? Her mind was
playing tricks on her.

Frances settled into the driver's seat, stretched her
arms above her head, and then circled her head on her
neck. As she turned the key in the ignition, she reached
for her cell phone, but the message signal was already
on. Three unanswered calls, all from Elvis. "I'll meet
you at the ME's office. Maggie's got her report."

20

Frances's mind raced as she drove. She turned on the radio and searched for a country station, a familiar Lyle Lovett song, something to calm her down, but the noise blaring through the airwaves only exacerbated her anxiety. She wanted to feel strong, in control, but for reasons she couldn't articulate, her emotions seemed to be getting the best of her. Hope's death had triggered reactions she'd never expected to have, ones centered on the shattered image of her aunt's perfect family, and she held onto the steering wheel with both hands to keep them from trembling.

She saw the sign for Storrow Drive up ahead and turned on her blinker. "Frances Taylor Pratt, pull yourself together." But despite her forceful tone of voice as she admonished herself aloud, she wasn't the least bit confident in her ability to listen.

Dr. Mallory sat cross-legged on top of her desk, wearing shiny leather pants and a black mohair sweater that stretched tight across her chest. She'd curled her hair with rollers so that her face was encircled in blond ringlets and her half-glasses balanced on the end of her nose. As Frances entered the room, she looked up from the pages she'd been reading. Elvis came toward her, dismissing with a nod the policeman who had escorted her from the information desk. "Have a seat."

She'd barely sat down when Maggie began to speak. "Here's the deal. I'll be blunt, as I said I would. There aren't many ways to candy-coat an autopsy."

Frances nodded. She wanted the straight story, although she could feel her stomach knot in anticipation.

"External examination revealed the following: significant evidence of fingertip bruises around the neck. Although there were ligature marks as well from the rope, the larynx and hyoid bone were fractured." Maggie looked up, as if to gauge Frances's reaction.

"All that means is that there's evidence of manual strangulation," Elvis clarified. "Fingertip bruises are small but deep in the tissue and intense in color from the pressure. Plus you don't see those kinds of fractures in a death by hanging."

"Are you doing this or am I?" Maggie asked.

"Sorry," he said, faking a look of humility.

"Cause of death was strangulation. Whoever killed her, hanged her afterward, presumably to make it look like suicide. Someone who obviously wasn't expecting an autopsy. There's no other external bruising, and tissue samples from under her nails revealed nothing."

Frances actually felt relief as Maggie uttered those

words. No signs of a struggle. That Hope hadn't fought off her aggressor meant she hadn't known her death was coming. And that would be easier for everyone, especially Adelaide. But it also pointed to the overwhelming likelihood that she had known her killer.

"Can you tell us anything else about the condition of her body?" she asked.

"Yes. First off, internal examination revealed several tears in the esophagus, as well as a fair amount of inflammation in the esophageal wall."

"What does that mean?"

"She had an eating disorder. That was obvious from the very low body-fat ratio and a weight almost twenty-five percent below normal for her height. Based on the condition of her esophagus, as well as evidence of a significant amount of decay in the tooth enamel, I'd say she was bulimic. Probably an electrolyte imbalance if we tested for it."

Frances sighed. Having seen Hope's near skeletal body and heard of her eating disorders from both Penelope and Fiona, she wasn't surprised by Maggie's findings. The diary entries, the condition of her body, all evidenced myriad demons that hadn't been exorcised. Now it was too late.

"Toxicology tests were run. A phosphatase color test was positive for the presence of semen in her stomach. A male with blood type O negative."

She glanced at Elvis.

"Jack's type is AB." He shrugged his shoulders.

"How'd you find that out?"

"His polo team's got its own medical supervisor. He

keeps pretty extensive records on the physical condition of the players. And let's just say that guy is a
friend of a friend." Elvis didn't need to add that the
supervisor apparently was friendly enough to disclose
confidential information without Jack's consent.

"How long had the semen been in her stomach?"

"Sperm don't survive long. The sample was suffi-
ciently brittle. But I'd estimate within twenty-four hours
of death." Maggie consulted the sheet in front of her.
"She also had approximately two thousand milligrams
of something called meprobamate in her blood. That's
the generic word for the drug – an antianxiety med –
but it's marketed under the name Equanil. It's prescribed short term, usually no more than four months
at a time because longer use results in severe depen-
dence. The normal adult dose is twelve hundred to
sixteen hundred milligrams a day, so the amount she
took is high, but not what I'd consider overdose level,
even with her low body weight."

"Is this the same drug the police found in her bedroom?" Frances asked, remembering the pills from the
inventory list.

"I'll have to check," Elvis replied.

"Presumably you know that Hope had had a hysterectomy," Maggie continued.

Frances was shocked. She'd had no idea. Wouldn't
she have heard about such serious surgery? It didn't
make sense. "Why?"

"I can't tell you that. Judging from the condition of
the scar tissue, it was a while ago. There were also
several small scars on her vaginal wall, but they may

have been from the surgery. It's hard to say. It's not relevant to a medical determination of the cause of death, but I thought you should know."

"Not or probably not?" Elvis asked.

"You're the investigator. I'm just giving you the medical facts that I see."

Hysterectomy. The word resonated in Frances's ears. Her thoughts instantly returned to Fiona, who had known of Hope's infertility and who had also objected to the autopsy. Did she know too of Hope's other lover? If she hadn't wanted her son to marry, would she have taken any steps to prevent it? Frances wondered whether her suspicions arose from her intense dislike for the woman or from inculpating facts.

Silence fell as they all contemplated the import of the report.

"What can you establish about the order of events leading up to her death?" Elvis asked.

Maggie looked up and removed her glasses. She chewed on one arm of the rim. "Sex, drugs, and rock and roll. She performed fellatio on someone other than her fiancé, took a hefty dose of pills to calm herself down, and, moments before she was scheduled to be married, was murdered by someone wanting to make her death look self-inflicted."

"Is it possible that the killer drugged her first?"

"I doubt it. I couldn't find one thing to suggest the pills were forced down her throat."

"And the esophageal tears couldn't be consistent with that?"

Maggie paused for a moment, considering the scenario

Frances had presented. "It's a very remote possibility. So remote I'd say no. But it certainly made it easier for the killer."

"We've gotten some information back from the crime lab," Elvis said. "There's a good fingerprint from the closet doorknob that we're running now to see if we can find a match, and a partial print on the top of a medicine bottle that doesn't match the victim's. A soiled Kleenex has come back positive for traces of meprobamate, as well as for the victim's saliva. It may be that she almost took the pills, changed her mind, but then later did swallow them. As if someone or something interrupted her." He paused, appearing to reflect on his own words. "There are also a couple of white silk fibers from the carpet near the dressing table, which we're checking against Hope's wedding gown. If it's a match, they may be from her having been dragged to the closet."

"Do you know about a key that was seized?" Frances asked, remembering the inventory list.

"A key? No."

Maggie shot them a stern glance. Clearly she was impatient and wanted the rest of their discussion to happen outside her office. Her job was done, and the next cadaver was undoubtedly waiting in line.

"See you tonight," Elvis said, kissing her goodbye.

"Good luck," she said to Frances. "I'm sure this is hard."

As they were walking out, Elvis reached for his pager, which apparently had been set to vibrate. He checked the text file. "Well, I stand corrected!" he exclaimed.

"What is it?" France asked.

"Our brothers in blue picked up Michael Davis, the fleeing caterer. He's over at the Charles Street precinct." He flipped open his cell phone, dialed a number, and pushed buttons through a series of prompts. Finally someone on the other end picked up. "It's Elvis. We're on our way."

"Who's handling this for the DA's office?" Frances asked a few minutes later. Elvis was speeding, and she wondered how much longer his Cadillac could survive. She saw the Public Garden on her left as they raced down Charles Street South. Scores of tourists waited on line to be paddled around the pond in swan-shaped boats. It was a Boston tradition, and Frances had enjoyed a similar ride with her father and sister on a trip years before.

"Mark O'Connor. He's a good guy, very experienced. I know he's got his application in to the judicial nominating committee, but so far nothing's happened. No one wants a Caucasian male on the bench anymore."

Alone in a windowless room with a linoleum floor, Michael Davis sat bent over a Formica table. Through the thin fabric of his worn T-shirt, Frances could see his ribs. Long brown hair covered his face, and his elbows rested on the tabletop. His feet were bare. Watching from outside the soundproof glass stood a broad-shouldered redhead. His striped shirtsleeves were rolled, and his suspenders had the seal of the Commonwealth of Massachusetts running up and down them. Elvis introduced Frances to Mark O'Connor, chief of violent crimes, who had held that position through two different administrations. "He managed to survive not only a change in district attorney but a change in party affiliation as well. Now that's talent," Elvis said in a stage whisper. Mark blushed.

The uniformed officer beside him was Tony Angelino. He explained that Michael had already been advised of his constitutional rights. So far he hadn't requested a lawyer, but he wasn't talking, either.

"Where'd you find him?" Elvis asked.

"I stopped him at the Tobin Bridge for skipping the toll. Also his truck had a broken tail light. When I approached, I saw what I determined based on my training and experience to be a marijuana roach on the floor of the passenger side, and I detected a strange odor. The suspect appeared nervous and glassy-eyed. Based on this probable cause, I arrested him for possession. When I ran the plate, the APB came up, so I notified Detective Mallory." Officer Angelino recited the facts as if he were testifying at trial. Cop talk, Frances thought. It always contained cover-your-ass phrases, euphemisms for, "I thought the guy looked shady, so I found an excuse to haul him into the precinct." In any event, this time it had worked.

"He's had three cups of coffee and a pack of Camel nonfilter cigarettes. He's made no phone call."

"Where's the truck?" Elvis asked.

"Downstairs in the lot."

"We've got enough probable cause to search, but we

thought we'd wait for you since we knew you'd be coming," the officer added.

"Why don't you take Ms. Pratt down and show her the car. Mark and I will try to talk to the guy."

"Is that okay with you?" Mark asked, turning to Frances.

"Sure. Thanks, though," Frances replied. No prosecutor she'd ever known was this deferential, and she wondered whether he and Elvis just didn't want anyone watching as they pulled the blinds and interrogated Michael the old-fashioned way. No, they didn't seem like the type. Elvis might be unpredictable, but Mark had a soft-spoken tone of voice and he wore suspenders. If she had to guess, his shirt was custom. That ruled out any possibility that he'd get himself dirty over a witness interrogation.

Frances followed Officer Angelino back out onto the street and to a guarded parking lot surrounded by chicken-wire fence topped with curls of barbed wire. The black truck parked away from the street had a neon orange tag in the window, designating it as police property. He pulled a pair of latex gloves out of his pocket, struggled slightly to get them on, and then opened the driver's-side door. Inside, empty cans, packs of cigarettes, food wrappers, jumper cables, loose popcorn, and CDs lay strewn in the backseat and on the floor. The upholstered interior was stained, and the crack in the front window had been sealed with duct tape.

The ashtray was open. Inside were several butts, as

NANCY GEARY

well as something gold. He reached in and removed a man's signet ring with a thick band. He held it up to his eye and then pointed it toward Frances. She could see the seal of an angel with a sword. "It's Saint Michael," Officer Angelino offered in explanation. "Patron saint of the weak and downtrodden. He was pretty fierce, courageous, a protector. You definitely want him on your side." He smiled.

He returned his attention to the truck. On the floor of the passenger side lay a dark green duffel bag.

"Shall we start with this?" he asked, removing the bag.

Frances shrugged.

Officer Angelino unzipped the bag and began to sort through the contents: a pair of blue jeans, leather sandals, and a navy sweatshirt; a couple of pairs of Fruit of the Loom briefs; a spiral address book and $40 in cash; a small plastic bag of green "plant matter," as he referred to it; and a copy of Tom Clancy's *The Hunt for Red October*. No more than the contents of an overnight bag. He frowned, obviously disappointed. Perhaps he was looking for this to be his first big case, a chance to work with the chief of violent crimes, maybe even to get his name in the paper. With what he'd just found, that was unlikely.

"Can I take a look?" Frances asked.

"Sure."

Frances gazed in at the empty duffel. She ran her hand along the interior canvas and the seams. As she did, her finger felt something hard. She stopped and felt again. Slowly, holding onto the lump, she turned the

266

bag inside out. The light instantly sparkled on the large brilliant-cut diamond in a platinum setting. The magnificent ring had been sewn into the bottom of the bag. She knew without having to call Jack for confirmation that it had been his gift to Hope when he'd proposed. There was no time to lose. They needed to get a forensics team on the car. She wasn't about to risk jeopardizing the preservation of any more evidence.

Mark paced before the soundproof glass, watching Elvis with Michael. "He's amazing," Mark commented as Frances approached. "Just never stops. One moment he's cajoling a suspect and we're all in there laughing, and the next he threatens to eat him alive. I guess that's why he's effective. Everyone stays off balance."

"We found something." She opened her palm, revealed the diamond ring, and quickly explained that it had been missing. "According to Jack, she would never have taken it off voluntarily."

Mark took it from her and held it up to the light. He turned it around and squinted to look at the other side of the stone. "That's it," he announced. "Davis's print matched the doorknob, too. We've got him dead to rights on a larceny charge, but I'm willing to bet we've got our killer." He clapped his palms. "Yesss." Then he slipped the ring in his pocket and opened the door to the interrogation room. Through the intercom, Frances listened. "Michael Davis, you are under arrest for the murder of Hope Lawrence," he announced. Even Elvis, who had been standing over Michael with one foot propped on the edge of his seat, stood up, startled. He shot a glance back through the one-way glass, but a response was pointless since he couldn't see whatever facial expression she might return.

"Get me a lawyer," Michael muttered. With those words, the questioning was over.

21

It took Frances more than a few moments to reorient herself when she opened her eyes. Manchester; the same twin bed that she'd always slept in; her aunt's guest room. The curtains had been drawn, but light still filtered through the lace. She pulled the covers up under her chin and focused on a speck moving across the ceiling. It was a ladybug, a symbol of good luck. Ironic, she thought.

She heard footsteps in the hallway and watched the turn of the doorknob to her room. She debated closing her eyes and feigning sleep for a few more minutes, anything to avoid the onslaught of another torturous day, but when Adelaide appeared on the threshold she sat up. Her aunt carried a tray.

"I wasn't sure you were awake."

Frances tried to smile. "What time is it?"

"Nearly noon. I thought you might want some break-fast." She rested the tray in front of Frances. The coffee smelled delicious, and even the overbuttered English muffin and two small sausages looked appetizing. Frances couldn't remember when her last meal had been. Nor did she recall ever having slept so late. She'd refused to admit how exhausted she was.

"We've had so much to do with the funeral arrangements," Adelaide said. She spoke seemingly to herself, unaware of Frances's presence. "The planning is endless, but I think I'm just having a difficult time making decisions. Should the flowers be pink or white or yellow or blue? What hymns, what prayers? Choices I would have had no difficulty making a week ago. And the Cabots call incessantly about that trust. Now they want us to meet with their lawyer. I know they're being kind." She paused, apparently distracted by a loose thread on her skirt. "I really don't know what charity makes sense. Probably the money should go to the church. That's where Hope's heart was." She lifted her hand to her mouth and appeared to cover a quivering lip.

"The church seems as good as anything else, if that's what you think Hope would have wanted."

"I suppose. I did discuss it with Father Whitney. He said the money could be put to good use – to fund the food pantry or update the Sunday-school curriculum. It's a lot of money, especially for a parish this size . . ." She broke off and walked over to the window to stare out at the lawn below. "Life seemed so simple a few days ago. My biggest worry was whether the caterers could prepare tenderloin for three hundred people and not have it be overcooked. Medium rare, I kept instructing. I wanted it medium rare. Medium rare," she repeated, and her voice cracked. "What was I thinking? All the attention and effort and energy we pour into meaningless activities. I would rather have had one extra hour with my daughter than three hundred medium-rare steaks."

Frances pushed the tray to one side and swung her feet to the floor. She walked over to her aunt and put her arms around her, embracing her from behind. They stood for several minutes, neither one saying a word, only the sounds of the various birds outside breaking the silence. Then Adelaide extricated herself and turned to face her niece. "How will life ever be normal?" she asked.

"It won't. It can't. You and Bill will have a long struggle ahead to figure out what kind of new life you can make together. It won't be normal because normal included Hope." As she said the words, she realized how true a sentiment it was. No one ever really recovered from a tragedy. People just learned to move on because there was no other choice. "I wish I could help."

"You do. And I'm sure you'll continue to help us if we have to face some awful trial of that man." She wiped her eyes and turned back to the window.

Adelaide's words reminded Frances of all the developments of the day before, some of which she hadn't had an opportunity to share with her aunt and uncle. When she'd returned from Boston the previous evening, the hours had disappeared in conversation of the stolen ring, news of the arrest of Michael Davis, and speculation on what would happen now. It had been after two in the morning when Adelaide and Bill finally admitted they could hear no more and retired to bed.

She hadn't had an opportunity to question them about the medical examiner's findings or to show them Hope's diary.

Frances took a gulp of her coffee and felt the hot liquid scald the back of her throat. The pain actually helped to orient her; the burning sensation was an experience that made the day real. "I hate to talk to you about the autopsy, but something came up that was . . . curious," she said, struggling for words.

In response to the comment, Adelaide turned to face her, but she said nothing.

"Hope's hysterectomy, why was it done?"

Adelaide clasped her hands and bent her head as if in prayer. "Why does it matter?" she asked.

Frances thought for a moment. Her aunt was right that the condition of Hope's body couldn't be relevant to the prosecution of a jewel thief, some lowlife who happened to slaughter a bride for the sake of her multicarat diamond. But for reasons Frances couldn't articulate, she had a sense that the information was important, that she wasn't looking simply to satisfy some morbid curiosity. A hysterectomy in a young woman was highly unusual, and she had enough experience to know that in an investigation, the unusual was often the most important.

Adelaide lowered herself onto the seat of a small wooden chair. "It can't possibly have anything to do with her death."

Frances felt a strange reaction akin to fear pulsing through her system. Her aunt was avoiding the subject, and with each moment that passed she had the nagging sense that the truth would be shocking. "How old was she?"

"It was a long time ago. Before Hope and Jack even got involved."

"What was wrong?" she prodded.

"I just can't discuss it."

"But Hope had scars!" Her frustration boiled over even as she knew she wasn't being fair. Her perseverance was inflicting a great deal of pain. Adelaide was right. Whatever happened a long time ago, whatever secret she was dead set to keep, couldn't be relevant to Hope's murder, could it?

Her aunt's face looked haggard and worn, much older than her years. "It's not something I can discuss. Not with you and not with anyone. I'm sorry. Please don't ask any more."

"Does Bill know?"

"Yes, but don't talk to him about it," she said, standing up. She seemed frozen, with her eyes slightly bugged and her hand resting on the door frame. The color had drained from her face. "Please. I beg you. Leave the subject alone."

"I'm sorry. It's none of my business. I'm truly sorry," Frances repeated. She wanted to add that she was also saddened by the fact that her aunt hadn't felt comfortable enough to ever tell her that Hope was adopted, but she refrained. What was it about this family that so much went unsaid? Then she remembered the diary, the other development that she had yet to share. She wondered for a moment whether its production would only make matters worse, then decided she had no choice. She had no right to withhold Hope's thoughts and feelings from her parents.

"There's something I want to give you," she said, removing the book from her knapsack. "Father Whitney brought it over yesterday for you. Here. It's Hope's journal." She extended her hand.

Swaying slightly, Adelaide took the small volume and held it to her chest. "How did he get it?" she asked.

"Hope apparently left it with him the day of her wedding."

"She kept a diary for years. There must be hundreds of them, unless she threw them out. She liked little books just like this one." Adelaide placed the spine on one palm and let the pages fall open.

"I've only read parts," Frances volunteered.

Adelaide's shoulders slouched, and she seemed to struggle to stabilize herself. Frances supported her around her waist and steered her back to the chair. As she rested the book on her knees, she flipped through the dimpled pages and stared at the words without any sign that she was processing their content. Glancing over her shoulder, Frances could see that she had paused on the August 14 entry. "Perhaps if he hits me or lashes out, it will be easier . . . His violence is easier, easier than his sorrow." Adelaide's eyes filled with tears.

"Is there anything I can do?"

Adelaide swallowed. Her breathing was shallow, and Frances could see her chest rise and fall in a flutter. "This can't be," she whispered. "These aren't Hope's words."

Frances could only imagine how unbearable it was to

read Hope's self-flagellation. As her adoptive mother, Adelaide had to wonder whether self-loathing was genetically programmed or whether something in her environment, something about the manner in which she'd been raised, had dictated her self-image. Had it been fate? But there could be no denying that the diary reflected her sentiments. "I'm sorry."

"No. It's not possible. I know she loved Jack, and he would never be violent. I don't believe it. I can't. That boy wanted nothing more than to make her his bride. I saw how he was with his father. He was willing to jeopardize everything for her."

"But Hope's feelings weren't reciprocal."

"You're wrong. I know my daughter, and I don't believe this. It isn't how she felt. Jack was the center of her universe. He would never hurt her. She wouldn't have been with someone who did. I just know that. And if he was, Hope would've told . . ." Adelaide put her face in her hands. "Someone put her up to this. Someone made her say these horrible things. This diary's a fake."

Frances said nothing. She could think of no way to confront her aunt's denial without upsetting her further.

"I want you to do something for me," Adelaide said. Frances leaned forward to catch her request. "I want you to prove this isn't Hope's diary."

What was she asking? To have the pages analyzed? If so, for what? It seemed a futile exercise under the circumstances. "Does it look like her handwriting?"

"I don't know what it looks like. Maybe I'm losing my mind. God knows I can hardly remember my name these days." She looked up, staring intently at Frances with an expression of terror in her eyes. "Help me find out whose words these are. Tell me this wasn't Hope. Tell me that after all we've been through she wasn't afraid of her fiancé." She reached out and clasped Frances's hands in her own. "Please do this for me, whatever it costs."

Did Adelaide need to hold onto this fantasy? If so, how could she cope if it was authentic? It seemed a ridiculous task, but at this point Frances was willing to appease her. "I'll get it analyzed," she replied. "And maybe you'll be right," she added, wishing more than ever that her words could be true.

22

Frances, Bill, and Adelaide stood before the Cabots' front door and rang the bell, hearing its timbre resonate inside. Adelaide fingered the buttons on her pale cardigan. Glancing at his watch, Bill remarked, "I hope we can eat right away."

"It's very kind of them to have invited us," Adelaide said, seeming to force an air of appreciation.

"Maybe," Bill replied. "But I don't understand the need to go over all this paperwork. The memorial foundation was their idea, not ours."

Frances thought the same thing but had been hesitant to speak aloud lest she upset her aunt. Perhaps the Cabots wanted to reach out to the Lawrences, to make a supportive gesture; but given her conversation with Fiona the day before, she doubted there was such an altruistic motive. However, Adelaide had asked her to join them, and she didn't want to disappoint.

Expecting the pinch-faced maid of her earlier visit, Frances was surprised when Jack greeted them at the door. Dark circles ringed his glassy eyes, and his skin looked pale. The tails of his Oxford shirt hung out over his wrinkled khaki trousers, and his blue blazer seemed to hang askew on his frame. With one hand, he held onto the door frame for balance. In the other, he clutched a crystal tumbler filled with a brown liquid. "There's been a change in plans. Dad wants to have dinner on the boat. They're over at the Yacht Club."

Although the Manchester Yacht Club was less than a five-minute drive away, it still seemed ungracious of the Cabots to have left before their guests arrived.

"Aren't you joining us?" Adelaide asked.

"Yeah. But Dad takes a while to get the boat ready, so I thought I'd take a quick walk. I'll meet you over there."

"Would you like company?" Frances offered.

Jack gulped his drink, then nodded in her direction, seeming to indicate that he would. "We'll only be a few minutes," he said to the Lawrences.

"Take your time," Adelaide replied, touching Frances's arm.

Frances and Jack fell into stride as they walked down the winding drive. Neither one spoke. Realizing it was premature for conversation, Frances tried to enjoy the spectacular landscape, the thick green lawn, tall trees, and horses grazing peacefully, the sounds of crickets starting to come out in the early evening, and the changing light in the sky.

Just before they reached the road, Jack stopped. "Let me show you something."

He picked up his pace, extending his gait so that

Frances was almost jogging to keep up. She felt like a child scrambling beside a long-limbed parent and wondered how he could walk so fast without breaking into a trot himself. They raced across the lawn parallel to the road, then cut back up through a grove of willow trees in the direction of the house. He stopped abruptly in front of a low stone wall.

Frances looked around, trying to assess the significance of their locale.

"Hope loved this wall," Jack said, patting one of the stones. "We used to come here when we were first dating. She'd sit cross-legged on top, and I'd stand in front of her, trying to kiss her as she spoke. When she was determined to tell a story, though, I was totally out of luck. You couldn't distract her for a moment."

Frances smiled, wanting to share in his happy memory. "What kinds of stories did she tell?"

"When we were younger, it was mostly about friends. Who said what to whom, gossipy stuff. Occasionally she spoke of how hard it was to be an only child, the loneliness and the pressure of being the sole focus of your parents' attention. She and I had that in common, and I think she thought I could relate."

So even Hope had discounted Penelope's existence within the family, Frances thought.

"We hadn't been out here in a long time, months, but then we came twice just before our wedding. The first time was August 15. I remember because it was the anniversary of the day I proposed, and it was the last time I saw Hope happy, truly happy, or at least that's what I wanted to believe. She seemed ebullient, excited about being my wife. She wanted the ceremony over with – I think all the fuss, all her mother's planning, had finally exhausted her – but we talked about how wonderful it would be to live together, to make our own way. She told me how much she loved me. I wanted to think she meant it."

Jack's memory was painful to hear, especially in light of what Hope had written in her diary the previous day: her desire not to be married and her fear of his wrath. Frances remembered the words. Had Hope lost her resolve, or had something made her change her mind, even if only temporarily? Listening to Jack, she realized how difficult it was for someone on the outside ever to understand the dynamics of a relationship, the different but other equally legitimate perspectives. It still seemed odd, though, that Hope and he could have been so far apart in their thoughts.

"She wanted a different wedding from what had been planned. Only the two of us here, with this stone wall as the altar. 'The trees will bear witness,' she said. She felt hypocritical getting married in the church."

"Why?"

"I think she felt judged there. She'd gotten involved with Holy Spirit and Father Whitney after several of her poems had been rejected for publication and she felt dejected. She didn't think she could succeed as a poet, not that I cared. She didn't have to work or accomplish anything for my sake, but some creative or humanitarian outlet was important to her. In religion she saw the opportunity to help others, and she thought that would give her some direction. She craved a sense of spirituality in a way I've never seen before. There was an obsessive quality to her drive to find some higher meaning to life. Then, recently, her attitude seemed to change, almost overnight. It was as if she suddenly realized the church was just like everything else. There were personalities and politics, good and bad people, ambitions. You name it. And it seemed to destroy her. She wanted to discover a world of angels, or perhaps of saints, and they weren't there."

Frances shrugged. "Maybe that's the problem with religion. People expect too much – everything from forgiveness to salvation. And what institution can live up to that standard?"

"Maybe." Jack clenched his jaw. His agitated eyes fixated on hers while his left hand slapped repeatedly at his thigh. "But I think she also thought the church could protect her."

"From what?"

"Her demons. Her past."

"Why did she need protection?"

"I don't know exactly. Something from her childhood seemed to torment her. She had all kinds of fears, nightmares. I kept telling her she should switch shrinks."

"She was seeing a psychiatrist?"

"Yeah. Some guy at the Avery Bowes Institute. If you ask me, he didn't help her one iota. She'd been in therapy since she was a teenager, and I often thought it was making her worse."

"Was her doctor named Peter Frank?"

Jack curled his nose. "I think so. The name sounds familiar."

Frances decided not to ask him if he knew his mother had consulted with him, too. The coincidence was haunting. They stood for a moment in silence before Jack said, "You must think my family's horrible to have asked for a prenuptial."

"It's not my place to judge," she offered, taken aback by the sudden shift in conversation.

"I didn't want it. It wasn't necessary. Frankly, I couldn't imagine life without Hope as my wife, so the last thing I cared about was what happened to my money. And then this."

"Did you and she discuss it?"

"Not like you might think. A prenuptial was my father's brainchild. He wanted it to protect the Cabot riches, whatever they are. But if you ask me, it really had to do with Carl. My father distrusted Hope and resented that I'd agreed to marry her despite that relationship."

"Did you know him?" she asked, surprised that he even knew *of* him.

"Hope talked about him, but we never met." He paused and gave Frances a quizzical look, appearing to wonder how much he could say. When he spoke again, his words came slowly. "I knew they were still having sex. I'm sure that sounds bizarre, since we were about to get married. I always told myself I could never deal with someone who was unfaithful, but reality doesn't work that way. I couldn't turn off my feelings just because she was sleeping with another man. Carl gave her something I couldn't, and I wanted more than anything for her to be happy. I'd take whatever part of her I could get."

Frances was stunned. It had never occurred to her that Jack knew about, let alone tolerated, Hope's affair. She realized how often she'd had the same thought, that she could simply dismiss someone she cared about if he cheated on her. Yet Jack was right. Emotions didn't end with an off switch. "Did you expect their involvement to end when you married?"

"I don't know what I expected. The truth is that our relationship got better because of him, if you can believe that. We'd broken up because I couldn't stand that she was seeing someone else, too, but when we got back together, it was magic. She seemed liberated, freer emotionally and physically. We were doing stuff we'd never done before, and she was initiating it. It was as if some passion within her got unleashed and I was the beneficiary. How could I object?"

Frances no doubt appeared as startled as she felt by this revelation, because Jack quickly added, "You must think I'm the one who needs the shrink. I guess it's hard to explain if you didn't grow up around here. But it's a pretty puritanical bunch. I'm not sure anyone owns a copy of the *Kama Sutra*, if you know what I mean. And to find someone who's seriously into pleasure, who wants to explore – it just blew my mind."

Even though she was learning from another teacher, Frances thought. "How much did your parents know?"

"I don't know what they knew versus what they

suspected, but Dad definitely wanted to sabotage our relationship. It seemed as if he felt personally insulted by Hope's affair. As if she'd betrayed his biology or rebuffed his Y chromosome or something. I think he thought a prenuptial might do the trick. But I would never hurt Hope that way, by asking. So good old Dad spoke to the Lawrences himself, and they agreed. I think Bill and Adelaide were just as paranoid about the Carl situation – the idea that Hope might end up with someone from the wrong side of the tracks was too much of a slap in the face – so they basically agreed to whatever Dad wanted. There was this unbelievable negotiation between our parents over something we weren't going to do. Dad's lawyer even prepared a draft based on what they decided, although Hope never signed and neither did I. We spoke about the situation, being horrified by our parents, but that was the context. She knew I didn't doubt the strength of our relationship for one moment."

"What happened when you wouldn't sign?"

"Dad was livid. You see, the money's tied up in trust. It has been for years. I get the income and my children get the principal when I die. He thought if we didn't make it, Hope would have a claim to fifty percent of the income, which she might have. I'm no divorce lawyer. He thought this was some sacrilege."

"Did you know Hope couldn't have children?"

He nodded. "Not until recently, though. Mom found out somehow and threw it in my face as evidence of Hope's great deceptions."

"How did she know?"

"Don't ask me. For all I know, they were investigating Hope. They were constantly critical, suspicious, judgmental. But in the last couple of days before our wedding, that was their fixation. As I understand it, the way the trust documents are set up, my children have to be blood. If we'd adopted, those kids wouldn't be covered."

"Issue of the body," Frances mumbled, remembering the arcane scenario from law school. How could a parent, or in this case a grandparent, distinguish between a biological and an adopted child?

"That's it."

"So there was no prenuptial?"

"No. And there never will be," he said to himself. Silence fell between them as they listened to the crickets.

"You said you came here twice. What happened the second time?" she coaxed.

Jack blushed slightly and smiled to himself. When he spoke, his voice sounded wistful. "We met the morning of our wedding. It was early, around six I think, because Hope wanted to get back before anyone woke up. There was still dew on the grass. I thought Hope wanted to talk – she'd asked me to come – and I expected that she wanted to explain the odd way she'd acted at the rehearsal dinner. But she hardly said a word. Just took off all her clothes, lay down in the grass, and wanted me to touch her. She looked so beautiful, and she was incredibly aroused. Then, almost as if nothing had happened, she stood up, got dressed, gave me a kiss on the top of my head, and scurried off." He looked down at his topsiders and, reflexively, touched his hair, perhaps remembering where she had laid her last kiss.

Surprisingly, Frances didn't feel embarrassed at the intimacy of the conversation. All she could think was that she was happy for Jack that he had that memory of their last encounter to cherish. "Did Hope ever let you read her diaries?"

"No. I saw her writing in them all the time, but she was very careful to keep them private. When she finished one journal, she'd put it away in a safe-deposit box."

"Do you know where?"

"One of the banks in town."

Frances remembered the unidentified key that had been inventoried by the police. Perhaps that unlocked the box. She leaned against the stone wall next to Jack. There was a certain maturity in his expressions, an adulthood permeating his boyish face brought on by his immense sorrow. Listening to him talk about Hope, or various aspects of their shared dreams, she was struck by the thought that he might have been the only one who had truly appreciated and loved Hope for who she was.

Jack coughed to clear his throat and then spoke, almost as if he were thinking aloud. "I couldn't imagine life without her, and now she's gone. So I'm waiting for my imagination to catch up with reality. In the interim, here I am, missing her every moment."

"I guess you've heard about the arrest, the caterer's employee."

"Yeah." He bent over and pulled a long weed from the ground, then began to split its stalk with his fingers. "I guess it's better it's a total stranger."

"What do you mean?"

"Before the police found him, you know my mind was racing, trying to figure out who might have done it and why. I'd convinced myself it was someone Hope knew. Otherwise there would have been signs of a struggle, or that's what I told myself. Hope had much more of a fighter instinct than people gave her credit for. So I'd been racking my brain, thinking about all the anger and animosity that's been generated around here recently. In my craziness, I even got to thinking it might be Dad, you know, 'cause he was so furious about this stupid prenuptial. I figured if he was pissed off enough to skip his own son's wedding, he was irrational enough to do anything. I guess the possibility that some sicko snuck in and did this before she knew what was coming never occurred to me. I hope for her sake . . ." He couldn't finish his sentence. He coughed to clear his throat and, Frances thought, to cover the tears in his voice.

"We better head over to the Yacht Club," she said.

"Yeah. God only knows what fire has already been started."

The pink sky illuminated the silhouette of the *Lucky Day* as it swayed slightly on its mooring. As Frances approached the dock, she could see Jim rigging the sails. With his Oxford shirt billowing in the wind, he moved quickly and easily about the deck, hoisting the enormous triangles of canvas up to the tops of the masts. Fiona scurried about behind him, seeming to await instructions that never came on how she could assist. With a yellow-and-orange scarf tied around her head, Adelaide sat in a teak deck chair, holding a wineglass. Alone, Bill stood at the bow, gazing out to sea.

The harbor was full of boats, and the symphony of clanging masts filled the evening air. While Jack rowed the dinghy, Frances glanced back at the shore. People milled about the porch of the domed clubhouse with beers in hand, and several children played tag on the hill sloping down to the sea. She could hear the high-pitched laughter, the glee emanating from the small bodies and drifting through the air. The serenity of the evening could have made her forget, but for the nautical flags flown at half-mast in remembrance of Hope.

Jim was waiting by the ladder as they approached. Jack threw him a line, which he quickly belayed to a cleat. "What took you so long?" he asked as they climbed aboard.

"We lost track of time," Jack muttered.

"Well, hurry up then. Let's get off this mooring. We're losing a great sunset."

"I can see it from here."

Jim leaned toward Jack to pat him on the bottom. "Don't be smart with me," he whispered. Given his low tone, Frances couldn't tell whether the comment was a jest or a reprimand.

Jim went to the helm as Jack swung himself around a cable. She could hear his topsiders squeaking as the rubber soles gripped the deck. He walked to the bow and released the mooring line. The diesel engine turned over, and they were under way, motoring out of the harbor. "We'll get under sail as soon as we're past the lighthouse," Jim called to his passengers, his words somewhat muffled in the wind.

"I actually prefer motoring. It's a lot smoother," Fiona said as she made her way into the cabin. "Excuse me. I'm going to get hors d'oeuvres."

Jack perched against the side of the boat and fingered a loose piece of rope in his hands. He knotted and unknotted the string.

"Hope should be here," Adelaide said to no one in particular.

But could she have been? Frances thought, recalling how afraid Hope apparently was of the sea. It was an unusual phobia for someone who had grown up on the water, who was part of a Yacht Club society, where boating – under sail or by motor – was how people spent their free time. Wasn't familiarity supposed to have the opposite effect? But then she remembered that one fateful voyage, the capsized sailboat that had nearly cost Hope her life. Perhaps her fear hadn't been irrational after all.

She settled in the chair next to her aunt and poured herself a glass of Pinot Grigio from one of several uncorked bottles in a cooler. Maybe the wine would help her think of something to say, something comforting, but it was doubtful. Jack's wistful words, his description of his last romantic moment with Hope, filled her mind.

"Here," Jack said as he leaned over her shoulder and handed her a piece of rope. "This is a bowline knot. This is what I'm talking about. Pull," he directed. As she did, the knot tightened. Even though it was only a sample, the exercise made her uneasy. "Pretty simple. But not common knowledge."

Frances thought of Michael Davis, wondering whether he had nautical experience. Even though Mark appeared convinced he was the killer, and everyone else seemed relieved that an arrest had been made, she had serious reservations. It didn't make sense. Various questions tumbled over and over in her mind, and she could come up with no rational answers. If he had strangled Hope for her ring, why would he go to the trouble of making her murder appear to be a suicide? He'd clearly intended to skip town – he was on his way when he was arrested – so why the cover? The time and effort had only increased the likelihood that he would be caught. She'd assumed the murderer was someone who couldn't leave Manchester and therefore wanted to throw the police off. What the killer didn't want was an investigation.

There was also the issue that Jack had raised – no evidence of a struggle. She'd thought of that fact as she wondered how Michael could have murdered her without even a scratch. Strangled without the slightest resistance. Could two thousand milligrams of meprobamate achieve that level of passivity?

All of these logistical inconsistencies aside, that

someone would kill a bride for her engagement ring seemed remote. He had a criminal record. Was the value of a diamond worth the risk? Then again, people killed for a lot less – a pair of Nikes, a baseball jacket, a Timex watch. The cases she'd heard about in the district attorney's office never ceased to amaze or sadden her.

The purr of the engine stopped abruptly, and the enormous sails flapped for a moment as Jim positioned them to catch the wind. The boat listed slightly as they filled. The *Lucky Day* picked up speed. "Come here, Jack," Jim commanded as if addressing a dog. "You steer." Robotically, Jack took over the helm while Jim moved about the deck, tightening winches and adjusting cleats. Frances remembered the frantic sense she'd experienced whenever she'd been in charge of a sailboat, the overwhelming stress caused by the speed, the required strength, the multitude of tasks to perform simultaneously; but Jim seemed completely at ease. An experienced captain, he controlled his ship the way he appeared to control the rest of his life.

When he'd finished, he joined the group of passengers seated in the stern, made several vodka tonics in plastic tumblers, handed one to his wife, and took a sip of the second. "Ah. I've needed a stiff drink."

"You have a beautiful boat," Frances remarked to make conversation.

"A Sou'wester 59. It's a Hinckley design that's been around for more than a decade. They don't come much better. Have a look around the interior if you'd like."

"Thanks." She forced a smile without getting up.

"Shall we go over the details now?" Fiona asked as

she spread cream cheese draped with chutney on assorted crackers and offered them around. That she had no takers didn't seem to bother her. "That way we can try to enjoy the rest of the sail. I mean, if that's possible."

"Good enough," Jim said, rubbing his palms together. "Lloyd's drawn up documents to create a charitable trust in Hope's memory. As soon as he obtains 501(c)(3) status, we'll make an initial contribution of one million dollars."

Can't forget the tax deduction, Frances thought, then chastised herself for her cynicism. With or without a benefit from Uncle Sam, it was very generous.

"We wanted your input, but our thought was to make you two the trustees. That way it really gets turned over to the Lawrence family."

"Why not Jack?" Adelaide asked.

Jim took a step closer to his wife before answering. "I don't know how best to say this," he began, "but . . . but . . . his team's planning on making a substantial donation. Beyond that, it's clearly best to leave him out of it. He's young. He shouldn't be saddled with the administration."

"I can't believe he wouldn't want some role," Bill said, looking in Jack's direction.

"If you asked him today, I'm sure he'd agree. But I'm trying to be realistic about the future. The trust will continue *in perpetuity*, but he shouldn't be burdened by memory any more than he has to."

"Jim and I both feel that Jack's pain—"

"Don't interrupt," Jim admonished his wife. "Look. Let's be sensible. We want to memorialize Hope and have done everything as quickly as possible to achieve that end. But Jack . . . well . . . I expect he'll have a family someday. It's not a good idea for him to be acting as trustee for his former fiancée's trust once he's married."

Adelaide and Bill exchanged glances before she diverted her gaze and covered her mouth with her hand.

"I'm speaking from a practical standpoint," he added.

"Administering a charity that Hope would have wanted might be soothing for Jack," Frances offered. She didn't understand why the Cabots continued to treat their grown son as a child. His role, if any, should be his decision. But the undercurrent of ugliness in the conversation made her comments irrelevant.

"He'll get all the comfort he needs," Jim retorted.

"Why are you trying to distance him from us?" Bill asked.

"Please don't," Adelaide said quietly, reaching out to touch his pants leg.

Bill put his hands in his pockets. "Our children loved each other. They were going to make a life together," he said, ignoring her efforts to silence him. "You can't deny that your son wanted to marry my daughter. You can't minimize his devastation or ours. The violence has destroyed us all. You may choose to ignore how people feel, but I'll be goddamned if I'll allow Hope's memory to be obliterated."

"Calm down," Jim said, taking a step forward and resting his hand on Bill's shoulder. "I don't know what you're talking about."

"Don't touch me." He took a step away and turned to look at Jack, who seemed lost in thought at the helm.

Frances hoped that the wind prevented any of the conversation from drifting his way.

"We care about him," Bill continued. "If you had some problem with my daughter, you picked a fine time to raise it."

"You're overreacting. What happened is an unfathomable horror. We all agree on that."

"Stop," Adelaide pleaded. She was trembling all over. "Please bring us back to shore."

Frances felt a surge of anger. She knew it wasn't her place to intervene, but the Cabots' insensitivity toward her aunt and uncle in their most vulnerable moment seemed beyond inhumane. She was about to interject when Fiona spoke in a softened tone. "I think you've misunderstood. No one's being critical of her. We just want to help."

"Help? Is that what you're doing? We don't need your help. We don't want your pity. Forget your trust. We don't need a memorial to remember—"

"My parents had three problems with Hope that they never wanted to admit. They couldn't bear the thought that if our marriage didn't work out, she might end up with some of the Cabot wealth, as dear Father refers to it."

The sound of Jack's voice silenced the group. Nobody

had noticed he'd abandoned the helm and moved to within inches of his father.

"And they recently discovered she couldn't have children. That seems to have agitated them further, the idea that we couldn't perpetuate some noble lineage. But most of all, they couldn't accept that she was also in love with another man. That's why they want me to stay out of the trust. They want me to move on. To find some other woman who will be forever grateful for my affection. But there's nowhere I can go and nothing I can do to avoid thinking of her, and part of thinking of her is thinking of Carl."

Fiona gasped at the mention of Hope's lover.

"I won't hear this," Jim said.

Jack turned away from the group and stared out to sea. "Hope loved me, too. In the end she loved me more. She wanted to be *my* bride, not his. I had won. At the end of the day, we would have made each other very happy. But because I gave her a ring, she was murdered. Some killer thought her life was worth less than a diamond. So we'll never have a chance."

Nobody said anything. Frances saw Fiona pour more wine, resorting to ingrained social convention when conversation became painful. Jack looked lost, and Frances wanted to move to embrace him, but she feared such a gesture would be seen as too forward. Instead she reached for her aunt's hand, pressing the chilled fingers between her two palms. Bill got up and moved gingerly to the bow. She watched him stand with his legs apart for balance and his Gore-Tex jacket flapping.

It seemed hard to fathom that such animosity had been hidden behind this façade of social etiquette, forced smiles, and endless pleasantries. Even with Hope's murder and Michael's arrest, the Cabots and the Lawrences were still locked in a debate over the union between Hope and their son. Was this how every set of future in-laws reacted? Was every marriage surrounded by discussions of whether one party was worthy of the other? If so, it seemed hard to imagine how anyone ever wed.

The wind gusted, sending a chill through her whole body. Please, she thought, get us back to solid ground.

23

"Ricki Manning and Associates," read the gold plaque on the outside of the brownstone. Before ringing the bell, Frances rested her shopping bag of documents on the threshold, turned her back to the door, and let the sun shine on her face. She glanced up and down Marlborough Street and admired its beauty, the rows of town houses with iron-gated gardens in front, the narrow brick sidewalks buckled by the roots of magnolia trees. A woman in black leggings, a white T-shirt, and wedged sneakers pushed a baby stroller toward her. A second child, a girl of perhaps four with reddish pigtails and a lime green sundress, skipped along beside, chatting to her mother. Ms. Manning's office, located in this decidedly residential area, was appropriately discreet.

The door buzzed and she pushed her way into an expansive, carpeted foyer. Lit only by an ornate crystal chandelier, the room was dark, especially in contrast with the bright light of outdoors. A cleanly shaven receptionist came around from behind his desk to greet her. "Ms. Pratt, welcome. Ricki is just finishing up on a call. She'll be with you in a moment."

Frances sat in an armchair upholstered in gold brocade and flipped through the materials that Adelaide had collected of Hope's handwriting – letters she'd sent her parents, her checkbook ledger, scribbled lists on pieces of notepad, anything and everything that evidenced her actual penmanship. Then there was the red leather diary. Frances had looked at the lettering several times since her aunt had raised the issue of its authenticity, but she could find no great differences. The deviations in the loops and dips seemed no more than the normal variations that could occur in anyone's handwriting. Out of desperation, her aunt was willing to pay Ricki's exorbitant fees to have the book examined because she couldn't accept the truth of its contents.

The door to the left of the reception area opened, and out stepped an elegant woman with long gray hair tied in a loose bun. Around her neck hung two pairs of eyeglasses as well as a silver-handled magnifying glass. As she walked toward Frances, the flowing fabric of her beige pants swirled around her slender legs. "I'm Ricki Manning," she said with a slight smile and an outstretched hand. "Won't you come in?"

Ricki and Frances settled themselves at a round conference table in the bay window of her spacious office, and Frances began unpacking her shopping bag. "I should have showed you upstairs before we got started," Ricki said. "That's where the hard-core science takes place, the forensic handwriting analysis that tends to impress people." She smiled. "But you know the ropes."

Although it was said in all innocence, Frances

cringed at the expression. Ricki apparently didn't notice. "Some think because I'm a graphologist that I can't do the forensic work, too, but they're wrong. I've got ultraviolet light tables, stereoscopic microscopes, you name it. You won't find a more state-of-the-art facility anywhere in the country, I can assure you."

"That's what I understand," Frances said. In her years as a financial crimes prosecutor at the Suffolk County District Attorney's Office, she'd had her share of cases involving forged or fraudulent documents. She understood the various techniques, the tools experts used to analyze details such as ink luster and pressure, erasures, watermarks, and other signs of authenticity, as well as the distinguishing characteristics of an individual's penmanship. But none of the handwriting experts she'd used on Long Island had either Ricki's personal presence or her exceptional professional setup. Elvis claimed she was unparalleled. "No one can hold a candle to that broad, and once she forms an opinion, she won't waver. She's about the best witness out there."

Furthermore, Frances had never sought the services of a graphologist. Largely considered a pseudoscience, graphology involved an evaluation and assessment of an author's personal and emotional characteristics from penmanship, grammar, and stylistic flourishes. Margin size, word slant, and letter height revealed educational background, personality traits, and mental illness. Frances hoped that such a comprehensive analysis would satisfy her aunt.

"So," she began as she put on one of the pairs of

glasses and glanced at a legal pad in front of her, "aside from what you told me on the telephone, what can you tell me about the diary?"

"Not much. It was given to me after her death by Father Whitney, the Episcopalian minister who was to perform the marriage."

"And she had given it to him?"

"Yes. Shortly before her wedding. All he said was that he'd found it in his office with a note asking him to keep it safe for her. When I made this appointment, I called him again to see if he remembered anything else about it, any mention Hope might have made of her diary, anything at all, but he just repeated what he'd said the day he gave it to me. When he learned that Hope had been murdered, he gave it to us because he hoped it might contain something helpful. In any event, he didn't think it was his place to keep it."

"Someone's been arrested, isn't that right?"

"Yes. This has nothing to do with that. In all honesty, I think this may be a waste of your time. Her mother, my aunt, questions its authenticity. As I'm sure you understand, she's very fragile at the moment. She and her husband are very close to Hope's fiancé and can't bear to think that she was unhappy with him. So she's searching for another explanation for these sad words. I look at the other stuff I've brought – everything from a to-do list to letters she sent home from camp ten years ago – and I don't see anything in the handwriting that looks suspicious."

Ricki crossed her arms in front of her chest and leaned back in her chair. "Well, that might mean one of two things: either the diary is authentic and was written by Hope, or it was re-created by a good forger."

"Or I just can't see the difference."

Ricki smiled.

"I've brought a lot of exemplars, more than you probably want or need." Frances handed her the diary while she spread out the remaining documents on the table in front of them. "Actually, I guess they're collected standards rather than exemplars," she corrected herself, recalling the difference. Standards referred to everyday documents whose authenticity wasn't at issue that could be used for comparison against the questioned document; exemplars were specific writing samples obtained from suspects that contained specimens of the entire upper- and lowercase alphabet.

Ricki looked at several letters under her magnifying glass. "When were these written?"

"Unfortunately, a while ago. Adelaide looked for more recent correspondence but couldn't find much. She wrote her poetry on a word processor," Frances added somewhat apologetically.

"What about these?" she asked, pushing several Post-it Notes toward Frances.

"Those are recent. Written in the last week or so before she died."

"And perhaps written in more haste than her diary."

Frances nodded.

"See this descending baseline?" Ricki asked, pointing out the downward slope of Hope's words. "It indicates depression, fatalism, and fatigue. The slope is alarming." She produced some colored tabs from a drawer

301

under the table and stuck them to various documents, making notations on each that Frances couldn't discern. "See how these sentences drop off at the end?" she said, pushing a letter toward Frances. The last words pitched down, falling off the line. "You tend to see this in people with suicidal tendencies. Had there been anything terribly upsetting to her in the weeks before she died?"

"I'm not aware of anything specifically. But that doesn't mean there wasn't."

Ricki held several documents up to a light board, squinted through her magnifier at numerous others, and thumbed through several pages of the diary. As she did, she made slight sounds but offered no information. Finally, she pushed her chair back from the table. "It's interesting to me that the slant, or word tilt, changes quite a bit. Most people have a more or less consistent slant, but Hope's diary is quite vertical, and her quick notes have a pronounced left slant. At times the words look almost flat."

"What does that mean?"

"Well, I'm not sure at the moment, but I think it's worth exploring." She stood and turned to an oversize calendar that hung on the wall. Each day was marked with entries in red, green, or navy pen. She sighed. "Give me a couple of days. I'll call as soon as I have anything definitive."

"I appreciate your help," Frances said, standing up to leave. She thought momentarily about whether to apologize. It did seem absurd to utilize the services of this expert to placate Adelaide, even though she would be

REDEMPTION

well compensated for her time. But nothing in Ricki's demeanor made it appear that she resented the task in the slightest.

Adelaide held the lid of the teapot secure with one hand as she poured with the other. Steam rose from the porcelain cup, and the strong smell of mint filled the breakfast room where the two sat despite the noon hour. Frances had left for Boston before eight and had missed an early morning meal, which she now needed. Her stomach growled. She reached for the creamer as well as a raisin scone from the stack arranged on a plate. Through the window she could see a grove of freshly planted cherry blossoms in the center of the immense lawn. It was Adelaide and Bill's personal memorial to their daughter and would be the burial place for her ashes. The grove was to be dedicated following the memorial service.

"I never thought I'd live to see this day," Adelaide said, leaning against the cushioned window seat and pushing a wisp of hair off her face. "You're not a parent, but I'm sure you can understand. You do the best you possibly can to raise your children with the hope that you give them the strength, courage, and resources to live a happy and productive life. You expect that they'll bury you but go on with their lives, full of the joys and inevitable share of sadness that we all experience. The order's not supposed to be upset. I feel as if the whole purpose of my life has ended. Everything I tried to do, to accomplish, is ruined. I look around. I see people

303

being sympathetic but also managing to carry on, and I don't know how I'll find the strength."

Frances closed her eyes. Hearing her aunt articulate her sorrow made the enormity of the tragedy unavoidable. In a few phrases, she'd captured both the pleasure and pain of parenthood, an experience foreign to Frances. Neither she nor Penelope had children. Hope was dead. Someone or something larger than all of them had left the fate of the Pratt bloodline up to Blair alone.

"I was so shocked by last night, I could hardly speak. I tried to tell myself that the Cabots are nervous around us and don't know how to help, but they seemed so cold, so calculating, saying, 'My son is alive and I want him to have a future.' Here Fiona professed to love Hope as much as I do, and we haven't even . . . before . . ." Adelaide glanced out at the cherry grove, then covered her face with her hands, emitting the tiniest of muffled sounds.

"Did you and Fiona talk often about Hope?"

"Not really," she said, sniffling. "Although there was one conversation I remember well. She asked all kinds of questions and seemed genuinely concerned about Hope's well-being. I remember talking and feeling this relief wash over me. Like a dam breaking and suddenly the water rushes out. But I regret opening up to her. I shouldn't have done it. I was just so thankful to have someone to talk to. It's difficult here. I have wonderful friends, don't misunderstand, but it's almost as if there are rules in place. You can't be too honest, too emotional. Everything is supposed to always be all right, better than all right, really, perfect. If you falter, if you have problems, you keep them quiet or it will come back to haunt—" She cut herself off.

"What sorts of things did you say to her?"

"I told her the truth about Hope's eating disorder. I told her Hope had been diagnosed with clinical depression and possibly bipolar disorder. I remember the conversation so clearly, because as I was talking, I was thinking, Why is this so secret? Why have I been ashamed? It's my daughter. I love her and I want to do whatever I can to help her. It seemed almost as if there were a disconnection between the words I uttered and the feeling inside." She paused, then got up from the table and moved to the sideboard. She returned with a pot of raspberry jam and another of clotted cream, each with its own dollop-size porcelain spoon. She placed them on the table near Frances. "I'm sorry to say that around here seeing a psychiatrist is a scarlet letter. Worse, perhaps. Bill got apoplectic whenever I mentioned the words 'bulimia' or 'depression.' He was frightened of the stigma."

"What do you mean?"

As she responded, her gaze seemed to drift past Frances. "Years before, we'd had problems with Penelope."

"What were they?"

"She was horribly jealous of Hope and, in several episodes, had shown herself to be somewhat . . . violent. I'd had to come to Hope's rescue. One time she tied her to a tree and left her for hours, claiming not to know where she was. Poor Bea Bundy next door eventually heard her crying and called Bill, who went and untied her, but we were both so distraught, as was poor Hope. Sweet thing. I can still remember her little tear-stained face, her body limp from exhaustion as Bill carried her inside. For nights afterward, she'd awaken screaming in fear, but during the day she remained ever faithful to Penelope, following her around like an adoring puppy. Another time, the gardener found Penelope spreading liquid fire starter around the bottom of Hope's little playhouse. Do you remember it, the one with the green windowboxes and gabled roof? He asked her what she was doing, and she said she wanted to burn off the weeds around the edge of the house, but we were all alarmed. So at least for a long while, she posed a real danger."

"What did you do?"

"She went to see some therapist, a woman who was a specialist in adolescent development. But after one session, Bill didn't want her to return. 'Talking about issues until we're all blue in the face only magnifies them. Let's keep this in perspective,' he said. It was then that I realized he was fearful of psychiatry, the process and the label."

"But Hope saw a therapist?"

"Her physical health was in jeopardy. That was easier for Bill to understand. Even so, he was very apprehensive. Dr. Bentley, our family physician, wanted her on antidepressants. He's an older man and I'm sure conservative in his approach, certainly not prone to over-medicate. My initial reaction was to follow his recommendation, but Bill said antidepressants were out of the question."

"Why?"

"He didn't want a permanent record. He kept telling me that once Hope was married and set up in her own home with Jack, she would get better. He didn't want to allow what he saw as a demerit to exist forever. He didn't want her and Jack to begin their life together socially handicapped."

"Do you remember what medication Dr. Bentley wanted to prescribe?"

"Something called an SSRI. I remember that."

Selective serotonin reuptake inhibitors, like Prozac or Zoloft, were commonly prescribed to alleviate symptoms of depression. Since clients of the Coalition Against Domestic Violence had benefited from these drugs, Frances had at least anecdotal information about their efficacy. "How did you find Hope's psychiatrist?"

"He was recommended by Dr. Bentley."

"Dr. Frank?"

"How did you know?"

"Jack mentioned the name. Did you know Fiona Cabot went to see him as well?"

She looked surprised. "No."

"Did you or Bill ever see him?"

Adelaide pursed her lips, obviously reluctant to answer. When she spoke, her voice had softened considerably, and Frances leaned forward so as not to miss a word. "He'd wanted us to come initially. He believed it was important for those involved in Hope's life to share in therapy. It seemed reasonable enough to me, especially with Hope still living at home, but I could tell it didn't sit well with Bill. He went once, and that night when he got home, he sat in the library and drank. It was the only time I've ever seen him drink like that. I couldn't get him to talk about what had happened, and I couldn't get him to come to bed. The next morning the Scotch decanter was empty and he was asleep in a chair. After that he started making excuses for why he couldn't make his appointment, and eventually he just refused to go back. He said the doctor was blaming him for all of Hope's problems."

Frances could see the sadness on Adelaide's face. "After your conversation with Fiona, did Hope's emotional state ever come up again?" she asked, redirecting her aunt's focus. She had pushed her aunt to open up before and failed miserably; she'd decided to tread lightly if the opportunity arose again.

Adelaide shook her head. "She never asked. It was hurtful to me that she didn't, but I couldn't be the one to bring it up." Again she stood and walked over to the corner hutch. She opened several drawers, removed a stack of yellow-and-blue print napkins and began refolding them, pressing the fabric with the palm of her hand. Her restlessness seemed to magnify the fragility of her psyche.

As Frances sat watching her aunt's homemade form of occupational therapy, she felt a nagging sense of unease. "What were the terms of the prenuptial Hope was supposed to sign?"

The look of shock on Adelaide's face made clear it wasn't a question she'd expected. "Why do you ask?"

"Jack was talking to me about it. He said his parents were insistent that Hope agree to certain terms prior to their marriage and that he hadn't wanted anything to do with such a contract. He also told me that when he couldn't be persuaded, they turned to you and Bill."

"It's . . . not . . . something . . . I'm . . . proud . . . of," she stammered.

Frances leaned closer to her and, without meaning to, spoke in a whisper. "What happened?"

Adelaide's eyes welled with tears yet again. "It felt as if we were conspiring against our own daughter. We served the Cabots vodka tonics and shrimp cocktail out on the veranda while we discussed financial arrangements between Hope and Jack in the event of a divorce. Here they weren't even married. I'm so appalled, embarrassed."

"Why did you do it?"

"If I say it was Bill's idea, you'll get the wrong impression. But his rationalization made sense to me. It actually seemed to be in Hope's best interest."

"What do you mean?" Frances prompted.

"Ever since Hope got involved with Carl, Bill was very anxious about her. He's of the view that relationships need similar backgrounds, similar frames of reference, in order to survive. Hope and Carl were night and day. I think Bill feared that if she ended up with Carl, he'd lose her because she would have to abandon her roots to hold onto her marriage. And abandoning her roots meant abandoning us. Does that make sense?" she implored.

She thought about her aunt's words. Frances never put much stock in familial backgrounds, economic, ethnic, or religious. Sam's experiences had been completely different from those of her own childhood, yet she felt without a doubt that he knew and understood her better than anyone else she had known. His capacity for empathy, his sensitivity, was particular to him, not the Oregon farmlands upon which he was raised. But she knew she was being naïve. Plenty of people couldn't surmount the enormous hurdles of difference to find a common ground, even if their passions ran deep.

"When Hope and Jack rekindled their romance, Bill was ecstatic," Adelaide continued, apparently not willing to wait further for Frances's reaction. "He had confidence in Jack – confidence that he could protect her from the outside world, insulate her, keep her safe. Because Bill recognized Hope's fragility, his primary concern was that she marry a man who could take care of her. Part of that care was financial – and Jack is very well off – and part was a mentality that Bill believed Jack had. So he was willing to do anything possible to make sure the marriage took place. Although we never spoke about it, I think he also wanted to make sure the marriage happened before the Cabots learned that Hope couldn't have children."

"They didn't know?" She was shocked.

"No, or at least not until very recently. Bill knew they'd try to get Jack to change his mind. Bloodline is so important to them. I told him several times I thought it was a mistake, but his response was always the same. 'I married you when you couldn't have children, and we've been happy,' he said." She smiled meekly. "I suppose that's his way of complimenting me."

Frances said nothing. Such deception seemed obscene, yet Bill had managed to convince his wife that their situation was comparable. "But you didn't know you wouldn't have another baby when you married him?"

"No, I didn't. Penelope had happened without anyone thinking twice, just a blink of an eye. And there wasn't the kind of medical assistance available then." She opened a drawer and neatly laid the refolded napkins inside, then returned to her seat. "Anyway, that's the long story for why Bill supported whatever the Cabots wanted, including the prenuptial." She sat back down. "It's difficult for you to understand because you grew up with wealth. You'll never want for anything, I'm sure. But our circumstances were different. How can I say this delicately? I do so hate to discuss money."

"Don't we all," Frances said, trying to put her aunt at ease.

"For most of our marriage, Bill and I have been more than comfortable. When he worked at Hale and Dorr, he earned plenty. He'd inherited this home, and we had everything we needed. But when he had to leave the firm, when he had to start all over, the situation changed. Taxes and upkeep on this house seemed overwhelming. We fell behind. And this is a difficult community to fall behind in. Even when Teddy moved in and began to help us out, something I'm ashamed to admit, it wasn't enough. I'm sure you've noticed all that needs to be done around here. As if the house were collapsing with us in it." Her eyes filled with tears again. "Hope had been raised in affluence, like you, but it was coming to an abrupt end. Bill and I will probably have to sell this place now. Some 25-year-old broker type will buy it, bulldoze it, and build an enormous house with Palladian windows. It will kill him, his family home . . . But I'm rambling. Suffice it to say that he wanted Hope to be taken care of, and Jack could do that. Maybe he hoped that Jack would take care of all of us, I don't know. But he wanted the marriage to happen, and he'd agree to any condition to see that it did."

"I'm sorry," Frances said.

"Me, too," she replied, standing up. "I can't tell you how sorry I am."

Frances watched her leave the kitchen and pass into the dining room. As she did, she stooped to pick up something – a leaf, a piece of lint – off the well-worn rug. Even on her way to dress for her daughter's funeral she noticed, and corrected, the imperfections. How much had her elegant touches been able to mask?

24

Frances inched closer to Sam and reached for his hand as they sat together in the pew. Unexpectedly, he'd arrived just moments after her conversation with Adelaide; she'd been alone in the dining room, staring at platters of cold cuts, cheese, and dips set out for after the service and rearranging flowers in a vase that was too small in proportion to the long Chippendale table, when she'd heard a knock. There was Sam on the threshold in his yellow slicker, khakis, and canvas sneakers, wearing a baseball cap and holding a bouquet of calla lilies. Her eyes had welled with tears as she'd embraced him, and the feel of his strong arms around her had made her want to collapse. "I know you never need anyone," he'd whispered in her ear, "but I wanted to be at the memorial service for you just in case."

The Church of the Holy Spirit was filled to capacity. Except for the sea of dark clothing, little had changed with the crowd that had gathered for the Lawrence-Cabot wedding just days earlier. Votive candles burned on every window ledge. Each pew was adorned with a bunch of white spray roses, and two enormous bouquets of white lilies dominated the altar. The mahogany box that would eventually hold Hope's ashes sat in the middle. Although Hope was to be cremated, her body was still with the medical examiner. Since Adelaide didn't want the guests to know, the empty box provided the necessary deception.

The organist played Pachelbel's Canon while Adelaide and Bill proceeded slowly down the aisle. She held onto his arm with both hands and took several small steps for every one of his strides. He held his head high, but hers was positioned to avoid all eye contact. His breast pocket had no handkerchief. Apparently it had been needed even before the service started.

Clutching several sheets of paper, Penelope followed behind, escorted by Jack. His cheeks were drawn and he stared ahead vacantly as he shuffled, seeming to lack the energy to lift his feet off the ground. Bringing up the rear, Teddy made her way down the aisle with the help of her silver-handled cane. When they had all settled into the first pew Reverend Whitney approached the altar, bowed his head slightly, and turned to face the congregation. Dark rings circled his eyes, and his fingers trembled slightly as he clasped his prayer book. "The Lord be with you," he began.

"And with thy spirit," the crowd mumbled in response.

"Let us pray. Oh God, whose mercies cannot be numbered, accept our prayers on behalf of Hope Alexandra Lawrence and grant her an entrance into the land of light and joy."

Frances listened to the order of service, realizing how much of it she recognized. That the words would be familiar surprised her, and she felt comforted, although she couldn't tell exactly why. "Yea, though I walk through the valley of the shadow of death, I will fear no evil . . ." The oft-repeated words of Psalm 23 washed over her. Perhaps rote memorization did quiet the mind.

After Father Whitney completed his opening prayer, Penelope stood up and made her way to the podium. She arranged her papers, then grasped the lectern for a moment, adjusted the microphone to the height of her mouth, and paused to look up at the crowd. That she was to give a eulogy seemed surprising, but perhaps the task had been too difficult for those closest to Hope. Or maybe she had decided to seize this occasion to assuage her guilt. It was a testament to Adelaide's generosity that she had allowed her to speak at what she surely wanted to be a momentous, graceful occasion.

Penelope cleared her throat, glanced down again at her notes, and then crumpled the sheet of paper into a ball. She held it in both hands, as if to offer it up in sacrifice. "I had some prepared remarks about my sister, Hope, but I don't want to deliver them. They are not the words I should say. I don't want to tell you canned stories about our childhood. All of us have our own memories of her. Those individual memories will be the things that sustain us in the months and years ahead as we return to our lives without her. As her older sister, I'm sure my memories are colored by sibling rivalries, perhaps even jealousies, moments when she and I didn't get along." She paused and seemed to look directly at Jack. "And we are all horrified by her murder. That her life was taken is such an outrage that it still feels unreal, impossible. Weren't we all just here for what was to be her wedding? No one suffers more over her absence than Jack. I think I share the views of all of us when I say to him that I love him and want to help him heal, if such a thing is possible. Hope would have wanted that, too."

Frances glanced at Jack, but he didn't appear to react to her words.

"I will take this opportunity in memorializing my sister to share one moment with you, a recent one, a conversation she and I had the night before she was to marry, a moment when she reached out to me as her sister."

Frances felt Sam squeeze her hand.

"Hope told me that she feared becoming Jack's wife because she didn't know if she could be all he wanted. She didn't know whether she could meet his expectations."

Adelaide gasped, and Bill put his arm around her shoulders for comfort. For a moment, Frances regretted that she hadn't told them about Penelope's continued interest in Jack or of how critical she'd been when speaking of her sister the night after her murder. It hadn't seemed necessary at the time and would only have added to their pain. But now she wondered whether she should interject, even if it meant interrupting the service her aunt had planned.

"It startled me that she had such insecurities. I was

astounded that after all the good fortune she'd had in her life, she could still fear failure. At the same time, her vulnerabilities made me see her in a light I never had. Hope was a woman who struggled with perfection – what it meant and how to achieve it – first with her parents and then with her husband-to-be. She looked for direction; she sought guidance in this church. What she didn't realize was that her goal had already been attained. It wasn't in front of her. It was in her grasp. We all thought she was perfect. There were no unmet aspirations. My sorrow at her death is that she didn't ever see herself in the light in which the rest of the world saw her. If I had the opportunity to speak to her again, as I did that evening, I would tell her she was perfect, she needn't worry."

As Penelope stepped down from the podium, her lip quivered. At the first pew, she stopped and stood in front of Jack. For what seemed like forever, neither of them moved. Frances wondered whether everyone was holding their breath as she was, trying to interpret Penelope's gesture. Then, unexpectedly, she bent down and embraced him. After several seconds, his arms reached up to encircle her waist. They seemed to hold onto each other for a moment that was slightly longer than appropriate under the circumstances.

Adelaide's shoulders shook, but she stifled any sounds of tears. Did she have any sense of Penelope's true feelings for Jack? Could it actually be that they wanted one of their daughters to have him, and she was next in line? It seemed too soon to be passing the proverbial hat.

Frances heard the heavy doors open. Glancing back at the church entrance, she saw a figure leave, but the doors swung shut before she could see who it was. Had Carl come? No one in the Lawrence–Cabot clan would welcome his presence, except perhaps Teddy, but it was certainly possible that his desire to pay his respects had compelled him to risk being recognized.

She turned her attention back to the altar as Reverend Whitney got up from his chair and adjusted the cincture over his cassock. The candlelight reflected off the black polish of his shoes, and Frances was reminded of the song "Walking on Sunshine," an odd thought given the solemnity of the occasion. He moved to the front and stood with his hands crossed in front of him. "Adelaide and Bill have asked me to say a few words about their wonderful daughter, and I feel privileged to do so," he began. "I'll begin with a passage from the book of Job, a passage that marks Job's continuing recognition of the power of the Lord. 'I know that my redeemer lives and that he shall stand at the latter day upon the earth. And though after my skin worms destroy this body, yet in my flesh shall I see God.' As all of you know, Hope had an inner beauty that matched her physical beauty. She came to this parish anxious to be of service, to help her community, and at the same time find a place of peace herself, but it didn't take me long to recognize that her capacity to love and her generosity of spirit were marks that she had been chosen by God. Despite the difficulties she faced, her belief in the Lord never faltered, because she knew that in her own flesh and blood she would see God. And she did. So as she finds her place in heaven, her mission has been accomplished. Let us pray."

Frances and Sam stood on the small patch of lawn as the other mourners ambled slowly out of the church. Neither said a word. Frances felt the odd vibration of her cell phone, the ringer of which she'd turned off, and reached into her jacket pocket.

"Fanny, I hate to bother you. I know you're at the funeral." It was Elvis.

"What is it?" she said in a voice barely above a whisper.

"Michael Davis and his lawyer are meeting with the ADA tomorrow morning."

"On a Saturday?"

"We work harder than you give us credit for. But more to the point, I don't think you should head home." Hearing his words, Frances sighed. She'd been gone more than a week; with Michael's arrest and the funeral over, she was eager to return to Orient with Sam. There was nothing more she could do for her aunt. Her own life and work beckoned.

"Why?"

"You'll want to hear what he has to say." There was a brief pause, and Frances wondered whether the cell signal had faded. But when Elvis spoke again, his voice was loud and clear. "Michael Davis is not our killer."

25

"How come there's been a change?" Frances asked. She sat beside Elvis in his convertible as he wove along back roads en route to the Essex County District Attorney's Office. Construction, a seemingly endless problem in and around the northern suburbs of Boston, precluded use of the major thoroughfares. Time was precious. The interview with Michael Davis was scheduled for ten.

"He got a lawyer who wants him to talk. A gal named Percy Lukewarm."

Frances raised her eyebrows. The name sounded as if it belonged to a character from a comic book.

"Everyone has the same reaction, but it's unfortunate for her. She knows her stuff. In my humble opinion, she's one of the best criminal lawyers around."

"How could Michael retain her?"

"Apparently the Davis family isn't quite as derelict as the son. Daddy is a patent lawyer at a downtown firm. So he makes a decent enough living, probably better than most, and has enough to pay an expensive ticket. Mama Davis is an administrative assistant at Boston

320

College Law School, where Percy teaches criminal procedure. She's been Michael's lawyer since his juvenile troubles."

"Pretty lucky."

"I'll say. Anyway, Percy and Mark are old friends. If I had to venture a guess, they dated once, but at least he still respects her." Elvis chuckled.

Frances decided to let the comment slide. She wasn't feeling her usual sense of urgency to defend the female gender. Her thoughts were fixed on the oddity of a Saturday morning interview.

"Michael was arraigned yesterday in district court on the murder and larceny charges. The case hasn't been presented to the grand jury yet, so there's no indictment. I think Mark had set aside grand jury time on Wednesday next week."

That made sense. Presentation of a case to a grand jury required preparation. More often than not in the case of violent crimes, charges were filed by a police officer in district court so that the suspect could be arrested immediately and held on bail. Michael had been charged with one count of murder and one count of larceny in an amount more than $250 for the theft of the diamond ring. When indictments were issued out of the superior court, the lower court charges against him would be dismissed. But none of these procedural niceties helped explain why Elvis now concluded that Michael wasn't the murderer.

"After the arraignment, Percy called Mark to tell him she wanted to proffer some information. She said Michael did take the ring but didn't hurt Hope. What he could offer in exchange for some sort of deal is information about who really killed her."

"Do you believe him?"

"My conversation with Mark was extremely brief. But it's my understanding that the DA is willing to negotiate something."

She was silent. There was nothing to say. They both knew they were losing their only suspect.

Overhead fluorescent bulbs illuminated the windowless conference room. Mark was in a corner talking in hushed tones on the telephone while he paced in semicircles the length of its cord. Michael sat in a folding chair with his elbows resting on his knees. Beside him at the long metal table was a woman in a denim skirt and peach polo shirt holding a legal pad covered in handwritten notes. Her calfskin briefcase was open on the table in front of her. A tousle of red curls spilled from a loose bun and tumbled about her freckled face. When Frances and Elvis entered, she stood up and removed the oval spectacles she'd been wearing. Even when she was standing, her skirt remained at least six inches above her knee, providing a view that Elvis made no pretense of ignoring. Introductions were brief.

"I'm sorry about your cousin," Percy said in a voice that jurors loved, deep and raspy. "My condolences, and my client's as well, are extended to you and your family."

Frances felt self-conscious. While she appreciated

Percy's sentiment, she preferred to keep her personal involvement out of the investigation.

"Let's get down to business," Mark said as he replaced the receiver in its cradle and joined the group at the table. "No one wants to be here on a Saturday, I'm sure." Frances thought she saw him wink as he produced a document from a folder he'd been holding and extended it to Percy. Reading upside down from across the table, Frances could see it was an agreement for immunity: Michael could not be prosecuted for crimes in connection with Hope Lawrence's death in exchange for his full and complete cooperation, including his testimony at trial, if necessary. A broad grant of freedom, immunity agreements were an important weapon in the prosecution's arsenal; it was often the only way to extract invaluable investigative information. If Michael Davis wasn't the killer, then he knew an awful lot about who was.

Percy took her time reading the document. "You'll find it's exactly as we discussed," Mark offered. She looked up and shot him a "that's what prosecutors always say but let me be the judge" smile. She made several notations on her pad, as well as one on the original, which she asked him to initial.

"Okay?" he asked.

"Looks good."

Michael, Percy, and Mark all signed the document, and Mark returned it to its folder. "Don't worry," he said as Percy started to speak. "I'll get you a copy before you leave."

"Aren't you the good guy," she said, smiling. "Shall we begin?"

Mark walked over to a tripod and switched on the camcorder that had been positioned to face Michael. He returned to his seat, announced the date and time, and identified those present. Frances and Elvis, who had been sitting quietly while the immunity agreement was being finalized, leaned forward in unison.

Mark began by asking a series of leading questions designed to establish that Percy Lukewarm had advised Michael of his legal rights, that he understood the nature of those rights, and that he was being offered immunity from prosecution in exchange for his cooperation with the government in its ongoing investigation of the murder of Hope Lawrence. With these legalities established, Mark sat back in his chair.

"Go ahead, Michael." Percy rested her hand gently on his shoulder. The deep red polish of her manicured nails reflected the light. As he looked up for a minute and met Frances's stare, he appeared younger than he had in the police interrogation room, perhaps no more than twenty-five. His dark eyes seemed vacant, the blue irises rimmed red from what had surely been a series of sleepless nights. Now was the moment of truth.

"I . . . uh . . . I . . ." he stammered. He turned to Percy, obviously in search of guidance.

"I'm going to walk him through. It'll be more efficient, I assure you."

Mark nodded his assent.

She warmed him up with questions about his date of birth and other preliminaries. With an encouraging voice or supportive smile, Percy seemed to reward even his most basic answers. She certainly had skill. "Now, Michael, tell us what you were doing at the Lawrence house last Saturday."

"I was working for Best Laid Plans. They had the catering job for the wedding."

"Had you worked for that company before?"

"Yeah. This was my third job. First time I actually did some serving, passing, but that didn't go too well, so I settled for gruntwork, carrying shit – I mean glasses, dishes – to and from the trucks."

Percy laid her hand on his. "It's okay to say 'shit.'" Michael forced a laugh, but Frances could see the tension ease as he dropped his shoulders and leaned back in his chair. "And Saturday you were at the Lawrences'?"

He nodded.

"Did you ask to go there?"

"Nobody lives on Smith's Point without big bucks. So when we were signing up for Saturday jobs, I picked that one. You know a lot of guys don't want night work. They want the catering stuff in the afternoons. Christine – she's the owner – was happy to give me the wedding."

"And why did you want to work at what you perceived to be a wealthy location?"

Michael gave her a bemused look, as if anyone in his right mind would seize the opportunity to steal from the rich. When she didn't respond, he added, "I thought there might be something in it for me besides twelve bucks an hour."

"Tell us what happened while you were at work."

"Well, we finished setting up and had a little time to spare. That's the thing about Christine. She's extra cautious about time, but as long as I'm getting paid, it doesn't bother me. Anyway, she packs these big pans of lasagna for the employees' chow. Most guys were hanging in the kitchen, filling up before the party began. I thought it could be time to check out the house."

"At this point, were you planning to steal something?" Michael said nothing.

"We need to know. Under the terms of your agreement with the prosecution, they can't use any information you tell them today against you in any way, but that means you must cooperate and answer all my questions. Their questions, too. Do you understand?"

He nodded.

"So answer my question."

"Not right away," he mumbled.

"But you went into the house because if there was something valuable that you could take, you were going to do that. Isn't that right?" Percy's client was squirming, but this time she didn't seem to notice.

"Had you met any of the members of the Lawrence family before?" Mark asked. Michael shook his head. "Were you introduced to any of them that day?" Again he indicated no. "Go on," Mark urged. "I didn't mean to interrupt."

"Well, I went inside, and the place was pretty quiet

because the reception was all set up under the tent on the lawn. I was a little nervous being downstairs with all the Best Laid Plans people in the kitchen, so I thought the second floor would be safer. I looked in a bunch of rooms. They must have been for guests or something, because there was no personal shit in them. Unless I was after some scented candle or something."

"What in particular *were* you looking for?"

Michael paused, again seemingly reluctant to answer. "Jewelry?"

"Yeah."

"What else?"

"Basically that's it. Jewelry's the easiest to take and the quickest to unload."

"As you were going in and out of these various bedrooms, did you see anyone?"

"Yeah. At one point when I was in the hall, I heard a door open and a woman stepped out of a bedroom . . . the bedroom," he said, looking at Percy.

"You mean the bedroom of Hope Lawrence?"

"Yeah."

"What did she look like?"

"She was pretty hot, actually. She had on a bright suit. Green I think."

"Do you remember her hair color?"

"Dark."

"How old would you say she was?"

"Thirties. I'm not that good with ages."

Mark stepped forward and produced a manila envelope from the same folder that contained the immunity agreement. He opened its clasp, removed a handful of photographs, and arranged them on the table in front of Michael. All eight of them were of pretty women appearing to be in their early thirties with straight dark hair. "Do you recognize the woman you saw leaving Hope's bedroom from among these pictures? Take all the time you need." He stepped back.

"I do." He handed Mark one of the photographs.

"Are you sure?"

"Positive."

Mark made a notation on the photo Michael had selected and handed it to Frances. He put the others back in his envelope. She could barely contain her reaction as she stared at the face of Penelope. She looked up to see his reaction, but he had none. Apparently it was no coincidence that her picture had been included in the photo array.

"After you saw this woman leave Hope's bedroom, where did she go?" Mark continued without a moment's hesitation.

"Down the stairs."

"Did you see her again?"

"No."

"Did you see anyone else?"

"Yeah. I checked out another room, which turned out to be a bathroom, and I was about to go back out into the hall when I heard a voice. I looked out and saw Mr. Lawrence, or I assumed that's who it was. He was all dressed up in his wedding stuff, what's it called?"

"A tuxedo? A morning suit?"

"A morning suit, the kind that has stripes on the pants. Anyway, he was knocking on the door and calling to Hope, asking her if she was ready, telling her they were late."

"Could you hear any response?"

"No."

"How long did he stay outside the door?"

"Couple of minutes. Then he headed downstairs."

"What did you do?"

"I figured that was the bride's room but that she'd already left. I waited for a couple of minutes, but nobody came back. The room was a mess when I went in. There was stuff all over the dressing table and the rug was kind of askew and pillows from the bed were on the floor."

"What did you do?"

"I started opening drawers in the dressing table, the bureau. You know, checking out the kinds of places people keep jewelry. There was a pair of pearl earrings, but they weren't big enough to go for more than a hundred or so. Not worth the risk. Otherwise, I didn't see much."

"What about the ring with the insignia of St. Michael, the one that the police found in your truck?"

"That was on her dresser. I didn't think it was worth all that much, but the sword was cool, so I took it for myself. I'm Catholic," he added, as if that provided some excuse.

"Then what did you do?"

"Well, I thought I heard voices in the hall again, so I opened a closet door to hide just in case someone stuck their head in. And, well . . . I can't tell you what it was like to see her."

"You mean Hope Lawrence?"

"Yeah. She was in a wedding dress. And she was hanging there." He closed his eyes and wrinkled his nose as if to squeeze the image out of his mind.

"Were you able to determine whether she was dead?"

"I don't know. I assume she was. She looked horrible. Her face was kind of tilted with her tongue hanging out. You know, maybe I should have checked, but I was so freaked. And as I said, she sure looked dead."

"Did you move or touch or alter the body in any way?"

Michael diverted his gaze. They all knew what was coming. "I saw the ring. The diamond was huge. Worth a fortune. At least fifty grand, even at a pawnshop. And it just slid right off her finger."

Frances felt a well of saliva surge into her mouth. *Don't be sick.* But it was hard to imagine someone callous enough to steal an engagement ring off a bride's finger and not even bother to check for a pulse. Although it wouldn't have made a difference. As the medical examiner had reported, Hope was dead before she'd ever been hanged.

"So you in no way harmed her."

"No. As I said, she was dead. I know she was. And I sure as hell had nothing to do with that."

Percy looked up at Mark and bit her lip.

"Do you recall what her finger felt like when you touched it?" he asked.

"What do you mean?"

"Well, whether it was warm or cold?"

"I don't remember. I was creeped out, you know. Here's this broad just hanging there."

Frances felt all eyes on her for a moment, perhaps trying to assess whether she could handle such a matter-of-fact discussion of her cousin, but the crudeness of his narrative hardly mattered. Her interest in him was limited to whatever information he could provide. So far, nothing he'd said seemed particularly helpful to the investigation. His claim of innocence didn't even exonerate him.

"While you were in the Lawrence house, did you see or hear anyone else come or go from Hope's bedroom?"

"Yes."

"What did you see?"

Michael rested his chin on his hands for a moment and appeared to contemplate the question. "When I was in the closet, I heard the door open. Not the closet door, which wasn't all the way closed, but the door to the hallway. I had to pretty much hold my breath. I was scared to be in there with that body, you know, wondering whether someone was going to find me. I saw a guy come in and go over to the dressing table."

"What did the man look like?"

"Tall, dark hair, forties maybe, although the guy was pretty buff. He was wearing a T-shirt and jeans. He was kind of foreign looking."

Again Mark produced an array of photographs from the folder and spread them out on the table in front of Michael. This time each image showed a handsome man with dark brown or black hair and tanned skin.

Frances could see that one picture was of Carl. "Do you recognize the man you saw in Hope's bedroom? Take your time."

It didn't take long for Michael to identify Hope's lover. Mark collected the photographs and marked the one he had selected.

"What did you see him do?" Percy continued.

"He went toward the dressing table, which was out of my sight, but I heard rummaging. I don't know. I figured he was looking for something."

"How long was he there?"

"Couple of minutes, maybe. It felt like days 'cause I was shitting in my pants wanting him to leave so I could get out of there."

"Did you see whether he took anything?"

"No. But he stopped at the door and used a red bandanna to wipe off the doorknob. I could see his hands doing that."

"Anything else you noticed about his appearance, his clothes?"

"No. Look, I was pretty damn scared."

"What happened then?"

"I got out of that house as fast as I could, jumped in my car, and didn't look back. I knew I had to get out of Manchester as fast as possible. Figured I could get lost in Boston for a while, sell the ring, and live pretty comfortably, maybe even with my folks, until I figured out my next move. Then I got busted on the Tobin Bridge and here I am." He smiled, obviously pleased to have finished his narrative.

"Why didn't you go to the police?"

"I've got a record. You think anyone's going to believe me? I'd be the first one they'd finger. Plus I had the ring."

There was silence for several moments before Percy said, "If any of you have any questions, feel free to ask."

Frances replayed in her mind what she had just heard. Something didn't seem right. The interview had been so well choreographed, the photo arrays so perfectly planned, that she wondered whether Mark was overlooking details in his rush to prosecute. Assuming Michael was credible, an assumption that she wasn't at all sure she was willing to make, all he'd been able to say was that Penelope had been in Hope's room around the time of her murder and that Carl had gone in looking for something after she was already dead.

Questions spun in her head. What had Carl been looking for? She thought of the St. Michael's ring – a man's ring – and remembered the band of pale skin around his finger that she'd noticed the day she'd gone to his boat. Was that the ring he'd been missing? If so, when had he left it in Hope's room? And why? Were they to assume that Carl returned to Hope's room after he killed her to remove some sort of evidence that linked him to the crime? She glanced at the faces of Elvis and Mark, wondering what they were thinking. How could Mark be so sure of Carl's guilt that he was willing to give immunity to a known felon?

There was also the issue of Penelope. Shouldn't she have been at the church by the time Michael said he saw her leave Hope's bedroom? Frances remembered her late arrival, how she'd settled into the pew beside Sam and offered some excuse. What had she been doing before that? Was there a connection between Penelope and Carl? She shuddered to think. Did Penelope's jealousy of her baby sister extend to wanting to share both lovers? This already small world seemed to be closing in on her.

Plus, she now remembered, she'd had to pick the lock in order to get into Hope's room. But if Hope was dead when Michael left, who had locked it behind him?

"Did you actually lock the door when you left?"

Michael looked at Frances, obviously surprised to have a question come from her. "Yeah," he mumbled.

"Why?"

He glanced at his lawyer, who nodded for him to answer. "I had the ring. I had to buy myself a little time to get away. I figured if someone came looking for her, they'd be stuck outside at least temporarily. Most North Shore types aren't skilled lock pickers."

Frances refrained from any further questions. The criminal never ceased to astound – or sicken – her.

Mark turned off the video. Percy stood up and smiled, obviously pleased with the results she'd achieved for her client. She thanked him, nodded goodbyes to Frances and Elvis, and left with Michael trailing a few feet behind her. Although his stooped posture didn't reflect it, he had to know he'd just gotten a very sweet deal.

*

Mark's office was larger than those Frances had seen in the world of government employees. His metal desk was piled high with stacks of papers, unread memos, files, and copies of legal cases from the advance sheets. On one wall hung his diplomas – a bachelor of science from the Massachusetts Institute of Technology and a doctorate of jurisprudence from Boston University Law School – and several plaques, distinguished awards from various law enforcement agencies and task forces. He snapped the plastic lid off a paper cup of coffee and took a long, loud sip.

Frances crossed her legs, trying to get comfortable in the well-worn armchair but feeling instead the jab of springs through the foam cushion. Elvis paced back and forth in front of the plate-glass window. He seemed to be doing calculations on his fingers.

"What can you tell us about Carl LeFleur?" Mark asked.

Frances recounted the little she knew, including her uncle's suspicions and their failed effort to talk to him. "From what I understand, Hope loved him very much. Even her fiancé admits that."

"I guess so. Carl's blood type – O negative – matches the semen found in Hope's stomach."

"We checked emergency room records last night," Elvis explained. "He went in about eight months ago for a fairly serious swordfish puncture."

"How'd he get that as a lobsterman?" she asked.

"Don't know. I can only tell you what the records said. But O negative is relatively rare."

Mark flipped through several pieces of paper on his

desk. "Forensics tells me the key that was found in Hope's room belongs to a boat engine. We should have been able to guess that, given the cork. Apparently it's pretty common to attach keys to something that will float, just in case they drop overboard. Anyway, we're preparing a search warrant for the . . ." – he paused and glanced at a yellow Post-it Note – "the *Lady Hope* – cute name, by the way – to see if it's a match. I'd put money on it. Only problem is that we need to track down a judge to sign the warrant, which is going to be tough today. There's a charity golf tournament for an officer killed several years ago in the line of duty, and virtually the entire criminal justice system is participating. I'd be there too if it weren't for this."

"I appreciate that," Frances said in recognition of his efforts.

"What about Penelope Lawrence?" he asked, changing the subject.

"She's my aunt's daughter from her first marriage. She's quite an accomplished lawyer. My aunt says she works prodigious hours. Single, no children."

"What was her relationship to Hope?"

"Not close, from what I understand. There was some jealousy." Frances realized as she spoke that she was minimizing the extent of the animosity between the half-sisters, including the event to which she bore witness. For the second time in as many days, she thought about that ill-fated sailing expedition, the three girls in a capsized boat, the desperate effort to save her cousin, and the look in Penelope's eyes as she'd stood on the beach, the stare of hatred, evil. *Why didn't you go for help?* Frances had never said anything further. She'd wanted to believe that she'd misunderstood the meaning of Penelope's actions. Penelope had been young. Perhaps she'd been so frightened that she'd been unable – not unwilling – to help. But what if, as Frances reluctantly suspected, she'd wanted Hope to drown? She'd failed that day, but had she harbored such rage over the years that she would kill her mother's other child? It seemed far-fetched. "She'd also had a brief relationship with Jack Cabot."

"Her prints were on the bottle top we recovered, the one we assume belonged to the meprobamate prescription." He looked up. "I'm not sure where that leaves us, though."

"Can I ask you something?" Frances said, realizing that she would do it regardless of their response. "Wouldn't Hope's ingestion of the drugs have made her relaxed, even dopey?"

"Yeah. Meprobamate is a pretty serious antianxiety medication, and her dosage was up there."

"And there wasn't any evidence of a struggle, that's what Maggie said, which is consistent with the fact that Hope was probably unable to put up much resistance."

"So?" Mark asked.

"It means that even someone who was not significantly stronger, someone who might not ordinarily be able to overpower her, could have strangled her," Elvis said, finishing her thought. "Including a woman."

"You're telling me Penelope's the killer?"

"I'm not telling you anything. I just don't want to overlook anything. Has there been any follow-up on the

recovered money?" she asked, thinking of the ten thousand dollars that the police had found at the Lawrence
home.

"No fingerprints, if that's what you mean. Where it
came from and why it was there? Well, I guess you
could say those are open questions. Could be entirely
unrelated. We'll be getting subpoenas for bank records,
but I'd bet Carl's won't show anything like that amount
of cash."

"But that's the point. No one knows where it came
from, and you're telling me it's unrelated to your suspect. Then what was it about?"

"Maybe some guest at the wedding was planning a
drug buy. There could be a hundred explanations. But I
think we're getting sidetracked."

Frances disagreed. The North Shore crowd was cautious about money; people were unlikely to have that
amount of extra cash on hand, and it wasn't part of
Episcopalian tradition to slip greenbacks to the bride
and groom at the reception. "Why are you so convinced
of Carl's guilt?" she asked.

"Who said anything about convinced? But I like the
way the evidence is falling into place." Frances's face
must have further revealed her skepticism, because he
added, "What makes you think he's not?"

"Aside from the fact he loved her?"

"Come on, Frances. This isn't a fairy tale. Crimes of
passion. They happen every day."

"Then why'd he go to the trouble of staging a
suicide?"

"Maybe he had some reason to think a suicide was

plausible. Then he wouldn't get caught. Most people don't understand that the police would investigate anyway."

Maybe. Her impression of Carl was that he had a pretty good idea of how law enforcement operated.

"Is your uncle willing to go forward with the A and B charge?" Elvis asked, referring to what Frances had described as the discord between Bill and Carl the day of Hope's wedding, conduct that certainly supported a charge of assault and battery.

"I asked him after we discussed it," she replied. "He was reluctant, very reluctant." She thought back to the brief conversation she'd had with Bill and realized that the paucity of her description didn't begin to capture his reaction. He'd been emphatic.

"I want nothing to do with that man," he'd said in a voice that bordered on a yell. She'd tried to explain the value in pressing a charge, that if nothing else, it would allow the police to pick him up for questioning, but he'd dismissed her pleas. "I know he's dangerous, but the police shouldn't be looking at me to give them a reason to get him off the street." His response had seemed odd, given his initial suggestion that the police focus on Carl, but with Michael's arrest, the issue had become moot.

"Maybe when he hears what we know now, he'll change his mind," Elvis said. "After all, who wouldn't want to go after the person who killed their daughter?"

26

The law offices of Hallowell and McKenzie, situated on the twenty-eighth through thirty-first floors of Exchange Place in the center of Boston's financial district, exuded success. In the mahogany-paneled reception, Frances and Elvis perched on couches covered in deep-hued stripes as they waited with the weekend receptionist for Penelope's secretary to escort them back to her office. On the wall hung rows of formal black-and-white photographs of men in suits and neckties, all eyes seeming to survey the visitors. Brochures on the coffee table outlined the firm's many areas of expertise, the strengths and accomplishments of its partners, and the cutting-edge services they could provide. Several casually dressed attorneys passed briskly through the reception area en route to the library just beyond.

After Frances and Elvis had left the district attorney's office, she'd called Penelope at her Back Bay home. When there was no answer, they'd decided to pay a visit to her at the office. Most lawyers in private practice spent at least some part of the weekend at work, and it was worth the gamble that they would find her there.

Besides, they had at least several hours to wait while Mark prepared the search warrant for Carl's boat and tracked down a judge to sign it.

It turned out they were in luck. Penelope had been in the office since just after ten a.m., according to the receptionist's log.

Maria, a heavyset woman with black hair and thick-rimmed glasses, appeared in pink Bermuda shorts and led them down the hall to a small, rectangular office. It was sparsely furnished with a slipcovered couch, a bookshelf with carefully organized files, and a large desk with a collection of corporate tombstones arranged on one corner, the souvenirs given to the various legal and financial participants in every deal. Dartmouth College and Harvard Law School diplomas framed in black lacquer adorned the otherwise bare walls. The desk held an ashtray with several cigarette butts and a vase of orange roses. Penelope waited, standing at attention behind her desk in wrinkled linen pants and an untucked shirt. She looked pale and her eyes were red. Frances forced a smile, which she didn't return, and Elvis extended his hand in introduction, similarly without response. She remained frozen with her arms crossed in front of her chest.

"What do you want?" she asked abruptly.

"I'm sorry to have to do this," Elvis said as he began to read her the Miranda warnings.

"I know my rights. Just tell me what you want and why you're here." Elvis reached into his pocket to produce a waiver form. "I'll sign whatever you've got. Let's just get this over with. You've caused me terrible

341

embarrassment already, although I suspect that was part of your plan or you wouldn't have come here."

"We just wanted to find you," Elvis replied before Frances could. "We weren't expecting such a crowd."

"It's hard enough to make partner. Just try not showing up on the weekend."

"I'm sure," he said, trying to be placatory.

"What do you want to ask me?"

"What were you doing in Hope's room just before her wedding was scheduled to begin?" Elvis answered.

"I don't know what you're talking about."

"I don't mean any disrespect, but that's where you're wrong. We've got an eyewitness placing you in Hope's bedroom less than an hour before she was discovered."

"Oh, you do, do you?" she replied sardonically. "Isn't that grand." She opened her desk drawer and removed a pack of Marlboro Lights. "Mind if I smoke?" she asked, although her tone made clear she didn't care about their preferences. She lit a cigarette and took a long drag, tilted her head up, and exhaled smoke toward the ceiling. "That catering guy murdered Hope. Please leave me alone. This has been hard enough on my family." She glared at Frances.

"Penelope, why don't you just tell us what happened, what you know."

"Why would you think I know anything? Am I my sister's keeper?" Penelope turned her back on them and stared out the window.

"Perhaps the voice of your sister's blood cries from the ground," Elvis suggested, picking up on her biblical reference.

"What were you doing in her room?" Frances asked. The crack in her voice revealed her uneasiness. The invocation of the most famous of sibling rivalries seemed particularly ominous.

"I don't understand what this is all about."

"We need to know what you saw in Hope's room, what you remember. It could really help." She sounded more imploring than she'd intended.

"I want you to go," she mumbled, although her voice contained no shred of resolve.

"Look. We're trying to do this the easy way. But believe you me, things can get much more complicated," Elvis said. "Hope's murderer is still at large, and we're quite sure you know something you're not saying."

"What can I tell you?" she asked as she slumped into her chair. Her fingers gripped the arms, and her knuckles turned white. "My sister's dead, but I didn't hurt her. And I don't know who did. Yes, I was in her room, but I never saw her." She sighed, a mixture of exhaustion and despair.

"Why'd you go in?"

Penelope's shoulders slouched and she dropped forward, covering her face with her hands. "The morning of her wedding she'd asked me to bring her some medication, a prescription that Mom had. I don't even remember the name of the drug. She said she needed it badly." Her words seemed to echo in the room, and neither Frances nor Elvis responded immediately, waiting for the sound to diminish.

"Did you get it for her?"

Penelope looked up. "She wanted the pills. She was in pain, anxious, truly a mess of nerves. She knew what they were and where they were located. All I did was bring them to her. I was a gofer, nothing more."

"Did you see her take any of them?"

"No."

Frances thought for a moment. Had Hope been tranquilized at lunch with Teddy? Frances had attributed her oddity to prewedding jitters. "What happened when you got them for her?"

"She gave me that sweet smile of hers. Then thanked me. Thanked me for being her sister. That's it. I left."

Frances took a few steps toward her cousin and lowered her voice. "Did Hope know about your feelings for Jack?"

Penelope's eyes widened at the reference. Then she shook her head. "No, or at least I don't think so. I never said a word."

"Did you know Carl LeFleur?"

"Hope's other boyfriend? I never met him."

"Did you tell anyone you'd given her the prescription?"

"No."

"What you're talking about is several hours before the relevant time period," Elvis said. "Why did you go in her room shortly before the ceremony was scheduled to begin?"

Penelope started to cry. Her sobs grew louder, and she gripped her hair with her fingers, pulling it hard. She blew her nose and wiped her eyes, obviously trying to regain composure, only to be overcome once again with tears. When she finally spoke, she gasped for air between words thick with mucus. "I knew Hope was in trouble. Anyone could tell that. She was frantic about getting married. When she asked me for the medication I got it for her, not because I wanted to help, but because I wanted her to make a fool of herself. If she was drugged, I figured she'd fall asleep in her plate, say something wildly inappropriate, be unable to dance. I wanted Bill and Mom and most of all Jack to see how imperfect she could be. I wanted her to fuck up in some way that no one could forget." Penelope shuddered, as if her own words were difficult to hear. "I'm not proud of what I did. But I didn't hurt her."

Elvis shot a glance at Frances, obviously surprised by this disclosure. She closed her eyes for a moment, realizing how painful these words would be for her aunt and uncle to hear.

"You must be thinking, why? I'm her sister, after all. Why would I wish her harm? Frances knows. She knows I wanted Hope's husband. I wanted Jack for myself. But I didn't have a prayer. He was so enamored of her that she could do no wrong. A public display of her inability to function would be his punishment, his reminder that he should have picked me."

She turned away and walked over to the window, seeming to stare out across downtown Boston and into Faneuil Hall Marketplace filled with tourists. "I'm not Bill's daughter, and that half difference between me and Hope represented a chasm between us, our circumstances, and how we were perceived. My whole life I've come second," she said, gritting her teeth. "You know,

if you look at me, at what I've accomplished, it was
never good enough. I was elected to Phi Beta Kappa. I
graduated from law school. I'm on track for partnership
at a good firm. I earn a good salary and own my home.
But nothing I did changed our relative worth. Hope was
the cherished child. No one told me that she was
adopted until after her death. Bill simply announced
before the memorial service for my half-sister that we
weren't blood relatives. How sick is that? All I remember as a child was that I went to stay with Teddy, and
when I returned home, Mom had a baby. I didn't know
about gestation. I didn't put two and two together. I was
three years old. But suddenly they were the perfect
family, and I was the extra, the one who didn't fit, just
like that *Sesame Street* song kids sing about 'one of these
things is not like the others. One of these things doesn't
belong.' That was me. The fourth grid that didn't belong
in the picture."

That there could be such anger within the embracing
home Adelaide had created was incomprehensible to
Frances. But she had to admit that her time in that
house had been brief; perhaps her sporadic visits captured the illusion rather than the essence of family life.
And she knew as well as anyone what it meant to be
the product of a first, failed marriage.

"I'm never going to have children because it's too
easy to damage them. A forgotten field-hockey game, a
perfect test score that goes uncelebrated, each time I
was filled with shame and a sense of inadequacy. It's
taken me my whole life to accept myself – to not hate
who I am each and every day – because of how Bill and

Mom treated me. And then when Jack rejected me and chose her, I felt the same sense of failure all over again. I hate them all. Now Mom and Bill have lost the symbol of their special bond, and nothing can bring her back." She sat back down at her desk, pushed a stack of papers to one side, and rested her head on her forearms for a moment before sitting upright again. "And maybe they deserve it."

Frances listened, numb. The power of anger, the intensity of emotional damage imbued Penelope with self-righteousness. She seemed possessed.

"But when she didn't show up at the church on time, I panicked. I don't know what I thought, but she'd seemed desperate and I suddenly feared she'd take too many pills. So I went back to look for her, to look for the pills. I never saw either." She walked over to the window and looked out at the city of Boston below. "I went into that bedroom out of a guilt I didn't deserve, a guilt that said, 'What if she harms herself? And if she does, will I be blamed?' I decided I should take the pills away. When she wasn't there, I figured I'd overreacted. She'd gone to the church. I never dreamed . . ." Her voice dropped off.

Her cousin's hatred, a hatred born out of low self-esteem, was shocking, but Frances didn't know whether to be enraged or saddened. Although its manifestations differed, both Hope and Penelope had suffered tremendously from some misdirected force within their family. She needed to call Sam, to hear the voice of kindness, of consideration, to be reminded that such qualities still existed in people she knew. As she and Elvis departed, she told him that she would catch the commuter rail back to Manchester. As considerate as he'd been to play chauffeur, she needed to be alone.

The nearly three-mile walk from the train station back to the Lawrence home invigorated her. She moved at a brisk pace, swinging her arms and stretching her muscles. She paused at the entrance to the driveway and inhaled deeply, feeling the salty sea air fill her lungs. Both her aunt's and uncle's cars were in the driveway, and she knew she should go inside and apprise them of the status of the investigation, but she couldn't bear the conversation. Michael's arrest had provided a sense of closure for all of them, and the latest developments were certain to cause tremendous pain. Meanwhile, how could they be expected to go on with their lives knowing that one family member had turned against another and that the way they'd chosen to raise their two daughters had contributed to such bitter animosity?

Frances's thoughts wandered to the murder of Clio, her own stepmother, more than a year before. She'd felt detached at the time, numbed by the experience yet driven by the urge to prove to her father that she could help, that she would find the killer. All she'd discovered was a family so fragmented and emotionally bruised that it had turned on its own members like a wild animal that eats its young. But she'd never expected the violence, the hatred, to spread beyond her nuclear family. That Adelaide's family was equally beset by animus seemed inconceivable. Perhaps her only salvation was to say goodbye once and for all to the torment of her father's gene pool.

Instead of going inside, she turned up the dirt path to the guest cottage that Teddy called home. She had wandered along it hundreds of times as a child, feeling the pine needles beneath her bare feet. The narrow path had a magic quality as it wound its way through the trees, and she remembered how easily it had stimulated her imagination; she'd pretended to be Hansel and Gretel leaving bread crumbs in the woods, or an ornithologist tracking a rare species of bird, or a detective searching for clues. Infinite possibilities. That's what summers in Manchester had been about. Her imagination could soar because life itself was simple: there was a routine to the day, a fixed universe, and few surprises. The ice-cream parlor offered only five flavors – vanilla, chocolate, strawberry, mint chip, and peppermint – and a quarter actually bought twenty-five pieces of candy. The bike shop inflated tires for free. A tragedy was getting her kite stuck in a tree or losing a tennis ball in a patch of poison ivy. Twenty years didn't seem long enough for that world to have changed.

"Teddy!" she called as she opened the screen door. She stepped inside, and it swung shut behind her. Her grandmother's three dogs pulled themselves up off the braided rug and wandered over to sniff the newcomer. She leaned over to rub their heads. "Teddy!" she called again.

"I'm in here."

With the dogs padding slowly behind her, she moved

through the living room in the direction of the voice. She heard odd electronic sounds followed by a computer-generated America Online voice: "Welcome. You've got mail." Peering around the corner, she saw her grand-mother in a pink quilted bathrobe and matching slippers, seated at a small wooden table and staring at a monitor. She had pulled the discolored lace curtains shut to block the reflection of the afternoon sun on her screen but still kept her face only inches away. With her arthritic right hand, she navigated the mouse and clicked on an icon.

Frances chuckled.

"What do you find so amusing?" Teddy asked without a trace of humor in her voice.

She didn't know how to respond. Although her grand-mother had always struck her as progressive, the idea of Teddy on the Internet seemed incredible.

"This blasted machine is so slow. Bea was telling me just yesterday that I should invest in some sort of high-speed access through the cable company, and I think she's right. I'm just not sure whether I can get it up here."

Frances covered her mouth to try to squelch a further outburst. She imagined the group of women, all over eighty, discussing the pros and cons of cable versus telephone connections over lunch at the Singing Beach Club or a game of mah jongg. "How did you learn this?"

"Don't sound so surprised. I learned the same way everyone else does. I asked Bill to get me a computer, and he ordered this one. He found some nice fellow, a what-do-you-call-it . . ." She paused to think. "An ITS consultant, that's what he was. He came and set everything up. He explained the basic information to me and left me with several books for beginner computer users. I taught myself the rest."

"You get e-mail?"

"Absolutely. Perhaps I'll send you one if you take that smirk off your face."

"You never cease to amaze me," Frances said. "What are you doing now?"

"I'm looking to see whether the Chancellor has responded to my inquiries."

"Chancellor?"

"Of the Episcopalian Diocese. He's a glorified lawyer. But he's a terribly nice man at a firm in Boston."

"How did you meet him?"

"I didn't meet him. We've just communicated by e-mail. I thought he might be less inclined to think I'm some old coot if I limited contact to the computer. He probably thinks I'm both younger and more reasonable than I am." She glanced back over her shoulder and smiled at Frances. "I'm trying to find out about Father Whitney."

"Find out what?"

"Whatever I can."

"Why?" Although Teddy had mentioned several times over the last week that she had reservations about the Church of the Holy Spirit, her comments had been limited to the negative impact it had on Hope.

"The Cabots have set up that foundation in memory of Hope, and Adelaide is wanting the money to be turned over to the church. Between you and me, I think they're trying to tithe their way to heaven. I say good luck. But the real issue in my mind is whether a church of that small size is equipped to deal with a lot of money and a serious responsibility. I want to know whether dollars will be spent redecorating the parish hall or whether we're going to get some good Christian service for the money. I would hate to see it wasted," Teddy replied.

"Father Whitney doesn't give that impression."

"He may be quite devoted to his flock, but money can have a distorting effect. Some say you have to be better than a priest not to let it go to your head."

"I thought money wasn't supposed to matter to the truly pious. Isn't there a 'God takes care of everything' mentality?" Frances said with more than a hint of sarcasm.

Teddy sighed. "I see you inherited one thing from me." With that, she turned back to face her screen. "Now, I'm extremely busy, if you don't mind."

"Good luck." Frances patted her back and left her to her attempts at cyber-communication with the Episcopalian Chancellor.

Frances slipped in the back door, stopped briefly in the kitchen to grab a homemade chocolate-chip cookie from the green Bremmer wafer tin by the toaster, and mounted the stairs to the second floor two at a time. She wanted to get up to her bedroom unnoticed. She pushed open the door and saw that everything had been tidied in her absence; the bed was made, a stack of clean towels was piled on the chair, and her laundry had been washed and folded. The miracle of a housekeeper.

On the bedside table by the telephone, Frances noticed two messages. One indicated that Elvis had called. The other was a note from Adelaide saying that dinner would be at seven. She glanced at the numbers on the electronic clock. Only thirty-three minutes remained. It had been a long day, and what she really needed was a hot bath, a glass of wine, and an early bedtime.

She flopped down on one of the twin beds, kicked off her shoes, and stretched her arms over her head. Then she reached for the telephone and dialed Sam. He picked up on the second ring.

"Are you all right?" he asked.

Frances bit her lip, realizing that just the reassuring sound of his voice was enough to make her eyes fill with tears. The combination of stress, exhaustion, and sadness had taken its toll. He repeated his question. "I'm fine," she replied. "Just missing you."

"Fanny, you can't fool me. 'I'm fine' is your least favorite expression in the world. It means you're not fine but you don't want to talk about it. You're not Atlas."

"How are the dogs?"

"Great. I'm sure they miss you, if that's what you want to hear. I had them out on the tractor all day, and they came home and crashed. They must have done fifty laps around that field. Herding instincts gone amuck."

Frances closed her eyes, imagining the scene of Sam

riding his John Deere, plowing the soft brown earth to ready it for the fall planting while her crazy mutts chased their tails. She wished she were there.

"Any leads?" he asked.

"So much has happened," Frances began, and relayed what she had learned thus far. What she described had an almost surreal quality; reporting details aloud reinforced the strangeness of recent events: Michael's arrest, then his accusations against Penelope and Carl, and still the many unanswered questions. When she finished, Sam was silent for several moments. She listened to his breathing on the other end of the line.

"I'm sorry," he said finally.

"There's nothing for you to be sorry about," Frances replied, trying to sound in control. "But thanks."

"I'm sorry for you because I know how hard this investigation is. Once again it's your family, and I think, from what you're telling me, some childhood illusions are being shattered and that's probably worse than anything."

Sam had a capacity to sense how she truly felt without her having to articulate her feelings. He was the most intuitive person she knew. Once again he was right. She'd struggled to have her memories seen through a specific filter, and now the lens itself was distorted. "Could I ask you something?"

"You can ask me anything you like."

"Did you and Rose ever consider having children?" She heard the hesitancy in her voice, her reluctance to bring up Sam's first wife.

"We did. And I'll tell you, after Rose died, I wished

more than anything that we had. I wanted to still have someone who was a part of her."

"So why didn't you?"

There was a moment of silence on the other end of the line, and Frances wondered whether she should drop the subject to relieve him of the need to relive his past. Just as she was about to retract the question, she heard his voice.

"At the time that we were building our life together, we talked incessantly about whether we could do it, what kind of parents we would be. And we got nervous. We were insecure about whether we were good enough to create life, let alone care for a person with the combination of stability and creativity that we both recognized a child should have. We questioned whether we were smart enough or imaginative enough or loving enough to nurture a child's development. And so we abandoned the idea."

He paused, and Frances could hear some shuffling in the background, then the water running. "By the time we decided we actually were ready to embark on such an extraordinary endeavor, it was too late. Rose was already sick."

Now it was Frances's turn to be sorry. She shouldn't have asked. Her head had been spinning with issues of Adelaide's relationship to Hope and Penelope, of her conversation with Fiona about Jack, of parenting and all it implied. The thoughts had prompted her to stir up an obviously painful subject with the person she cared about most.

"Just goes to show you, there's never a perfect time

for anything important, so you can't wait around for it to come," he said.

"Yeah."

"Hey. Take care of yourself. If you need me, I'll be there in an instant. And if not, you know where I'll be waiting."

"Thanks." She paused and then added, "I love you." Tonight she wanted to say it first.

"I love you, too, Miss Fanny."

Frances replaced the receiver and stared at the message from Elvis. She preferred to go to sleep with Sam's words in her mind, but she forced herself to dial the number of his cell phone.

"We got a criminal complaint for assault against Carl," Elvis began as soon as she identified herself.

"Did Bill do that?"

"Yeah. An officer took his statement over the telephone."

"And the search warrant for the boat?" she asked.

"We've got a couple of guys executing it now. I'll keep you posted. But FYI, the key we recovered in Hope's bedroom turns the ignition on the *Lady Hope*."

As she hung up the telephone, she felt hollow. She remembered her conversation with Teddy, the discovery of their secret affair. What had been her grandmother's words? With Carl, Hope had found the "kind of mesmerizing chemistry that can leave a girl breathless." Teddy had recognized the special bond they had, the rarity of their connection, and so had supported the relationship way beyond what was proper. For what? So he could kill her?

REDEMPTION

Carl destroyed the person he loved because he couldn't have her. It was the oldest story in the world.

Why was being in love so dangerous? Her relationship with Sam seemed so simple, so easy. He was gentle, kind, comforting. She trusted him to do everything in his power to nurture her, and she hoped she did the same in return. Did that mean it wasn't real?

She crumpled the message slip in her hand, put her head in her pillow, and abandoned any notion of staving off tears. That she was alone was a relief, because it allowed her to cry without fear of being discovered. And for that she was thankful.

27

The windowless conference room was hot. State buildings rarely ran the central air-conditioning past three o'clock on Fridays, so by Sunday afternoon the temperature reached well into the eighties. Mark sat backward on a chair, his legs straddled, briefing Frances on the myriad developments that had occurred in less than twenty-four hours. They were alone. Although Elvis was supposed to be present, he had called several minutes before to inform them he would be late.

Mark reported that the prior evening, the police had carried out the search of Carl's boat. They'd found one key piece of evidence: in the bottom right-hand corner of his medicine cabinet, they'd discovered an orange plastic bottle with its cap missing. It was filled with small pills. He passed her the bottle and its contents sealed in a heavy-duty plastic bag. Even in its police packaging, she could read the label on the bottle: "Equanil. 800 mg. Take 2 per day as needed. Contents: 60. Refills: none." The name on the prescription was Adelaide Lawrence.

Carl had spent the night in custody. The supervising

officers reported that he'd eaten nothing, drunk nothing, and made no requests. He hadn't contacted a lawyer or said a single word, other than to make one telephone call to a local number.

He'd been arraigned before a magistrate at eleven a.m. The court-appointed lawyer assigned to represent him at his bail hearing had little to report in support of an argument that he wasn't a flight risk. His only asset was his fishing boat; he'd worked in the area his whole life. However, he had no criminal record, and although the prosecutor talked about his suspected involvement in Hope's death, he hadn't been charged. The magistrate set bail at $100,000 despite his lawyer's argument that imposition of such an enormous financial condition was effectively an illegal pretrial detention. What lobsterman in a rental had that kind of cash to post for his freedom? But he'd had access to funds that nobody realized, and now he was free.

"Do you know where he went?" Frances asked.

"No. The probation officer didn't bother to notify us when he made bail. He's not on his boat and he's not at home. But he can't be considered a fugitive because he has a right to be anywhere in the commonwealth. That's what making bail is all about. Until we can arrest him on a murder indictment or he fails to show up at his next court appearance, which isn't for another three weeks, there's nothing we can do."

"Have you searched his apartment?"

"Yeah. Guy's neat as a pin. There were a couple of pictures of him and Hope together, and a wedding invitation in a blank envelope, but otherwise nothing."

He may not have been on the guest list, Frances thought, remembering her conversation with Bill. But Hope had given him an invitation anyway. Could she have actually thought he'd come? Frances tried to imagine what must have gone through Carl's mind as he stared at the smart lettering. Rage? Sorrow? The traditions that accompanied a wedding were endlessly evocative, but of what she could only speculate.

Just then the door swung open and in walked Elvis. "Well, I'll be damned," he said. "You'll never guess who posted the cash for Carl's hundred thousand bail bond."

When he told her, Frances couldn't believe her ears and made him repeat it.

"That's right. Theodora Pratt. Your grandmother set him free."

"Teddy!" Frances called, as she let the screen door swing shut behind her. She had exceeded every speed limit on the way to her grandmother's cottage. Panic had set in as twice she'd tried to call from the road, only to get a busy signal. What was happening? What was her grandmother thinking to bail out Hope's killer? Realizing Teddy could be in serious danger, Frances had called the Manchester police from the road. She'd expected them to be there when she arrived, but there were no police cars or other indications of the presence of law enforcement. "Teddy!" she called again.

"You don't have to shout. I'm here on the porch," came the reply.

Teddy sat on a chair with her ankles crossed in front

of her. She wore a pink-and-green wraparound skirt and a matching polo shirt, a large straw hat, and her signature pearls. In one hand she held a glass of ice tea overflowing with mint, and in the other was a cigarette.

"Where are the police?"

"Are you the one that sent them? Bah. A couple of officers showed up – nice young men, very polite, although one of them did have an earring, I noticed – and I invited them in, but frankly I didn't know why they were here. I'm fine."

"But you bailed out Carl LeFleur!" she blurted out.

"I did. That's true. But I'm not in danger from him, if that's what you're thinking." She took a sip of her drink and smacked her lips. "He didn't kill Hope. And he shouldn't have to wait in jail on some fabricated charge just because he can't afford to post his own bond."

"You don't know what you're doing. The police have found evidence linking him to her murder. Listen to me." She was about to begin a recitation when she saw a shadow in her peripheral vision. He stood on the threshold, bare-chested, his hands holding onto each end of a towel wrapped around his neck. Her adrenaline surged. She should have known he'd be here. How could she have been so stupid? She felt helpless, realizing that she was unable to protect her grandmother. There was no way that she could overpower him physically. She felt for the cell phone in her pocket, then realized an attempt to call for help might precipitate a reaction. Why hadn't the police officers stayed?

Teddy glanced over at Carl. "Come sit down," she instructed him. With the towel he wiped a spot of shaving cream from his chin and then perched on the edge of a chair next to her, resting his elbows on his knees.

"Fanny, there's no reason to be afraid for me or for anyone else," Teddy said. "Carl hasn't hurt anyone. Once he tells you what happened, you'll understand. He needs your help."

"Help? I don't think—"

"The police will build a case against him," she interrupted. "I know they can place him at the scene. He's the perfect person to blame – he's an outsider in this town, and he doesn't have an alibi. So unless we find the real murderer, he'll be convicted. Certainly that dimwit appointed by the court won't mount a decent defense. His only chance is to give the police the true killer."

The determination on her grandmother's face made clear that she would not be dissuaded. Frances's words were futile. Carl stared ahead blankly with no acknowledgment of what Teddy was saying. She wanted a moment to speak to her grandmother alone, but she didn't dare say or do anything that might upset him. She tried to remind herself of all the people who worked tirelessly for prisoners on death row, defense attorneys who spent hour after hour alone with murderers and never feared for their own safety. Or did they just put up a good front?

"Go on," Teddy said. "Tell her."

He covered his mouth with his hand and coughed to clear his throat. "I know what you must be thinking," he said in a voice that was flat, devoid of expression.

REDEMPTION

"The last time, the only time, we've spoken, I hardly gave you any reason to believe in me. And maybe you never will. I'm so angry that I don't know whether I believe in myself. I knew Hope would marry Jack, and yes, I was furious . . . beyond furious: I was in an absolute rage at her, at him, at her family for pressuring her not to be with me. But I loved her more than I ever loved anything in the world. If I could take her place now, wherever she is, I'd do it in a moment."

He pulled a handkerchief out of his back pocket and blew his nose. Then he rested his face in his hands and rubbed his eyes. Teddy put out her cigarette in a lighthouse-shaped ashtray. She rested her liver-spotted hand on his back and rubbed him in slow, reassuring circles. This maternal affection toward the 44-year-old suspect in Hope's murder seemed beyond strange; it was disorienting. What had Carl done to win her over? Nobody said a word.

In the distance she could hear the sound of clanging masts rocking on their moorings. Even though the evening was clear, a foghorn blew. Her muscles were tense and she tried to relax. For her grandmother's sake, she would hear what he had to say. Besides, where could she go? She could hardly walk out and leave Teddy with a suspected killer.

"Please, Carl, tell Frances about the day Hope died. Tell her what you know."

Frances could see his Adam's apple move up and down as he swallowed. When he looked up his eyes had softened. His posture, his demeanor, and even his facial expression registered defeat; he looked broken, so different from the way he'd appeared a week before. Could someone change so dramatically, or was this chameleon-like behavior an act? She wanted to remain suspicious, to stay on guard, but she felt the first slivers of doubt creeping into her mind. Perhaps the police had been wrong.

"I don't really know where to begin," Carl said, looking to Teddy for direction.

"Just tell her what you've been telling me."

"I guess you know that Hope and I have been involved – were involved – for a long time." He spoke in a deliberate manner, as if selecting each word carefully. "We met at a fish market. I was in a fight with the owner over the price per pound he was willing to pay, and she was waiting in line to buy lobsters for some family function. As I'm getting angrier by the second – the guy was a cheap son of a bitch – this beautiful woman just comes up to me and offers to take mine directly from me. She'd pay me the retail price. I'll never forget the look on the fucking owner's face. He went ballistic, but I didn't care and neither did she. She had this expression, kind of bad, as if she were pleased by the hoopla. We went outside to the parking lot. I needed the money, and frankly, I thought she felt sorry for me. But we started talking, and the more we spoke, the way she was, I realized she was flirting, wanting something to happen." He paused, letting the words "And it did" go unspoken.

"When we first got together, she couldn't bear to be apart. She was so fearful, so fragile, and sometimes I felt as if she clung to me for her life. There were nights when she just wanted to sit in my apartment, not even talking. I didn't understand her moods. She'd be really excited and happy and sexy one day and then very withdrawn, quiet. One day she announced that our relationship had to end."

"When was that?"

"About fourteen months ago. She'd been under a lot of pressure from her family to stop seeing me. I wasn't what they had in mind. Bill had already shown up once at my apartment with the cops. He'd dragged her kicking and screaming out of there. That was a few months before. I'm not sure exactly of the timing. When Hope and I were together, particular days or months never mattered." He paused, seeming to dwell on a private memory he didn't wish to share.

"So why did she end your relationship?" Frances asked.

"I thought it was because of Jack. The perfect guy," he said sarcastically. "I suspect she knew he was going to propose. But what she told me had nothing to do with him or her parents. The reason she gave me was horrible. I couldn't believe it."

Frances realized she was holding her breath as she waited for his explanation.

He spoke slowly. "She told me she'd been abused, sexually. I understood it was a while back, but there'd been complications and she'd been left unable to have children. I'd seen the scar on her stomach but never asked. I didn't want to know the details, and she didn't offer them, so I can't tell you exactly what happened to her. But she felt crippled, defective, 'a Jonesport without a trap,' she said. I asked her over and over who'd hurt her, but she wouldn't tell me. All she said was that she'd trusted him. Like she trusted me. She said that as we got more and more involved, memories of those experiences returned. My age had a lot to do with it, she said, so I assume the guy was older, but it was also something else, something about the way we were physically. And it had frightened her. She felt dirty, like she was evil, and she thought it was my fault. It sounded bizarre, and frankly I thought she was spending too much time at that church she went to; it was making her feel guilty about everything. She might as well have been a Catholic."

He rubbed his forehead with his long, strong fingers. "I tried to get her to change her mind. I promised to protect her. I promised to keep her safe. I told her I'd kill whoever had hurt her, and I meant it. If I knew today, I'd do it now."

He cleared his throat again, obviously trying to contain his emotions. Listening, Frances felt numb. What exactly had happened? When? How long had it gone on? Had Adelaide and Bill known? Did they know now? How was it possible they didn't? What façade had been maintained all these years? Frances, Blair, and their father had visited the Lawrences' home, laughed, played on the beach and in the canoe, while Hope – the darling baby – had lived in hell.

"My begging sort of worked, although she'd never admit who'd hurt her. But at least she didn't cut things off with me completely. She'd see me every once in a while. We'd meet here." He glanced over at Teddy, who didn't respond. "After she got engaged to Jack, things got a lot worse, more tense. She felt even guiltier. And her family discovered that she was still seeing me."

"How?"

"I don't know. Maybe she said something. Maybe they saw us together. It doesn't matter. They knew and were furious. And I was mad. Really mad. I couldn't believe she'd agreed to marry Jack. And I know she did everything to try to keep me from losing my temper. She kept trying to get me to understand. But I couldn't. I loved her more than anyone could. I wanted her to be mine."

Frances felt an involuntary shudder. The defendant had just articulated a motive for the prosecution, and it sounded compelling.

"Her family was getting pretty desperate about me. Then in June Bill offered me ten grand to stay away. Here's the guy who locked Hope in the closet when she was little telling *me* to stay away. Like I'd take his money."

"Locked her in the closet?" Frances asked.

"Yeah. Apparently that's how he dished out punishment. The prick." Carl looked as if he were about to spit on the floor, but he caught himself as he remembered where he was.

"He offered you ten thousand dollars?"

"Cash. Shows up on my doorstep with money in an envelope and tries to bribe me. I gave it back to him."

Frances remembered the envelope that the police had recovered from the Lawrences' house, the one that both Bill and Adelaide claimed to know nothing about.

Had Bill's feigned discovery been a way to deflect attention? Was he clever enough to realize he could eliminate the evidence against him? She doubted he could be so calculating, but then again, the chasm between what she had perceived and what she was learning widened by the minute.

"Did you see Hope the day of her wedding?"

"Yes. She begged me to come over. I'd tried to see her the night before, but Bill kept me out. Then she called the next morning, desperate that I'd refused to come. I explained what had happened, and she asked me to come back, to come in the service entrance. I agreed."

"What happened when you saw her?"

"I gave her back a ring she'd given me about a year ago. It had a St. Michael emblem on it. She said it would protect me. She believed in all that stuff, but I didn't want her shit anymore. When I took it off, she got hysterical. She was crying and said she couldn't bear to lose me. She said she'd been wrong to associate me with her past. She said everyone had betrayed her, and she needed me more than ever. Then . . . then she kind of lunged at me and, well . . . I don't know how to say this." He looked again at Teddy.

"They were intimate," she said matter-of-factly. "In a manner of speaking."

"What about the pill bottle? How did you get that?" Frances found herself engrossed in his story. The tone of his voice and his demeanor were convincing – she could almost imagine how a jury would hear his tale –

and now she wanted to know how he would explain the evidence that the police had collected against him.

"I saw the bottle on her dressing table. I asked her how many she'd taken, and she said only a couple. I told her to forget the wedding. We'd run away together and I'd marry her, but she refused. She said she had to marry Jack, it was too late. So basically nothing was going to change. I found myself getting angrier and angrier. She wanted Jack *and* me. Maybe Jack was willing to go along with half her affection, but I wasn't. I left. I took the bottle with me."

Frances remembered the crumpled tissue that the police had found, the one containing traces of mepro-bamate. Elvis had hypothesized that Hope had been interrupted, spat the pills out, and then later ingested them. Was that before or after her last encounter with Carl? "Did you see any other pills anywhere? Ones that weren't in the bottle?"

He shook his head.

"Did you take the bottle because you thought she was going to kill herself?"

"I wasn't going to take the chance. And there's been more than one day in the last week when I've debated taking them myself."

"What about your key?"

"When I got back to my boat, I didn't have it. I figured I'd lost it in her room. It had been in my pants pocket. I had to go back to get it because it was the only one I had. I assumed everyone would be at the church. I never saw Hope again."

"And you didn't find the key."

"That's right."

Frances debated for a moment whether to ask about the bandanna, his seeming admission of guilt. She hated to disclose all that Michael could say about Carl, but she needed to know his response. Perhaps it was her grandmother's conviction wearing off on her, or perhaps it was the manner in which he spoke, but she found herself wanting to be convinced of the truth of his story, and this conduct was the most suspicious. "Why did you wipe off the doorknob?"

"What?"

"The prosecution's witness, the one who identified you to begin with, says he saw you wipe the doorknob with a bandanna as you left. Why?"

"I don't know," he said softly. "It's a lame answer, but I can't tell you why. I just had a feeling something was wrong, and I didn't want anyone to be able to place me back in her room . . . alone." There was a long pause, and the silence felt oppressively heavy. "I know what you're thinking. I know it doesn't look good. But I swear it has no significance."

Was that the truth? Could such a deliberate act have happened without an explanation? She doubted it. And that doubt made her more than uneasy. Carl had admitted his rage, admitted that he'd been alone with Hope around the time of her death. Perhaps he was the last person to see her alive. Even if the evidence linking him to the crime was circumstantial, even if he had an explanation for most of it, he couldn't explain everything. And that wasn't good enough.

Besides, who else was there? Frances thought of all the people who had been around Hope shortly before her death. Jack had thought it was his own father, the man who didn't come to the church. Where had he been while he was missing his son's wedding? Then there was the peculiar information that Fiona had consulted extensively with Dr. Frank, Hope's psychiatrist. Hope had been medicated enough that even someone not substantially stronger than her could have strangled her. She tried to recall when she'd seen the unhappy mother of the groom take her seat in the pew. Finally, Carl's story of sexual abuse highlighted the medical examiner's findings. Who had done that? Was the person still around? If so, and if he was still involved in Hope's life, had he been involved in her death?

"Why should I believe you?"

"Stop it, Frances. You should believe him because I'm telling you to," Teddy interrupted. "I'll vouch for him."

"What?"

"You heard me. When he left Hope's room, he came here. He told me what happened, exactly as he's just told you. When he mentioned the pills, I got apprehensive and called over to the house, to Hope's number. She answered. She wouldn't say much, we hardly spoke, but she was still alive after he'd seen her and already dead by the time he returned." She lit another cigarette, and Frances watched the smoke curl up from the tip and disappear into the evening air. Was her grandmother making that up? Was she so convinced of his innocence that she was willing to fabricate? Frances wanted to believe her but knew even the telephone records couldn't fully corroborate his story, given the vagueness of the time sequence. Nothing could prevent the prosecution from theorizing that Carl murdered Hope sometime after the call and before Michael Davis saw him return for his key. His case didn't look promising.

"He's an innocent man. And I want you to prove it. Don't do it for him if you don't want to, but do it for Hope. She wouldn't want the man she loved – the man she adored – to go to prison for a crime he didn't commit. Least of all if that crime was her murder."

28

"Why did Bill leave his law firm?"

Frances sat with her aunt in the library while Adelaide worked on a small needlepoint pillow. Although the windows were open, there was no sea breeze to dissipate the thick, humid air. She could feel herself starting to perspire. She knew her question seemed out of the blue, but as she'd begun to unravel the sad story of the Lawrence family, she'd wondered repeatedly about Bill's decision to leave a well-established law firm to set up a small practice on his own. Didn't most lawyers aspire to the power, prestige and remuneration of partnership? Why give that up? Frances had been involved in investigations long enough to know that seemingly irrational behavior usually wasn't.

Adelaide put down her canvas. "Please don't ask me. I can't discuss it."

"Why not?" Frances got up from her chair and moved to the love seat so she could sit beside her. She took hold of her aunt's hand and felt her thin, cold fingers. "Why can't you talk to me?" she asked.

"It's part of the past, Fanny. I can't resurrect it. I wish more than anything in the world I could rewrite history, but I can't. I can't talk about what's happened with you or anyone else."

"Please don't do this. Please tell me, Adelaide."

"You wouldn't understand."

"Try me!" Frances pleaded. "If Dad were in better health, you know he'd be here now, and he'd be urging you to tell him what was wrong. You're his sister and he loves you. I know that. But he couldn't be here. So I'm his poor stand-in."

"Telling you won't change anything. Why don't you just accept that? I appreciate your concern, your help, I really do. Having you here has meant more to me than I can possibly express, but I can't expect you to know how I feel."

"Is it that Hope was adopted? There's no shame in that. Who cares? You loved her, you made her a wonderful home, and she loved you. What more could anyone want?"

"Don't do this, please. I've lost my daughter," she said in a voice that reflected her disbelief. "Carl took her life. Our past isn't relevant anymore."

Frances took a deep breath and closed her eyes. She hadn't wanted to break the news of Carl's confession, of Teddy's insistence on his innocence, at least until there was another suspect. She wasn't at all sure her aunt's psyche could handle the emotional roller coaster caused by the various false arrests. They all needed closure. But the more Frances thought about what Carl had said, the more she'd come to realize that whatever abuse Hope had suffered in her past might well be connected to her death. An escalation of violence couldn't be ignored. "Carl didn't kill her, or at least it doesn't appear that he did."

Adelaide sighed, but she seemed too weary to react.

"Did you know Hope was abused?" Frances squeezed her aunt's hand, trying to convey in a simple gesture that her questions were an attempt to help, not to hurt; but she knew the mere mention of the words stabbed Adelaide.

Her eyes were vacant as she stared straight ahead. "How did you find out?"

"Carl told me. Hope confided in him."

"What did he say?"

"Not very much. He didn't know the details. He also didn't know who'd done it."

"Hardly anyone does." Her hands shook as she took a sip of her tea. "Why is this important now?"

"Someone hurt her, terribly, when she was young. If that person is still around, the police need to talk to him. Sexual abuse isn't about sex; it's about violence. He may well be involved in her death."

"No. No. That's impossible. He can't be involved. Bill loved her." Tears ran down her cheeks.

Bill, Bill Lawrence, Hope's own father. He couldn't have done such a thing. For a moment, Frances wondered whether she'd misheard, that in fact "Bill" was someone else, a stranger, someone Hope didn't know, didn't trust. But she knew from the look on her aunt's face that her ears hadn't deceived her. Struggling to maintain her composure, she stood, retrieved a tissue box from a side table by the window, and brought it to Adelaide.

"You must promise what I tell you will stay a secret. For Hope's sake, but also for the sake of our family. My daughter's gone. I can't lose Bill, too."

Frances nodded. "You have my word," she said in a voice that she didn't recognize.

Her aunt sighed, obviously struggling. "It wasn't what you think. He made a mistake but didn't hurt her. She did it to herself. He . . . I . . ." she stammered. "Please give me a moment," she said, looking away.

They sat in silence for what seemed an eternity. How had this happened? Why? Frances's mind raced as she realized that no matter what her aunt said, she could never look her uncle in the eye again. Sexual abuse was no mistake.

"You must try to understand," Adelaide said in a voice that had steadied. "If you can ever try to put this in perspective, you must listen. You have to understand our background – my background."

Perspective! Frances wanted to cry out. The idea was absurd, deranged. What was Adelaide thinking? Why was she so desperate that she would accept any rationale for what had happened to her daughter?

"My first husband was a handsome drunk, a beautiful man with a violent temper. Your father warned me, but I was so young, so enthralled, I wouldn't listen, and then I got pregnant. Poor Richard; he ended up paying our rent, paying for a nanny, practically putting food in our mouths because Morgan couldn't hold down a job. Eighteen months after we married, he died in his sleep.

He'd apparently had a serious vitamin B deficiency – common in alcoholics – and he developed nutritional cardiomyopathy. His heart just gave out. I woke to find him lying next to me."

Morgan Fairchild. She remembered the name but had no recollection of this uncle. Her father must have decided to keep her and her sister away from this relative.

"When I met Bill, I felt blessed. Truly lucky. I'd been working part-time at Richard's firm, although we both knew he was doing me a favor. I was his charity. I had no skills beyond impeccable manners and a good background in art history, and I hadn't gone to college. I couldn't type more than a few words a minute. I'd never expected to work, never wanted to be anything but a wife and mother. But he had me stuff envelopes and get coffee so that I wouldn't feel indebted, although I certainly did anyway. Your father's a good man." She stood, walked to the window, and fiddled with the tiebacks on a set of drapes, readjusting the folds ever so slightly. "Bill was counsel for one of the parties in a deal of Richard's. From the moment we met, he was warm and wonderful and kind. And he loved Penelope. He didn't care that I'd been married before, and I can't tell you what a relief that was. A single woman back then . . . it was different. He wanted to have a family, to be a family." She leaned against the wall. "It was only when . . . when . . . when we couldn't have our own child . . ."

"What happened?"

"I'd never seen Bill angry before. He was furious, as

if I had control. My doctor told me that such a reaction was common. He probably felt humiliated, ashamed. I'd been able to have a child with Morgan, why not with him? So we arranged to adopt Hope. We went away for the last six months so that no one would see that I hadn't been pregnant, and had this wonderful trip around Europe. Penny stayed with Teddy in Ann Arbor, and it felt like a second honeymoon. Your father and Clio met us in Paris for a few days. When we returned, we went through Nevada and picked up a beautiful little girl. She was two days old, and the tiniest, most precious creature in the world. Nobody knew she wasn't ours."

Listening, Frances realized this was her family, too. Her father had known the true story and had been a part of preserving the secret of Hope's history. Why? Couldn't the truth have been shared? Were they so proud of their family line that they couldn't include an outsider? For some reason, in order to accept Hope, they'd all needed to pretend she was one of them.

"Bill was quite enchanted with her as a small child; he treated her like a doll, lavished attention on her, dressed her and bathed her, and took her with him to the office. Those years were truly blissful. But around the time she turned twelve or thirteen – I wasn't really paying attention at first – he became increasingly concerned about her lack of discipline. One time he saw her on her bicycle in front of the penny candy store with her friends, and he became enraged. He had some notion that she was too good to be loitering, that standing around on a street corner was for commoners. He had a similar fit when he picked her up from a school dance and thought she'd had a cigarette. But something was odd. He refused to accept that she was on the brink of adolescence. It was what kids did, I tried to explain, but he wouldn't listen. And then the punishments began, ones that didn't fit the crime. He'd lock her in the closet in his upstairs study. I begged him to stop, but then he only got angry with me. He told me her rebelliousness, her lack of discipline, was my fault, and that he'd teach her to comport herself like a lady, to honor her parents. I thought about asking your father to talk to him – after all, he'd gone through it with you and your sister – but I didn't want to worry him. I kept hoping it would pass, that Bill would come around. I should have tried harder, but he seemed so emphatic that he was doing the right thing. I didn't know . . . I truly didn't. You have to believe me. I didn't know until it was too late."

"What? Tell me what he did."

Adelaide could barely speak through her tears. "He . . . he . . . had sex with her. They had sex in the closet."

A chill ran through Frances, and her feet and hands tingled as she struggled to process what her aunt had just confessed. She felt dizzy and wanted to pinch herself to make sure this conversation was real.

"She was fourteen when she got pregnant. I don't know how long it had been going on. She blamed herself, I think, and couldn't bear for anyone else to know. She managed to lose the baby, but in the process caused so much internal damage that she was rushed to the hospital. They did a hysterectomy that night. It was the only way to stop the bleeding."

Frances found it almost impossible to listen. The image of Hope trying to terminate her own pregnancy was sickening. She couldn't bear that her young cousin had suffered such pain alone. "Did she talk to you?"

"No. I remember standing in the hospital with Bill, watching her sleep and wondering what in the world had happened. It was so frightening it was hard to imagine. We'd almost lost her. We just kept holding each other and thanking God that she would be all right."

"How did you find out?"

"I didn't, not until much later. Every time I tried to discuss it, she got hysterical. The doctors had explained the medical complications – they knew she'd been pregnant – but even they didn't know who the father was."

"What about Bill?"

"He never said a word, either. He actually seemed happier than I'd seen him in years, and I remember at the time being scared by his behavior. It seemed so peculiar. In retrospect, I think he was happy he'd impregnated someone." She bent her head and sobbed. "I . . . know . . . that . . . sounds . . . . horrible."

Yes, it does! It is! Frances thought. What about Hope? What about protecting your own daughter? Were her aunt and uncle so concerned with appearances that they'd been willing to sacrifice her emotional and physical safety?

380

"I only found out after she'd been seeing Dr. Frank. After the surgery she began to starve herself. We realized she needed help, professional help. He explained to me that he wasn't surprised. She was a driven girl who'd suffered a terrible trauma that in her own mind was associated with her sexuality. She blamed herself, her body, so she wanted to disappear."

"So Dr. Frank told you about Bill?"

"He filed something with the state, reporting Bill. There was a hearing, and that's when I learned. Dr. Frank testified. I couldn't believe what he said. I couldn't believe what had gone on, and I couldn't believe that both Hope and Bill had kept it secret."

Frances felt as if her throat had closed, and she took a sip of tea in an effort to regain her composure. She couldn't find words.

"Because Hope was adopted I don't think Bill thought of it as incest. Or at least that's how he justified it. Was it so wrong to be attracted to her? He kept asking me that. She wasn't his blood, he said. She wasn't his child. I was so confused, so uncertain. We argued, but eventually . . . eventually I gave in. I wanted to believe he wasn't evil."

"And he convinced you of that?" The words came out before Frances could stop herself.

"I know," she sputtered. "I know what you're thinking. That I'm a horrible woman, a worse mother. Don't think a day hasn't passed without my sharing your views. I think a part of me was so horrified, I denied it had happened. I couldn't accept the truth. I wanted the whole experience to be some awful nightmare, some concoction in my head, because I looked at Bill and he was the man I loved. And I couldn't get myself to stop loving him, so it was easier to make myself disbelieve."

Frances knew she should say something comforting but couldn't bring herself to. "Did Hope ever tell you how she felt?"

"Not at the time. She refused to testify at the hearing, which took place before the Board of Registration in Medicine. The whole focus was whether Dr. Frank had violated her confidences. Bill didn't say anything, either, on the advice of his lawyer. But he had to tell his partners and they asked him to leave the law firm immediately," she said, almost as an afterthought.

How had Adelaide and Bill managed to keep his abuse secret? How come there hadn't been some kind of public outcry? A respected lawyer raped his minor daughter, and nobody knew?

As if reading her mind, Adelaide continued, "The hearing was closed and the records sealed because Hope was a minor. Bill's exit agreement included confidentiality provisions on both sides. He was lucky the firm agreed to that, but I think his partners were as anxious as he was to keep all of this out of the press. There were a few months when people talked, or at least I thought they did. I'd get an occasional odd look, or we wouldn't get an invitation that I'd expected. But basically it passed. Bill's been a member of this community for a long time. His friends weren't looking to find the worst."

She paused and stared directly at Frances. "I know what you must think of him. But he was destroyed. He begged me not to leave him. He said he would make it up to me, to her. He promised to redeem himself. And he did. He was a wonderful father to her after that. He was loving, careful. I know he never did anything inappropriate again. And it's why he went to extraordinary lengths to see this marriage happen. He knew it would be best for her, and he wanted her to be happy, to be safe."

Frances cringed. *And what about you?* she wanted to ask. How could Adelaide have called Bill her husband? How could they have lived day in and day out with the consequences of their conduct? How could she think that redemption was even possible?

"I love Bill. I know that must seem incredible to you after all I've said, but I do. Perhaps none of us can ever understand each other's relationships, what makes two people attracted to each other, care about each other, and want to build lives together. But he took me in when I was alone. He helped me to come to terms with Morgan's death. He gave me a life here in Manchester, and I was scared to be alone again. He's not evil. He's a good person. Ever since Hope's emergency, he's tried to make up for what happened, and now it's too late. He'll never know if Hope forgave him."

"So you and Hope never discussed it?"

She paused. "Yes. Once. About a month ago, she actually climbed onto the window ledge above the patio and started screaming. 'How could you allow it? How could you not protect me? How can you live with yourself?' Kathleen went running upstairs to Bill's office to try to get her back inside. I just stood there frozen, listening, begging. 'I can't trust my own mother,' she hollered. 'I hate you. I hope you rot in hell.' That's what she said. And then all of a sudden, she stopped. When I went inside she was curled up in a ball in Kathleen's arms, in tears. We never mentioned it again."

Adelaide looked exhausted, as if her confession had taken every ounce of energy she had. As she stood, she stumbled and had to catch her balance by holding onto the arm of the sofa. "I don't know what to say," she said, although her comment wasn't directed at Frances. "I must be some kind of a monster. Who doesn't protect their own child from the worst possible assaults? There isn't a day that I don't ask myself that question. But I didn't know what to do, and I convinced myself that we could remedy the situation. Here I threw myself into this wedding so that she would feel celebrated, special, and beautiful. She was supposed to finally recognize how much her parents loved her. And how sorry we were. We are."

Adelaide's knees buckled, and she struggled to remain upright. Frances didn't move. She knew she should assist her, comfort her, but she couldn't. The image of Hope hanging in her closet filled her vision, the torture and pain she'd endured in life finally over. For a moment the thought that her killer had actually been compassionate flashed through her mind, a mercy killing of a girl whose life had been filled with demons. She leaned back in her chair and felt the spindles against her spine.

"Please don't tell a soul," Adelaide murmured. "All of this can't possibly have anything to do with her death."

29

The Avery Bowes Institute was an impressive white stone building with a slate roof and two pairs of thick columns marking the entrance. To the left, a brick path led away from the structure and into a generous lawn dotted with wrought-iron benches, a marble fountain with a sculpture of Neptune from whose mouth the water percolated, and a cedar-mulched loop of track for jogging. To the right, an asphalt parking lot was filled with large practical cars and SUVs. Frances pulled into one of the marked spots.

But for a pair of white-coated doctors crossing the parking lot, the grounds were deserted. There was no trace of patients, health-care providers, nurses, or anyone else enjoying the beautiful afternoon. Her footsteps as she walked up the wide wooden stairs echoed in the exceptional quiet. She opened the large black door and stepped into a dramatic circular entrance. In the center was an oversize burl-wood desk with no one in attendance. A small white sign on the front of the desk instructed her, "Please ring bell for service," which she did.

"May I help you?" came a woman's voice over an intercom.

Frances looked around, startled by the sound, and saw the black speaker propped next to a large ledger. "I'm here to see Dr. Frank. Peter Frank."

"First door on the right," the voice replied. For a moment, Frances felt as if she were Dorothy in *The Wizard of Oz* about to discover the pudgy fellow behind the curtain pretending to be a wizard. Why have a reception desk if no one was there to man it? Nonetheless, she heeded the instructions.

The door opened into a sunny but otherwise generic waiting room filled with simple oak furniture and two potted palms. One woman wearing a cropped tank top, hip-hugging jeans, and a nostril ring sat reading a well-worn copy of *Redbook*. She looked up briefly with big blue eyes and cast a vacant stare before flipping the page and returning her attention to the magazine.

Frances approached an interior window and stared through at a cramped secretarial station, where a heavy-set woman sat eating a meatball sandwich. The buttons on her white uniform were stretched to popping across her stomach. "Just take a seat. The doctor will be with you shortly."

Frances settled herself into a chair opposite the *Redbook* reader and stared at a poster outlining the Patients' Bill of Rights. CONFIDENTIALITY. There it was, listed in large print.

The door into the waiting room opened and a tall, thin man stepped through. He wore a wrinkled dress shirt and a pair of black pleated pants. He extended his hand and introduced himself. "Peter Frank."

"Thanks for agreeing to see me."

He glanced at the young woman, then down at his watch. "You're early again," he said. "I'll see you at quarter of."

She didn't respond.

He shrugged. "Why don't we step outside," he said. "I could use a little fresh air."

Together they retraced Frances's steps back out through the entrance. Dr. Frank led the way across the lawn to the track loop. "Is it all right to walk while we talk?"

Frances nodded. "How long have you been at Avery Bowes?"

"Too long, most would say. There's so much work to be done here, people in a great deal of need, that the days have turned into months, which have turned into years. I think I'm into my second decade." He chuckled to himself. "Emotional illness is an amorphous beast. There's so much we don't know. And the funding is either nonexistent or mediocre at best, so progress is slow. But for the research departments at several major pharmaceutical companies – everyone's looking for another Prozac – we'd be quite stymied."

Frances knew little about the politics of mental health care, so she thought it best just to listen.

"The other major hurdle facing those of us who try to deal with the realm of emotional disease is societal ignorance. People don't understand it. It's less tangible;

you can't see bipolar disorder on an X-ray or schizo-
phrenia on an EKG. I can't tell you how many parents
of severely disturbed adolescents or spouses of very
sick adults have said to me, 'If she would just get out of
bed and get some exercise,' or, 'That isn't any reason
not to help with the children,' or, 'Our life is so perfect,
I just don't see what there is to be upset about.' It
astounds me. I wish I could point to a broken bone or a
tumor, but I can't. The eyes of loved ones glaze over
when I raise an issue of chemical imbalance or serotonin levels. But this is real. As real as anything else we
have to battle." He turned to her. "It's a thankless job, a
thankless profession. I've started to ask myself why I
ever got involved."

Dr. Frank reached out and grabbed her elbow, pulling
her toward him just as a man in gray sweats jogged by.
"People around here won't necessarily avoid you," he
said, releasing her arm and stepping farther away as if
embarrassed. They walked for several yards in silence.
"I'm very sorry to hear about Hope's death, but I don't
know how I can help you. Although it's sometimes hard
for me to imagine after everything the Lawrences have
put me through that I still have any obligations to them,
Hope was my patient."

"I respect that. You testified at a hearing about sexual
abuse that Hope had disclosed to you. Abuse she'd
suffered. Adelaide told me what Bill did, and she can
probably get copies of those transcripts because Hope
was, at least arguably, a party to the hearing. I can't
imagine the Board of Registration would deny her that.

I was just wondering if you could talk to me to save me some time."

"I'm not sure I understand the connection to her death."

"And I'm not sure I can explain it," she said. That Hope was vulnerable, that she put herself in the way of danger, that she'd been abused before, all were characteristics that made her a prime victim. The question was, who had exploited that now?

"Well, I suppose that's why you're doing the investigating and I'm not." He made a clicking sound with his jaw as he thought for a moment. "It was actually more complicated than what you've described. I'll give you the procedural history for starters; it doesn't involve any patient–therapist disclosures."

"I'll take what I can get."

"I filed what's called a 51A report. It's actually Chapter 119 of the Massachusetts General Laws. Section 51A mandates that a health-care worker or various other professional people notify the Department of Child Welfare if he or she has reasonable cause to believe that a person under eighteen is being abused or is at substantial risk of harm. Based on my therapy with Hope, I felt obligated to report."

Frances stopped in her tracks. "Did you have reason to think the abuse was continuing? You started seeing Hope almost a year after her hospital emergency."

Dr. Frank ran his fingers through his hair and looked down at the ground. He kicked a few of the pine needles back and forth between his scuffed loafers.

"That's true. But my understanding of the requirements of 51A covered this circumstance. Bill Lawrence and his attorney disagreed. They filed a complaint before the Board of Registration in Medicine, accusing me of violating my statutory duties to protect patient confidences. That's what the hearing was about. In order to assess whether I'd done something wrong, the board had to examine my underlying concerns for Hope."

"I see. So there was no hearing on your 51A report?"

"That's right. It's my understanding that DCW investigated, found no problem, and closed the case. I seriously doubt whether Hope would ever have said anything."

"But her pregnancy—"

"By the time the agency got involved, enough time had passed. Nothing in Hope's hospital records identified Bill as responsible for her unwanted pregnancy. DCW's concern is immediate harm. They've got too many kids sitting in their own feces waiting for food that isn't coming to worry about what happened years before. So I became the defendant, not him, a brilliant piece of legal strategy. The issue was my conduct, my disclosures, not the fact that he'd had sex with his fourteen-year-old daughter. Frankly, it was obscene."

"What happened at the Board of Registration?"

"It eventually found in my favor in a split decision. The one member who disagreed wrote a lengthy and scathing decision. I emerged with my license intact, but barely; it was an expensive and emotional battle that took nearly a year of my life. My marriage suffered. I hardly saw my kids. I was fortunate to have the support of several close colleagues here, but it was a difficult time professionally, too."

"Do you have copies of the transcripts?"

"Yes."

"Will you give them to me?"

He thought for a moment. "There's nothing that precludes me from sharing them with you, if that's your question. And you know what? Part of me doesn't care anymore. I knew the world of mental health care was screwed up, but that hearing was a mockery."

They walked a few paces in silence. His set jaw made his face look hard, unforgiving. She understood his bitterness. Bill, whose outrageous conduct was the issue to begin with, had tried to take his medical license. How could he not be angry with the Lawrence family? He'd tried to help, and it had nearly cost him his career.

"But Hope continued to see you?"

"It wasn't continual. When Bill brought the Board of Registration action, I stopped seeing her. She and I both knew our conversations couldn't be confidential and that there was too much discord between her family and me for me to be an effective therapist. I hadn't heard from her for years. After she got engaged, she contacted me. Perhaps she realized that I'd done nothing improper, that my only concern was to help her. Perhaps she came back because there was nowhere else to turn. Her therapy had been beneficial, and I believe she trusted me. Oftentimes major events like a pending marriage can trigger old emotions. It's not uncommon for people to return to therapy when their lives are on the brink of change."

"And you agreed to start seeing her again?"

"I wasn't going to penalize her for her father's conduct, but I had nothing further to do with her family. I'm surprised the police found the report. Records from the Department of Child Welfare are supposed to be confidential unless the findings warrant pressing criminal charges."

"The police haven't found anything as far as I know," Frances replied. A report filed a decade earlier from a closed case was probably gathering dust in a state storage facility, if it hadn't been destroyed. "Could I ask you one more thing?"

He turned to face her.

"What sort of consulting did you do for Fiona Cabot?"

"I don't know what you're talking about."

"She paid you five thousand dollars for a series of consultations. Did those have anything to do with Hope or the Lawrences?"

"I can't answer that."

"Did you tell her Hope couldn't have children?"

"Why would I do that?"

"Isn't it considered improper to see related patients without their consent?"

He didn't answer for a moment. "I've already made one mistake."

"Might I suggest more than one?" Frances stared into his eyes, wondering what secrets he knew and wouldn't share. She wanted the transcripts; she wanted an explanation of Fiona's visits. It seemed an odd coincidence that Hope and her future mother-in-law would share the same therapist, and she didn't believe in coincidences. Furthermore, from the invoice she'd seen, Fiona had paid Dr. Frank $1,250 an hour, more than six times what most well-qualified therapists made.

"Why?" Dr. Frank asked, interrupting her stream of consciousness.

"Why what?"

"Why are you doing this, undertaking this investigation?"

It was a question she'd asked herself more than once, and the answer still eluded her. She wondered whether she'd ever have the kind of understanding of herself and her motivations that she wished she had. She'd never seen a therapist before; in fact, she'd considered the idea of paying someone to listen to problems a narcissistic self-indulgence. But at various times in her life she'd had moments of reconsidering, only to dismiss the thoughts as quickly as they had come. Maybe she'd been too hasty. Self-awareness, or at least the ability to answer simple questions about why she agonized over the investigation into Hope's death when the district attorney's office was competent to handle it, seemed worth the premium. But judging from Hope's experience with Dr. Frank, psychiatry only made matters more complicated.

"I could probably make something up to sound good, but in all honesty, I don't know," she replied. "It just seems like something I have to do . . . for my family."

"Then I hope for your sake you find your answers."

"Me, too."

*

The Church of the Holy Spirit was empty. The sun had faded, and the gray light of dusk partially obscured the designs in the stained glass. Frances sat in the last pew and stared at the altar, the large Bible propped on a stand, the gold cross, and the series of candles in brass holders. The simplicity was beautiful.

She'd returned to the house at Smith's Point only to receive a note from Adelaide asking her to come here. But there was no sign of anyone, and she wasn't sure how long she could sit still in the growing darkness. She'd swallowed two cups of 7-Eleven coffee on the drive back from the Avery Bowes Institute. Although the coffee had tasted weak, the caffeine had gone straight to her nerves. She felt wired.

She removed the stack of papers from the crinkled brown bag that she held on her lap. It was only a small portion of the transcript in *Board of Registration in Medicine v. Peter Frank, MD*, but it was all she had until she received the rest of the materials that Dr. Frank had promised could be copied. She flipped past the cover page and began to read what appeared to be a prepared statement by Dr. Frank.

> I had been the patient's therapist for more than nine months before she chose to share with me the tragic and traumatic events that transpired between her and her father. Prior to her recitation of her full history, we had explored numerous issues involving self-loathing, self-destructive behavior, shame, and other feelings of intense inadequacy. It is clear to me that the patient's history had severely damaged not only her self-image, but also her ability to trust.

Although the patient repeatedly expressed that the sexual relationship with her father ended when she was hospitalized for complications related to a terminated pregnancy, I felt that my obligations under section 51A were triggered nonetheless. This patient went to severe lengths to attempt to cover up the abuse that had been inflicted upon her. In doing so, she had caused herself irreparable harm. Yet on several occasions, she relayed that she'd found the sexual experience pleasurable. She missed the intimacy with her father.

I am not confident of her accuracy as a reporter. In my professional opinion, were the relationship to begin anew, she would not come forward. Disclosure in my opinion was warranted to protect her future safety.

Her reading was interrupted when she heard the click of a lock echo in the empty room. She turned to see Father Whitney and Adelaide enter the building together. The minister held her aunt's arm and almost seemed to be keeping her righted. He glanced around and smiled as he recognized Frances. They shuffled over to where she stood. Adelaide sank into the empty bench.

"Your aunt needs you to take her home now," Father Whitney said. Adelaide pursed her lips, and Frances couldn't tell whether she was about to speak or cry.

Frances nodded. "Of course. My car's outside."

"I know this has been a very difficult day for all of you. These are trying times."

"I gather Adelaide's told you what's transpired."

"She needed comfort and prayer. I fault myself for

not better ministering to Hope. The sins Bill committed are egregious. The betrayal of a child's trust is difficult for us to even comprehend. I had spent so much time with Hope that I would have thought she could share her struggles, but I was wrong. Her confessions were incomplete. She kept the full truth hidden from everyone but God. Today Adelaide has spoken for her."

Adelaide's eyes were closed. It seemed as if she were present in body only. Her face registered no comprehension of the conversation.

"Adelaide and Bill have a difficult path ahead. But the Lord forgives us all. Even those who inflict terrible harm."

Frances wanted to object. She understood rationally that Father Whitney's role as clergy was to console, but she found it impossible to believe that anyone could forgive what Bill had done to his daughter. It was the worst kind of violation. What about the wrath of God, the God who punished? When did that God appear?

"She also shared with me developments in the investigation. I'm saddened to hear that a murderer is still free in our community."

"Me, too."

"Are you certain Carl's not responsible?"

Frances shrugged. "I'm not sure of anything. But I've heard his story, and we may be able to corroborate at least part of it. He loved Hope; I am convinced of that. And she trusted him, apparently even with her closest secrets."

"What do you mean?"

"She confided in him things that no one else knew –

the abuse and betrayal she'd experienced in her life. I believe there's a lot he's still hiding because he wants to protect her."

"Such as?"

"You mentioned her incomplete confessions to you. As far as I can tell, she confided in Carl and in her diaries. That's it. Not even Adelaide knew how much she was suffering. We haven't found the journals other than the one you gave us, but they have to be some-where. We have to find out what happened, and I'm now wondering whether they could help."

He rubbed his nose with his knuckle and furrowed his brow. After a moment he spoke in a voice barely above a whisper. "I want to believe in the innocence of all mankind, but I haven't heard you say anything that would convince me Carl didn't murder her."

"Maybe I just want to believe in his innocence and I'm really wrong, but something tells me I'm not."

"Perhaps you put too much faith in the fact that he loved her. But don't let him blind you. Crimes of passion occur over and over, and all the love in the world won't stop them. Only faith can do that. Faith is our healer, our redeemer."

If only it were that simple, Frances thought as she reached for her aunt's hand.

30

Frances sat on the edge of the bed and dialed Sam's number on her cell phone. She hadn't spoken to him for two days, and she needed to hear the sound of his voice, the solace he would inevitably provide. She listened to the ring over and over, but there was no answer. He wasn't home, and Luddite that he was, he had no answering machine. Disappointed, she dialed her house. Perhaps he had gone to feed the dogs. But when her own voice came on to announce that she was unavailable, she refrained from leaving a message.

She was about to turn off the power when the little envelope in the lower-right-hand corner of the phone's screen indicated she had a message. She retrieved it. "Frances, this is Carl. There were some things that I couldn't say the other day in front of Teddy, but I think we should talk. I have Hope's diaries. Please come alone." His voice cracked and she heard a cough in the background. "My phone's out, so I'm calling from a pay phone. But I'll be on my boat if you can make it here."

The message had been left at 5:34.

She replayed it, wanting to decipher clues from the

intonation of his voice, but the static on the line and his monochromatic tone gave her no hints as to what he might have to say. She got up, walked to the window, and looked across the expanse of lawn leading to Teddy's cottage. A part of her yearned to go sit with her grandmother, to hear the familiar rattle in her voice, to smell her menthol cigarettes, and to enjoy the inevitable offer of a glass of wine or a vodka tonic.

Why couldn't she and Teddy believe in the police work that had been done? Why was she digging up the horrors of Hope's past? She was struggling for some connection, some way to order the mysteries she'd uncovered, but so far she'd only been saddened and defeated by what she had learned. Nothing had brought her any closer to finding the killer. She, like her aunt, needed closure, to put the investigation behind her and return home to her life. What could another trip to Gloucester achieve? Could Hope's diaries help in this roundabout investigation? What could Carl have to say that he hadn't shared with Teddy, the only person who had believed in him from the very beginning?

The fishing pier seemed unusually quiet even for the late hour. Other than a green Oldsmobile and a black truck with a rusty body, the parking lot was empty. Unlike her last visit, this time there wasn't the activity of boats unloading and trucks loading the day's catch. Frances headed down the walkway to the dock where the *Lady Hope* was tied, wishing all the while that there was some evidence of human life besides herself and the temperamental lobsterman she was about to meet.

"Carl?" she called as she approached his boat. Other than a stretch of police tape dangling off one side, the deck looked just as it had before, with an array of tools scattered near the entrance to the interior cabin and a collection of lobster traps stacked at the stern. "Carl," she said again, but there was no answer.

Frances glanced back up toward the parking lot, wondering for a moment if he'd come to meet her. Or perhaps she'd arrived too late. Or maybe she should have checked his apartment. But he'd specifically said that he would be on his boat. She'd replayed his message on the drive north and had no doubt about his precise words.

She debated going aboard but thought it best to wait, to not be too intrusive. She glanced at her watch: 8:13. Trying to will the minutes to pass, she paced back and forth along the dock, gazing down at the black water below. *Go home*, said a voice inside her. She'd doubted the wisdom of this journey before she'd ever set out for Gloucester.

She paced back and forth on the slightly swaying dock for nearly half an hour and checked her watch one more time. He'd invited her to his boat. Could there be any real harm in taking a look around? She doubted that the police would have missed anything when they'd executed their warrant, but she was curious to see for herself. She swung her leg over the side and stepped aboard.

She opened the swinging doors and peered inside the

cabin. A tin pot smoked on a small burner in the galley kitchen. An opened and empty can of tomato soup rested on the counter, but its contents had been reduced to a blackened tar on the bottom of the pot. She shut off the flame and looked around. Other than a radio handset dangling from its cord the interior of the cabin seemed undisturbed. A collection of maps and navigational documents, a kerosene lamp, and a copy of Shakespeare's sonnets were arrayed on a table surrounded by a banquette. A small washboard-style door at the far end of the cabin was ajar, and as Frances approached, she could see the boat's enormous engine. "Carl," she called again, uneasy now. She looked inside. Nothing seemed out of place. A greasy rag and a screwdriver on the ground evidenced Carl's efforts to fix something. She remembered the clanging and banging she'd heard the last time she'd been on his boat.

She moved to the head and opened the latch. Nothing seemed disturbed. She peered inside a mirrored wall cabinet and scanned the contents of the two shelves: shaving cream, a razor, Band-Aids, nothing unusual.

Just then she heard footsteps on the walkway. She hurried out to the deck and saw a figure descending to the float. A baseball cap obscured the face, and she felt a momentary rush of panic. "Carl?" she called.

"No, I'm afraid not," said the male voice. To her surprise, it sounded familiar.

"Father Whitney?"

"Yes," he replied, removing his hat.

Relieved, she climbed out onto the dock, quickly approached the reverend, and extended her hand.

"Good to see you," she said, realizing that she truly meant it. The eerie quiet of the fishing pier, the discovery of the burned pot, and the mysteriousness of Carl's message had conspired to make her imagination race. Seeing the minister calmed her.

"What are you doing here?" he asked, taking Frances's hand and holding it in both of his.

She realized the same question could be posed to him. "I'm meeting Carl."

He lowered his voice to almost a whisper. "And I, too. He called me at the parish house earlier today and asked me to come here this evening. He said he wanted to meet with me to discuss some things about Hope's passing, some details he thought I should know." Father Whitney removed a watch from his pocket that was attached to his belt loop with a gold chain. "I'm a little late, but I couldn't get away earlier. We have many parishioners who are anxious to talk. They need to talk. The Lawrences are special people. It's times like this that we need to come together as a church family."

"Did he tell you what he wanted to talk with you about?"

"He said nothing beyond what I've just told you. Was he more expansive with you?"

"No." Frances scanned the boats once more.

Reverend Whitney walked to the *Lady Hope* and leaned over, peering onto the deck. "You're sure this is his boat?"

"Yes," she replied.

The minister held onto the handrail and lowered himself onto the deck. Having climbed on, he remained still, adjusting to the slight sway of the boat in the water. Then he moved to the cabin entrance and stuck his head in. "There's something cooking," he remarked. "Or at least there was. It appears rather burnt."

She didn't reply.

"I had the distinct impression that there was some urgency to this meeting. I do hope the man's all right," he said when he reappeared.

Frances perched against the stack of lobster crates. She agreed with the reverend that something felt amiss. His charred soup only heightened her uneasiness. She scanned the black sea, searching for an answer in the tide.

"What did Hope tell you about him?"

Father Whitney turned to face her. His expression was difficult to read. "Hope was a member of my parish, an important one, although I shouldn't draw distinctions because everyone is important. She and I spoke often. I was very fond of her."

"Many people were."

"Yes, that's true. As for Carl, I believe that Hope had very complex feelings toward him, feelings tied up with both his age and her family's disapproval. Based on what Adelaide confessed to me yesterday, I now suspect her difficulties were closely related to Bill's conduct. But our discussions centered around how attached to Carl she was and yet how sinful, how unclean, she felt when she was with him."

"In what way?"

"She didn't want to elaborate, and it's my role to hear only what a person chooses to tell me. God hears all, though, and she knew that. We're all mortal, I told her over and over, but she was her harshest critic by far. Just this spring she asked me to perform a reconciliation of the penitent, which we did together."

"Which is?" Frances asked. Then she thought to add, "Sorry I'm not as up as I should be on my Episcopalian ceremonies."

He smiled. "No reason you should be if the church isn't a big part of your life. Frankly, even many of those who profess to be good Episcopalians couldn't tell you much about rituals or liturgy. They come to Sunday services, but they don't understand. In any event, reconciliation is a pastoral service to help parishioners seek forgiveness. It's a spiritual cleansing of sorts. Hope told me she had squandered the inheritance of our Lord's saints and wandered far in a land of waste. The reconciliation was a way to bring her back."

"Did Carl talk to you, too?"

"I've never met him. That's why I find it confusing that he thought to call me. If anyone, he should speak to Adelaide and Bill."

Frances shrugged. A silence fell, and her eyes wandered back and forth over the deck, looking at the assortment of buoys, ropes, lines, crates, bait buckets, all the equipment to catch a lobster. As she looked, she noticed a rope, one end of which turned several times over a metal cleat while the other end disappeared into the water below. An anchor line seemed unlikely given that the *Lady Hope* was well fastened to the float. A lobster trap so close to the dock seemed similarly implausible. She took hold of it and began to pull, dragging it slowly out of the water. The task grew more difficult with each hoist. The wet rope was slippery, and she had difficulty maintaining a grip.

"Could I offer assistance?" Father Whitney asked.

She nodded. Although it felt awkward to ask a priest for help with such a laborious endeavor, she had no alternative. No one else was around.

He positioned himself between her and the water, leaned in, and grabbed hold about a yard below where she held. His long sleeves were wet, but she watched him wrap the rope around his strong hands, securing a grip. Together they pulled. Harder. She felt the sweat of exertion break out on her forehead despite the cool breeze.

Suddenly the rope emerged. They stumbled backward from the release of tension. Reverend Whitney held the frayed end in his hand. There was nothing attached.

"I'm sorry," Frances said. "I don't know what got into me. I should have left it alone. And now you're wet."

"There's no need to apologize," he said, leaning over and gently kissing the top of her head. The familiarity of the gesture startled her, but she had to admit that there was something soothing about the tender touch of a paternal figure. He stood and rolled up his wet sleeves.

Just then her eye caught something, a flat bluish white surface. She gasped. "Oh no!" she heard herself scream, but the voice sounded far away. She closed her eyes, knowing full well what the ocean was about to disgorge. A body. Blue jeans. A bare torso. Bare feet.

Dark hair on the back of the head, swaying in the water like seaweed. Carl had been wrong. Men did float face-down, pointing into the black abyss of their own destiny. Or at least he did.

"Dear God."

Her legs couldn't support her weight, and she collapsed. She heard the splinter of wood as she crushed a lobster crate and felt a sharp pain in her side. It didn't matter. Sinking down, she put her head between her knees, struggling to breathe, and felt wetness seep into her clothing. She heard Father Whitney scrambling on the deck, the clatter as he untied a line hook to drag the body out of the sea, and the thump as the lifeless form landed on the boat.

She glanced up only once, long enough to see a reddish brown stain covering most of the back of Carl's head. As the world went dark around her, she heard the minister's breathless voice, "May your rest be this day in peace and your dwelling place in the paradise of God."

31

Frances and Elvis stood on the deck of the *Lady Hope* listening to the sound of yellow police tape flapping against the side of her deck. The police had finished their official search of the vessel, but the harbor master had moved her to a slip away from the marina's main activity until such time as the police released her and she could be sold. In the meantime, she rocked gently beside other seemingly lost vessels. The salty air blew cold on Frances's cheek, and she felt a sorrow saturate her skin as she scanned the horizon. If Carl hadn't made bail, he'd be alive today.

After the emergence of his body events of the previous night blurred. Father Whitney must have called the police, because she remembered sounds of sirens, flashing lights, and people moving about the deck of the boat. Someone had escorted her into an ambulance, taken her pulse and vital signs, but the faces and specifics escaped her. It wasn't until she'd returned to Smith's Point that she remembered Carl's words. *I have Hope's diaries.* That's what they were here to find.

As Elvis updated her on the details of Carl's death, the words of his narration sounded distant. Cause was a blunt-force injury: brain hemorrhage, compressed skull fracture, a hit on the left side of the head. There was no water in his lungs, which meant that he had died before he was thrown overboard. The night before, the police had recovered a large sledgehammer covered with Carl's blood from a Dumpster behind the harbor master's office. Forensics had lifted a thumbprint off the handle, but there hadn't been a computer match in the commonwealth's database, so the print was being sent to the FBI, where the computerized information was more extensive.

"We went to his apartment around six this morning, but someone had gotten there first," Elvis said in a raised voice, an obvious effort to get her attention. "The place was ransacked. The door was busted in, not that it took much. Stuff broken, thrown off the shelves, clothes pulled out of the closet."

"Did anyone see anything?"

"The kid in the first-floor apartment said she heard footsteps on the stairs around three or four in the morning, but she assumed it was Carl. Apparently he kept weird hours, so she didn't think anything of it. She didn't hear or see anyone leave."

"Did they canvass the neighborhood?"

"It's a pretty tight-lipped community. You're not going to see much cooperation between the fishermen and the cops, but one woman across the street did mention seeing a guy in a foreign car asking for Carl. She hasn't seen him since."

"Any description of the driver?"

"Only that he looked rich – like that narrows the field."

"Was anything taken?"

Elvis shook his head. "We can't figure out for sure because there's no one around who can tell us what was supposed to be there. According to the landlady, he had no family. Never got any mail except for bills. It doesn't look like a robbery – several items of value were still there: a small stereo, a pair of aquamarine cuff links, a silver frame. I'd say whoever broke in wasn't looking for something to hock."

Her mind wandered as she stared out to sea. Mark's opinion, which Elvis included in his rendition of events, was that Carl had killed Hope and his death was revenge. But that assumed a fact she wasn't willing to accept.

"Where do you want to begin?" Elvis asked.

"I'll take the berth and you can search the galley."

They both went below, and Elvis began a systematic opening and shutting of cabinets, peering and checking. Frances pulled open the bifold door and stepped inside the forward cabin. She closed the door behind her, wanting to have a moment to assimilate the cramped space, the single berth with its cotton blanket rolled at one end, the single porthole window. Perhaps they'd come here when Hope felt she could no longer impose on Teddy. She ran her fingers along the thin mattress, the place that they had undoubtedly lain together, and tried to imagine their afternoons. They would have lain sideways to fit two bodies, and she imagined that Carl would run his hand along Hope's thin body as they snuggled like spoons. They would have shared stories, sometimes laughing, sometimes whispering, perhaps even crying, as the tide gently rocked the bed back and forth. As they glanced out the porthole, they would have seen the sky or the stars. For a moment she wished she could have had the same experience, the kind of quiet intimacy that for her was more passionate than anything else.

She shook her head and turned her attention back to the problem before her. She opened the storage cabinets and removed clothes, books, assorted fishing equipment, and an extra blanket. She knocked on the walls of the hull, wondering if a secret storage compartment had been installed to safeguard Hope's diaries, but she discerned no change in tonality. She lifted the mattress. The underside was empty. Although she was frustrated, it wasn't surprising that there were no diaries. Carl's boat had been searched once after his arrest, and combed over again by forensics just hours before. It was unlikely that anything important had been missed.

Frances sat on the berth and, without thinking, lay back against the pillow, detecting a faint smell of mildew. As she settled back, she felt something lumpy, a hard protrusion, and she shifted her position. No, she hadn't imagined it.

She got up and pressed her palms firmly into the mattress, moving them over the entire length of the canvas. She could feel at least five volumes, the hard corners and the flat covers. She should have known. Where else would a man store his lover's secrets?

She knew she should notify Elvis, but for one final minute she wanted to take in the peacefulness of the space and the romance that it must have encapsulated. In a moment it would be torn apart, the mattress violently split open and the diaries revealed. She wondered once again why all this sorrow had come to pass.

"Elvis," she called, although her own voice sounded foreign. "I found them."

"Teddy!" she called as she swung open the screen door. When she'd telephoned from the road to tell her grandmother she needed to come by, needed a favor, Teddy's irritation had been obvious. The death of Carl was more upsetting to her than she'd ever be willing to acknowledge, and Frances was quite sure she wanted to be alone. But this was important.

After dropping her knapsack on a chair by the door, she walked back to her grandmother's office.

Teddy sat with a pillow propped behind her back to soften the discomfort of the straight wooden chair. Although she leaned forward so that her eyes were less than a foot from the monitor, she gazed through a magnifying glass at the words on the screen.

As Frances leaned over her shoulders, she could smell the familiar talcum powder that Teddy used to coat her body after every shower or bath. She applied the powder with a giant satin puff, an item that she had refused to share even with her persistent, begging grandchildren. The ritual had seemed exotic, and Frances wondered whether her skin had absorbed so much over the years that the odor was permanent.

"What are you reading?" she asked.

"The Chancellor's reply. It sounds like Father Whitney will be canonized before long," she replied, resting her magnifying glass by her keyboard.

Frances read the message that filled the e-mail screen.

Thank you for your recent inquiry regarding Father Edgar Whitney and the Church of the Holy Spirit. The Episcopal Diocese is always happy to answer any questions concerning its clergy or any of their parishes. Your contemplation of making the church a beneficiary of your foundation is a blessing to us, but must only be done if you are fully satisfied and free of concerns.

Father Whitney completed seminary and was admitted to the priesthood in 1983. While an assistant rector at Christ Church in Barnstable, he requested a transfer within the Diocese. Because of a lack of available openings, he went initially to work at a camp for underprivileged boys in Orleans. He was very popular with the children, and he was able to demonstrate a great capacity for counseling and ministry. After that service, he was made rector of First Episcopal Church in Lynn. It is one of the most disadvantaged of our parishes and he performed a masterful job of making it a vital part of the community. He implemented a nursery school, ran a kitchen to provide meals for the homeless, and ministered to parishioners plagued by poverty, substance abuse, and broken homes. He certainly knows how to control costs, run outreach programs, and provide much-needed services on a fixed, limited budget.

The Diocese feels blessed to have Father Whitney as part of its clerical family and gives him the highest of recommendations. We think it is appropriate for you to place your faith in him and his parish as you contemplate your most generous gift. My thoughts and prayers are with you and your family during this time of suffering.

"Well, I suppose that debate can be laid to rest," Teddy remarked. "All I can think is that there won't be any foundation in Carl's memory. If I didn't have to live with your aunt and uncle, I'd consider starting one myself. That poor man."

"The police haven't been able to even find a next of kin to notify," Frances said, echoing her sentiment. Carl was someone whom no one would miss. She rested her hands on her grandmother's shoulder. "Could you ask the Chancellor one more thing for me?" she said.

"What's that?"

"I need to know about an Episcopalian minister named Roger Burgess. He worked somewhere on Cape Cod." Her grandmother gave her a quizzical look. "It may be a wild-goose chase, but you were the one who asked me to help Carl. I know nothing can change what's happened—"

"Hope's dead. Now Carl's dead," she interrupted, although the words were somewhat garbled by the frog in her throat.

"And we don't know who killed either of them. Please help me. Worst case is that I'm wrong, and this leads nowhere. But there won't be any harm done."

"That's what you think. All that gets done around here is harm," Teddy said as she leaned back toward the screen, clicked the reply box with the icon, and began to type Frances's request.

"Can I get you a sparkling water while you wait?" Henry asked. Dressed in a black turtleneck, black jeans, and motorcycle boots, he hardly looked the part of an office assistant. He paused from sorting through a stack of index cards and took a sip from a bottle of Perrier.

"No, thanks," Frances replied. The intercom buzzed just as she settled into the chair.

"She'll see you now," he said, motioning toward the door.

Inside, Ricki sat at her conference table with Hope's documents spread out in front of her and a cashmere blanket draped over her knees. She removed her glasses to greet Frances, then indicated for her to sit. "I have to apologize for a bad cold. It usually hits me when the seasons change." She covered her mouth just in time to block a sneeze, then dabbed her nose with a silk handkerchief. "How is the investigation going?"

"I wish I had more to report." *We've gone through two suspects and one's dead and we're no closer to finding Hope's killer*, she wanted to add.

Ricki leaned back in her chair and crossed her arms in front of her chest. "You said you were bringing other diaries, ones whose authenticity you don't question, so it would be a great help to take a look at those. But I can tell you now that this diary is forged." She patted the leather journal. Frances realized her jaw had dropped, as she couldn't contain her surprise. "I thought it would come as a shock, but there are several things that make me quite confident in my opinion. First, there's the slant issue that I raised when you first delivered the materials. The angle and degree of slant tends to be relatively constant in the same author. But in this diary there are dramatic fluctuations. Even accounting for someone with –" she paused, searching for the right word – "emotional troubles, these variations are material. Second, the baselines in the diary are straight. Virtually all of Hope's samples have a sloping baseline. Third, the pen pressure is quite different. The pressure on the diary is so intense that the pages have buckled. If you look at the samples," she said, pushing several toward Frances, "you'll notice a much lighter touch. At times, Hope's pen barely seems to touch the page."

Frances stared where Ricki indicated. It was true. She could see a difference after all.

"Finally, and most important, under a high-intensity magnifier you can see that even though the letters are connected in a script, each one has been done separately and attached afterward. The magnifier shows gaps that aren't readily visible to the naked eye." She flicked a switch on the microscope and slid a page of the diary between the viewfinder and the light. For a moment, Frances was reminded of observing leaves, bugs, and butterflies in elementary school science class.

Ricki adjusted the lens. Then she offered Frances a look. Sure enough, the white of the page could be seen, indicating slight breaks between each letter.

"So it's a good job."

Ricki pursed her lips. "Yes and no. The writer is obviously very familiar with Hope's handwriting. But he nor she is not a real forger. If I were to venture a guess, the person had extensive writings from Hope and was able to create a master alphabet to copy from. Do you see how thin the pages of this diary are?" Ricki held a single page up to the light. "If the forger had a stencil that could be placed behind each page, the letters could be traced. It's time-consuming, but not hard."

Frances tried to process all that Ricki was saying. Who had gone to the effort of creating a false diary for Hope? And why did someone want to do that? If anything, the text of the entries blamed Jack for her death. But if the purpose was to divert attention from the true killer, why wasn't the narrative stronger? Why leave so much to innuendo?

"I can't tell you much about the forger because I have nothing but imitated letters. Since the style is completely consistent, there are no idiosyncrasies in the penmanship to give me any clues into the personality of the author. However, if you have a suspect and provide me with samples and an exemplar, I may be able to help you. There could be similarities between aspects of the handwriting – the pressure, for instance – or the ink type on a sample may match. I'll certainly help if I can."

Frances stood to leave. Ricki cupped Frances's right hand in both of hers for a moment longer than was customary between strangers. "I know this complicates things for you and your family. I'm sorry," she said.

"Things were complicated long before you got involved," she replied, forcing a smile. And long before I did, too, she thought.

32

Frances watched the speedometer flutter at sixty-five. She'd been to Cape Cod only once before, to attend a debutante party in Osterville, and was basically unfamiliar with the hook of land that jutted out into the Atlantic. Scrubby pine, nice beaches, traffic, and more than a hundred college students gathering to celebrate their friend's ostensible coming out into society were all she remembered of the champagne-saturated weekend.

As she drove, she thought of the e-mail the Chancellor had sent to Teddy.

> In response to your inquiry, please be advised that Roger Burgess was defrocked more than a decade ago. He has never applied for reinstatement, and the Diocese has no further information to provide.

An Internet search of periodicals on the missing minister turned up a single story from the *Cape Cod Times*. The picture showed a dark-haired, smiling man in his mid-forties leaving the Barnstable Superior Court. He wore dark glasses and a large wooden cross around his neck. The caption read: "An act of God? Father Burgess found not liable in wrongful death action brought by Virginia Bailey's family."

But that had been all she needed. Hope's diary from the previous June and July – the most recent volume found in Carl's mattress – contained several references to "Ginny" and the "Bailey family." The most haunting sentences of an entry dated June 28 still resonated in Frances's memory; "She and I are soul mates in our suffering. Why is it that wherever we turn for protection, we are betrayed? Can anyone be safe? Does anyone care whether we are?"

She hit the accelerator.

Cove Road – the address for Ruth Bailey – was one of several streets within a golf-course subdivision called Cove Hollow just off Route 6 at the Centerville exit. Frances drove through a set of large gates and past an oval sign, careful to steer clear of the many battery-powered golf carts weaving across the road. Past the fourth hole, the houses began to crop up: uniform Capes with dormers on the back side, nonfunctional shutters, and attached garages set on square lots. Many had quarter board signs over the garage doors with names in gilded letters. The color of the mailbox out front and slight variations in landscaping marked the only differences in this residential community.

The garage door at 1313 Cove Road was open, and she could see a maroon Plymouth with its driver's-side door ajar and the engine idling. Frances parked her car and walked up the driveway just as an elderly woman appeared from the house and got in the car, pulling the door shut loudly.

She tapped on the window, and the woman started. Her right hand gripped the steering wheel as she cracked the window and looked out with terror in her hazel eyes. She was in her late sixties, with auburn hair, red cheeks, and deep crow's-feet. She wore a navy dress. A small gold cross necklace was visible beneath her lace collar. On the seat beside her was a basket with knitting needles and balls of yarn protruding.

"Ruth Bailey?"

The woman nodded.

"I'm sorry to bother you. I truly am. But I very much need a moment of your time. I believe my cousin Hope Lawrence was a friend of your daughter's."

Ruth turned her head away from Frances and peered out over her steering wheel for a moment before speaking. When she spoke, her words were slow and deliberate. "That name isn't familiar. And my daughter's been dead a long time."

"I know, and I'm so very sorry." Frances paused, wondering how to explain to a total stranger that the connection between Hope and Virginia Bailey was the key to discovering Hope's murderer. She'd convinced herself of that. "Please, can you spare five minutes? That's all I ask. I just have a few questions about Father Burgess and his connection to your daughter. I would have called, but your number's unlisted."

"There are very few people whom I want to find me these days." Ruth glanced at her knitting, then turned to Frances. The few freckles on her nose gave her a girlish quality despite her age. "I was off to a knitting group. We make children's sweaters to sell at the Christmas fair at our church. We have one of the most successful booths. Usually everything gets sold."

"I can come back," she offered.

"No, that's all right. If your cousin was a friend of my Ginny's, then you're welcome in my house." She turned off the engine and got out, leaving her basket behind.

Frances followed her through the side door into a sun-filled, wallpapered kitchen, a linoleum floor that sparkled, and an embroidered banner mounted about the windowsill that read: "God Bless This Home." The room was impeccable. Clean potholders hung on color-coordinated plastic hooks over the stove. Nothing cluttered the rose-colored counters. A single place mat and napkin in its ring were the only objects on the round table.

"Could I offer you anything?" Ruth asked, putting her car keys in a small basket by the entrance to the garage.

"No, thank you."

"Why don't we sit where it's more comfortable?"

They walked through the kitchen, past a half-bath papered with a nativity scene repeating every six inches, and into the living room. The shades were drawn, and the dark upholstered furniture had doilies draped over the backs and arms. Ruth offered her a seat, and as she sat in a rocking chair facing the fireplace, Frances noticed an eight by ten portrait of an attractive young woman set against a studio cloud background. She had an oval face, light brown hair tied back in a ponytail, and deep blue eyes. "That's Ginny," Ruth said, following Frances's gaze. "She was twenty-one in that picture. Two years before she died."

"You're kind to talk to me. I appreciate it."

"Why don't you tell me why you're here and what I can do."

Frances quickly summarized. She explained that her cousin had been murdered. In searching for anything that might lead them to the killer, they'd looked in Hope's diary and found references to Father Burgess and Ginny, whom she'd determined was Virginia Bailey. From her knapsack, she produced a computer printout of the newspaper article and picture. "In all honesty, I don't know how they knew each other or knew of each other, but Hope wrote about your daughter as if they had a spiritual affinity."

"Almost everyone who met Ginny did," Ruth replied. She walked over to a chest of drawers to the left of the fireplace. From the top one, she removed a rectangular box, which she kept on her lap, unopened, after she returned to her seat. "My Ginny was a wonderful girl. You wouldn't find a sweeter child, a more giving daughter. But when she graduated from college – she went to the University of Massachusetts at Amherst and graduated with a degree in psychology – she just seemed to have trouble. I'm not sure whether it was the difficulties of finding a job. There weren't too many opportunities for her here on the Cape, but she kept saying she wasn't ready to leave home."

"That's understandable," Frances remarked, wanting to say something reassuring.

"I think it was in part that her father had passed away her junior year. He had a heart attack. It was the first real pain in her life, and she had a very difficult time adjusting. We'd been a very normal family. Or perhaps I should say unusual in this day and age in that we were so ordinary. Charles and I had been married nearly twenty-five years. He'd had a wonderful job working at Polaroid, and I stayed at home to raise our children, Virginia and her younger brother, Charlie. They were actually Irish twins, just ten months apart." She laughed. "We were comfortable living in Dedham. Do you know it?"

Frances shook her head.

"It's a suburb of Boston. A beautiful town. We moved to the Cape when my husband took early retirement. Charlie never really lived here. He had gone to West Point and then joined the air force. He's a pilot now."

"Congratulations."

"Yes. He's quite accomplished." She smiled. "Please forgive me. I don't have many visitors," she offered, apparently in explanation for her digressions. "Ginny started to have issues after Charles's death. She stopped calling home. She didn't return my calls or respond to my letters. Her grades dropped. When she came home for spring break her junior year she seemed different, distant. She wandered about at night, unable to sleep. She lost her appetite. Shortly after she returned I got a call from her student adviser. She thought Ginny had some adjustment problems and should see a therapist. It was a very difficult conversation for me. Don't misunderstand me. I wanted nothing more than for my child to be happy but having a stranger tell me she needed a psychiatrist was hard. My husband and I didn't do things that way."

"But Virginia was a psychology major?"

"Yes. The difference between two generations, I suppose. Although when this started, she'd been an English major. I guess she'd taken enough psychology classes to switch at the last moment. In any event, I drove up and took her out to lunch and tried my best to have a conversation with her about her troubles. She didn't want to talk and just sat at this booth at Friendly's, pushing the pieces of a fish sandwich around on her plate. I'll never forget it. She didn't look me in the eye once – my own daughter." Ruth's voice cracked, and she cleared her throat to compose herself. "The spring of her graduation, she seemed worse than ever. She wouldn't work. There's a floral shop here in town that has a lot of business in July and August, what with all the weddings in this area, and they take on seasonal employees to help out. But she wasn't interested."

"Did she say why?"

"No." Ruth removed the lid on the box on her lap, sorted through contents that Frances couldn't see from where she sat, and produced a small photograph. She extended her hand to Frances, who got up to receive it. The picture showed Virginia in a tasseled cap and graduation gown, but her cheeks were pale, her lips were clenched, and her eyes stared vacantly at the camera. "I was scared, frustrated. It seemed unfair that I should be going through such difficulties with my only daughter when I'd recently lost my husband. I had no one to turn to for help. So I went to speak to Reverend Burgess."

"Your priest?"

"Yes. We've always been churchgoing people. Charles was on the vestry at the church we belonged to in Dedham. It was important to us. When we moved, we joined Christ Church in Barnstable. Reverend Burgess was very welcoming. We thought he was a good man. And his assistant was also very kind." She produced a piece of paper from her box and again handed it to Frances.

It was a newsletter from Christ Church. Volume XV, no. 3, dated September 1985. In the upper-right-hand corner was a picture of two men in cassocks, holding wooden spoons. They both smiled. The caption read: "All for the grace of God. Our Fathers help out with lunch for the Retired Men's Club." Frances lifted the paper slightly closer, thinking that her eyes were playing tricks on her. She studied the two faces, recognizing the one on the left from the newspaper clipping she'd seen. But the other man was also familiar. She lifted the picture closer. Staring out at her was Reverend Whitney.

"Is this Edgar Whitney?" she asked.

"He was our assistant rector."

"You know he's the minister now at the church where Hope belonged."

Ruth cocked her head slightly and fingered the contents of the box in front of her. "I wasn't aware of that.

I didn't follow his pastoral career after he left." She gave Frances a knowing look, as if she'd figured out something that was still beyond Frances's comprehension.

"In a diary she kept, Hope mentioned several times that she felt Father Whitney was responsible for something that happened to your daughter. Does that make sense?"

Ruth fingered the fabric of her skirt, and glanced away. After several minutes of silence, she turned back to Frances. "Hope wasn't alone in that view. But I'm getting ahead of myself."

"I'm sorry. Please continue."

Ruth cleared her throat and seemed to struggle to recapture her train of thought. "As I said, I spoke to Reverend Burgess about Ginny and her difficulties. He came by the house a day or two later to meet with her. He convinced her to come and volunteer in the church office so her summer wouldn't be wasted. I don't know how he did it. I wasn't part of the conversation. But I remember looking into this very room and seeing them sitting on this couch together. He held one of her hands in both of his, and she was totally engrossed, more so than I'd seen her since before Charles died. The next day, she was up even earlier than I."

"He never talked to you about what he'd said?"

"No, but it didn't matter. Ginny went off to work every day, went to church with me every Sunday, and seemed genuinely happier. I didn't want to pry. I was so relieved. I think I thought it reflected the power of faith, something that I hold very dear." She paused, and her eyes welled with tears. "In August she told me

Father Burgess had offered her full-time employment and that she'd accepted. I was disappointed. Her education had been expensive, and I thought she should aspire to something more than clerical work at the church office, but I was afraid to confront her. I didn't want her to feel that I was being judgmental."

"Did you talk to the minister?"

"I did. Perhaps I shouldn't have, I don't know."

"What did he say?"

"He said that Ginny was a very special girl. God had chosen her for the work at Christ Church, and I should be very proud of her. She was invaluable to him and Father Whitney. That was his word. 'Invaluable.'" Ruth hung her head and covered her mouth with her hands. When she spoke again, her words were muffled with tears. "So I went along. Who am I to question the word of the Lord? She and I lived in this house together, but she spent more and more time at the church. She had inquirers' class. She volunteered for every activity. She spent several weekends away on retreat. I couldn't keep up with all she did, but it seemed an awful lot of time for fourteen thousand dollars a year in salary."

"Did you talk to anyone about your concerns?"

"I mentioned it once or twice to Reverend Burgess during coffee hour, but he reassured me about the wonderful work she was doing. He said that with all the good Ginny was doing, she'd deliver our whole family into heaven. And people in the church were constantly coming up to me praising her. 'She did everything for the Christmas fair,' someone would say. 'The Youth Group loves her.' The compliments abounded. It seemed the first positive thing that had happened since Charles's death. So instead of being skeptical, I filled with pride, too much pride. My darling daughter was special. But pride comes before the fall. And then I found her."

Ruth looked up and stared directly at Frances. "It was Ash Wednesday, the start of the Lenten season, where we atone for our sins." She reached into the box once more and this time produced an off-white card with a cross on the cover. "This is Ginny's note. What she left behind for me to find."

Frances opened it. The rounded letters looked as though they'd been written by someone considerably younger than twenty-three.

> I have examined myself and found it despicable. I have repented, prayed, fasted, and meditated on God's Holy Word, but I cannot be redeemed. I have been filled with lust for Father Burgess, and I have acted on that perversion. I am the sinner, not he. I am Satan taunting Jesus in the desert; I am the snake in the Garden of Eden. Now I am the lamb. In my sacrifice, I seek forgiveness.

Frances got up and joined Ruth on the couch. Without saying a word, Ruth passed her the box. For the first time she could see all it contained: yellowed newspaper clippings describing Virginia's death, the discovery of her body, and the ensuing trial; handwritten notes, condolence letters and prayer cards, several photographs of Virginia, including one beside her brother in dress uniform, a lock of light brown hair, and the copy of the death certificate. She picked up a thick document and read the caption. It was the amended complaint filed in *In re Estate of Virginia Bailey v. Christ Church et al.*, with a Barnstable Superior Court civil action docket number from 1987.

Frances scanned the paragraphs.

This action for wrongful death and breach of fiduciary duty is brought by Ruth Carlton Bailey, Executrix of the Estate of Virginia Bailey (hereinafter "Executrix") against Christ Church, an Episcopal Church located in Barnstable County, Reverend Thomas Burgess, in his capacity as Rector, and Reverend Edgar Whitney, in his capacity as Assistant Rector (hereinafter collectively "Defendants").

Paragraph 54
Knowing of Virginia's susceptibility to influence, knowing of the power he held over her as her spiritual adviser, and knowing of her fragile emotional and physical condition, Reverend Burgess abused his position of trust by (a) insisting that she engage in almost daily sex acts with him; (b) instructing her that she would go to hell if she refused; and (c) threatening to expel her from the church if she informed anyone of what they had done.

Paragraph 66
Reverend Whitney knowingly aided and abetted the rector's abuse by (a) failing to bring it to the attention of the Vestry; (b) abdicating his pastoral responsibilities by leaving the parish hall during regular hours of operation so that Virginia would be left alone with Reverend Burgess; (c) reinforcing to Virginia the importance of silence.

Paragraph 80
Because of the power Reverend Burgess exerted over her, Virginia saw no escape from her misery other than to take her own life. This violation of his position of trust was the direct and proximate cause of her death.

Ruth returned to the chest of drawers and removed several volumes of what appeared to be trial transcripts. "I do need a cup of tea after all. Please excuse me one moment. Perhaps you'd like to take a look at these while I'm gone," she said, handing the volumes to Frances.

Alone, Frances flipped through the second day of trial. Skimming pages, she found a portion of the testimony of the medical examiner.

Mr. Dailey
Dr. Harvey, could you describe for the ladies and gentlemen of this jury what this photograph depicts?

Ms. Kessler
Objection. It speaks for itself.

Mr. Dailey
Fine. Withdrawn. Did you go to the Bailey residence on October 22?

Dr. Harvey
Yes.

Mr. Dailey
And did you see Virginia Bailey there?

Dr. Harvey
Yes.

> Mr. Dailey
>
> Was she dead or alive?

> Dr. Harvey
>
> She was dead by the time I got there.

> Mr. Dailey
>
> How did she appear?

> Dr. Harvey
>
> She was hanging from a noose tied to a beam in the Baileys' basement. Her head was tilted, her tongue was hanging out. Blood had pooled in her lower legs.

> Mr. Dailey
>
> Was she completely suspended from the ground?

> Dr. Harvey
>
> No. Her feet touched the floor.

> Mr. Dailey
>
> I'm showing you a photograph that's been previously marked Plaintiff's Exhibit 14 and I ask you whether that's a true and accurate representation of the condition of Virginia Bailey's body at the time you first saw her?

> Dr. Harvey
>
> Yes.

Attached to the back of the transcript was a photocopy of Exhibit 14. Frances forced herself to look at the image of a distorted face with bulging eyes, the limp body clothed in a flowered skirt and T-shirt, and turned ankles pressed into the floor. In the background were the normal contents of a basement: tools, paint supplies, boxes, a bicycle. She sat motionless and closed her eyes, wanting the image to vacate her brain. The similarities between Hope and Virginia Bailey were more than spiritual.

Ruth returned with a cup in her hand, walked to the fireplace, and touched the portrait of her daughter. "The trial wasn't about money."

The thought hadn't occurred to her. "What was the verdict?"

She held onto the mantelpiece as if for balance. "For the defendants. Reverend Burgess confessed to their relationship but looked me straight in the eye and said it was consensual. That it was what Ginny wanted and that she'd been so unbalanced that he hadn't known how to say no. His testimony was horrible, lies about Ginny's promiscuity, lies about things she asked him to do to her. They said she'd been the seductress. And there was nothing I could do. There was no way to guard her honor or protect her memory. Charlie was so mad, I thought he'd kill the man himself, but we had a sense of right and wrong even if he didn't. The jury believed him." Her lips quivered and she began to cry, but she kept talking, stammering out her words. "They . . . didn't . . . think . . . there . . . was . . . anything . . . wrong with what he did . . . to . . . my little . . . girl."

"What about Reverend Whitney?"

She coughed. "He testified. That . . . that man had the nerve to apologize to me and say he'd exercised poor judgment. But he claimed he didn't know Ginny was damaged by the relationship. He said she always seemed so happy when she was around Reverend Burgess."

"And the church?"

"The church couldn't be liable without the ministers. The vestry began a search for a new minister and sent me a ten-thousand-dollar 'gift' in Ginny's memory. That's about it. Reverend Harris, who's there now, is a wonderful man, full of compassion and concern. He checks on me all the time. He brought me back into the fold, so to speak."

Frances didn't know what to say. Having an affair with a parishioner probably wasn't enough to make Father Burgess responsible for her death. Unlike the Catholic Church, the Episcopal Church didn't require its ministers to practice celibacy. But that didn't minimize Ruth's pain.

"I'm sorry if this question seems insensitive," Frances said, "but was an autopsy done?"

"Yes."

"And there was no doubt about the suicide?"

Ruth sighed. "No. There was nothing to indicate otherwise." As she struggled visibly to contain her tears, she looked at Frances with imploring eyes and flared nostrils.

"How did you ever find out? I mean, how did you even gather the evidence to bring the lawsuit?"

"Well, Mr. Dailey, our lawyer, did most of the preparation. But there was one person who really made us aware. He was the church custodian, a kind older

gentleman named Jerry, who'd taken care of the buildings and grounds for years. He knew Ginny, was fond
of her, and was truly distraught by her death. Several
weeks after her funeral, he came to this house. He told
me he'd seen her with Father Burgess on several
occasions. He'd actually . . . found them, you know,
being intimate one evening. He'd been very concerned,
but when he said something, the minister threatened to
fire him. He'd also spoken to Father Whitney, who said
it was nobody's business, that what happens between
two people is private. And he even told Jerry several
times not to come to the church on days he was
supposed to work. Jerry knew it was to let them be
alone, but he didn't know what to do. He felt tremendous guilt that he hadn't done more to try to protect
her. We thought his testimony would convince the jury,
but that lady lawyer who represented the defendants
did quite a job discrediting him. She made him out to
be a crazy old coot, an alcoholic who fabricated stories.
But he was a good man. He hadn't made anything up.
The jury just didn't want to believe the horror of the
truth."

"I'm so sorry."

Ruth half smiled. "Ginny was a wonderful person.
She should still be with us. And she is in spirit. No court
proceeding can take that away."

As they said goodbye in the driveway, Frances
embraced the elderly woman. It was an awkward gesture, made more so because Ruth initially stepped

backward, startled by the affection, but after a moment the gentle lady put her arms around Frances's waist and held tight. Frances could hear the sobs.

"I needed to understand what it was about Ginny's life and death that made my cousin feel connected to her," she whispered in Ruth's ear. "You've explained that. And I can't thank you enough."

33

Frances stood just inside the sacristy, trying to settle her nerves. Her heart pounded and her palms were clammy; she'd tossed and turned, trying to piece together the fragments of information she'd gathered over the last week. But as the sun came up and the night's restless exhaustion dissipated, one thing was clear: the betrayal Hope had experienced from Bill's abuse had shaped her life long after the physical wounds had healed. She'd identified with Virginia Bailey because they'd both been hurt by people they trusted: the father Bill and Father Burgess. The paternal bond turned out to be fraught with peril.

She wished her mere presence in the church now could provide some sense of tranquility. Instead it increased her agitation. All the baptisms, weddings, and joyful celebrations of so many holidays that had transpired within the walls of the Church of the Holy Spirit did nothing to negate the pain and cruelty of human interaction in the outside world. Or even the failings of people within.

Elvis joined her. "Come on," he advised. "He's in his office."

She'd considered coming to speak to Father Whitney unaccompanied. In many respects it made more sense. The questions she needed to ask about what had happened in Barnstable didn't require Elvis's presence and he might be more inclined to open up without a policeman present. But something had made her reconsider.

She followed Elvis through a back door into the church office. The adjacent door to Reverend Whitney's private office was ajar. He stood behind his expansive desk as they entered and extended his hand in greeting. He wore street clothes, dark pants, a white button-down shirt, and a crimson cardigan. She could see the dark circles under his eyes.

"I didn't realize you were here with Detective Mallory," he said.

"Call me Elvis," she heard behind her as she took a seat across from the minister.

"What can I do for you?"

Elvis looked over at Frances. Earlier, over coffee and a stale sweet roll from Dunkin' Donuts, she'd explained what she knew about Virginia Bailey. They'd speculated on Father Whitney's involvement, how much he might have known, and his potential reaction to being questioned so many years later; but now that the moment had arrived, they both seemed apprehensive. Reverend Whitney selected a cashew from a bowl of trail mix and chewed slowly.

"What do you make here? Your salary, I mean?" Elvis

asked offhandedly as he picked up a copy of the church newsletter and seemed to skim through it.

"Sixty-five thousand," Father Whitney replied.

"Plus housing?"

"Yes."

"And a car?"

"Yes. I'm not sure what you're getting at."

"And the parish gives you something for food and utilities too, doesn't it? Isn't that part of the church budget?"

"What is your point?"

"It's a good deal here," he said, replacing the stapled papers. "Pre-tty sw-eet."

"I am more than compensated for my work with the Lord, if that's what you mean. But I have never asked for a raise, never asked for more than what I've been offered."

"Can't imagine you would," he said. Then he smiled, a big grin. He was the cat ready to bat at the vole caught between his paws.

"We need to ask you about Virginia Bailey," Frances said. She knew Elvis had wanted to warm him up and then make him feel uneasy. Elvis at his best.

He cleared his throat. "Why have you been looking into my past?" he asked. His voice sounded calm, but he spoke with forcefulness.

Neither of them responded.

"If you're asking, I suspect you know the answers then, as well. Ginny Bailey was a very kind, very devoted girl, whose death was a tragedy. I testified at the civil trial brought by her mother against the church and its clergy, which included me, after she killed herself. I was under oath, and I took that oath seriously. In retrospect, Father Burgess and I might well have tried to offer her more help, more counseling, more compassion, but her physical involvement with him was consensual. If anything, he was more frightened of it than she. He should have exercised better judgment, more control, but she was a passionate girl and hard to resist. We are mortals. We all yield to temptation at various times. Or are you free of sin?" He leaned toward Elvis. "Fortunately, the Lord forgives."

"But it's against the canons. And you didn't report it to anyone at the diocese. You let it continue. Didn't you feel *any* obligation to come forward?"

"Adultery is against the law. Does that mean no one commits the sin? People know about their friends' extramarital affairs and do nothing. For a policeman, you're naïve. The relationship between Father Burgess and Ginny appeared to hurt no one. It was not my place to expose it."

"When did Hope find out about what happened at Christ Church?"

The minister was silent. He reached for another nut and split it down the middle with his front teeth. Frances watched him chew for a moment before speaking. "Several months ago."

"How?"

"She'd been gathering some materials to send into the diocese. I can't remember what it was she couldn't find, but she'd been looking for something and discovered a box of documents I have about the case."

"What was her reaction?"

He spoke slowly as he gazed out the window into the garden beyond. "She came into my office, obviously disturbed. Anyone would be upset, I knew that. But we discussed it, talked at length about what happened, what I knew and didn't know, and what I could and couldn't have done. Even if she didn't agree, I believe she understood."

Elvis glanced at Frances, who opened one of the leather diaries at a page she had tabbed and began to read.

I asked Father Whitney about Ginny. Why? Why did he do nothing to protect her? Why did he sit idly by? Why wasn't this his business? I could tell my questions angered him. "I did my best," he replied. "And there hasn't been a day since Ginny's death when I haven't repented." That's not good enough! I want to yell out. My mother's said the same thing, and it's not good enough.

Father Whitney set his jaw. "Whatever impression you may have, you're mistaken. Hope and I were very close. I understood she was upset. She thought I should have reported my superior and ended the affair. She thought I could have saved Ginny. But she was wrong."

"Did Hope threaten to report you to the diocese?" Frances asked.

"Never."

"What does the Bible say about liars, Father?" Elvis asked. "I'm no acolyte, but I seem to recall something about blistering tongues."

Frances felt a jolt from Elvis's words. She hadn't expected him to be so confrontational. "Can you help us to understand this? It's an entry from Hope's diary, one we found aboard Carl's boat." She flipped several pages in the diary and read aloud.

> I cannot live with myself if I do nothing. This parish trusts Father Whitney. He has heard our confessions. We turn to him for help, for guidance, for safety. He has betrayed us. Nobody here knows what happened on the Cape. He's never told the congregation what he allowed to transpire. Now that I know, I refuse to be like the others. I won't be silent.

Father Whitney stood up. The color had drained from his face. "You don't understand. Hope hated her father for what he did, and she hated her mother even more for letting it happen. She'd turned to this church; she'd relied on her faith to help her to heal. Quite understandably, she was upset with me. But her mother's conduct and mine weren't equivalent. I tried to explain that to her." He held onto the back of his chair, seemingly for balance, although Frances saw the whites of his knuckles as he gripped. "God is my judge," he mumbled.

"How did you feel about her threat to expose you?" Elvis asked.

He took a step back as a look of alarm passed over his face. "You can indict me any way you want, but I will not confess to what I haven't done. I have served this parish to the best of my ability. I have done everything in my power to help this community through good times and bad. I have reached out to our

441

parishioners. You can ask anyone about me and hear the same thing. I am proud of my work."

"A good minister. Was it to make up for the bad?" he persisted.

"This is satanic. Why have you come here?"

"Hope wasn't wrong to blame you. You were as critical of yourself as she was," Frances said.

"I am critical of myself. You're right about that. Ginny Bailey's death nearly destroyed me. I was ashamed. I questioned my faith. I questioned what sort of God would allow a minister to treat a vulnerable young girl in such a way. You can't tell me I haven't suffered over that whole affair."

"But you thought you'd suffered enough. You didn't think you should be punished anymore."

"Punishment is for God to do. It is not our place to dispense it."

"That's exactly what I'm saying. And Hope was going to do just that." Frances felt her breath coming quickly as she realized the truth. "Hope wasn't going to leave you in God's hands. She was going to break the special bond, the trust between you and turn you in to the vestry, the parish, whatever. And you feared that if they knew, the members of this congregation wouldn't want you anymore. You may have underestimated the tolerance of this community, but perhaps not. That's hardly the point. You weren't willing to accept the consequences of your own actions, to accept responsibility for your past."

"I didn't hurt her."

Frances refused to listen. Her rage felt uncontrollable. "Did you expect that simply because you'd repented that you'd be redeemed? Did you honestly think that anything you could do would make up for the loss of a life?"

"Why are you persecuting me?"

"Persecuting *you*? Is that what you think?" She swallowed hard and found that the sensation of her own saliva passing along her throat gave her strength. This was real, now; she had to confront evil standing before her. An evil that wasn't metaphysical or metaphorical, that had nothing to do with the Bible, the Book of Common Prayer, or anything about faith. There stood a selfish man, one who had inflicted harm to protect his own interests. This crime was no different from any other. That the passion was spiritual instead of physical didn't change the intent to kill.

"Why, Father? Why didn't you take the risk that your parishioners would accept your follies, your failings, and accept you anyway? How could you preach acceptance of oneself if you didn't believe it?"

"I have spent my life in toil, in service to God," he interrupted. "He will protect me from your baseless allegations. If anything, I helped her. I helped her as I helped others come to terms with the horrors and injustice in this world. She found solace in the church, in our prayers together, in the Bible. Nothing I did contributed to her death."

"You killed her!" Frances screamed. She refused to let him hide behind his cloak of piety any longer. Just as Hope apparently had, she wanted to punish him for the pain he had inflicted. Now was the time for God's wrath, His fury, and she found herself praying for it.

"Stop! Enough, I say." He walked around to the front of his desk and put his hand against one of her shoulders, seeming to hold her off. They stood frozen, staring into each other's eyes as she felt the pressure he exerted. She held her ground. Now she understood. He'd seen a suicide before, the suicide of a confused girl, one not too dissimilar to Hope, and he knew that no one suffered consequences because of it. Father Burgess hadn't been held responsible; with suicide, only the deceased was to blame. So he'd gone to every effort to make Hope's death appear self-inflicted. He wanted to preach to the congregation and sing with the choir every Sunday. He too wanted to escape responsibility. He thought he could deviate from pious conduct because the state wouldn't catch him and the Lord would forgive him. Apparently, anything could be forgiven with adequate repentance. What kind of moral code was that?

She recalled him appearing at the dock the night they'd discovered Carl's body, and the sense of security she'd felt when she'd seen his face in the light. He'd already been to the boat; he'd already killed the lobsterman. No doubt, as soon as the minister could be fingerprinted there would be a match on the handle of the sledgehammer recovered from the Dumpster.

And then she remembered. The conversation came rushing back, making her dizzy in a sea of words. She'd been the one to tell him what Carl knew about Hope's past. She'd been the one to tell him of the existence of other diaries. That information must have led him to believe Carl knew much more than he did. Her willingness to believe in the piety of a man of the cloth, her need to confess to someone whose trappings made him seem trustworthy, had led to Carl's execution. How could she have been so stupid? Carl's face as he'd been pulled from the black sea, his vacant stare, burned in her memory. It was her fault, and she would have to live with that responsibility. Only Carl could dispense forgiveness, but her very conduct had deprived him of that ability.

Father Whitney knelt down, clasped his hands, bowed his head, and seemed to pray.

"Edgar Whitney, you are under arrest for the murders of Hope Lawrence and Carl LeFleur," Elvis said as he stood and removed a pair of handcuffs from his jacket pocket. He walked around the desk as Father Whitney rose, put his hands behind his back, and hung his head. "You have the right to remain silent. You have the right to an attorney . . ."

The words blurred as Frances stared at this priest. He was supposed to serve God, to execute as best as possible God's will on earth. She'd seen many criminals led away, heard many tales of abuse and greed, but his crimes seemed worse. Perhaps he shouldn't be held to a higher standard – he was human like everyone else and shared the same ugly characteristics – but she wanted him to be better, more moral, more selfless. Isn't that why people went to church? To find something and someone to guide them in their everyday lives, to help them find answers to the struggles they faced, to teach them to walk in Jesus' shoes. He was certainly no better, and probably worse, for abusing the trust vested in him. Now two people – one who had turned to him for guidance and the other the man who had loved her and kept her secrets – were dead. He was responsible.

She closed her eyes for a moment and thought of Sam, remembering his voice during their last conversation. His words, his tone, gave her strength. Then, clutching Hope's diary tight to her chest, she followed Elvis and his defendant out of the church.

SEPTEMBER

34

Frances rested her elbows on the railing and stared overboard, feeling the salty wind on her face. As the Cross Sound Ferry churned its way through Long Island Sound, white tidal pools lightened the blackish green water. The noise of the engine blurred all other sounds and she watched the pull of the current under the boat. The last seagull leaving port out of New London had turned back, the shoreline had disappeared, and the huge ship carrying dozens of cars and passengers seemed alone in the vast ocean.

Sam returned from the galley with two Styrofoam cups of coffee and handed one to Frances. "The line was endless," he said, handing her one.

She took a sip and felt a burn in the back of her throat. The liquid was bitter, a taste she remembered well from the previous day as she'd sat with Elvis in Mark O'Connor's office, reviewing all the evidence against Father Whitney that had been compiled over the last two weeks. Forensics had found two fibers in Carl's ransacked apartment that matched a jacket from the minister's office closet. With a fingerprint match off

the sledgehammer, the case against him for the lobsterman's murder was strong.

Whether he'd be tried for Hope's murder too was
now up to the grand jury. Mark had presented the case
as best he could: police had found the most recent
volume of Hope's diary in his apartment – the one he'd
taken in order to create a forgery. One of the final
entries had been read into the record:

> I turned for help so many times, but ultimately no one
> was there, and now I understand why. Even when the
> hurt is right before us, even when Father Whitney
> witnessed Ginny's pain, silence prevailed. Now he's
> angry with me for wanting justice, for wanting those
> who turn to him to know how quickly he will betray
> them. He told me yesterday that he would force me to
> keep quiet if I wouldn't make that choice on my own.
> "There's nothing I could do. Why do you want me
> punished now?" If I hear that refrain one more time, I
> will scream.
>
> My insides have been destroyed, and even my
> dreams aren't my own. I want to be held, rocked in
> gentle arms, protected from the hurt, but my night-
> mares, my memories, forced me to give up the one
> person who might have saved me. I'll become Jack's
> wife, but nothing will change. I'll be free from this
> family, but not this community. I'll remain immersed
> in a world of façades.
>
> Why don't we stand up for the people we love? Why
> isn't that worth the fight? But I too am guilty. I've let
> Carl go because I no longer have the strength, because
> I'm plagued by my fears. Maybe I do understand my
> mother better than I thought.

Upon hearing the words, two grand jurors had cried.

Ricki Manning was able to find some striking similarities between Father Whitney's handwriting and the forged pages, including an ink match, although it was from a common type of pen available for fifty-nine cents at most drugstores or supermarkets. Jack testified that there was never any discussion of eliminating a portion of the planned wedding ceremony; Father Whitney had fabricated his story about changing the service as a ruse to get Hope to leave her lunch at Singing Beach and meet with him alone. Although he had not killed her until later in the day, the inference was that he and she had had a final confrontation. Perhaps he'd threatened her.

The best evidence, though, came from a religious vestments supplier in East Boston. He explained that the silky rope of the noose was actually a cincture and that he sold that type of belt to various Episcopal churches, including the Church of the Holy Spirit.

As the sky had darkened, Elvis drove Frances back to Manchester, where they said their goodbyes for the immediate future with promises of communication and visits that both knew would never transpire. Watching him wave from his lilac convertible, she'd felt sad. How often the most horrible situations brought people together, only to have the relationship dissipate when the crisis resolved. For a moment the image of Kelly Slater flashed into her mind. They'd gone through a war together when Kelly left her husband and yet had had no contact since she'd relayed her decision to return to the man who abused her. This cycle of intense experiences and abrupt endings characterized her professional life and, in many ways, her personal one, too. It made her yearn for something consistent, someone constant.

"Adelaide and Bill told me they wanted to come see the farm," Sam said, resting his free hand on her back and rubbing it gently in small circles.

"Bill's not welcome in my house," Frances replied. Honoring her aunt's wishes, she hadn't shared Hope's history with Sam, but that didn't mean she would forget. "As for Adelaide, I wouldn't count on it. She wants to think we'll stay connected because she wants something positive to come out of Hope's death."

"What about Teddy?"

"We can still talk. And now e-mail, too." She cradled her Styrofoam cup in both hands and took a sip of the coffee. "You know, when I was a child, I always imagined them in that beautiful house overlooking the harbor. I wanted so much to be a part of Adelaide's world. She seemed to bestow love and comfort wherever she went. But it was a fantasy with no basis in reality, a wish born of too many trips to the ice-cream parlor. It was a nightmare there . . . too."

"It's all the same family."

"That's the problem." They both laughed.

"I heard tell once that the best family is the one you get to make yourself, not the one you're born into."

"Wise words." They were silent for a moment. "I wish once, just once, my dreams wouldn't be total fiction, that accurate perceptions could form the basis of a fantasy. But enough philosophy." She saw the coast of Orient Point off in the distance. "We're almost home."

"Fanny," Sam said, "you're always the one to say, 'Can I ask you something?' But now there's something I need to ask you."

"Anything." She turned toward him and was startled by the serious look on his face. Her pulse quickened, and she felt a lump in the back of her throat. When he rubbed his eyes and pushed a stray lock of hair off his forehead, she thought she saw a tear.

"I don't know how else to say this. I'd be honored if you'd marry me." Sam reached in his pocket and pulled out a small velvet box. "I guess I'm supposed to add, 'At least consider it,' but I'd rather you didn't. I'd rather you just agreed. I may not be the most brilliant or the most successful man on the planet, but there's no one who could love you more than I do or more than I will."

She stood up and put her arms around him. Inhaling deeply, she smelled the musty scent of his skin and kissed his neck. She felt his embrace as he squeezed her closer to him. She couldn't imagine being anyplace else in the world. Her only prayer was that the feeling would never pass.